Girl Friday

JANE GREEN

PENGUIN BOOKS

PENGUIN BOOKS

Published by the Penguin Group
Penguin Books Ltd, 80 Strand, London WC2R 0RL, England
Penguin Group (USA), Inc., 375 Hudson Street, New York, New York 10014, USA
Penguin Group (Canada), 90 Eglinton Avenue East, Suite 700, Toronto, Ontario, Canada M4P 2Y3
(a division of Pearson Penguin Canada Inc.)
Penguin Ireland, 25 St Stephen's Green, Dublin 2, Ireland (a division of Penguin Books Ltd)
Penguin Group (Australia), 250 Camberwell Road, Camberwell, Victoria 3124, Australia
(a division of Pearson Australia Group Pty Ltd)
Penguin Books India Pvt Ltd, 11 Community Centre, Panchsheel Park, New Delhi – 110 017, India
Penguin Group (NZ), 67 Apollo Drive, Rosedale, North Shore 0632, New Zealand
(a division of Pearson New Zealand Ltd)
Penguin Books (South Africa) (Pty) Ltd, 24 Sturdee Avenue, Rosebank,
Johannesburg 2196, South Africa

Penguin Books Ltd, Registered Offices: 80 Strand, London WC2R 0RL, England

www.penguin.com

First published by Michael Joseph 2009
Published in Penguin Books 2010

008

Printed in Great Britain by Clays Ltd, St Ives plc

A CIP catalogue record for this book is available from the British Library

ISBN: 978-0-141-03863-6

www.greenpenguin.co.uk

For Heidi
With blessings and love

Acknowledgements

Thank you to the various people in the various places that, knowingly or otherwise, hosted me during the writing of this book, namely the staff of the Westport Public Library, and Michael, who kept me in delicious cappuccino at Cocoa Michelle.

My universally wonderful agents and teams at Penguin, Ford Ennals, Dina Fleischmann, Sally Ann Howard, Elise Klein, Clare Parkinson, Karen Siff, Martha Stewart, Nicole Straight, Paula Trafford, my ever-wonderful 'Goddess Posse': Heidi Armitage, Jennifer Brockman, Tina Gaudoin, Dani Shapiro.

My family: the Warburgs, the Greens and all of our children.

And Ian, my beloved husband, who fills me with joy and has changed the way I look at the world.

I

One of the unexpected bonuses of divorce, Kit Hargrove realizes, as she settles onto the porch swing, curling her feet up under her and placing a glass of chilled wine on the wicker table, is having weekends without the children, weekends when she gets to enjoy this extraordinary peace and quiet, remembers who she was before she became defined by motherhood, by the constant noise and motion that come with having a thirteen-year-old and an eight-year-old.

In the beginning, those first few months before they worked out a custody arrangement, when Adam, her ex, stayed in the city Monday to Friday and collected the children every weekend, Kit had been utterly lost.

The house suddenly seemed so quiet, the huge new colonial they had moved into when Adam got his big job in the city, the house they thought they had to have, given the entertaining he now wanted them to be doing, the investors he wanted to invite over to dinner.

She still blames the house for the ending of the marriage. A huge white clapboard house, with black shutters, and a marble-tiled double-height entrance, it was impressive, and empty. Much the way Kit felt about her life while she was living there. The ceilings were high and coffered, the walls panelled. Everything about the house shouted expense, and it never felt like home.

There was nothing cosy about the enormous Great Room, the expansive master bedroom suite complete with his 'n' hers bathrooms and a sitting room attached that no one ever sat in.

There was nothing comfortable about the formal living room, with its Persian rugs and hard French furniture, a room that they used perhaps three times a year, although no one lasted longer than twenty minutes in there before moving into the kitchen and crowding round the island in the one room in the house that felt welcoming and warm.

The kitchen was the room that Kit lived in, for the rest of the house felt like a mausoleum, and the day they moved in was the day it all started to go wrong.

Adam started commuting into the city during the week, leaving on the 'death train' at 5.30 a.m. to avoid the crowds, getting home at 9 p.m.

From Monday to Friday he didn't see the children, didn't see her. She rattled around in that huge house, growing more and more used to being on her own, resenting his presence more and more when he was back for the weekends, feeling like he was invading her space, attempting to mark a territory that, without her knowing, or wanting it to, had undoubtedly become hers.

They became like strangers, ships that pass in the night, not able to agree on anything, not having any common ground, other than their children, and they'd make dinner plans on the weekend and beg people to join them, so they wouldn't have to sit in restaurants in silence, looking around the room, wondering how it was they had nothing to talk about any more.

When they separated, then talked divorce, Kit knew the house had to be sold. And she was glad. There was nothing in the house that felt like hers, no good memories, nothing but loneliness and isolation within its walls.

During the early days she felt, mostly, lost. For so many years Adam had been her best friend, her lover and, even towards the end, when they barely saw one another, she still knew he was her partner, she still always had someone to phone when she needed an answer to a question.

After the separation, during those first few days, when Adam and the kids pulled away from the house in his Range Rover, Kit would stand in the driveway watching them go, not knowing who she was supposed to *be* without her children, what she was supposed to *do*, how she was supposed to fill two whole days without mouths to feed and small people to entertain.

She lost her partner, her lover and her identity in one fell swoop.

She didn't have the energy to go out, although her social life shrank to almost nothing anyway. A single woman, it seems, doesn't have quite the same appeal in suburban Connecticut. Their couple friends initially invited her out, feeling sorry for her, or wanting to hear what had happened, but the invitations petered out, and she quickly realized that the friends she and Adam shared, *their* friends, would not necessarily remain her friends, because the chemistry just wasn't the same.

And she couldn't even think about dating (although it was extraordinary how many people offered to set her up on blind dates, within what felt like minutes of her separation), so she went to bed.

Days would pass when she barely emerged from the comfort of her cocoon in the grand master suite on the second floor, aided by Ambien at night and pointless reality shows on the television during the day. She once watched almost eight hours straight of *Project Runway*, even though she wasn't the least bit interested to begin with – but by hour three she was desperate to know who was next going to be *auf wiedersehen*ed off the show by the glamazonian Heidi Klum.

And then, when they finally agreed a custody arrangement, she had the kids every other weekend, but by that time Adam had agreed to sell the house and split the proceeds, and the resulting house-hunt was like a well-needed injection of energy.

They were lucky. Their house sold quickly, and Kit found a small cape on a pretty street behind Main Street, that was easily big enough for her and the children, and Adam rented a small farmhouse on the other side of town.

It took the best part of a year for Kit to start feeling like herself again after the divorce. And at the end of that time she was not the self she was during her marriage – the wife she had tried so hard to be – but the self she was before her marriage: her true self, the identity she lost in her quest to be the perfect wife.

*

It is extraordinary, she thinks, picking up the phone and scrolling back through the numbers to see who has called, how much her life has changed. She was a wealthy Wall Street widow in a large house, with immaculate children dressed in French designer kiddie wear, complete with Land Rover, a wardrobe stuffed with Tory Burch and a social life that involved going to the gym with the other Wall Street widows, then coming home to shower and change before attending a trunk show in someone's home.

The trunk shows varied. Designer stationery featuring cute colourful cartoons of women who were supposed to look like Kit and her friends, or jewellery made by a local once-high-powered-but-now-looking-to-find-her-creativity mother, charging exorbitant prices for semi-precious gemstones strung together with pretty clasps. Some held children's wear sales and displayed tie-dyed funky yoga pants for three-year-olds, sparkly navel-baring tops for toddlers. Others filled their homes with children's clothes from the catalogues, trying to induce mothers to order copious amounts of clothes. Whatever the trunk show, what they all had in common was the aim to satisfy the instant gratification gene that all Wall Street widows seemed to have.

As soon as she and Adam separated, Kit knew she needed to work, but she didn't want to go back into teaching. She had loved it while she did it – teaching at a Montessori school until she became pregnant with Tory – but she didn't want to be an employee, as such, of *anyone*. She wanted to make some money, and retain her freedom. Adam paid child support, and the alimony was just about enough to live, but not enough to live the life she had grown used to in Highfield, heart of Connecticut's Gold Coast.

It wasn't even as if it was a big life, not compared to some of her friends. Certainly, her life was bigger when she was married, but one of the lovelier changes that occurred post-divorce was that she suddenly saw no reason to feel insecure around the women who used to cause her nervous breakdowns while waiting in the corridors outside the classrooms in pre-school.

She doesn't see the need to dress to impress these women any more, because who else had she been carefully applying make-up for, popping diamond studs in her ears, carefully coordinating her ballet pumps with her bag?

She had felt those women looking her up and down, judging her, deciding whether or not she was good enough based on the cost of her handbag or the number of carats in her ears, and she had shrunk with inadequacy every time she walked in.

Since the divorce, she has found she doesn't want to wear make-up any more. Her daily uniform has become jeans and boots in winter, and shorts and flip-flops in summer. Sure, she still dresses up on the rare occasions she has to, but now if she bumps into one of the scary gala-obsessed women in Stop and Shop and she is in shorts with her hair shoved back in a ponytail, she doesn't mind, doesn't have an urge to hide behind the grapefruit stand.

She has taken up yoga, joining the new yoga centre that has opened on the outskirts of town, and is finding not only is she calmer, more centred, but she has found new friends, women like her – grounded, down-to-earth women – not to mention Tracy, the charismatic owner of the yoga centre, who has swiftly become one of Kit's favourite newer friends in town.

Kit has been avoiding the charity circuit, choosing instead to focus on the handful of friends she trusts and adores. Getting divorced in a small town, she discovered, was no walk in the park. For a while there, she and Adam were the subject of various gossipy lunches. The rumours shocked and upset her. In the course of one week she heard the following different reasons for their divorce:

1) That Adam had been unfaithful
2) That she had been unfaithful
3) They had run out of money so now she was leaving him.

None of it was true. The truth, that they had simply grown apart, was far more prosaic, and didn't seem to make sense to people, hence the need to embellish. The rumours had hurt Kit far more than she let on, and it was only when she met Tracy at the yoga centre that she became willing to expand her social circle again, beyond Charlie, her oldest friend in Highfield.

For a long time after the divorce, she had stopped being invited to things. She doubted Adam was being invited either, but that was largely because he was rarely in Highfield these days. She realized that however much people liked her while she was married, even though she was effectively single in those days because Adam was hardly ever around, it was different now that she was actually *divorced*. People seemed to become frightened of being around her too much, as if, she sometimes thought, some of her bad karma might rub off on them.

Not that she felt as if she had bad karma. Not any more. She felt as if she had had bad karma during her marriage, when she would go to bed at night and feel that she was drowning in loneliness. Since the dust settled, and once the children were fine again, she has woken up every morning looking forward to the day, trusting that it will be good, knowing that she has finally discovered who she is, and with a sense of peace.

When Kit first saw the house she bought for herself and the kids after the divorce, she fell in love. Instantly. White clapboard with sea-green shutters that had little starfish cut-outs, the window boxes bursting with impatiens that tumbled over the sides, it was the prettiest house she had ever seen.

She recognized that she was falling in love with a lifestyle rather than with a house, but she didn't care. She wanted that lifestyle. She saw herself swinging on the porch swing, hosting dinners around that kitchen table, kneading dough on those marble countertops.

The kids would curl up on the huge, squishy, mushroom-coloured sofas as a fire blazed in the grate and she merrily made dinner while sipping a glass of ice-cold Pinot Grigio, and the three of them would all live happily ever after.

It was something of a shock to do the walk through

on the day of closing, to realize that without the smells of cinnamon buns rising gently in the oven, the sounds of soft jazz filling the air, without the mushroom-coloured sofas, softly lit table lamps and fresh blue and white curtains, the house was just ... a house. A nice house, admittedly, but Kit couldn't help but feel a swell of disappointment.

She knew the sellers were taking the furniture, of course, but she didn't think it would make the house feel so ... different.

By the next morning, she had forgotten that. She had forgotten it because she woke up after their first night in the house, the sun streaming through the curtainless windows, and realized that it was hers. All hers. And more than that, her *life* was hers.

There was something so different about living in a small, manageable house, living a life that felt *real*, rather than a pretence. Never again would she have to squeeze into high heels and dresses because that's what her husband liked. Never again would she have to sit through boring dinners with people she didn't under-stand, people with whom she had nothing in common, because Adam was doing a deal with them, or needed to befriend them, or impress them.

She didn't have to take the kids on vacation to only the smartest and best hotels, hotels that always intimi-dated her, where she never felt she belonged. For the first time in a long time – fifteen years to be exact – Kit didn't have to please anyone other than herself.

Of course there were the children too – dramatic, strong-willed Tory, and easy, easy-going Buckley, and she always had to consider them, but she didn't have to change her way of living, change her life for them.

And while she knew there would be times when she would feel vulnerable and lonely and scared, she also knew that the more time that passed, the less she would feel those things, and when she did, she would breathe through the feeling and remind herself it always passed.

So she woke up, made coffee and climbed back into bed, sipping slowly and looking out of the window at the tree tops, refusing to be daunted by the boxes all over the house, relishing the feeling of being free.

They spent the day unpacking, Tory miserably until Kit promised her a cool sofa bed from PB Teen, and then, towards dusk, there was a banging on the door and it was flung open before anyone had a chance to even get up. A small, wiry, very tanned old woman with long white hair in a ponytail came striding into the living room holding a stack of plates with a pie balanced precariously on the top.

'I'm Edie,' she said. 'I live next door in the purple house.' Tory caught Buckley's eye and suppressed a grin – they had been wondering who lived in the bright purple eyesore next door. 'And before you ask, no, I won't paint it. I love the colour purple and you'll get used to it.'

'I . . . I hadn't noticed,' Kit lied.

'I've brought you a home-made rhubarb and cherry pie –' Edie put the plates down on the counter – 'and some plates for us to eat it off as I figured you wouldn't have unpacked yet.'

*

'You need a job,' she said, half an hour later, after the group had swapped small talk and licked their plates clean. She peered at Kit as Kit pretended not to be disconcerted by this tiny, white-haired bundle of energy who had made herself instantly at home.

'I do?' Kit said, wondering how Edie had known; for it was true, it was just that Kit hadn't got around to telling anyone.

'Why yes.' Edie got up, opened the fridge, found a carton of orange juice and helped herself. 'It's not good for all you young girls to give up your jobs once you've had children. You get bored and have far too much time to worry about things you don't have to worry about. Everyone should work, in my opinion. We need to exercise our brains just as much as our bodies.'

'Do *you* exercise?' Tory asked, somewhat mesmerized by Edie.

'I most certainly do,' Edie said, flexing her muscles. 'I do Pilates twice a week and play tennis every weekend.'

'How old are you?' Tory said.

'Tory!' Kit instantly admonished. 'You can't ask that! It's rude.'

'Not at all,' Edie dismissed Kit. 'I like people who speak their minds. I'm eighty-three years young.'

'Wow!' Tory said. 'You look amazing.'

'You see?' Edie beamed with delight. 'That's because I take care of my body and my mind.'

'So what do you do?' Kit couldn't help but ask.

'I'm a realtor.' Edie's chest puffed up with pride. 'The

star of the Burton Holloway group for the last thirty years.'

'Thirty years!' Tory, at thirteen, couldn't fathom doing anything for that long. 'That's a lifetime.'

'Almost!' Edie chuckled. 'I'm going to speak to my friend Robert McClore about you. He's been looking for an assistant for ages, and he keeps trying out these silly young things who haven't a clue how to use their initiative and don't have a bone of common sense in their bodies. He needs someone like you. Know how to type?' She examined Kit with a beady eye.

'I . . . of course.' Robert McClore! The famous writer! Kit grinned, thinking this was the most exciting thing to have happened to her since she once sat in the same restaurant as Ray Liotta.

Kit had realized that knowing she would have to get a job was very different to actually finding one. In the early days, she didn't have the strength to actively look, being too busy packing up the house, making lists of what was hers and what was Adam's. Too busy sorting out the books into his and hers piles, wondering what on earth to do with the Duxiana bed, and all the extra furniture that Adam didn't want, the furniture that wouldn't fit into a new, smaller house.

Too busy running, so she wouldn't have to stop and deal with the anxiety, the fear. Could she do this by herself? Was she really that strong?

But once she bought this house, she knew she would have to find something, and Edie's suggestion was a blessing in disguise.

*

Robert McClore is probably the most famous person to live in Highfield. Neighbouring towns have their share of movie stars and rock gods, but Highfield has one of the biggest names in literature today.

He is talked of in the same breath as Clancy, Patterson or Grisham. He is one of the giants in men's commercial fiction, and the airports stack his small, meaty paperbacks high every summer.

He is read by all the men who profess not to enjoy fiction. The men who read the *New York Times* and the *Wall Street Journal*, who, if they read books at all, read biographies, history books, business tomes, and who only ever pick up a blockbuster when they're flying to sandy destinations with their wives and families.

His books have been turned into movies, each one more successful than the last, and the script for *The Last Landing* is still studied by film students all over the country, lauded as an example, as *the* example, in fact, of the perfect thriller.

He moved to Highfield thirty-five years previously with his wife, Penelope, a model. They were part of the beautiful crowd, the artists and writers who summered in Highfield, who drove down on Friday nights with the back seats of their sporty little convertibles stuffed with cases of champagne.

They were the golden couple, until Penelope disappeared from their yacht while they were sailing, with friends, in the Greek islands during the summer of 1978. It was the biggest story of the year, and to this day there are people who believe Penelope was murdered, that there was far more to the story than met the eye.

Their friends, it was true, were there. Plum Apostoles, who had made a fortune in shipping, was rumoured to have been having an affair with Penelope. Plum's wife, Ileana, was thought to have been having an affair with Robert. Plum had, it later came out, served time in prison for assault. There was talk of huge rows, drunken parties, but Robert never spoke about it again.

Nor did he remarry. The parties and the high life stopped as soon as Penelope disappeared, and he became something of a recluse.

Hillpoint, the grand old house perched at the top of Dune Road, overlooks the calm waters of Long Island Sound. The house itself is approached by a long, gravel driveway. As the electric gates swing noiselessly open, and you round the corner, you catch a glimpse of the large white columns of the house before it comes into view in its entirety.

Gracious, regal, impressive, it is a house that is often whispered about, for few have actually seen it, few have ventured beyond those intimidating electric gates. Some of the mothers that Kit knows, women who have grown up in Highfield, say they went trick or treating there as children, that Robert and Penelope left the gates open every Halloween, when they threw huge parties for all their New York friends, and they let anyone come, lavishing delicious gourmet candy on all the local neighbourhood children.

The house was designed by Cameron Clark in 1929, but it is a house that hasn't been seen for years. Aside from the people who take care of Robert McClore, few are allowed beyond the gates.

Robert McClore spends his time writing a book a year, consulting on the movies, and occasionally, very occasionally, appearing at an event in town to benefit one of the local charities. His name appears far more often than he does, as a generous donor to everything charitable, including being one of the giant supporters behind the rebuilding of Highfield Library.

Kit sat in her kitchen and looked at her new neighbour.

'Of *course* I know how to type,' she said, despite not having typed for many, many years. Still, nothing that a spot of practice wouldn't cure.

'Know how to read?' Edie peered at Kit with a twinkle in her eye, while Tory burst out laughing.

'Is Robert McClore really looking for an assistant?' Kit asked.

'Yes, and he'd like you.'

'How do you know? You don't know me.'

'No, but I like you already, and that's always a good sign.'

'How do you know him?'

Edie smiled. 'I was his . . . well, not assistant, exactly . . . more like his Girl Friday. Oh it was hundreds of years ago, when he and his wife, gorgeous thing, first moved to Highfield. I used to cook for them, do a spot of cleaning, and even go on movie sets with him. It was quite the life.'

'It sounds amazing. Did you do it for long?'

A look of sadness came into Edie's eyes. 'A while. Until Penelope died. You know the story?'

Kit nodded. Everyone in town knew the story.

'Robert was a changed man when he came back. He went into hiding for a while, hence that ridiculous reputation he has as a recluse.'

'You mean he's not?'

'Robert!' Edie barked with laughter. 'He loves people! He's just private. There's a big difference. He couldn't stand the attention after Penelope's death, and refused to let anyone help him. Including me. That's when I decided to get my realtor's licence instead.'

'But you're still in touch?'

'Of course! I shall ring him tonight when I get home.'

Kit chose her clothes carefully, but it all went horribly wrong at the last minute. You're going for an interview to be an assistant to a novelist, she told herself, as she glared at her black skirt suit in the mirror, not an accountant.

She whipped off her suit and put on black pants and a blue shirt, then tore the pants off and pulled her chinos on. Too casual. Oh *God*. What on earth was she supposed to wear? She wanted to be professional, but not too professional. Casual, but not too casual.

In the end she settled on brown pants and a blue cashmere sweater with a pretty scarf, and all the way over to Robert McClore's house she fought the urge to run home and change.

'You will be fine.' Edie was driving, and kept chuckling to herself about how nervous Kit was. 'He's terribly nice, and you'll charm him. You'll see.'

But as soon as they pulled through the gates and Kit

saw, for the first time, the grandeur of the house, she almost went to pieces.

Edie bypassed the front door and marched straight in the back – 'He never keeps it locked,' she whispered to Kit, 'but don't tell anyone' – striding through the kitchen and calling out a loud, 'Hellooo?'

'Edie!' It was slightly surreal, this man who was so famous suddenly standing before her. He gave Edie a huge hug, then turned to Kit with a warm smile on his face.

'I'm Robert,' he said. 'You must be Kit.'

She was instantly disarmed by his warmth, although now, eight months later, she knows that it is only because of Edie that he was relaxed; more often, with strangers, he is polite and always gracious, but distant – the price of fame meaning he has to truly trust before he can let anyone get close.

And so, for the past eight months, Kit has been his assistant. Initially, she went in three days a week, just for three hours, to tidy up, answer fan mail, sort out his bills. Robert McClore wasn't around much while she was there. She'd be in the large office downstairs, while he was in his writing office, a former sunroom attached to the side of the house.

She would knock tentatively when she needed him, intimidated by his greatness, but slowly they began to chat, slowly they began to relax with one another, and now he brings her coffee when he makes his, and sits in the 1920s art deco armchair in her office, chatting to her about life.

Three hours a day became five hours a day, four days a week, and Robert told her, just the other day, he didn't know what he did before she came along. Her chest swelled with pride.

Finally, for the first time since the divorce, it feels like everything in life is in place. Her kids are settled, her home is calm, she loves her job. She wakes up every morning and cannot believe how lucky she is.

2

Robert McClore wanders in and places a mug of coffee on the desk to one side of Kit's computer. She looks up and smiles gratefully, reaching over for the mug and sliding her chair slightly away from the desk so she can sit more comfortably.

'How's the research coming along?' he asks.

Kit has spent the last two weeks trawling the Internet for information on Navy SEAL training. Every day she collates the most relevant facts, cuts and pastes them, and gives them to Robert. She doesn't read the books as he writes them, but reads the outlines, the synopses and the research. She never thought this kind of book would interest her – she is much more likely to pick up a book with a pink cover featuring a pair of glossy high-heeled shoes – but since working here she has read most of Robert's work, and is surprised by how much she likes it.

This latest features a martial arts expert brought in to train the Navy SEALs. Only he's not quite what he appears, and mayhem ensues when his terrorist links are discovered.

'It's fascinating,' Kit says, for it is, and that is the true beauty of the job. Not that she is gainfully employed and earning her own money for the first time in years, but that she is learning something new every day.

Frequently, she leaves feeling that her brain has physically expanded in the few short hours she has spent there. 'I love learning about all these new things,' she says with a smile. 'I never expected I'd be finding out so much when I took the job.'

'That doesn't mean you regret it, then?' Robert says, sipping his coffee.

'God! No!' She is forceful, and slightly embarrassed. She looks away, then turns to him again, wondering how it is that such a kind, successful and – yes, okay, she has to admit this, even though he is many years older than her – very *handsome* man, is on his own so much of the time.

There are times, particularly like now, when there feels such intimacy between them that she wants to blurt out the question: why are you on your own? But she would never cross that line, would never dare be so presumptuous.

But she doesn't understand it. She knows about the terrible tragedy with his wife, yet it seems there has been no one serious since then. Rumours abound about covert affairs with wives of wealthy men, but in eight months here she has never seen evidence of anything.

There is talk in the town that he might be gay, but she thinks that unlikely. Just as there have been no women, there have been no men either, and she just doesn't believe it, realizing that he is a target for gossip, false rumours, simply because of his fame.

She studies him as he leafs through the papers she has collated for him. He has a craggy, handsome face, tanned from the hours he spends in the garden. She watches him through the windows sometimes, knows he is taking a break from writing, but that this is part of the process, that gardening is a meditation for him, and he would not relish being disturbed.

His hair is more salt than pepper these days, but the silver-framed photos scattered around the house show Robert and Penelope decades ago, Robert squeezed next to Warren Beatty and Meryl Streep at the Academy Awards, and when he was younger his looks weren't just handsome, they were breathtaking.

'I wonder whether you would come to the reading tonight.' Robert suddenly lays the papers on his lap and studies Kit over the top of his glasses. 'You haven't been to one of my readings and I think you would enjoy it.'

'I thought you didn't like turning up with "people",' Kit says and grins, thinking of the stories Robert has told her, how he turns up for book signings, lectures, television shows, with no one, and is usually ignored because people don't believe it's him, don't believe a writer of his calibre could possibly have no ego, ergo no entourage.

Her favourite story, one that he told her just recently, laughing all the while, was when he turned up to a talk show that featured another author, this one female, young, who had enjoyed great success with her very commercial first novel and was suffering from an advanced case, Robert said, of 'first novel syndrome', which meant all the attention had quite clearly gone to her head.

Young, beautiful and charming on the surface, she

had arrived with her assistant, her publicist, her editor, her manager, her hair and make-up artist, her sister and her sister's friend. The production team, panicking, put her in the best dressing room, the one that had home-made pastries and fresh coffee, baskets of fresh fruit on every surface. The one that had two plush sofas and a fridge filled with chilled white wine.

Robert arrived alone. He was shoved into someone's office, which they had decided to turn into a makeshift dressing room for the day.

'See?' Kit had been horrified but had laughed. 'You need *people*!'

'Oh pshaw,' Robert had brushed her off. 'I can't stand all that *look at me, I'm a star* business. I don't need people, but I wouldn't have minded some of those home-made pastries.'

Robert grins at Kit now.

'I don't want you to come and assist me. I want you to come and be a member of the audience. Come and enjoy.'

'I ... I'd love to,' Kit says. 'I just have to see if I can get a babysitter.'

'Isn't Tory thirteen? Couldn't she babysit?'

'Yes, but she's already got plans tonight. Let me ask around this afternoon at yoga and see if I can find someone.'

Later that day, at her yoga class, Kit inhales, sits back on her ankles as she stretches forward in Child's Pose, then swoops slowly through Chataranga and into Downward Dog.

She catches the eye of Charlie, who grimaces at her and makes her smile, then she forces herself to stay focused on her breathing.

The room is absolutely quiet, save for the soft, tinkling music in the background, and Tracy's melodious voice, taking them through the yoga movements.

Kit never would have thought she would become addicted to yoga. She remembers first trying it when she was pregnant with Tory. She went to a pre-natal yoga class, armed with all the right gear because she was convinced it was going to change her life. She had cute maternity yoga pants, the matching vest with a painted Buddha on it, and a brand-new hot-pink yoga mat.

She had entered at the back of the class, a little surprised that when she smiled at the other mothers they didn't smile back, but perhaps, she thought, they were already in a meditative state and didn't quite see her.

Kit was looking forward to lying flat on her back and breathing deeply, anticipating an hour of rest and relaxation, of going through the movements in a slow and measured way. After the thirtieth consecutive Downward Dog, she knew she'd made a terrible mistake. It didn't help that she was using her pregnancy with Tory as an excuse to eat whatever the hell she wanted and was subsequently the size of a small whale (she liked to think it was normal that six out of ten people asked her if she was having twins, but she very much doubted it).

She huffed and puffed her way through the class, threw the yoga mat in the back of the closet in the mudroom when she got home, and forgot all about it until the yard sale when they moved, when someone paid $2 for the mat.

Since the time of that first class, yoga seemed to sweep the country. Everyone Kit knew was raving about either Pilates or yoga, but it wasn't until she and Adam separated that she actually decided to give it another go.

And even then she didn't really want to, she just did it because Charlie was going, and this, more than anything, was an opportunity to see Charlie more often and grab tea or coffee or lunch, depending on the time of the class, afterwards.

Charlie had been her lifesaver when she first moved to Highfield. Their girls, Tory and Paige, were in pre-school together, and the minute Kit walked into the pre-school and saw Charlie's mass of curly red hair, her large open smile, she knew they'd be friends, made it her mission, in fact, to be friends.

She got Charlie's number from the school, phoned her the next day and invited her over so the girls could get to know one another before they started school. Given that Tory and Paige were turning two, it was unlikely they'd find much in common, but that's what mothers of pre-schoolers did, particularly ones who were new to the area – they looked for mothers they liked the look of and invited them over.

Months later, when she and Charlie were firm friends, Charlie confessed she had no idea who Kit was when she phoned with that initial invitation. 'And you still came?' Kit was aghast but Charlie shrugged and said, 'I needed friends as much as anyone else.'

The girls had been best frenemies until Charlie sent her daughter to private school, and this had, unwittingly, split them up. Until then, if they weren't obsessed with one another, unable to breathe or live without the other in her sights at all times, they were having huge and dramatic arguments, which Kit and Charlie tried to laugh about, but in truth they found all rather exhausting.

Charlie's husband, Keith, worked, as did most of the husbands in Highfield these days, in finance, and he and Adam instantly bonded, so for a while the four of them were inseparable.

They went out for dinner every Saturday night, sometimes with others joining in, did classes with their kids at the library and YMCA, and had brunch every Sunday, usually at Kit's house because, as Charlie said, she was a horrible cook.

'It's brunch,' Kit said in disbelief. 'Bagels, scrambled eggs and bacon. What's to cook?'

'Have you tasted my scrambled eggs?' Charlie said, and Kit shook her head. 'Exactly.'

'I'll make them!' Kit offered, but the tradition, for a long time, remained brunch at Kit and Adam's.

On the night that Kit and Adam decided to divorce – both of them had been waiting for their unhappiness to pass, waiting for things to get better, until they realized that they had been living this way for two years and it wasn't going to get any better, that they had in fact drifted so far apart they couldn't see how to find their way back, even if they had wanted to – Charlie and Keith were the first people Kit turned to.

Kit moves gracefully out of Plank as her mind flits back to walking into Charlie and Keith's kitchen, sitting at their table as Keith brought over a bottle of vodka. Not for her, but for himself. He was so shocked he was almost numb, just kept shaking his head in disbelief.

'But we've been unhappy for years,' Kit kept saying. 'Couldn't you tell?'

'No!' Keith insisted. 'I thought all that bickering was just, well, just part of your relationship. I didn't think it meant there was something wrong with the marriage. I didn't think you would split up.'

Kit remembers Charlie saying, afterwards, that Keith had been heartbroken. She said that for both of them, but particularly for Keith, having their best friends break up was like losing a friend, and Keith had to grieve.

Charlie understood, though. She had liked Adam, but after they split up she confessed she could see that they weren't perhaps a great match. Adam was very caught up in working on Wall Street, and all the trappings that came with that. And Kit? Well, Charlie realized that the labels and the jewels weren't her, and Charlie knew how unhappy Kit was, living in the huge house.

Things had been a little awkward for a while with Keith because Kit knew he still saw Adam – had lunch with him regularly in the city. And although she and Adam had approached their separation and subsequent divorce determined to be friends, ironing out the finances and custody agreement was so horrible that for a time Kit actually hated him.

Her first priority was to protect the children and she

had hoped that she and Adam would be able to come to an amicable arrangement, but Adam's lawyer, the Rottweiler, as she came to call him, was so aggressive that she is convinced to this day he deliberately made things as contentious and awkward as possible, dragging the proceedings out far longer than was necessary, in order to get more money.

They are friendlier now. Adam is dating up a storm in New York City, which Kit thinks should bother her more, but in fact she is grateful she does not have to spend time going to the smartest, trendiest restaurants any more, and grateful for her quiet life in Highfield.

Perhaps it was simply that they married too young, she realizes now. They met at twenty-three, married at twenty-five, long before they knew who they were going to grow into, long before they knew whether they were going to share their journey or find that when they came to a fork, they would both choose a different direction.

There had been many forks in their marriage, and many different directions chosen, but Kit had never thought seriously about the possibility of leaving because the idea of being on her own again, of handling this life all by herself, was not just overwhelming, but terrifying.

True, Adam had never been around very much during the marriage, and for most of the time, particularly during the week, she felt like a single mother, but that wasn't the same as actually *being* a single mother, having to deal with everything herself, not having any support when the going got tough – and there were times when the going certainly got tough.

The class finishes and Tracy bows her head in Prayer Pose, then looks at each of the women in the room intently. 'Namaste,' she says to all of them in turn.

'Namaste,' they say and bow their heads in reply.

'So?' Tracy gives first Kit then Charlie a hug. 'Anyone for a smoothie?'

'Love one,' they both say in unison, turning to one another and laughing.

'I saw in the paper that Robert McClore's giving a talk tonight,' Tracy says, as they walk out of the yoga studio and up the stairs towards the smoothie bar. 'I thought I might go. You'll be there, right?'

'Thanks for reminding me!' Kit turns to Charlie. 'I meant to ask you. Is Keith around tonight? Can I borrow Amanda?' Amanda is the wonderful Brazilian babysitter who moved into Charlie and Keith's house six months previously, and has changed their lives.

'Where's Edie?'

'Pilates tonight.'

'Oh damn. The kids have sleepovers and Amanda's going out. I'm so sorry. What about Adam? Do you think he could take the kids?'

'I don't know.' Kit sighs. 'Adam's so busy sowing his wild oats he doesn't tend to be around any more than he needs to be, and certainly not at the last minute. But you're right, I should try.' And she reaches down into her bag and brings out her mobile phone to send him a text.

'I can't believe we're finally going to meet your reclusive boss,' Tracy says with a smile as they sit down at a table in the corner.

'Uh oh!' Charlie casts her a sideways glance. 'I know that look.'

'What do you mean?'

'I mean that predatory, cougar look. You've got your eye on Robert McClore, haven't you?'

Tracy laughs. 'Don't call me a cougar!'

'Why not?' Charlie is all innocence. 'It's a compliment!'

'No it's not. Anyway, isn't a cougar a woman who goes out with younger men?'

'No. A cougar is a sexually active and confident woman who's a predator. Tell me you're not flattered.'

'I'm not flattered.'

'But you wouldn't mind getting your hands on Robert McClore?'

'Well, he is attractive and single and seriously successful. Why exactly would I not be interested?'

'You're talking about my boss!' Kit says. 'I don't even think of him that way. Anyway, he's not interested, and why would you be? He's in his sixties, Tracy! That's much too old for you.'

'I'm forty-one,' Tracy says. 'And I've always liked older men. Just say you'll introduce me, that's all. Oh go on ... please?' She leans her head on Kit's shoulder and Kit laughs.

'Tracy, like you need anyone to introduce you. Men go crazy for you.'

'In my dreams!' Tracy snorts. 'Since that freaky ex-husband of mine left, I only seem to attract the losers.'

'Cute losers,' Charlie says and grins, remembering a guy who was with Tracy one time when she and Keith had bumped into them. That one had turned out to be a drug addict who ended his many clean years soon after he and Tracy started dating.

'Yes, well. I've never been able to resist that lethal combination of black hair and green eyes.' Tracy remembers the ex with a shrug.

'Doesn't sound like Robert McClore would be your type,' Charlie teases.

'Maybe he's not.' Tracy grins. 'But I wouldn't mind finding out.'

'You're both incorrigible!' Kit laughs, but she is thrilled to have found Tracy, thrilled that she now feels part of a 'gang', feels like she belongs; and how lovely it is to have someone to share things with, to call up out of the blue or have them drop in unexpectedly for coffee.

She hadn't realized, for many years during her marriage, quite how much she had missed her female friends. Not that they fell out deliberately, but she no longer lived in Concord, and nor did any of her school friends, and distance, more than anything else, had forced them to drift apart.

She was in Connecticut, others were in New York, still others scattered across the United States, and even some in Paris and London. From time to time they exchanged emails, and Facebook had done wonders in reintroducing her to faces from her past, but it wasn't the same as having that close-knit group of friends, people who knew you back before you grew into your self, people who had known, and loved you, for years.

Charlie she has known for eleven years. They have

shared history, laughter, tears. When Charlie suffered three miscarriages in a row after Paige was born, Kit was the one on whose shoulder she cried.

And when Emma was born, it was Kit who threw the baby shower, Kit who gathered her friends together and made beautiful favours of miniature bassinets stuffed with embroidered goodies, Kit who took care of Emma when Charlie had to be somewhere for Paige.

They met Tracy at an event called Cocktails, Creators and Chat, just over a year ago. In aid of one of the local breast cancer charities, it was a monthly event that had guest speakers, and women all over Highfield insisted their husbands get the earlier train home, or found a babysitter, and they filled the hall of the local theatre, sipping Cosmos and chattering excitedly, so thrilled to be away from their families for the night.

Tracy stepped up to the stage, gorgeous with her long, blonde hair, her fresh-faced Californian beauty, and she talked about her love of yoga, her journey from being a girl who leaped from one drama to another, to a woman who had finally found peace.

Her speech affected Kit, particularly. She was coming out of the haze of her divorce, and was starting to enjoy her life, to feel serenity during the weekends she was all alone, rather than a crippling fear.

Kit had approached Tracy afterwards, a little intimidated by both Tracy's confidence and her beauty. 'I loved your talk.'

'Thank you.' Tracy smiled. 'I love being able to share some of my journey with women, especially those of us who are on a similar path.'

'Well, I just got divorced, so it was more than a little relevant.'

'How are you doing?' Tracy asked, placing a hand on Kit's arm, and Kit found herself talking to Tracy as if she were an old friend, an instant bond between them.

Part of the gift bag that night had been a free yoga session at Tracy's new studio, Namaste.

'Will you come?' Tracy said, as she was being pulled away to talk to other women.

'Sure,' Kit said, thinking, suddenly, and sadly, that Tracy was only being a good businesswoman.

'No, seriously. I want you to come. I don't often meet other single women and I think it's really important to have girlfriends. Honestly, I could do with some single girlfriends. Will you come? Make sure it's one of my classes and we can have some tea afterwards. Can we do that?'

Kit's face lit up. 'I'd love to,' she said.

The following week she and Charlie did exactly that, and by the time they had all finished their tea and had sat chatting and laughing for over an hour, they were firm friends.

3

Edie is stooped over, pulling at the roses to bring them closer so she can deadhead them, when she hears Kit's car pull into the driveway.

Many years ago, Edie knew all of her neighbours. She grew up in this same house, and remembers sitting on the front porch every night, watching the procession of neighbours pass the house, all of them stopping to wander over and say hello, most of them with dogs by their side.

She, and all the other kids on the street, would leave the house at dawn and rarely reappear until dusk, zipping around the neighbourhood on bikes, taking pitchers of iced water to the fields across the street and collapsing under huge weeping maples when they got too hot and bothered.

'Don't misbehave,' their mothers would tell them as they ran out through the back door in the morning. 'One of us will see, and you know we'll tell.' And it was true, for every mother on the street was at home, and all of them considered the children of the neighbourhood their own children – if someone misbehaved, it was their right to reprimand, no matter who the child in question belonged to.

When it rained they would sit under the covered

porches playing Sorry, Monopoly, or Chutes and Ladders.

Summers were filled with cookouts, and if you were spotted in the street, you were invited in, friend, neighbour or stranger. It didn't matter.

Over the years, Edie has got used to seeing fewer and fewer people in her street. She spends time in her front yard, carefully training the roses over the picket fence, weeding the beds, cutting back the bayberry, and every time she hears a sound she looks up hopefully, but not so many people walk past these days.

The daily routine around here seems to be the same. Edie sees the husbands leave for the city any time between five and seven o'clock, driving purposefully to the train station, their *Wall Street Journals* beside them on the passenger seat.

Then the children come straggling down the road, backpacks falling off, kicking stones, barely mumbling a response to Edie's loud and ringing 'Good morning'.

And lastly, once the children are off to school, the mothers appear, striding down the road in pairs, for their morning power walk. Always dressed in black, with baseball caps and sunglasses, they stride past Edie, not even looking over, certainly not saying anything to the old lady with the white ponytail who they probably think is a little bit nuts.

Thank God for Kit! Edie lays down her pruning shears and walks over to the car. It isn't that Edie was lonely exactly – she still has her job, after all, and goes to the YMCA regularly for her exercise classes – but she didn't realize quite how much she missed having a friend next door, until Kit moved in.

Despite the age difference of over forty years, Edie now considers Kit to be a close friend. More than that; Kit is the daughter she never had. It is a special relationship, and one she has only ever experienced once before, many years ago. It didn't end well, and she tries not to remember.

Edie was careful not to impose too much on Kit, after that initial visit, but then Kit got the job working for Robert and was so grateful to Edie she brought her beautiful flowers to thank her, and now Edie finds she has a family, complete with blooming thirteen-year-old Tory, and adorable, adoring, eight-year-old Buckley.

And if you ask Kit, she would say she would never have expected to adopt a mother but, in truth, Edie is the mother she always wished she had. Not that Kit's mother is bad, but she has never been particularly interested in Kit, never available for her in the way Kit always wanted.

There are times when Kit would love to punish her for being so unavailable – by keeping the kids from her – but she is relieved that the children enjoy her so much, and that they are able to have a relationship with her mother she never had.

But Edie? Edie is something quite different. Edie is the one she can rely on, Edie is the one who will drop everything to go and pick Buckley up from school if he's sick and Kit can't get to him. Edie joins them for dinner, at least a couple of times a week, firmly instructing

Buckley not to talk with food in his mouth, and even, on occasion, forcing Tory to spit her chewing gum into the waiting hand Edie holds at Tory's chin level.

'Disgusting habit,' Edie mutters, as she heads to the trash can to get rid of the offending substance. 'Not in my presence.'

Amazingly, the children don't seem to mind being told what to do by Edie. In fact, they are far more likely to listen to Edie than to Kit. Many's the time Buckley has requested that Edie put him to bed, not Mom, and Kit has no idea what she would do without this surrogate grandmother, mother and friend who has become so indispensable in her life.

'I saw in the paper that Robert's giving a talk tonight,' Edie says, opening Kit's car door for her, as the children shout their hellos and run into the house to switch on the television set. 'I have Pilates but I thought perhaps I could miss it for once.'

'No! You'd miss Pilates? I thought you never missed Pilates.'

'Well, I don't,' Edie grumbles. 'But this is special. It's not often that Robert gives talks any more and I'd like to hear what he has to say.'

'It's such a shame, isn't it, that he rarely does this these days?'

'I agree,' Edie says with a sigh. 'I think the press gave him such a hard time after his wife died, he just decided to keep to himself. Can't blame the poor man, really. Terrible thing to happen to him, and there he was, trying to recover from the tragedy, and then all those rumours started. I would have probably gone to live in South America.' She follows Kit into the house.

Kit laughs. 'And then everyone would have assumed you were guilty.'

'True, but you'd be living in a lovely hot climate, sunning yourself on a tropical beach. Who cares what people might think?'

'Only you would think like that. Well, I'm going, and I'd love you to come with me. Adam, miraculously, said he'd come home early and take the kids, so he should be here at around quarter to seven, and then we could head over there.'

'Lovely!' Edie's face lights up. 'I'll just go and get ready.'

When Kit and Adam were first divorced, most of the time when Adam showed up to get the kids, or Kit drove over to his house to drop them off, it was like being with a stranger. There was something so familiar about him, and yet they were so stiff with one another, so awkward, she sometimes got out the wedding album and flicked through, just to check that she actually did marry him, that it wasn't just a figment of her imagination.

For a long time, Adam appeared to be furious with her, and during the divorce negotiations it was fair to say they pretty much hated one another, but as soon as the divorce was finalized it seemed they both started to heal.

And now, a year on, there are times when Kit realizes they can be friends. Times too when she wonders whether things could have turned out differently, whether there was an opportunity they didn't take, therapy perhaps, couples' counselling, something that could have brought them back to one another before it was too late.

She still remembers, so clearly, how she met him, on 4 July 1991, at a party in Concord.

She noticed him as soon as he walked in, nudged her girlfriends and pointed out the cute stranger who had entered with a guy they'd all been at school with.

'Hey,' Samantha, one of her bolder friends called over. 'Who's the new cutie?'

'This is my cousin Adam,' he said. 'He's from Connecticut.'

'Hey, Adam from Connecticut,' Samantha said, all big eyes and flirtatious smiles. 'I'm Samantha from Concord.'

'Hey,' he said, then turned his gaze to Kit. 'Who are you?'

'Kit from Concord,' she said, and she blushed, looking away quickly so he wouldn't see. He saw.

The rest of the night passed in a blur of drinking, laughing and dancing. As did the rest of that summer. At twenty-three, Kit was mostly interested in having fun, and Adam made her laugh more than anyone she'd ever met.

At the end of the summer he invited her to Connecticut to stay with him, and during her trip she rang her mother and told her where she was, and Ginny demanded they both come into the city and have lunch with her.

She sent a car for them, and positively swooned when she met Adam. Kit tried to tell herself it didn't matter, but now, all these years older and with the hindsight that comes with age, she realizes she phoned her mother because she wanted her approval, and Ginny quite clearly approved of this good-looking graduate of Harvard Business School who was evidently going to be a success.

Could it have been that simple, Kit sometimes wonders. I married him to please my mother? She tries not to dwell on the answer.

Almost immediately, once the partying and drinking stopped and they settled into being newly-weds, Kit had a horrible feeling that she had done the wrong thing. Sure, he still made her laugh, and sure, they still had fun, but now that the excitement of planning a wedding had passed, now that they were just getting on with life, they really didn't have much to talk about at all, didn't, in fact, seem to have anything in common.

Adam was climbing the corporate ladder, and Kit was happy to just stay at home, more so when she found she was pregnant with Tory. She wasn't interested in any kind of social climbing, had had quite enough of that with her mother, thank you very much, and much of the time when Kit said she couldn't attend a function in the city – pregnancy was an extraordinarily useful excuse, particularly when she invented a morning sickness she didn't actually have – Ginny turned out to be a wonderful and gracious partner for Adam.

Everyone was happy.

Except perhaps Kit. But she tried not to think about it. Tried to focus on all that was good, and who, after all, wouldn't want what she had? A charming husband who all her friends adored, an impressive house, a beautiful daughter. How could she possibly expect more? What right did she have to feel there was something missing? How selfish to even dwell on that for a second.

So she tried not to. Until it became too hard to ignore.

Yet, post-divorce, and now that Adam is back out there in the dating scene, he has been friendlier, chattier, and there are even times when she looks at him and wonders what was wrong with her, that she couldn't be happy when she was with him.

She hears his car from the bedroom as she's slipping on her shoes, and comes down the stairs yelling towards the kids, both holed up in Tory's bedroom, watching something on the computer.

'Tory! Buckley! Computer off. Get your stuff. Dad's here.'

'Hi.' Adam grins and raises an eyebrow as he looks her up and down, making her feel instantly self-conscious. 'You look great. Got a hot date?'

Despite herself, Kit laughs. She has made an effort tonight, it is true. Her light brown hair, now streaked with gold from the sun and a few strands of her natural grey, is silky on her shoulders, straight and shiny instead of her usual natural wave.

A touch of eyeshadow brings out her blue eyes, and she is wearing a wrap dress that shows off her figure perfectly. At five foot eight, she has always been tall and rarely wears heels, far happier in her clogs and Merrell slides, but tonight she stands tall, feeling feminine and flirty, pretty in her dress-up clothes.

'I'm off to a book reading.'

'That's it? You dressed like that for a book reading?'

He has a point.

'Oh God,' Kit groans. 'Is it too much?'

'Are you kidding? You look amazing. Nice dress.'

'Thanks.' She twirls awkwardly, wondering if it is as strange for Adam to see her in unfamiliar clothes in her new environment, as it is for her to see him in his.

When she drops the kids off, she can see into the house, all the furniture that used to be theirs, paintings they bought together, books she remembers from their bookshelf.

She had always bought everything in the house, decorated herself, chosen the furnishings, Adam trusting her taste and style, leaving her in charge; so although she didn't miss the things she saw in Adam's house, they were familiar, they had her imprint on them.

Then she started seeing new things. A rug, some cushions. Paintings. Things she not only didn't buy, but things she would never have bought. Not her taste. And then his clothes. Unfamiliar shoes, jackets she hadn't seen before – and that was perhaps the moment she realized he had moved on.

This dress she is wearing tonight, a navy and white printed wrap dress, is new. One of the first things she did, after her divorce, was sort through her wardrobe and get rid of all the clothes she thought of as belonging to her previous incarnation as a rich housewife.

The little bouclé suits, the matching heels. The silk shirts and cashmere capes. It was a look that was far more her mother than her, and when she dropped them off at the consignment store, she felt the weight of trying to be someone she is not, finally lift off her for good.

Her mother was horrified. 'Darling!' she said. 'Who gets rid of Chanel?'

'I do,' she said simply, knowing that her mother would never understand her daily uniform of Gap capris and Old Navy vests, although she has to admit, she has made an effort tonight, and not because of the possibility of meeting a man, but for her friends.

Kit thinks of the few times that she, as a new singleton, Charlie and Tracy, plus a number of other girls from the yoga studio, have had nights out, and how she determined, at the first one, that she would never again be the frumpy friend.

She had shown up, straight from work, at the Mexican restaurant on Main Street, expecting to have a quiet dinner with the girls.

In jeans and an L. L. Bean shirt, she realized her mistake as soon as she walked in. This was a Girls' Night Out, and these Girls were definitely making the most of it. Tracy, who has the best body of anyone she knows, was in a skin-tight aqua dress, high heels, her blonde hair tumbling in rollered curls down her back. Charlie was in a green and white print dress with flat jewelled sandals, and the other girls were in an assortment of cute dresses and tight jeans, with lots of make-up and jewellery.

Frozen margaritas were being downed by the dozen, and when the lights were dimmed and the music was turned up, the girls were the first to grab the waiters and dance raucously on the tables, while the rest of the restaurant cheered and clapped, before joining in.

Kit was self-conscious, at best. She had never been a big girls' night out person, but she had to admit she had fun, once the margaritas had loosened her up a bit; and the next time they arranged a night, she went all out with a flippy pink mini-dress and sparkly eye-shadow.

'That's more like it!' Tracy had hugged her approvingly. 'Now you look like one of the girls.'

'As opposed to what?' Kit said, bemused. 'One of the boys?'

'I just meant you look gorgeous,' Tracy said, and Kit, who hadn't ever managed to quit her search for approval from other women – thank you, *Mother* – had beamed.

Kit shouts up the stairs to hurry the children as their father is waiting, giving Adam an apologetic shrug. He smiles in return, and they both stand there, awkward suddenly, waiting for the children to thunder down the stairs.

'See you, Mom!' The kids whirl past her, not even stopping to give her a kiss goodbye.

'Hey!' Adam roars. 'Go back and give your mother a kiss.'

'Sorry, Mom,' they say sheepishly, and she catches Adam's eye as she straightens up from kissing Buckley and thanks him with her eyes. He nods, and for a minute she feels a pang of loss.

Then his phone buzzes, and he quickly reads through a text, a small smile playing on his lips as he does so.

She has heard through the grapevine that he is dating many women and she realizes this is from one of them.

Oh screw him, she thinks. Saying goodbye, she goes to clean up the kitchen while she waits for Edie.

4

Tracy is the first to arrive at the bookstore, and seeing no one there she knows, she heads over to the coffee bar and orders a mint tea while she waits.

She has dressed carefully today. Not one of her usual skin-tight colourful dresses that show off her yoga-toned body to perfection, but something far more subdued. A white shirt tucked into jeans, and a big silver-buckled turquoise-studded western belt, suede ballet flats on her feet, her hair drawn back in a low, elegant ponytail, and glasses.

She wasn't sure about the glasses, put them on, took them off, put them on again. Was it too contrived, perhaps? Too *Why, Miss Jones, I never realized you were so beautiful?*

She has worn contacts for years, was thinking about now investing in Lasik, except the thought of it terrified her, and she was so used to the contacts they never really bothered her. Wearing glasses has always made her feel like the nerdy schoolgirl she once was, long before she discovered the transformative effects of yoga, when her hair was dark and frizzy, and her thighs rubbed together when she walked.

At the ripe old age of forty-one, Tracy has mastered the art of transformation, morphing into a serene, peaceful yogini now she is in Highfield, and finally away from the storm of her early life in California.

Occasionally, Tracy will pull her pictures down from the attic of her house. She keeps them under lock and key, doesn't want anyone to see who she was in any of her former lives, and even now she is stunned when she flicks through, studies the unhappy, chubby girl, the sullen teenager, the promiscuous twenty-something party girl and the wealthy, polished thirty-something housewife.

She had never been frightened of forty, had always felt that forty would give her the greatest transformation yet, lead her into the best years of her life, and so far this has been partly true, although there are pieces of her past she is not able to shake, no matter how hard she tries.

To look at her, you would never recognize her from the old photographs. True, there is something in the eyes that remains, a sadness perhaps, but almost everything else has changed. The dark untamed locks were finally tamed into a mass of tumbling curls in her twenties, when she also joined Weight Watchers, lost thirty pounds and discovered, for the first time, her power over men.

A series of rich boyfriends, then Jed, the long and painful love of her life. He rang her doorbell one day, selling wholesale gourmet food out of the back of a van, and she was taken in by his good looks and the twinkle in his eye. Soon he had managed to charm his way into her kitchen, then into her life.

He had been exactly her type. Tall, tanned, black hair and green eyes, and irresistibly confident, with a confidence that Tracy had always lacked, even though you would never know it, to look at her.

He piled boxes of food into her freezer, then threw in more because, he said, she was so pretty. She guessed he said that to all the girls, but the next day he rang her doorbell again, and this time, instead of holding a box of crab claws, he held a bouquet of flowers.

For a while, it was everything Tracy had ever dreamed about. He was loving, attentive, lavishing her with attention and presents. He adored her so much, he couldn't bear for her to even talk to another man, and, in the beginning, she found it endearing to be loved so much.

Until the night they had run into an old friend whom she had hugged – and Jed changed. He said nothing, gave her the silent treatment until they got home, and as soon as the front door closed, he screamed at her.

She had humiliated him, he said, flirting with another man. How dare she, he spat, as she tried, in disbelief, to defend herself. He pushed her against the wall, hard, and she was so shocked, she told him to get out.

He left, coming back two hours later, weeping and telling her he didn't know what came over him and he would never lay a finger on her again.

She should have left that night. Now, looking back, she thinks so often of how her life would have been different if she had left that night, but how did she know? How did she know what was to come as she sat on the sofa with this wreck of a man, who she knew she loved, weeping in her arms?

The pushing happened again. And again. And more.

So much more. Each time he swore it would never happen again, and as time went by she became too scared to leave, tried to keep her head down. He told her he was insecure because they weren't married, so they got married, and things got worse. She was now his. His property. His to abuse as he pleased.

Eventually, Jed started having affairs, and he left her, as she always hoped he would, for she knew she didn't have the strength to leave him.

She moved house, changed her name, got a new job working as a secretary for Richard Stonehill, who had a penchant for redheads, and a penchant for her.

She became a sleek, glossy redhead, deeply tanned (aided by an excellent self-tanning spray), with huge diamond studs in her ears and an even larger ring on her finger.

It was easy to be a rich housewife, easier still to be married to one of the biggest movie executives in Hollywood. And it was fun, to go to all those parties, to have all those stars over for dinner, to call them friends, even though she knew the rules, knew that the friendship was entirely due to Richard's power. As soon as they divorced she wasn't surprised the friends all disappeared.

The divorce was easy. Setting it up wasn't quite so easy. Under California law, spouses are automatically entitled to fifty per cent, but not when they have signed a watertight pre-nup.

Luckily for Tracy, she knew about Richard's secret before she married him. Hell, it was part of the reason he married her, for he believed she accepted him, loved him; she was able to dominate him like no one else, not even the mistresses he had paid over the years.

She often felt like giggling, in her costume of black latex, as she and several others tied Richard up and smacked him until he was sore and red; and soon she began to find Richard rather ridiculous.

She no longer needed saving from Jed, and she no longer needed Richard. The pre-nup she had signed was indeed watertight, but his reputation was not, and when Tracy decided the time had come for them to move on with their lives, all she had to do was produce some photographs she had taken over the course of some of their more ... *elaborate* parties, and Richard was offering her whatever she wanted.

His manager stepped in. Tried to tell Tracy he would ruin her, but Tracy had laughed and said she was only a housewife, what did she have to lose.

In the end she got a settlement she was reasonably happy with, and a chance to reinvent herself. She grew her hair long and highlighted it blonde, let her skin tan in the sun, carried on learning more and more complicated yoga, Hatha, then Vinyasa, then finally Ashtanga, the yoga she had started all those years ago when she first moved to California.

And then, when her past threatened to catch up with her – it started with an associate of Richard's, a regular presence at his parties, turning up at her house and requesting, no, in a menacing way *demanding* her continued participation, and this was followed by her phone ringing in the dead of night and no one being on the line – she decided to move.

She had had enough of California by that time, enough of Los Angeles, of the movie scene, and she went to New York for a couple of weeks, and found herself, one weekend, accepting an invitation to a beach house in Highfield, Connecticut.

She parked in the car park by the marina, walked down some of the cobbled streets in the old part of town, right by the beach, and stepped onto Main Street, where she saw the pelargoniums in full bloom, tumbling from the window boxes outside the high-end stores that lined the street; there were laughing teenagers strolling past with ice creams in their hands, sand on their ankles and flip-flops on their feet.

She had forgotten quite how much she had missed the East Coast. Not that she would ever go back to Long Island – God knows she had worked hard to lose that particular accent. But Highfield felt ... right. It felt like home. She stood in the middle of Main Street with a broad smile on her face, and when she reached her friend's beach house with a view of the water, she knew her days in California were over.

Tracy bought an old 1950s ranch out at Sasquatchan Cove and, thanks to her divorce settlement, promptly knocked it down and rebuilt a classic shingle beach house, with large picture windows that looked out over the water, and a huge open-plan kitchen/living room, with big squashy sofas for people to sink into with a glass of wine.

Some time after she moved to Highfield, she took over the lease at Navajo Hall. A former movie theatre, it had been a pizza parlour, a video arcade, and in its last incarnation a hang-out for teens, complete with pool tables and no-alcohol bar, but the wealthy teens in Highfield were far too busy taking drugs and throwing excessive parties at their parents' huge houses while said parents were in Nantucket or Block Island for the weekend, to bother with the shabby and somewhat decrepit Navajo Hall, and when Tracy made the owner an offer he couldn't refuse, he didn't refuse.

She had a vision for Namaste. A yoga centre that would be more than a yoga centre. A yoga centre that would bring people together, become a centre for the community. A place where people could hang out, have lunch, connect. A place that would attract all the best people in Highfield, Connecticut, and if any of them happened to be wealthy single men, well, what was wrong with that?

If only it hadn't been for Facebook. If only it hadn't been for one of those nights when she couldn't sleep, when she decided, just for fun, to look up some ex-boyfriends. Her life was going so smoothly until then.

In the small bookstore that is hosting Robert McClore for the evening, there is a palpable frisson that traverses the room as the author appears, walking slowly towards the podium. He thanks the special-events organizer at the bookstore for introducing him, clears his throat, and starts to read.

Kit, seated between Edie and Charlie, smiles. God, he's good, she thinks to herself. His voice is low and mellifluous, as he reads slowly, bringing the characters to life, pausing from time to time and looking up from the pages to catch the eye of someone in the audience, a couple of times Kit's, and she is surprised that her heart leaps a little.

But he is an attractive man, she thinks. He is so much older than her and yet he is someone she would have noticed on the street, even if she had not known who he was. She sneaks a glance to the side, and sees Tracy, rapt, and the other women in the audience, strangers to her, watching him with half-smiles on their faces.

They all want to know him, she thinks. And I do! With that, she closes her eyes, the better to lose herself in his soft, seductive voice.

'I know that you're a big Democratic Party supporter –' Tracy sits forward earnestly in her chair – 'and in fact you were one of the main reasons Bob Riverside is now in office, so I was surprised when you made Troy Jenkins, the Democratic congressman in *A Life Not Taken*, the villain. Particularly when the book you wrote immediately prior to that, *Safe House*, demonized the Democratic mayor. Can you tell us a bit about your choice of politics for your characters, and how that may conflict with your own personal beliefs?'

Robert smiles and raises an eyebrow. 'Good question, and although I tend to avoid talking politics at my book readings – I apologize in advance to any Republicans sitting in the audience – it raises an interesting point about how much of yourself and your own beliefs you should put into your writing . . .'

As he talks, Kit looks at Tracy in surprise. Kit

hasn't read *A Life Not Taken*, hadn't read any of Robert McClore's books before working for him, and still has not managed his entire collection. She had no idea Tracy knew his books so well, but look at her! Listen to her! She's not just listening to Robert McClore, she's having a discussion with him, asking him more questions and he is clearly appreciative.

Kit turns to see Charlie looking at her with a grin and a raised eyebrow. 'Who knew?' she appears to be saying, and Kit shrugs. How odd, she thinks, that Tracy never said anything before.

The line of people waiting for their books to be signed snakes back through the bookstore. In a small town such as Highfield, with an event as exciting as a Robert McClore reading, many people have turned out, some who have not seen one another for years, and there is a buzz of excited chatter as people run into old neighbours, old friends, people they haven't realized they missed until they see them tonight.

And many who have known Robert. Not friends, but people who have been on the periphery of his life, people who have turned up to re-establish a connection with him, all of whom want to talk to him, to explain how they know him, or knew him, how their grandson once mowed his lawn, or they met him thirty years ago at a party.

Robert is gracious with everyone. He greets each of them warmly and effusively, as if they are guests in his home, and Kit, standing on the sidelines with Tracy, Charlie and Edie, is impressed.

'Why doesn't he do this more often?' Charlie asks. 'I'd always heard he was a recluse, but look at him! He's chatting to everyone! He's not the slightest bit how I'd expected.'

'But I told you he was charming,' Kit says. 'Although you're right. I'd also thought he was overwhelmed by large crowds. What do you think, Edie? You're the one who knows him best.'

'You do?' Tracy looks at her keenly. 'How?'

'I used to be his chef,' Edie says. 'And house manager. I was sort of his Girl Friday for years. He loved my macaroni cheese, used to say it was even better than his mother's.' She smiles at the memory.

'When was the last time you cooked for him?' Kit says.

'Years ago.' Edie struggles to remember.

'You should have brought him some macaroni cheese tonight,' Kit says with a laugh.

'You're right.' Edie's face falls. 'I wish I had.'

'Oh Edie,' Kit puts a gentle hand on her arm, 'I was kidding. You have enough to do.'

'But you are right,' she says, worried now. 'I wish I'd thought of it.'

'You can always make some this week,' Kit says, 'and I'll bring it with me as a surprise. He'd love it.' And with that they step forward to join the back of the line, inching closer and closer to Robert McClore's table.

Robert McClore had forgotten how much he loves doing these events. He had forgotten how much he

54

enjoys talking to intelligent people, people who read his books, about their thoughts, their feelings. He had forgotten how much he enjoys discovering how his books have touched people, made them think about things differently, sent them off, on occasion, on journeys they would otherwise not have gone on.

He is not, naturally, nearly as much of an isolationist as his reputation would lead you to think. In fact, back in the day, he was as gregarious as they come. He loves people, what kind of a writer would he be, in fact, if he did not love people, was not interested in everyone, fascinated by how people think, the motivations that lead them to do the things they do?

But the press attention was so overwhelming after Penelope died. Even though it went away, eventually, recently it started again: a few years ago he was snapped coming out of hospital, just a colonoscopy, entirely routine, and the next thing he knew the *National Enquirer* had printed this terrible picture of him, looking thin, gaunt and old, and stated that he had colon cancer and weeks to live.

He didn't have colon cancer. He had two precancerous polyps, but they had been removed, and as far as he, his gastroenterologist and his internist were concerned, he had never been better.

For a while the photographers seemed to be everywhere, their long lenses poking over the high walls of Hillpoint, and some even rented boats and tried to take pictures from the Sound but the rocks prevented them from coming too close, seeing too much.

Robert stopped going outside to garden, kept the

blinds of the house down, and then, on the advice of his publisher, went on *Larry King Live* to correct the story that he was near death, brought his gastroenterologist with him, and used the opportunity to state the importance of regular and early colonoscopies.

The researchers, those eager, earnest young kids who telephoned him beforehand, brought him into the green room when he arrived, told him there was nothing to worry about, didn't tell him Larry King would bring up Penelope.

And not just Penelope, and the mystery and rumours surrounding her death, but they peppered it with photos of her, photos of her he hadn't seen for years, looking so beautiful it quite literally took his breath away, and he didn't know quite what to say.

Larry King had been gentle, had seen the discomfort in Robert's face, the grief that flashed in his eyes, and he didn't push as much as he might have done, but this, Robert realized, is the reason he avoids the press. Even now, all these years later, they still want to know whether there was more to the story, still want to hear if he's in touch with Plum Apostoles, still ask whether either of them had, indeed, been having an affair with the other's spouse.

It didn't seem to matter how many times he said no. They still refused to believe him, or perhaps they thought that truth was always stranger than fiction, and that a simple death was far too prosaic for a writer of the stature of Robert McClore.

The photographers went away after the *Larry King* appearance, but the intrusion worried him, and he told his publishers he wasn't going to do any publicity for the next few books. Not that he had to. His name, the covers that screamed his name in giant shiny orange letters, were publicity enough.

But these local events are different. He has lived in Highfield a long time, feels connected to the community, knows it is important to give something back. He has known other celebrities in neighbouring towns, actors who helped rebuild theatres, musicians who sponsored music festivals, who are loved and appreciated by the towns in which they live.

He has known others, actors or actresses who live in the towns but don't get involved, see themselves as separate from the rest. Better? Perhaps, he doesn't know, but they don't last as long, are written about disparagingly in the local papers, are not approached for fund-raising opportunities.

Robert has always tried to give back. He is a patron of the library, and regularly donates items to local charities – walk-on parts in the movies, dinner with Robert McClore, a complete signed set of first editions.

The owner of this bookstore is someone he has known for years, and Robert is aware that every independent bookstore owner is struggling these days. He is happy to help.

There is nothing flirtatious about Tracy's behaviour, yet it is absolutely clear that she is flirting with Robert McClore. Not by giggling, or flicking her hair, or making – heaven forbid – suggestive comments that would leave no one in any doubt, but by focusing intently on every word, by listening to what he is saying, and by asking intelligent questions, questions that clearly delight him.

'. . . you ought to come,' Kit overhears, as she heads back to interrupt the conversation, and she sees Tracy hand a business card – on recycled paper, of course – to a surprised Robert.

'I don't think yoga's quite my thing,' he laughs, embarrassed.

'You might be surprised,' Tracy says. 'My most committed clients are always the most sceptical.'

'But not old men, I would think.'

'You're not old,' Tracy says, without a hint of a smile. 'But thinking that you are, is certainly one way to hasten the ageing process,' and she raises an eyebrow.

'Touché.' He smiles, tucking the card inside his book. 'Perhaps I will see you again.'

5

'What?' Tracy giggles as the four of them cross the car park to the car. '*What?*'

'You know what!' Charlie nudges her. 'You little flirt.'

'I was not!' she says indignantly as Kit shakes her head. 'I was just being friendly.'

'Right,' drawls Edie, 'that's why you offered him – what was it I heard? A free yoga course?'

'Actually, that was my business head talking. It's always good for a business like this to have a celebrity clientele, and seeing that he's the biggest celebrity in town, I thought it would be no bad thing.'

'Oh great. So now you're using my boss. Thanks.'

'I'm not. Honestly. Okay, okay. You got me. I do think he's attractive. Far more attractive in the flesh, actually. And that voice! Kit! It was heavenly! How can you stand to work for him without melting every time he speaks?'

'How about, because he's the same age as my father? Which isn't just weird, it's pretty disgusting.'

'Excuse me, ladies –' Edie clears her throat – 'I'm eighty-three, and I can tell you Robert McClore isn't old, he's in the prime of his life.'

'Exactly. He's not old, just older than us. Anyway, I love older men. He's nowhere near as old as my father, and even if he were, you'd never draw a similarity. I'm starving. Where shall we go to eat?'

Hacienda is more than just a Mexican restaurant: it's a thriving bar with live music every weekend on the upper deck.

It's an institution in Highfield, with people coming from miles around to hear the bands; and more recently it has become even more popular because of its reputation as a singles' meeting place.

Not every night, but on Thursdays and Sundays the place is packed with singles ranging in age from twenty-something to fifty-something, all squeezed together, looking over one another's shoulder to see if anyone more interesting has just stepped into the room.

'This is horrendous,' Kit shouts above the music as Tracy muscles her way back from the bar with margaritas in hand. 'It's so damned noisy. How long did they say it would be for a table?'

'Forty minutes,' Tracy says with a grin. 'More time for us to have fun.'

Kit casts a glance over at Edie, who is clearly hating this.

'I'm sorry, ladies,' she says, 'but I can't hear anything.'

'Me either,' Charlie shouts. 'I hate to be a killjoy, but this really isn't my scene. I had no idea this place got so busy on a Thursday. I think I'm going to head home.'

'Don't leave me here!' Kit says in horror. 'I may be single but I'm not desperate.'

'Okay, okay.' Tracy nods her head. 'It is a bit loud. You want to go somewhere else?'

'This is more like it.' They settle at a quiet table in the corner of the Greenhouse, a brasserie next to a popular garden centre on the outskirts of town that opened last year, and has quickly become one of the most popular restaurants in town.

The English owners, Alice and Harry, have lived in Highfield for six years and, once the twins were in pre-school, Alice started to think about going back to work.

She had been a caterer, back in London, a few lifetimes ago, and every time she and Harry went out to eat they found the food mediocre and the prices astronomical.

'I don't think I'm being ridiculous,' Harry would say, 'resenting going out for a neighbourhood hamburger which costs twenty-six dollars. Twenty-six dollars! Even if it's organic Kobe beef with gold-leafed tomatoes, how can they possibly charge that much?'

'It's not the food,' Alice kept explaining, 'it's the lease. The landlords are charging so much the restaurants have to keep the prices high or they'd all go out of business.'

'What this town needs is a decent brasserie,' Harry kept muttering. 'Somewhere that serves fresh pastries for breakfast, great salads and sandwiches for lunch, and casual suppers.'

'They don't have that in suburban Connecticut,' Alice would say.

'That's the point. They ought to.'

'Well, why don't we start one?'

'We? Because I'm running the garden centre. I couldn't possibly find time to start a restaurant.'

'So,' Alice said, with a familiar twinkle in her eye. 'How about opening something *at* the garden centre? We could convert one of those big old greenhouses in the lower field.'

'What? So everyone could wilt in the heat? Do you have any idea how hot those things are?' Harry laughed.

'Hello? Air conditioning? And you can treat the glass now too. Plus, blinds. You could have lovely natural rush blinds.'

'And how do we afford air conditioning, a professional kitchen, lovely natural rush blinds?'

'Investors, my darling. Plus the money we have from the divorce.'

Alice came to America a long time ago, when she was married to Joe Chambers. So odd to think she'd had another life before this one, a life as the wife of a successful investment banker, who transferred to New York only for Alice to discover that their marriage wasn't as rock solid, or her husband as faithful, as she had once thought.

Joe, it turned out, was a serial philanderer. He loved Alice, or so he said, but he couldn't resist the charms of a pretty woman, and there were many, many pretty women.

Alice might have been able to ignore it, to pretend it wasn't happening, to stay in their pretty little cottage in Highfield while Joe spent Monday to Friday in New York City, gallivanting around at all the top restaurants and bars; but then she met Harry, and although nothing happened with Harry until long after she was divorced, it made her realize there was more to life than loneliness, more to life than being an accessory wife.

She had no children with Joe, and there are times when she forgets she was married before, had any life different to the one she has now with Harry, whom she adores.

They are a family, partners and parents, with George and Carly their six-year-old twins. Even though the stresses of life often get in the way, Alice still goes to bed, every night, snuggled into Harry's shoulder, and wakes up every morning happy to be next to him, in this bed, with this life.

The income they have comes from Harry's garden centre – he bought out his boss when he retired a few years ago – and Alice's private catering, but as soon as she came up with the idea for the restaurant, she knew it was right, knew it was exactly what this town needed.

For it was true, Highfield, despite being so close to New York, despite having more than its fair share of sophisticates, did not have a plethora of decent restaurants. Old-fashioned Italian ('Think Chicken Kiev Italian rather than Jamie Oliver Italian,' Harry would say), a few modern Mediterranean places that were fair but over-priced and never changed the menu, and of course the ubiquitous all-American burger joints that were usually filled with kids and people who simply weren't interested in real food.

'I want something that uses local food, seasonal, preferably organic,' Alice said. 'Things we can grow ourselves. I want a place that people can care about, where they know they'll get great food, fairly priced, but if they just want a cappuccino, that's fine too.'

'It should be something European,' Harry said. 'A true French brasserie.'

'Yes, in the sense that it will serve food all day, but not necessarily French, just ... comfortable. Unpretentious. Somewhere that people can come because of the food, the price and the service.'

'Do you have any idea of the work involved in running a restaurant?' Harry said.

'Well, no. Do you?'

'Not really. I mean, I've worked as a waiter, but everyone says it's a killer. You have to be there all the time otherwise everything goes pear-shaped pretty damn quickly.'

'I agree, it's going to be hard, but wouldn't it be wonderful? And we'd both be at the garden centre, so at least we'd be together.'

'I think we need to do our research,' Harry said. 'And take it very slowly.'

Now it's the most popular place in town, a place where, this evening, Kit, Edie, Tracy and Charlie are sitting comfortably in the corner, refilling their glasses and clearly having a wonderful time.

'Who's Jed?' Edie asks Tracy, who is in the middle of a story.

'What?'

'You just said Jed would do that too.'

'I did?'

64

'Yup. Who is he?'

There is a long pause.

'My first husband,' she says finally. Reluctantly.

'*First* husband?' Kit and Charlie say in unison. '*What* first husband?'

'How many have you had?'

Tracy flushes. 'Only two. I can't believe I never mentioned Jed before.'

'Neither can we!' Kit laughs. 'I think you'd better start at the beginning.'

Alice comes out of the kitchen and approaches the table to say hello, and Tracy shrieks with delight and stands up to give Alice a big hug.

'You know my friends,' Tracy says, and Alice says hello. She knows Kit and Charlie, has done a few yoga classes with them, but doesn't know them well, and has never met Edie before.

'You emerged from the kitchen at just the right time,' Charlie says impishly. 'We were just about to quiz Tracy on her first husband. We think she may have killed him off.'

'First husband?' Alice raises an eyebrow. 'You mean Richard Stonehill?'

'Well –'

'That's what we thought,' Charlie interrupts Tracy who is trying to speak. 'But no, it seems there was a mysterious man before Richard Stonehill who is known, simply, as Jed.'

'Jed? Sounds like a biker.' Alice smiles.

'He was, actually,' Tracy says, and sighs. 'I was very young, had no idea what I was doing, and married the first man who came along and asked me. He was tall, dark and dangerous, and I thought he was the most exciting man I'd ever met.'

'And was he?' They lean towards her, intrigued.

'Which? Exciting or dangerous?'

'Both.'

'Well, yes. He was. It was that crazy whirlwind first-love thing, and it didn't last, and honestly, I hardly ever even think about him. I can't imagine why his name would just come into my conversation.'

'Perhaps you're not quite as over him as you thought?'

'Oh please. This was years ago. I haven't heard from him in fifteen years.'

'What happened to him?'

Tracy shrugs. 'I have no idea. I'm sure whatever it is he's up to no good.'

'Was he up to no good then?'

'Yes. That was one of the reasons I left.'

Charlie sits back and shakes her head with a grin. 'God, you do have a habit of attracting the wrong men. They all seem to have terrible secrets.'

'This wasn't a terrible secret, nothing as perverse or strange as Richard. Let's just say honesty wasn't a priority for him.'

'Oh come on –' it's Kit's turn – 'you can't just say something like that and leave us all dying of curiosity. What happened?'

Tracy looks uncomfortable. 'Nothing happened. Okay, well, a small something. He stole some money.'

'From you?' Kit's eyes are as big as saucers.

'From me?' Tracy bursts out laughing. 'I didn't have any money. Neither of us did. He was working in a retail store and it turns out he'd been stealing from them. He was accused of grand larceny.'

'God!' Charlie says. 'That's pretty big. Did you know?'

'No! Absolutely not. That was the end. There were some other things too, things that had happened before that. We'd gone to see my parents and my mom had phoned afterwards and accused us of taking some stuff that was valuable, my grandmother's silver, things like that, and I screamed at her and told her she was crazy, and how dare she accuse us.'

'But presumably this ... Jed ... took it?' Alice has pulled a chair up to the table and joined them.

'Yes, I guess so, but I never found it. I think he'd sold it pretty soon afterwards.'

'Wow!' Charlie sits up and crosses her arms. 'What do you think it was in you that attracted bad men?'

Tracy laughs. 'My therapist in California said horribly low self-esteem.'

'We'll just have to find you a decent man,' Alice says with a smile.

'She's already got her eyes on Robert McClore,' Charlie tells Alice.

'Robert McClore the writer?' Alice is impressed.

'Yes. Robert McClore the writer, who's also my boss, which is just a tiny bit embarrassing.'

'Not embarrassing at all.' Tracy nudges Kit and says, 'Just think, if Robert McClore and I get married we'll see each other every day! Think how much fun it will be.'

'Okay, this is a little much for me,' Kit says, wondering just what it is that is making her so uncomfortable. Tracy is joking, after all, and even if she isn't joking about being attracted to Robert, why exactly is it so unsettling?

'Never mind about Tracy,' Edie pipes up, 'how about Miss Kit here? She could do with a decent man herself.'

'You're single?' Alice has seen Kit, but never had a conversation with her, knows little about her.

'Divorced. Two children.'

'I'll keep my eyes open,' Alice says. 'Although most of the men I meet these days tend to be Mexican gardeners. Cute, though. Interested?'

'My Spanish isn't up to par,' Kit says. 'But thanks for thinking of me.'

'Hey,' Alice says suddenly. 'Isn't Robert McClore about sixty-five? Isn't that a little old for you?'

'What can I say?' Tracy shrugs with a smile. 'I've always been into older men, and as Edie will tell you, sixty-five is positively a baby.'

Charlie gets home to find the house unusually quiet. It's not often she is in the house by herself these days, but with Keith away, the kids at sleepovers, and Amanda being out, it is a rare treat.

Not that she's going to take advantage of it. What would she do, in the house by herself, that she wouldn't otherwise do? Dance naked in the living room? Scream at the top of her lungs on top of the kitchen table just to feel what it would be like?

She does what she always does. Gathers the

children's shoes and sweatshirts, which are strewn all over the hallway. This infuriates her because not only does she tell the children, repeatedly, to put their shoes in the mudroom and hang their sweatshirts on the hooks, she also tells Amanda, repeatedly, to pick up after the children before she goes out, and to make sure everything goes back in its place.

She sighs out loud as she passes the TV room and sees Emma's Polly Pocket dolls and clothes all over the floor, kernels of popcorn scattered among them. Damn. Another thing she has told Amanda repeatedly. No food in the TV room. Why does she sometimes feel she is talking to no one at all?

What is the point of giving instructions when no one listens to her? And much as she adores Amanda, she has noticed a change: in the early days, when she asked Amanda to do something, or requested something be done differently, Amanda would just do it, no questions asked.

Recently, she has jumped on the defence. Charlie feels that instead of accepting things, Amanda argues with her all the time. Or blames the children. When Amanda is supposed to be the adult.

But that, of course, is the problem with having an au pair. Or a former au pair who calls herself a nanny because she is no longer with Cultural Care, or Au Pair in America, or whichever programme it was that brought her over here, except she is still only twenty years old, and is therefore far more like another teenage daughter, and certainly not a nanny in the sense that Mary Poppins is a nanny.

Charlie hates that she has become one of those women who sits with her girlfriends and complains about the nanny, but then again, she never thought she'd be one of those women who has a nanny.

And now that Emma is four, it's not really as if she needs one. Sure, Charlie has her flower business, but that's easily handled while the children are in school. The real reason they have a nanny is that Keith decided that if all the other wealthy Wall Street wives had nannies, then they must have one too, but Charlie didn't need much convincing.

It has made her life so much easier, allows her to do what she wants, when she wants to. It means that she can do a bit of impromptu shopping: on her way to pick up Paige, she may spot a sale in her favourite store in town, and can ring Amanda and ask her to collect Paige instead.

And really, isn't it a small price to pay, that she doesn't always pick up, or clean up, or put petrol in the car? And maybe, just maybe, the nanny will come home tomorrow and realize that Charlie was the one who cleared everything up, and maybe she'll feel so guilty she'll make sure it never happens again.

6

'It's me.'

'Hi, you,' Kit says, her stock response to women who phone up and say, it's me, who would doubtless be upset should she respond, as she is often tempted to, '*Which* me?' Although, in truth, these days the *me* tends to be Charlie, or, more frequently now, Tracy.

Today it's Tracy.

'So this guy comes in this morning and signs up for the yoga class at five, and he's adorable, and you have to get your ass over here this afternoon.'

'Thanks for thinking of me, but he's probably married with five children.'

'No! We chatted. He's just moved to town, he's single, and he doesn't know anyone.'

'Then he's gay.'

Tracy laughs. 'He's definitely not gay.'

'So if he's that cute, how come you're not interested?'

'Trust me, I would be, but I've already told you, I'm into older men and this guy must be late thirties, early forties. Not nearly mature enough for me. But I promise you, he is as cute as can be, and I want you to promise me you'll be in the class.'

'Five?'

'Yup.'

'Okay. Let me see if Edie can take Buckley.'

'And wear those lilac yoga pants and the matching vest.'

'Why? You don't think I look gorgeous in one of Adam's old oversized faded T-shirts?'

'I think you look gorgeous in anything, but honey, if you want the guys to notice you, you have to show your wares off to their best advantage, and no one's going to be able to see anything under one of those huge T-shirts you love.'

'Okay, okay. Point taken. I'll even do my hair.'

'Good girl. I'll see you later.'

'Damn,' Kit hisses under her breath as she riffles through her yoga drawer. Where the hell is that lilac outfit? She could have sworn she saw it in here the other day.

One word comes to mind.

Tory.

Damn.

When Tory was little, it was adorable how she'd come into her closet and play dress up with her clothes, telling her mom she couldn't wait until she was big enough to actually borrow them and wear them properly, and Kit had laughed, knowing that day was very far away.

Except now it seems that day has come. Tory is only thirteen, but their shoe size is exactly the same, and no matter what shoes Kit buys for her, no matter how cool the clothes – Abercrombie is all the rage – the only things she is desperate to wear are in Kit's wardrobe, and the more Kit likes them, the better.

Kit's favourite J. Crew flip-flops with the embroidered whales on them? The ones that were sparkling white and navy? Now they are filthy dirty, Tory having taken them, without asking, and worn them to a baseball match, getting them covered with dust and dirt.

Her pink cashmere pashmina that cost a fortune, that she wore to a wedding a few summers ago and hasn't had occasion to wear since? Disappeared, Tory swearing blind she hadn't seen it and hadn't taken it, only for Kit to find it, damp and crumpled, under a mountain of dirty clothes in the back of Tory's wardrobe.

Half the time Tory will lie and tell Kit, all wide-eyed and innocent, that she found the clothes in her own closet, as if a) that were true, and b) the fact that they are in her closet means they are automatically hers.

If Tory treated her clothes well, asked before taking them, put them back in the closet, Kit would have no issue with lending her things, but she can't stand this attitude of entitlement, this *what's yours is mine*, and *I'm going to treat everything of yours just as horribly as I treat my own things*.

It was funny when Tory was six. Anything sparkly or bright – hair clips, nail polish, make-up – would disappear from Kit's drawers and reappear in Tory's. Kit and Adam would laugh about how precocious their daughter was, coming down for breakfast with Nars blusher on her cheeks and Lancôme Juicy gloss thickly slicked on her lips.

Although heaven forbid Buckley gets his hands on anything of Tory's. Heaven forbid Buckley even enters Tory's room without permission. The screaming that ensues is quite unlike anything Kit has ever heard.

But the missing lilac yoga pants? There's only one place they can be, and by the time Kit has turned Tory's room upside down, finding two sweaters, three pairs of shoes, one pair of pants and four scarves that belong to Kit, she is positively fuming.

The bus pulls up at the end of the driveway, and Kit storms out of the front door. Buckley, seeing his mother in a rage, adjusts his facial expression from one of delight at coming home to his mom, to one of nervous anticipation. Tory shuffles towards the house, kicking up stray stones on the road, clad in none other than Kit's lilac yoga pants.

'Get those off right this second,' Kit says, trying hard to keep her voice calm.

'What?'

'You know what. Those are my pants. How many times have I told you not to take my things without asking? I've been looking for them all day, and I cannot believe you had the nerve to just help yourself.'

'Oh relax.' Tory shoves past her mother and starts heading up the stairs. 'I don't even like them that much.'

'Don't you dare walk away from me,' Kit yells, starting up behind Tory, who runs into her room, slamming the door. 'That's it. No more clothes. I'm not buying you anything else this summer.'

'I don't care,' Tory shrieks. 'Daddy will buy me stuff anyway, and he spends much more money than you. I wish I lived with him! I hate you!'

'You spoiled little brat.' Kit can't help herself; but Tory undoubtedly knew that her words were like a red rag to a bull. 'How dare you! I work my ass off to try and buy you nice things, to give you what you need, and this is how you repay me? By acting like one of those bratty spoiled girls you hang out with, who snap their fingers and get whatever they want? That's it. I'm cancelling the Jonas Brothers tickets.'

'Nooooooooooooooooo!' comes a wail from behind the bedroom door. 'You can't do that.'

'Oh no? Watch me. When you're rude to me, young lady, there is a consequence, and this, I'm afraid, is the consequence.'

'But how am I going to tell Paige?' The wail becomes louder. 'You can't do this to me.'

'You'll have to think about how to tell Paige. It's not my problem.' Kit's shoulders sag with the drama.

'I'm sorry.' The door opens and Tory appears, now contrite. 'I'm sorry, Mommy. I'm really sorry. I'm sorry I was rude and I'm sorry I took your clothes without asking.' Standing in underpants she hands Kit the yoga pants in a ball.

'Okay,' Kit takes a deep breath, 'I'm sorry I shouted too.' She opens her arms and she and Tory hug.

'So I can still go to the Jonas Brothers, right?'

Kit detaches and shakes her head. 'No.'

'But I just said sorry,' Tory starts to wail again. 'You said okay.'

'I did. And I accept your apology, but the consequence hasn't changed.'

'Nooooooooooooooooo!' The door is slammed again and Tory collapses in a sobbing mess on her bed.

Kit goes into the office, tired and upset, to find

Buckley doing what he always does when his sister starts screaming: sitting coma-like in front of the computer playing Club Penguin.

Thank God, she thinks, I'm going to yoga. Thank God I'm doing something for myself. Putting the lilac pants in the washing machine, she gazes out of the window wondering when her life became so damned hard.

Kit manages to calm down by the time she walks into Namaste. There is something about the incense, the ambient music, the soft lighting, and her breathing changes, always, as soon as she steps through the door.

She takes her place in the yoga class, waiting for the teacher to arrive. In her usual yoga class there are just the same five women that show up every week, but here she knows no one. A different crowd, who clearly know one another, who just smile at Kit but don't include her in the conversation.

The door opens and a stranger walks in, male, handsome. You can feel, instantly, the energy in the room shifting, and she knows this is the man Tracy was talking about.

He is impossible to miss.

Tracy isn't taking this class – she tended to teach the Ashtanga yoga and this is Vinyasa – but after he rolls out his mat, Kit notices Tracy peeking in through the round glass window in the door, grinning and giving Kit a discreet thumbs-up.

Breathing in and out, in and out, absorbing the peace and calm in the room, Kit starts to forget about the stress and drama at home, starts to feel the tension leave her body. These episodes with Tory are so disconcerting, so upsetting, it can often throw her for an entire day.

She has tried to talk to Adam about it. Tried to explain the problems she is having, but Adam has only ever seen Tory as his little girl, refuses to believe that she could ever be rude, or difficult, and if there is a problem with Kit, surely it must be something to do with Kit.

Kit recognizes that she plays a part in this. Tory can behave however she chooses to behave, but every time Kit reacts to her behaviour, she is making the situation somehow worse.

'This has nothing to do with me,' she tries to tell herself, during those moments when Tory flies off the handle. 'These are her hormones. I didn't cause it, I can't control it, I can't cure it.'

And her other mantra: 'Today I choose to be happy, irrespective of other people's behaviour.'

Life has been so much easier since she found yoga. Since she and Charlie now see one another several times a week because of these classes, since her burgeoning friendship with Tracy. So much easier since she discovered a place that's all hers, a place where she isn't a wife or ex-wife, a mother, an assistant, but Kit.

Just Kit.

She can't help but sneak a peek at the stranger. He is, just as Tracy described, adorable. But more than adorable, the phrase that Tracy used recently comes to mind: tall, dark and dangerous.

He glances up from Downward Dog to find her looking at him, and she blushes furiously and looks away, not before he smiles at her. A sweet smile. Shy, almost. Embarrassed.

The lovely thing about yoga, Kit thinks, as the class ends and they bow their Namastes to one another, is that it forces you to switch your mind off for an hour and a half. It becomes more than exercise, it becomes a meditation; all you are able to do is concentrate on your poses, your breathing, being in the present.

She watches the stranger walk over to talk to the teacher, thank her, explain that he has had some problems with his knee and could some of the poses be modified. Kit rolls up her mat and leaves, wanting to strike up a conversation of some kind, but not having the slightest idea how to start.

She had met Adam so young, had been married so long, she never thought she'd be single at the age of forty, never thought she'd have to meet men, tell her stories, be vibrant and fun and interesting in a bid to attract someone who may or may not turn out to be her soulmate.

She sees others do it, put profiles up on match.com, give their business cards out to men in bars. Business cards? Why would she have a business card? She has had a handful of dates, less perhaps, since the ending of her marriage, because she just doesn't know how to do this whole dating thing.

She has been set up, from time to time, but that is usually awkward, and although she never expects them to be interested in her, they usually call her afterwards, and she doesn't know how to tell them she doesn't want to see them again, so she procrastinates, or avoids picking up the phone, screening her calls until they get the message and go away.

'You're gorgeous,' Charlie always says. 'They'd be lucky to have you.'

But Kit doesn't see gorgeous very often these days when she looks in the bathroom mirror. Mostly she sees tired. She sees grey in her hair and bags under her eyes. She sees washed-out sallow skin and a deadness to her face.

Sometimes she looks at the old pictures, from when she and Adam were married, and she barely recognizes the girl in them, not because much has changed – same hairstyle but more grey, same figure, just slightly more padded – but because the bloom of youth, already fading when she gave birth to Tory, disappeared swiftly and suddenly when she went through her divorce.

Other things disappeared just as swiftly and suddenly. The ten pounds she had been wanting to lose ever since she gave birth to Tory, fell off her frame. She still has no idea how she did it, doesn't remember not eating, or dieting, but the stress seemed to make it melt away.

Occasionally, she can make herself look like the girl of old, the glamour girl she used to be when she was married to Adam. Like when she goes out with Tracy and Charlie, when she makes an effort, straightens her hair, brushes on blusher and lipgloss, concealer on the shadows under her eyes, spray-tan to give her body a healthy glow she doesn't usually feel. But most of the time she can't be bothered; she runs around town with hair shoved back in a ponytail, practical and no-nonsense, certainly not wanting to be mistaken for one of the glamorous, scary mothers at school who look down their noses at Kit (or at least did, until they discovered she works for Robert McClore).

Today, for yoga, she may not have managed the lilac pants – they weren't dry in time – but she wore the chocolate brown ones that are pretty nice, with a sky-blue tight vest. She washed her hair and blew it dry, then decided it was too over-the-top for a yoga class, so drew it back in a tight, swinging ponytail.

Adam always loved her hair back in a ponytail like this. He said she looked both elegant and young, and with her hair off her face you could actually see how pretty she is, how high her cheekbones, how full her lips.

But he hadn't noticed her, the stranger. Or at least, not enough to come and talk to her. Tracy is not at the desk when she walks out, and because this is not her usual yoga class, she does not know the women who are there and feels awkward about going to the smoothie bar by herself.

She is heading out of the door and towards her car, when she hears footsteps behind her, and turns to see the stranger following her out. Is he following her? Surely not. Why on earth would he be following her? But he flashes a big smile at her and she falters, awkward, giving a half-smile in return, not sure if he wants her to stop or not.

He approaches her. 'Hi, I'm Steve. This is my first yoga class here, I wanted to know whether there are any others you recommend.'

'Oh. Sure.'

'Do you have a name?' He peers at her, squinting in the sunlight.

She laughs. 'I'm Kit.'

'Nice to meet you.'

He takes her hand in his and she is shocked at how warm and masculine it feels, shocked at how she had forgotten what a man's hand feels like, looks like; she feels a thrill run up her spine.

'Um, are you still here?'

'Oh God!' Kit shakes her head, embarrassed. 'I'm sorry. I was just thinking about something.'

'No, I'm sorry. You're obviously busy. I just thought you looked like someone who could tell me about the town. I just moved here.'

'You did? Where are you from?'

'Originally, I'm from upstate New York, then I spent some time in California, and now I'm back.'

'Tracy's from California too. Did you meet Tracy?'

'The owner? Sure. I came in earlier. She's from LA, though, and I'm from just outside San Francisco. They may as well be different continents.'

'So what brought you to Highfield?'

'Business. What else? I just sold a big computer game company and there is a software company in Fairfield I've been involved with for a while, just as a share-holder and consultant, and now I've taken it over.'

'I know nothing about computers.' Kit smiles. 'But

I have an eight-year-old boy who would probably know all about your computer games.'

'Any other kids?'

'Yes. A thirteen-year-old girl whom I'm trying to forget about right now.'

'Ah yes. Thirteen. The fun years.'

'You have kids?'

'No. Unfortunately. I've never been married.'

Kit wants to ask if he has a girlfriend, but she can't.

'So . . . is there a husband to go with those kids?'

'An ex-husband.'

'Boyfriend?'

She blushes. Shakes her head.

'I'm surprised,' he says, but not in a lascivious way, in a sweet way. 'I know this may be a little soon, but I really don't know anyone here. Would you, perhaps, have, I don't know, a drink, or dinner with me?'

'Now?' Kit panics, thinking of getting back to the kids.

'Well, no,' he gestures to his shorts and T-shirt, 'now probably isn't the best time – I'm not exactly dressed for dinner. Maybe I could call you?'

'That would be lovely,' Kit says, rustling around in her handbag for a pad and pen. Is she supposed to give her number out to a stranger? Probably not. She doesn't know the rules any more, but how else could he get in touch with her? And he seems above-board. Sounds successful. Looks successful. And as she waves goodbye and gets into her Volvo, the car she bought soon after the divorce was finalized, she notices him walk over to a shiny black convertible, and climb into the driver's seat.

Oh my, she thinks to herself as she pulls down the mirror and checks that she is looking okay – although she must be looking okay or he would never have asked her out on a date. A date! A date! I have a date! And he's cute! Soooo cute! My ship may be coming in after all!

7

'So who is this young man again?' Edie looks at her suspiciously as Kit dashes around the bedroom looking for her new gold hoop earrings.

'I told you,' Kit says. 'His name is Steve and he's involved with some computer company in Fairfield.'

'Why isn't he coming to the house to pick you up?' Edie says. 'I don't like all this modern stuff. When a young man takes you out to dinner he ought to come to the door and collect you.'

'Oh Edie. Not any more. Anyway, this is safer. As you keep pointing out, I don't know anything about him, so the last thing I'm going to do is give him my home address.'

'Didn't you Google him?' Edie says.

'How do you know about Google?' Kit starts to laugh.

'I'm eighty-three.' Edie sniffs. 'Not dead.'

'Okay, okay. Yes, I Googled him and I found a Steve Macintyre who works in computers, but there are no pictures so I have no idea if it's the same one.'

'Just make sure you know something about him,' Edie says cautiously.

'I will. Promise. Buckley?' Kit dashes into the office, looking at her watch and hoping she isn't going to be late. 'Buckley? Have you seen my earrings?'

Buckley, glued to the computer screen from which beeps, peeps and crashes are emanating, doesn't move.

'Buckley! That computer's going off in two minutes. I asked you a question.'

'What?' Buckley stirs.

'Have you seen my hoop earrings?'

'Nah.' He shrugs, without turning round.

'Tory?' Kit goes into the family room where Tory is lying on the sofa, talking animatedly on the phone. 'Tory? Did you take my new hoop earrings?'

'Hang on,' Tory says into the mouthpiece. 'No, Mom. You were wearing them this morning, though.'

'I was? Oh God, I was. Thank you, darling,' and she leans down and plants a soft kiss on Tory's forehead before checking her watch. Does she have time to run to Dune Road and pick up the earrings?

She was wearing them this morning. Now she remembers. Robert had been so pleased with the local event, he had said he wouldn't mind doing a small book tour. Kit spent the day on the phone with his publishers, putting together a small tour of important venues – town halls, libraries, places that could easily bring together the few hundred people that would undoubtedly turn out to hear Robert McClore.

Her earrings were annoying the hell out of her. They were clanking on the phone so she took them off, and can see them clearly now, sitting neatly on the table next to the phone, exactly where she left them.

Of course she has other earrings, but she has a vision of what she wants to look like, and that vision includes those earrings. It just won't be the same with another pair.

She checks her watch again. If she leaves right now, she can head over and reach Dune Road within ten minutes. She might be a few minutes late to meet Steve, but isn't it better to be a few minutes late anyway?

She hasn't played these dating games for years, doesn't know the rules any more, but she knows it is probably better to be slightly late than to appear too eager by showing up early.

'Edie, you have my mobile phone number?'

'Of course. Off you go. Don't worry about a thing and have a lovely time.'

Kit kisses the children, neither of them looking up from their respective computer and phone call, and dashes out to the car.

When you turn onto Dune Road, you think you might have made a wrong turn, finding yourself on a narrow, sandy dirt track which doesn't appear to lead anywhere, but then you turn a corner and find yourself staring at those magnificent gates leading to Robert McClore's house.

Kit has tried calling to let him know she'll be coming. She doesn't want to disturb him, but then again, she won't be long, has all the codes to the house; he will probably not even notice that she has been there. She has left a message. There is nothing more she can do.

The house is, as expected, quiet. She rings the doorbell, hears a soft padding and the locks are opened.

'Miss Kit!' It is Maria, the housekeeper, a beaming smile on her face.

'Oh Maria! I'm so sorry to bother you but I left my earrings here this morning. They're on the desk in the office and I'm going out. Would you mind if I just got them?'

'Ah,' Maria nods approvingly as she notices Kit's outfit. 'You look lovely, Miss Kit. Of course you can go and get them. Mr McClore is just doing a class.'

'A class?' Kit starts to follow Maria through the house. 'What sort of class?'

'You know!' Maria laughs. 'A yoga class. With your friend.'

'What?' Kit has no idea why she stops suddenly, but she does.

'Yes!' Maria nods enthusiastically. 'They are in the living room. I am trying not to disturb them. Ssssh.'

'Is this –' Kit knows she shouldn't be asking, but it is so weird, that Tracy hasn't said anything. It feels ... covert, secretive, like she has just stumbled upon something she isn't supposed to know. 'Is this his first one?'

She feels intrusive asking, and it is only a yoga class. But why on earth would Tracy not have said anything about it? She saw her earlier today. Is it possible this was organized some time in the last two hours? But wait, Tracy had called while Kit was getting ready, to see what she was wearing, to share her nerves and excitement about the date that Tracy had, effectively, organized.

That was only forty minutes ago. How had she not

said anything? She must have just been leaving to come here. That's just ... more than weird. It feels horrible. Wrong. And deeply unsettling.

They walk past the living-room door, which is closed, and Kit glances through the glass and sees Robert sitting on the floor, cross-legged, breathing deeply. Tracy sits opposite him, doing the same. Both of them have their eyes closed.

It is a scene of absolute innocence. I am being ridiculous, she tells herself, as she goes to the office, grabs her earrings and, thanking Maria, leaves. Obviously they just forgot to mention it. Why would there be anything strange about it? It all looked completely fine. Normal.

But why does she still feel so odd?

By the time she reaches the Greenhouse, she is starting to feel better. She called Charlie on the way over there and told her what happened.

'So?' Charlie said. 'She obviously forgot.'

'But how do you forget something like that? She was desperate to get to know him and suddenly she's at his house giving him a private yoga lesson and she doesn't say anything when I'm not just a close friend, but I'm his assistant? I'm the reason she even knows him, for God's sake.'

'Okay, so it's a little weird, but Tracy is a little weird. I wouldn't worry about it. Do you think there's more to it?'

'What? What do you mean?'

'Well, did you see him sticking his tongue in her mouth, for example?'

'Ewww! Gross! Charlie! Do you have to?'

'That's my point. From your description it was a perfectly normal yoga lesson. You know Tracy. As much as she's a business whizz, she's also a bit of a space cadet. She was probably just focusing on you and what you're wearing and all that stuff, and didn't think to tell you.'

'You really think so?'

'I really think so.'

It is difficult to miss Steve when she walks in. The room is packed, buzzing with noisy chatter and laughter, and Steve is at the bar, better-looking than she remembered, almost impossibly handsome in a crisp blue shirt and chinos.

What can he possibly see in me, Kit thinks, praying that tonight will go well, praying he won't be disappointed by her, but he smiles widely as soon as he sees her, extending a hand to shake hers. She is pleased he didn't kiss her on the cheek. It would have felt too odd, and she is aware that people in the room are looking at them, for how could they not notice him, this good-looking man whom nobody knows?

'Is this place okay?' Steve asks, pulling out a stool for her then asking what she would like. She orders a Pomegranate Martini rather than the ubiquitous Cosmo. Cosmos seem so old-fashioned now, but until recently, until she read a magazine article about the new *in* drink, she hadn't known what else to order.

'I asked around and heard this was the hot place in Highfield right now.'

'It is,' Kit says. 'Everyone's crazy about it.'

'I know. I couldn't get a table until eight. Is this okay, that we sit at the bar and have a drink first?'

'Of course it is.'

Kit smiles, thinking how, all those years when she was married, she didn't ever sit at the bar for a drink before dinner. It was just one of those things married people didn't do, she thought. At least, not married people in Highfield.

'So ...' She tries desperately to think of something to say, so unused to being on a date, and so unused to being in the company of someone so intimidatingly handsome. 'How do you like living here so far?'

Steve laughs. 'It's ... different. I knew what I was getting into on some level. I moved from an incredibly vibrant place with a thriving social scene, where couples and singles all mixed, and I knew that Highfield was going to be much more like a suburb ... I guess I didn't anticipate how hard it would be to meet people.'

'It must be,' Kit says. 'I made all my friends here while I was married, and most of them through the children. We'd meet at the playground, or in play-groups, in pre-school. I can't even imagine how hard it must be.'

'It is, but I like that I'm working out here, rather than in Manhattan. It's beginning to feel more like home, the more familiar it becomes, and that would never happen if I were getting on a train every morning and coming back late at night.'

'That's what my husband did,' Kit says and laughs. 'As soon as we divorced he started spending more and more time in the city. I'm not sure he ever thought of Highfield as home, but he has to be here now when he has the kids.'

Steve looks at her intently. 'It must have been lonely, when you were married, with your husband gone all the time.'

Kit smiles ruefully. 'It was, and it wasn't. It was in the beginning, of course, and then I got used to it, and resented him for coming home and trying to take charge, when he hadn't been there all week and had no idea how anything was run.'

'So the moral of the story is, if I fall in love with you, I'd better make damn sure not to get a job in New York City?' Steve laughs, and Kit finds herself blushing furiously, not knowing what to say, where to look.

Did he really just say that, she thinks. And should I be pleased? Or scared?

By the time they have shared a melted-chocolate pudding, Kit is neither pleased nor scared. She is relaxed and happy, and – wonder of wonders – allowing herself to be gently flirted with, and flirting a little in return.

Alice comes over and says hello, then turns, so that Steve cannot see her, and winks at Kit, giving her a swoony look as she places her hand over her heart. Alice thinks he is handsome too, thinks Kit. And he is with me!

Weaving through the restaurant out to her car, Kit stops several times to say quick hellos to people she knows. 'This is Steve,' she says proudly, noticing how all the women look at him appraisingly, appreciatively.

'You look *great*!' people tell her and, for once, she believes them. She *feels* great tonight. She had forgotten what it was like *to* feel like this.

In the car park, Steve walks her to her car, and suddenly she feels slightly nauseous with nerves. Is he going to kiss her? Is she ready for this? Part of her wants him to, has spent the better part of this evening trying not to gaze at his lips, trying not to imagine what it would feel like, but she has not kissed anyone other than Adam for almost twenty years.

She is not ready for it.

'Can I call you?' Steve says, holding the door of her car open as she climbs in.

'I'd like that,' she says.

He leans down and kisses her on the cheek.

'Thank you for a great night,' he says, gently closing the door.

Kit drives off smiling, and smiles all the way home. It couldn't have been more perfect if she had scripted it herself.

'Hello?' The lights are blazing and there is the sound of laughter from the kitchen. Male laughter. Is she imagining it? 'Edie? Tory?'

Edie and Tory both look up, as does Adam. They are sitting around the kitchen table playing Life.

'Oh.' Kit is stunned to see Adam there. Looking so comfortable in her home. She is not annoyed, but surprised. Not sure how she should react.

'Dad called,' Tory is keen to explain. 'And when

I said you were out he asked if he could come over. Is that okay?' she adds quickly.

Kit rearranges her features. 'Of course it is,' she lies. For on one hand, it is. This is the father of her children: there is a part of her that always wants him to be welcomed, that wants them to be able to co-parent effectively; but there is a part of her that wants to say no. Wants to shut him out altogether so she can move on, not have these moments when she has flashes of times they were happy, times when they were a family, a family that worked.

And more, she wants to have been asked permission. Wants to have been given an opportunity to say no. For this is what Adam always did: take charge. It is not his place to do that any more.

She takes a deep breath and places her clutch bag on the counter.

'So, what are you doing?'

'Playing Life. It's so funny!' Tory babbles, gazing adoringly at her father, who looks utterly relaxed, legs sprawled out under the kitchen table, a bottle of Budweiser in front of him.

'I'd better go.' He stands, reaching down to give Tory a hug. 'Edie? It's been a pleasure,' he says. 'Goodbye.' And Edie watches him with evident delight as Kit walks him to the door.

'I'm sorry,' he says to her, as they reach the front door. 'I didn't think. Tory asked me over and I wasn't doing anything, and I just wanted to see the kids. I should have checked with you.'

'You're right,' she says, softening immediately, for it is so unlike Adam to ever say sorry. 'But it's okay. It looks like you had fun.'

'We did. And I put Buckley to bed. He was thrilled. You look like you had fun too.'

Kit smiles. 'I did.'

'I can tell. You're glowing.' And with a sad look on his face, Adam walks away from the house.

Kit watches him until he reaches the car, then softly closes the door. At times like this she honestly has no idea why their marriage didn't work.

8

Charlie ushers Emma into the car to take her to pre-school, and climbs into the driver's seat.

'Shit!' she says loudly, jumping out and feeling her wet bottom. 'I don't believe it!' She notices that, once again, Amanda has left the window open all night, and the summer rainstorm has soaked her seat.

'Mommy?' Emma's little four-year-old voice says loudly from the back as she wriggles herself into her car seat. 'What does *ship* mean?'

'You know, Ems,' Charlie forces her voice to sound normal, 'ships are like big boats, they sail on the ocean.'

'Why did you say "ship"?'

Charlie's heart sinks as she realizes Emma is not going to let this one go easily, for her daughter is nothing if not persistent. She thinks this must be what they mean by second-child syndrome: Paige was always so easy, then along came Emma who, from day one, was stubborn, strong-willed and determined to have her way.

'I just thought that we ought to go for a cruise one day and . . . and I should start looking for a ship.'

There's a pause.

'What kind of a ship?'

Oh God. Charlie just doesn't have the patience for this today. Goddamned Amanda. Goddamned nannies.

Thank heavens Emma will be in kindergarten next year and hopefully she won't need anyone by then.

Not that she needs anyone now, some would argue. She didn't work for years after Paige was born, but once Paige was in school she started her floral design company, initially just doing flowers for friends, and parties that friends held, but word quickly got out, and now she finds she has orders to fill almost every day.

Keith's career, his job on Wall Street, seems to be going from strength to strength, and it's true, she doesn't need to work, could do as most of her friends do – hit the gym after putting the kids on the bus, meet friends for lunch, fill the afternoon with charity meetings – but she likes being defined as something other than a mother, likes having a different role in life.

She doesn't have a store. For a while she thought about getting one, but the only place it would make sense, in terms of passing trade, would be on Main Street, and the rents are now so ridiculously high, all the independent stores are being forced to close their doors, the ubiquitous chain stores the only ones who can continue to afford to be there.

There are vacant spots by the marina, but the prices are too high there, and after a while she realized that even if, financially, it made sense to have a retail space, it would also mean taking the business a whole lot more seriously. It would mean accepting every order, no matter how much she didn't want to do it; it would mean actively shopping for new clients; and worst of all, it would mean getting up at four in the morning every day to make it to the big wholesale flower markets in the city, to ensure she got the biggest and the best.

Not that she doesn't go to the markets now, but it's leisurely, at her own pace and time, to fill orders as they come in.

A couple of years ago she and Keith converted an old, falling-down barn in their yard, into a work-space. It isn't fancy. It has brushed concrete floors and countertops, industrial track lighting, but there is a large refrigerated room to keep the flowers cool and fresh, shelves and shelves of vases of assorted sizes and shapes, and her tools of the trade neatly assembled, rolls of brown paper, spools of raffia.

A large cork notice board fills two walls – one has orders pinned all over it, various reminders, and the other is filled with pictures that inspire her: hand-tied bunches of peonies and lilacs, elegant gardens with clipped boxwood hedges, photographs cut from magazines of brides holding gorgeous bunches of hydrangeas.

In one corner is a wrought-iron café table with four chairs. They had been driving through Easton one Sunday, taking Paige, when she was around eight, to feed the animals at Silverman's Farm, when they passed a tag sale.

'Stop!' Charlie had yelled, and Keith, who didn't seem to have reflexes half as quick as hers, drove half a mile down the road before safely executing a U-turn and going back to the tag sale.

She had seen the table and chairs, then black, had

bought them for twenty dollars, brought them home, spray-painted them white, and this was now her meeting area, her portfolio on an old whitewashed pine sideboard next to it, a stack of photographs to provide her clients with inspiration.

Not that Charlie needs to impress. The only flower stores in town specialize in what Charlie has come to think of as 'petrol station specials' – straggly bunches of gerbera daisies, chrysanthemums, cheap imported roses and sprays of gypsophila, all filled in with bunches of green, and in the most garish colours you can imagine: purple with yellow with orange with red, all in the same bunch.

Charlie is careful with her colours, careful to put together only flowers of the same tone. She may put purple with lilac and pink, but they will all be of the same family, will all complement one another.

She has banished ribbons from her workshop – if you want ribbons, she tells people, perhaps you ought to try one of the florists in town.

She ties her bunches with brown paper and raffia, displays her arrangements in simple frosted-glass cubed vases of varying shapes and sizes.

She can go bigger – for a wedding late last summer, a local girl marrying a Scot, she had antique Chinese rice carriers in the centre of each table, filled to bursting with spiky pink heather, a hint of sphagnum moss drifting over the edges. They adored it.

Her workshop has become her refuge, the place where she is Charlie again. Not a wife. Not a mother. Not someone who spends all her time looking after other people, but an independent woman who loves her job.

And because she is so fulfilled by her work, she finds she is a better mother. She is more able to be present, to relax and be there for her children because she has had that time for herself.

The pre-school part of Highfield Academy is from nine until twelve. No extended-day options available, which, had Charlie known that at the time, would have precluded her from even putting Emma in, but it seemed so much easier to have her in the pre-school attached to the elementary school she would be attending.

However, the thought of spending every afternoon hustling Emma from playdate to playdate, or to music classes, or gym classes, or the museum, or the aquarium, filled her with horror.

She had already done it with Paige. She devoted herself to Paige for years, and vividly remembers the mind-numbing hours of sitting there watching Paige amuse herself, sinking into a coma of boredom, wondering whether she, Charlie, would ever have a life again.

And the playdates: sitting in mock-cheerful playrooms above garages that had been turned into fully-equipped wonderlands, complete with enough plastic toys, indoor swing sets, Little Tikes climbing equipment that would put, and *did* put, their pre-school to shame.

Forcing conversations with women she barely knew, trying to find some common ground other than they both had daughters the same age, knowing, by the end of that first playdate, whether you would become friends, or whether this was not an experience you would ever be repeating.

At least she and the other mothers were the same age then. Now, with Emma being almost ten years younger, Charlie has discovered that the mothers of the children Emma is in pre-school with are also ten years younger.

They remind her of herself when she moved here with Paige, standing outside the classroom waiting for the doors to open every day, more small talk. But this time she isn't invited to playdates, isn't included in the mommy and me groups, not least, she suspects, because she is older.

She isn't in workout gear when she goes to collect Emma, hasn't turned up to the school fund-raiser (because she felt so out of place), has little in common with the other women, so when, a few months ago, she heard of a fantastic Brazilian babysitter who was looking for a job, she almost sank to her knees in gratitude.

No more waiting outside the classroom for Emma! No more feeling like an old woman who doesn't fit in. No more forcing a smile on her face as the other mothers chatter about shared group playdates, to which Charlie hasn't been invited. Not that she would have necessarily wanted to go, but how awkward she feels, standing there, leaning against the wall, knowing that she isn't wanted.

Her life, these past six months, has been glorious. She still takes Emma to school every day, but drops her off in the car park, and the teachers, waiting with sign-in sheets, escort her into the building. Now she can get away with a friendly wave and smile at the young mothers, all waiting in line in their SUVs to drop their children, while Amanda is at home, cleaning up the breakfast mess.

And now Amanda is the one who waits outside the classroom door, Amanda is the one who takes Emma to her classes, to the museum, to playdates, bringing her home every day at around three. Amanda is the one who will collect Paige from school on days she has activities, who will sit and chat to other nannies while Paige hits softball.

And then it is Charlie's turn, and Amanda goes off to study, for she is at school in the mornings.

But there have been a few hiccups with Amanda. Nothing serious, but one of the other mothers phoned her the other day to say that Amanda was always late, and that Emma was often the last one in the class to be picked up, and her little face was so sad.

It was sod's law that it was this mother who should be the one to be there when Amanda was late. She was one of the ubermothers – a different breed to the wealthy women in town. She didn't have a nanny, claiming she would never bestow the care of her children to another; however, it was her financial situation that prevented her from having any childcare. She was from the Bronx, and although she had pulled herself up by her boot-straps, she could never get as high as she thought was her due. She couldn't have kept up with the chattering classes even if she wanted to (which she desperately did): she simply didn't have the means.

She was a gossipy, unpleasant busybody of a mother who stuck her nose into everyone's business, who judged all the other mothers as being inferior to her, and the fact that it was this woman who rang Charlie was irritating as hell.

Charlie knew that Amanda wasn't always as punctual as Charlie would have liked, and she sat her down and sternly told her it was unacceptable. That was at the point when Amanda actually listened to her instead of arguing back, and as far as Charlie knows, it didn't happen again.

Then there is the issue of the locked doors. Amanda has a busier social life than Charlie has ever had, and as a consequence is always the last one in the house.

'You must lock the back door,' Charlie has said, repeatedly, only to come down most mornings and find the door unlocked.

So it is mostly little things that bother her: climbing into the car to find there is no petrol. Nothing. Barely enough to get to the petrol station, and Amanda was the last one to drive it, not thinking of filling the tank for the next person.

Leaving the car window open so the rain soaks the seats, or leaving the sun roof open to do the same.

Helping herself to a healthy wedge of fruit pie that was sitting, perfect, in the fridge, waiting to be served at a dinner party that night.

But there are more pros than cons, Charlie has to concede. If only she'd remember to put up the god-damned car window.

*

'Hey!' Tracy looks up from the desk at the front of the yoga centre, hesitates for just a split second before running over to give Kit the requisite hug.

'How was the date?'

'It was good.' Kit is cautious, waiting to see if Tracy volunteers that she was giving Robert a private class last night. 'How was your evening?'

Tracy nudges her. 'I don't wanna talk about me! I want to hear about that cute guy! Did you have fun? Did he charm your socks off?'

Kit woke this morning bubbling with excitement and a slow smile spreads on her face. She has left three messages for Charlie, enormously frustrated that she can't get hold of her, and has been dying to talk to someone.

Tracy doesn't feel like her natural first choice, not after she knows Tracy has kept something from her, but she wants to share, needs to share, and although she's trying to stay calm, she feels like squealing with happiness.

'He's really nice,' Kit says.

'Oh come on. Look at you!' Tracy peers closely. 'You look like you're about to burst.'

'No ... it's just I had a really nice time. I'd forgotten what it's like to have a date that goes well.'

'So it did go well? You like him?'

'I think so. Although who knows what will happen? He seemed to want to do it again.'

She wants to say more, but doesn't, because things feel strange with Tracy, and until it's out in the open, Kit can't confide more in her. She takes a deep breath, hating confrontation, but it seems that Tracy is deliberately keeping this from her, and why would that be? Tracy's made no secret of wanting to get to know Robert better, so why would she not tell Kit she was at his house last night? Even if it were purely innocent, not saying something immediately throws a shadow of guilt.

'Tracy . . . there's something I need to talk about with you . . . I know you were at Robert's last night.'

'What?' Tracy looks shocked. 'I mean, well, yes, I was. I was giving him a yoga lesson.'

'But why didn't you tell me?'

'Honestly? I could tell you weren't happy when I was saying I had kind of a crush on him, and I didn't want to upset you.'

'But that's ridiculous. I'm not upset. I'm more upset that you didn't tell me; it makes me far more suspicious.'

'I'm sorry. I hear you and you're right. I should have said something, but it was all totally last minute. He called me yesterday and asked me –'

'He called you?'

'Yes. Why?'

Kit shakes her head. No need to say it, but she is surprised, would have thought it was the other way round.

'So I really wasn't planning it, and it was just a yoga lesson. I didn't think it was a big deal, not worth repeating.'

'Would you just tell me next time?' Kit says. 'Only because it feels weird not to know. I mean, I walked in and saw you both there, my friend and my boss, and no one had said anything which makes me feel ... I don't know ... irrelevant.'

'You walked in?' Now Tracy is surprised. 'I thought you were on your date?'

'I was, but I left my earrings at Robert's and wanted to pick them up before the date.'

'You're sure you weren't spying on me?' For a second, Tracy's face hardens, and Kit frowns, trying to figure it out, then Tracy breaks into a smile. 'Relax. I was kidding. Do you forgive me?'

'Of course I forgive you. I wasn't mad, I just needed to say something.'

'So now will you tell me properly how your date was?'

Kit pauses. She wants to tell her, and although Tracy seems to have been honest, and even apologized for not saying anything, Kit just doesn't feel entirely comfortable. It's as if Tracy is plugging her for information, but not because she has her best interests at heart.

'I guess I don't really date,' she says slowly. 'I haven't been looking for anything, and I'm sure it won't lead to anything anyway because I'm much too busy, but he's cute.'

'*Cute?* Is that it?'

'No.' She shrugs. 'He's handsome and funny and smart, and certainly seems to be interested in me.'

Tracy raises an eyebrow. 'You mean ...'

'No! I mean, he asked me tons of questions. He seems like he really wants to get to know me, which is probably a stupid thing to think on a first date, but ... it was nice.'

'So are you seeing him again?'

Kit blushes, and suddenly realizes what it is she's uncomfortable about. Tracy is tense. As tense as a wire.

And suddenly Kit knows why.

Single girlfriends aren't allowed to have boyfriends, she realizes. They may no longer be in tenth grade, but nothing much has changed. When single women bond, they bond firmly, and the advent of a new boyfriend is always a threat to that friendship.

No wonder Tracy is tense. In a town filled with married women, Kit and Tracy bonded precisely because of their shared single status. Charlie is friendly with Tracy too, but she can't bemoan her life in the same way, doesn't understand exactly what it's like.

And now that a man has finally entered Kit's life, a man who seems, on paper, to be about as close to perfect as you can get, Tracy is threatened.

Never mind that she was the one who introduced them. That part was the fun part, an adventure, something they could giggle about. Just as long as it doesn't get serious.

Kit doesn't want to tell Tracy any more. She doesn't want to tell her about the email Steve sent her this morning:

Kit — thank you for a wonderful evening last night. I don't remember the last time I had such a great time, and I hope I didn't ask too many questions! Are you around on Friday night? I have tickets for the theatre and I'd love you to come . . . Hope to hear from you soon and have a great day! Steve

A perfect email from a perfect gentleman. But a message she's not going to share with Tracy. Not now.

She looks at her watch. 'I have to go or I'll be late for the class,' and saying goodbye she walks wearily up the stairs, wondering at what age they will grow out of these silly, petty things.

9

Robert McClore is intrigued by this woman who is so much younger than he. There have been many women over the years, but there have been few that have charmed him as this Tracy has.

There is something about her that he recognizes, something about her that reminds him of himself – on the surface she is sweetness, a ditzy Californian blonde, but she is also a businesswoman, and there is a ruthless quality to her, a toughness that he cannot help but admire.

Years ago he might have been intimidated by her, but he has been around the block enough times, lived through enough things that he can more than hold his own with her. So, even though he might not trust her entirely, he finds that she creeps into his thoughts, and, given how long it has been since anyone has done that, it is something he must pursue.

These days, he doesn't often think about Penelope, preferring to let the past stay in the past, preferring to let the myth remain, that they had a perfect marriage, the golden couple, the people everyone wanted to be, or, at the very least, be around.

But it is true that you never know what goes on behind locked doors, and their marriage was troubled, to say the least, although time has eased the memories, and he tells himself now that it was the seventies, they were expected to be unfaithful, they weren't doing anything differently to any of their friends.

He met Penelope in 1971. She was part of the wave of hot, young models who graced the covers of all the hippest magazines. She'd been linked to Paul McCartney and Mick Jagger. Robert, a budding journalist who was spending most of his evenings working on his first novel, had been sent to interview her.

The world of models and rock stars wasn't one that Robert was familiar with, not at that time. He was quiet, studious, had graduated with a degree in English literature, and worked hard at his dreams of writing the Great American Novel, taking the job at the *Times* just to pay the bills.

He'd had girlfriends, of course, because although he saw nothing but *himself* when he looked in the mirror, and there was nothing he found particularly exciting, women had always found him attractive, and he had rarely had to pursue them.

No one had lasted, simply because work had always come first, and a news reporter had little time for relationships, although the news was simply a step towards features, and even that was a step towards getting his novel published.

The paper was finally giving him a chance, only because the writer assigned to interview Penelope – she was known merely as *Penelope*, already famous enough to have dropped her last name – had come down with the flu.

It was an important piece, a cover story for the new magazine, and he wanted to get it right. He spent hours scrolling through the microfiche, reading up on her, although there wasn't much he could find out, other than speculation and gossip about her romantic assignations.

These were, obviously, the days before the Internet. The days before a click of a button could bring up everything you would ever want to know, and more besides. They were the days when the press kept their distance, and celebrities had a private life, if they so chose.

The interview was scheduled at a photographer's studio in the Village. Robert was a little early but he walked in, standing quietly at the back of the room while he took in the chemistry between Penelope and the photographer – Lee Stewart, also one of the hottest photographers around, mentioned in the same breath as Helmut Newton, David Bailey, Francesco Scavullo.

'You're beautiful!' the photographer shouted as he moved around like a suntanned spider, crouching, standing, zipping from one side to the other. Janis Joplin blared from an eight-track in the corner, and various beautiful people stood around gazing as Penelope, posing in front of a white screen, pouted and smiled, and a wind machine blew her long hair in a stream of gold behind her.

She was, quite simply, gorgeous. Far more beautiful than in her pictures. He stood, mesmerized, watching her pose, and when it was over and she wandered over to him, grabbing an apple and biting into it, then grinning and introducing herself, he realized that, for the first time ever, he believed in love at first sight.

The interview moved from the sofa in the photographer's studio, to a restaurant, to Studio 54. All the while they were surrounded by other people, friends, acquaintances of Penelope, all of whom were beautiful and fashionable, and accepted Robert as if he were one of them, even though he had never met people like this, never had a desire to be part of this world other than, perhaps, as a curious observer.

The entire night, Penelope didn't take her gaze off Robert. What started out as a formal interview quickly became two people getting to know one another's most intimate secrets, two people who couldn't deny the extraordinary chemistry between them.

And from Studio 54 to Penelope's loft.

'I think you're my soulmate,' she murmured sleepily, after they made love for the second time, and he fell into a dreamless sleep, knowing that she was right.

They married three months later, a wedding filled with royalty from the worlds of music, modelling and movies.

Robert had already started to change, to become comfortable in Penelope's world, and now that he was brushing shoulders with the Great and the Good, his own name became known. Less than two months after their wedding he signed his first publishing deal.

For a while, they were giddy with their luck. Two of the most beautiful people in New York, at all the right parties, with all the right connections. Robert went from being a jobbing reporter to a household name, mixing with Tom Wolfe, Paul Newman, friends with Philip Roth.

But the tint from the rose-coloured spectacles quickly faded, and Robert and Penelope found that once the excitement of their wedding had worn off, those few times they were ever alone together, they didn't actually have anything in common.

He had thought Penelope was a free spirit, and was astonished to discover she was actually rather stupid. She had dropped out of school at fourteen, which everyone thought was wonderful, a hippy child who had chosen a freer way of life, but Robert came to discover she could barely read or write, showed no curiosity for the outside world, for anything in fact beyond her parties, her friends, and the ever-increasing drink, drugs and, eventually, sex.

She also had a temper that was truly terrifying. Fuelled by alcohol, she would pick up whatever was at hand during one of her rages, and throw it at him, as hard as she could. He learned to duck, to move quickly out of the way, but there were times when the side of a lamp would clip his cheek, or an encyclopaedia would hit him with full force in the back, and he would be bruised and sore for days.

Lust very quickly turned to hate, but he had made his bed and he honestly didn't know how to get out of it. It was his idea to buy in Highfield, and he thought that perhaps things would change, for there were still times when he looked at her and caught his breath because she was so beautiful.

She would never be what he wanted her to be, but if

he moved her out of the city, if they bought a country place, maybe she would settle down and they would have children, the quiet peaceful life he had always wanted.

He drove out of the city one Saturday when Penelope was at a photo shoot in Paris, with a list of properties the realtor had told him about, and spent the morning trudging through house after house, each one more pedestrian than the last.

'There is another house,' the realtor said slowly, just as Robert was beginning to feel despondent. 'Although it's more money than you wanted to spend.'

'Tell me about it,' Robert said, as they drove through town towards the beach.

The house on Dune Road was the last one on the list, and the most expensive. It was out of their price range, but the realtor said they had to see it, because it had been in one family for generations, and was, in her opinion, the most beautiful house in Highfield, and certainly a house worthy of a famous author and his equally famous and beautiful wife.

As soon as they turned onto Dune Road, the rosa rugosa overgrown, almost overtaking the sandy track, Robert's heart started to pound. And then around the curve, through the gates, and up a driveway to a large square house with elegant pillars which was the most beautiful house he'd ever seen.

He didn't need to go upstairs to see the views over the sparkling waters of Long Island Sound from the master bedroom to make his decision. He didn't need to appreciate the antique library, the many fireplaces, the high ceilings and gracious French doors that opened onto a terrace with a pergola covered by an ancient wisteria.

He knew, as soon as he saw the place, that this would be his home, and that he would never leave it, never live anywhere else, for the rest of his days.

'You will love it,' he told Penelope the next day, when he finally managed to get hold of her, and Penelope, when he drove her out there the following weekend, simply shrugged and said it was nice. She didn't have the yearning for a home that Robert had, didn't have, he realized with sinking heart, an ounce of nesting instinct, nor of domesticity.

Before they closed on the house, Robert sold a film and, for the first time, money was no longer an issue, so buying the house was no longer a stretch. They had staff from the beginning, needed them to pick up after Penelope, who would literally grind her cigarette butts out on the wooden floors, drop her clothes wherever she was standing, knock over a wine bottle and not bother cleaning it up.

The staff turned a deaf ear when they heard the screaming, learned to disappear if Penelope was in one of her rages. Picked up the pieces quietly, having signed confidentiality agreements, knowing that they could never tell anyone of what really went on in the McClore house.

The only times she would be okay, the only times she didn't resent him for dragging her out of New York, was when the house was filled with her friends and models and rock stars were draped over all the furniture. Robert learned to acquiesce, learned to accept the constant stream of people for it was easier than dealing with Penelope on her own.

Their parties swiftly became orgies. It was, in some respects, a sign of the times, or perhaps a sign of their marriage, because after a while Robert stopped caring and started sleeping with other people too, models who turned up, friends of Penelope, women who made themselves as available to him as the air that he breathed.

And it was becoming harder to breathe. There were nights when he would wake up and feel as if he was suffocating with unhappiness, with dread, with the fear of what was going to happen next.

But his fear, his nervous anticipation, his sense of dread fuelled his writing with the same, and each book became bigger than the last. And then came the first of the movies, starring Warren Beatty, and he was Hollywood's golden boy as well, the man who could do no wrong.

Then that invitation to sail around the Mediterranean on Plum Apostoles's yacht. They had already met a number of times, and Robert knew that Plum was Penelope's latest conquest. He had seen the hurt in Ileana's eyes when Penelope had led Plum upstairs, led him by the hand, turning on the stairs to kiss him fully and passionately in front of the rest of the people in the room, who applauded and laughed.

Ileana was attractive and sweet and so obviously ill at ease in this world. He took pity on her, took her to bed that night. Tried, with his actions, to apologize for the behaviour of his wife.

He hadn't wanted to go on the yacht, but Plum had decided he wanted to make it in the movie business, and was one of the major investors behind the smaller studio that was making Robert's next movie. It was a business move. Nothing more.

Penelope came to bed in the early hours of the morning, ignoring Ileana, who, embarrassed, scuttled out, not before hearing Penelope belittling Robert, laughing at him, accusing him of being hopeless in bed, and feeling sorry for Ileana.

'You are a joke,' she hissed, turning to go up to the deck, and this time, for the first time, Robert lost his temper.

Perhaps lack of sleep, perhaps the wrong combination of drink and drugs, perhaps the final straw, but Robert felt a surge of temper at being dismissed, yet again, in front of someone else, and he followed her up to the deck and stood over her, almost nose to nose.

'Shut the hell up!' he shouted, louder than he expected.

'Why? Because you know it's true? Because you're not really a man, you're just a pathetic little boy? A pathetic little boy who doesn't know how to keep a woman happy?' She glared at him, then spat at him, full in the face.

He grabbed her arm, and something about the look in his eyes suddenly told Penelope he'd had enough, and she backed away from him, stumbling as she hit the railing.

And Robert stopped. It wasn't worth it. They just

needed to divorce. To stop making each other so miserable.

'You're pathetic,' he whispered. 'It's not worth it.' He turned to go back.

Penelope flung out an arm to slap him, as she had so many times before, and she lost her balance.

No sound. Not a shriek, not a scream, nothing.

Robert heard the splash as he was walking down the stairs. He ran back up, and Penelope had vanished. He turned, his face white, to see Plum.

'Stop the boat!' Plum said. 'I saw her go over. Get the crew up NOW!'

By the time they were flown back, accompanied by the police, by the press, he was a changed man. Or perhaps unchanged. It was a terrible, tragic accident, and he blamed himself. If he hadn't lost his temper she wouldn't have backed away, wouldn't have been scared of him.

He ran the tape of that night over and over in his head for months. Finally, he started to forgive himself, started to understand that no amount of guilt could change what had happened.

As he healed, he began to live the life he had always thought he was going to lead, before Penelope came into it, just with more money, more people wanting more things from him.

For he had come to realize that his life with Penelope was not what he would have chosen.

He had felt like an impostor much of the time, had known he didn't fit in, only found peace when Penelope and the entourage that always surrounded her were travelling and he could be in the house by himself, build a fire and sit in an armchair with the papers, reading quietly, no need to be anywhere else, to see anyone else, to be doing anything else.

He stopped returning calls, burned the hundreds of condolences that arrived in his mailbox every day, didn't answer the door to the flowers that arrived. He also stopped writing for a couple of years, finding that there was only one story that needed to be told back then, and he couldn't tell that story, would never be ready to tell that story.

Until now. Until the idea of a mystery, of a series of mysteries raised its head. Last night, for the first time, he managed to stop worrying about where to find an idea for a mystery, and lost himself in the quiet breathing of his yoga class.

And afterwards, he mentioned to Tracy that he was thinking about a mystery, and she said what a wonderful idea, and pointed out, laughing, that he had been at the centre of a mystery of his own, and perhaps he could use his own story as inspiration.

The more he thinks about it, the more he realizes Tracy has definitely hit upon something – what better mystery than the one surrounding the death of Penelope?

It won't be his story. He will never tell his story entirely, but he can always write it, then change it. Write it as it was, then change the names, change the facts, make sure to disguise it so people don't know.

He can draw upon his life, write about that unique time in history, the parties, the people, the atmosphere of freedom, of possibility, that has never existed before or since.

He can write about a free-spirited actress, a woman whom everyone adores, who chooses to seduce a scientist, perhaps, a serious, quiet man who falls under her spell, who feels as though he is playing a part in a movie of his own making, until the movie turns dark and he doesn't know how to get out.

He will change the ending, of course. Not Plum and Ileana, but maybe Vladimir and Alla. Or Marco and Francesca. Or Serge and Jeanne. And it will not be a yacht sailing around the Mediterranean, but possibly a vacation at a villa in the hills above St Tropez, a vacation where it all goes wrong.

He will write about the mystery of Vladimir/Marco/ Serge. How he is a man of significant means, but has come about those means in dubious ways, rumours swirling about larceny, impersonation and deceit.

He loves the idea of writing it under a pseudonym. But not Robert McClore writing as someone else. A true pseudonym, one that will never be linked to him. What a genius idea, what a perfect solution to this book that will otherwise undoubtedly garner huge media attention.

He can also, he supposes, use a ghost writer, although might the subject matter be too sensitive?

As a writer Robert often puts his own life into his books, often without realizing it – but a ghost writer? How would he possibly know the details? He would imbue the writing with details of his own, details pulled from his imagination, or from his own life.

Robert could write the storyline, could draft each chapter, describe the characters, and then leave it up to a ghost writer to fill in the blanks.

He will have to decide which path to choose.

And in the meantime, he will have to give the yoga girl a call. He has met her a few times since the initial book reading, but his physical attraction for her increased enormously during their private lesson.

He keeps thinking of her pert bottom pointing up at the ceiling in Downward Dog, the way her T-shirt fell forward over her breasts, giving him a glimpse of her firm stomach. He shivers. He hasn't felt such a strong attraction for a woman for a very long time.

How can he possibly let this pass?

10

Kit opens her eyes and looks at the clock: 9.03. A brief moment of panic before she sinks back in the pillows with a smile. Of course. Saturday. The kids are with their dad, and she has the whole weekend to herself. No work, no phone calls, no rushing through breakfast to get the kids on the bus, just hours of wonderful leisurely time to do whatever she chooses.

Right now she chooses to stay in bed, to replay every wonderful second of her date with Steve last night.

He picked her up from home, and she could see from the look in his eyes that her choice of the gauzy navy form-fitting dress was perfect.

They went to the Highfield theatre to see the new David Hare play, and shortly after curtain up Kit realized how close the seats were: her leg was pressed up against Steve's, and there was nowhere to move it to. Suddenly she realized that the buzzing she was feeling, a buzzing that was so loud it was virtually drowning out the voices of the actors on stage, was lust.

It was so strong, it was almost palpable, like a current of electricity running between them; unexpected, entirely new, she spent the entire play lost in fantasies of her and Steve.

When the intermission arrived, she was so embarrassed at what he had been doing to her in her head for the past hour and a half, she could barely look at him.

They hadn't bothered with dinner. They had left the theatre, walking awkwardly to the car, Kit aware only of this incredible connection between them, and as they reached the car he grabbed her and started to kiss her, and – she swore she didn't think this could ever actually happen – her knees went weak.

They sat in the car for an hour, making out. He drove her home and they sat in the car for another hour, making out. Nothing more, not yet. She wasn't ready for more, and he didn't push.

But oh joy, oh the joy of feeling these feelings she thought were dead for ever. Oh the joy of finally meeting a man who may not be Mr Right, but is certainly good for Mr Right Now.

And more, the joy of feeling *heard. Seen.* She hasn't realized, until now, how low her self-esteem has been, first during her marriage, when she tried to turn herself into someone else, and then when recovering from the knock of her divorce.

Because however much she was a part of the decision to divorce, she still felt bruised and battered, never thought that she would have the energy or the will to go through all this again with someone new.

It has been so much easier, since she separated from Adam, to be cocooned with her family, to nest in her cosy home and allow life to carry on for others, outside the safety of her house.

Perhaps tonight will be the night, for the house is empty, and Steve said he wanted to see her this week-end. Perhaps she should get ready to finally do the unthinkable, to sleep with someone other than Adam, the only man she has slept with for almost twenty years.

She wants to, and doesn't want to. The truth – as hard as it is for her to admit it – is that the only man with whom she still feels truly safe, is Adam.

But Adam is her past. And Steve, if not her future, is certainly her here and now.

With a yawn and a stretch, she finally manages to drag herself out of bed, and opens the blinds in the bedroom to let the sharp autumn sunlight slice through.

A movement outside catches her eye and she moves closer to the blinds. There is a woman standing on the sidewalk opposite, who seems to be looking at the house. She turns briskly and walks off, but Kit is slightly disconcerted.

Not that it is unusual to see people walking in this neighbourhood, but this woman has no dog, no friends out on a power walk. In fact, she isn't even wearing walking shoes. And although there wasn't much time to see her face, there was something familiar about her.

By the time Kit has shrugged on her robe and gone downstairs to put coffee on she has forgotten about the woman outside. She lights a fire, collects the *New York Times* from the driveway and sticks a bagel in the toaster.

'Hello?' The back door opens and Edie walks in. 'Don't tell me you've forgotten about our date today,' she says, frowning, as she sees Kit in her bathrobe. 'You're taking me to the pumpkin patch, remember?'

'I didn't forget!' Kit smiles. 'Of course we're going. I just had a slow start this morning. If you let me finish this bagel I can be ready to go in ten minutes. Want some coffee?'

'Sure.' Edie sits down at the table and squints at Kit. 'What's going on with you?'

'What do you mean?'

'I mean, you can't stop smiling. You look like a girl who's fallen in love.'

'Oh Edie!' This time the grin stretches across Kit's face. 'That's ridiculous.'

'It may be ridiculous but you certainly look like the cat that got the cream. So go on, then, tell me if I'm right. Are you falling in love?'

'Well ... I'm definitely falling in like.'

Edie peers at her. 'And he likes you?'

'I don't know.' Kit shrugs. 'But I hope so. I mean, I think so.'

'So what do you like about him? Is it the fact that he's around six foot, six foot one, dark hair, tanned skin, very handsome in his brown suede jacket?'

Kit looks at her in shock.

'How do you know?'

'Because he just walked up your garden path and –'

The doorbell interrupts her.

'... I was going to say he's about to ring your door-bell.'

'Oh shit!' Kit says. 'What's he doing here?' She gestures down at herself in horror. 'I can't go to the door like this.'

'Run upstairs,' Edie says with a smile. 'I'll go. But be quick.'

*

124

'Hello.' Edie looks at him coolly.

'Hello.' Steve seems uncomfortable, holding a huge bouquet of red roses and clutching a bottle of champagne in the other hand.

'For me?' Edie, naughtily, sighs in pleasure and places a hand on her chest.

'Er ... actually, I was looking for Kit?' he says uncertainly.

'She's upstairs,' Edie says. 'Come in. I'm Edie. I live next door.'

'Lovely to meet you,' Steve says, putting the champagne down and reaching out to shake Edie's hand, looking directly into her eyes as he says it with warmth and meaning.

Wow, Edie thinks. He's good.

'Come into the kitchen,' Edie says, leading the way as Steve follows. 'Is it someone's birthday?' she asks.

He laughs. 'I just wanted to drop something nice off for Kit.'

'That's certainly very nice. I'm sure she'll be impressed.'

He frowns. 'I wasn't trying to impress her. I just wanted her to know what a lovely time I had last night. We went to the theatre.'

'I know. It sounds like a wonderful play.'

'It was.'

They sit in silence for a while, Edie quite comfortably, Steve looking around the room, clearly wishing that Kit would come downstairs.

'So how long have you lived in Highfield?' Edie says, finally.

'Just a couple of months.'

'Have you found it a good place to meet people?'

'I met Kit –' he smiles – 'so I'd have to say yes.'

'True. But uprooting becomes much harder, the older we get. Do you have any family or friends here?'

'I don't.' He shakes his head sadly. 'But I'm a pretty outgoing guy. I've joined the gym and I'm doing quite a bit of stuff. I hadn't expected everything to be so family-oriented here. It's not really the place for a single guy, other than, of course, the number of divorced women.' He laughs, then catches himself. 'Not that I'm looking at other divorced women.'

'Of course not.' Edie winks at him. 'Well, welcome to suburbia, I guess. That's what it's like. Tell me, do you play tennis?'

'Sure,' he says.

'Good. You can join my tennis game next weekend. We're one short. Len Blackman just dropped out.'

'I ... er ... when is it? My weekend is a little busy.'

'Nonsense,' Edie says sharply. 'It's Saturday morning, ten o'clock at my friend Rose's house – in View Point Drive. We'll expect you there and I won't take no for an answer.'

They both look up as Kit clatters down the stairs in jeans and a grey sweater, hair pulled back in a ponytail, face now washed and clear.

Standing up, Steve adjusts his expression to one of pleasure.

'Steve!' She walks over, catching sight of the roses and champagne, and blushes wildly. 'What are you doing here?' She stops in front of him, wants to kiss him, but feels awkward, and couldn't kiss him in front of Edie, anyway.

'I just wanted to thank you for last night.' He smiles down at her.

'Last night? But I didn't do anything.'

'You didn't have to. I just ... well ... these are for you.'

'Oh Steve. They're so beautiful.' Kit turns and opens cupboards, ostensibly to look for vases, but in fact to hide her face, red with embarrassment and pleasure.

'I should go,' he says, moving towards the door. 'I didn't mean to embarrass you by turning up unexpectedly. I was just going to leave them on the doorstep but I saw someone in the kitchen and wanted to see you. Maybe I can see you later?'

'That would be nice,' Kit says, beaming.

'I'll call you this afternoon.'

'Well?' She can't help herself. She expected Edie to pass judgement as soon as Steve left the house, but so far she's said nothing.

They are in the car, on their way to the pumpkin patch, and Kit is trying not to say anything, wanting Edie to bring up the subject first, but she just can't wait.

'Well, what?' Edie says innocently.

'What did you think of him?'

There's a long pause, and as they pull up to a light Kit turns to Edie, who sucks her teeth.

'I don't like him.'

Kit starts to laugh. 'No, seriously, Edie. What did you think of him?'

'Seriously? Kit, have you ever known me to mince my words or tell you anything other than the truth, even if I know it's absolutely the last thing in the world you want to hear?'

Kit's heart starts to pound.

Edie sees the expression on Kit's face and backtracks immediately. 'Oh Kit. I don't know him at all, which is why I asked him to play tennis next weekend. I want to see if I'm wrong, but my first impressions are almost always right. I'm a little bit of a witch, you know, and I pick up on things. I just don't trust him. And red roses and champagne? For no reason? It feels like he's trying too hard, and I'm not comfortable.'

Kit is shocked. She wants to say something, but she is stunned that Edie has been so ... disparaging. So honest.

'Kit, my dear,' she continues, 'I'm not saying don't see him, I'm just saying that he's walked into your life and you know nothing about him, and you need to be careful. For all we know, he's a con artist.'

'Oh Edie,' Kit snorts, 'don't be so dramatic. You've been watching those crime series on TV again, haven't you?'

'Well, yes, but they're true stories, and they mostly feature men just like this one. Handsome, educated, well-dressed and impossibly charming. How do you think so many people fall for them?'

Kit forces a laugh. 'Well, if he's looking to scam me, he won't get very far. A single mother who's scraping together a living?'

'He could be absolutely genuine,' Edie says,

softening. 'But you need to take it slowly, to try to find out a little more about him before you give your heart away. That's all I'm saying.'

'I thought you were saying that you didn't like him and didn't trust him.'

'Well, yes. That's true. I'm not sure about him, it's true. But all I really care about is you. That you're happy and that you're treated well. Let's see how he manages with the tennis game, and let's see what Rose thinks of him.'

'Why does it matter what Rose thinks?'

'Because not only is she, as you know, my tennis partner and one of my oldest friends, she also happens to be the best judge of character I have ever come across.'

'Okay. I'll take it slowly and be careful. But red roses!' Kit sighs, a smile back on her face. 'And champagne! No one's ever bought me red roses and champagne before!' She turns to Edie, hoping to see Edie's smile of validation, but Edie's expression is a frown, and she is staring out of the window.

It is true. Adam was never the romantic type. There were gifts, for birthdays, obviously, but mostly Kit would tell him what she wanted, and in the latter years, would simply go out and buy it for herself, telling him afterwards what it was he had bought her.

There were flowers on Valentine's Day, and she knew he only remembered when he climbed on the train at Grand Central Station, and found every other man holding a bunch of roses; then he would run in to the florist's, paying outrageous prices for his last-minute romantic gesture.

Kit has always secretly longed to be the type of woman men bought flowers for, and having never been that woman, not really, she is starting to discover just how seductive it is.

'How long, exactly, does it take to find the perfect pumpkin?' Kit tramps along behind Edie, dragging the wagon as Edie examines every pumpkin she sees, or so it seems.

Kit should be here with the kids, she thinks, seeing the hayride pass every few minutes, piles of children and their grown-ups sitting on hay bales, bumping along the dirt track as they drive slowly past the cows and horses grazing in the field.

There is a stand for food – apple cider, popcorn, caramel apples – and rosy-cheeked children are running up to the barnyard animals and shrieking with laughter as the cows moo.

Although Kit knows she will come back next week-end with the children, she feels a sharp pang of missing them, of knowing that this would be so much nicer with them here.

'Mom!' Kit looks up sharply – she is programmed to look up whenever she hears someone shout 'Mom!' and has been known to shout back 'Yes?' no matter whose child it is that is asking.

But this time she sees Buckley – her delicious Buckley! – running through the pumpkins, his eyes wide with delight, and she runs towards him and scoops him up, burying her face in his hair.

'Buck! What are you doing here?'

'We're here with Dad!' Buckley says, flinging his arms around her neck and hugging her tightly, showing her, quite unconsciously, how much he misses her. Most times when he comes back from his father's he is cool and offhand with her, refuses to kiss or be kissed, wants to be anything other than Mama's little boy.

But now, when he sees her so unexpectedly, he can't hide his joy, allows her to cover him with kisses, squeeze him tightly, shower him with love and affection.

'Dad! Tory! Mom's here!' Buckley shouts over, and both Adam's and Tory's faces light up, a fact which surprises Kit, and slightly confuses her.

'Mom!' Tory comes over and hugs her, which is yet another unexpected surprise, and Adam grins, then both kids run off to see a friend of Tory's on the other side of the field.

'Hey, Kit. Hi, Edie.' He reaches over and gives Edie a kiss.

Kit is astonished to see Edie practically simper. Why didn't she react that way with Steve?

'Did you borrow children for the day?' He looks amused; and it's true, they do seem to be the only adults there without small children.

'Edie is my child for the day.' Kit smiles.

'I'm afraid she's right. I decorate my house every year, and it's time for pumpkins. I need big ones for the porch, and a bunch of those little tiny ones to go above the front door. I'm thinking that I might also do a scarecrow this year. I thought Tory and Buckley could help. It would be a fun project.'

'Sounds great,' Kit says.

'Well, Tory's only going to be interested if the Scarecrow's clothes come from Kool Klothes and it has earrings that come from Claire's.'

'God, Claire's.' Kit shakes her head. 'What *is* this obsession with Claire's?'

Adam laughs. 'Every weekend she's with me, all she wants to do is have me take her up to Claire's. I won't go any more. Too much sparkly make-up in there. It gives me panic attacks. Last time I dropped her off on Main Street and left her there for an hour and a half. I thought she would have gone to all the stores, but she and Livvy spent the entire time in Claire's.'

Kit laughs.

'And have you heard the latest?' Kit shakes her head so Adam carries on: 'She's decided she wants her navel pierced.'

Kit gasps in horror. 'Not in this lifetime.'

'Her what?' Edie strains to hear. 'What did you just say?'

'Her navel –' he gestures to his own, nodding – 'pierced. Horrendous. I told her she's welcome to pierce whatever she wants when she's not living under my roof.'

'Jesus.' Kit whistles under her breath. 'Where did my little girl go? What did she say?'

'She said she lived mostly under your roof.'

'Typically smart-mouthed.'

'So then I said if she did that she'd lose her iPod, her phone and her right to go to any dances for six months. And I said that you agreed with me – hope that's okay?

If I hadn't said that she would have just presumed she could continue doing everything from your place.'

'No, that's fine. Absolutely right, in fact. I'm glad you said it. Thanks.'

Kit is grateful. The children have always listened more to Adam. When they were married, the worst punishment she could think of was to say, 'Wait until your father gets home.'

The children did seem to be far better behaved when they were married. Everything she has read has said that the transitions are the hardest, and it's true: when she gets Buckley and Tory back, they both take a while to recover their equilibrium.

Buckley is wild, doesn't listen to her at all, has a tendency to be sassy with her, and Tory is sullen and resentful, claiming her place as the Daddy's girl she has always been.

Discipline doesn't seem to stick when it comes out of Kit's mouth and Adam is not there to back her up, and although they get on well enough for her to be able to invoke him if necessary, she doesn't want to, doesn't want to not be able to deal with her own children herself, in her own way.

The latest behaviour that Tory is exhibiting is what Kit is calling the 'Whatevers'. Kit will be talking to Tory, and in mid-conversation Tory will walk out of the room, muttering, 'Whatever. Whatever. Whatever,' as she disappears.

'Don't you "whatever" me!' Kit has snapped, not knowing how to stop it, no longer knowing how to talk to her daughter. So, at moments like this, when Tory seems to be back to the sweet girl she always has been, Kit prays they will last for ever.

'Do you guys want to join us?' Adam gestures over to the kids, busy chatting with some other children they know. 'Seems silly for us all to be here and not doing it together.'

Kit looks at Edie who beams at Adam in delight. 'Sure!' she says.

The hayride bumps along with Buckley and Tory sitting in between Adam and Kit. Buckley is holding hands with both of them, across Tory's lap, and Tory has her hand resting on her mother's and Buckley's. Every minute or so, one or other of the children looks first at Kit, then at Adam, the smile on their little faces so wide Kit is concerned she may burst into tears.

At one point she looks over at Buckley, then raises her eyes to find Adam looking at her, and she knows he is thinking the same thing; when she looks away there is a lump in her throat.

She doesn't know, during moments like this, why it went so terribly wrong, but she knows that she can't go backwards. Too much time has passed, and she can't go back to being the corporate wife that Adam so badly wanted and needed her to be.

She can't go back to that life, that lonely life of being a Wall Street widow, with a husband who is barely there during the week, who whisks the children to all the weekend activities because of the guilt, leaving his wife at home to recover from a week of solitary child-rearing.

Adam was always like this when he was there. Fun. Involved. Engaged. But he was so rarely there; and then, when he started travelling for work, there were weekends when he was gone too, because he couldn't get a flight back until Saturday afternoon or late Saturday night.

They were a great family unit, but they were rarely a family unit. And nothing has changed, nothing would be different. Think of how many times Adam changes the schedule, moves things around because of work commitments, knows that it is always fine to change things around because Kit's life doesn't matter, Kit's primary purpose is still to be there for the children.

And in all the time that has passed, Kit has found that she doesn't look at Adam in the same way. There is a comfort in the familiarity that exists between them, but she doesn't look at him and find him physically attractive any more, not in the way she looks at Steve and wants to rip open his shirt and run her hands over his chest.

If anything, looking at Adam now, she wonders how she managed to sleep with him for so long. Not because she is repulsed, far from it, but because the intimacy that grows between married people is sliced away as soon as they divorce, and once the intimacy has gone, however well you may get on, however friendly you may become, it is hard to believe it was ever there.

'Mom? Dad? Can we go to the diner for lunch?' Tory asks suddenly, as the hayride bounces to a halt. They look at one another and both smile. This was their routine when they were married. Saturday lunches at the diner. Greek salad for Kit, pancakes, scrambled eggs and crispy bacon for Adam, waffles for Buckley and egg salad sandwich for Tory.

'It's fine with me,' Adam says. 'I don't know about Mom and Edie. You want to come with us?'

'Yes?' Kit isn't sure.

'The kids would love it.' Adam smiles, and it's genuine.

'So would we. Edie?'

Edie nods at her, a mischievous glint in her eye. 'We'd love to.'

I 2

Kit has never believed in time machines before today but she spends most of this sunny Saturday feeling as if she has stepped back to her life as it was three years ago.

The pumpkin patch with the family – the only addition being Edie, whom she didn't know when she was married to Adam and living in the big house on the other side of town – then lunch at the diner.

And at the diner they run into Charlie, Keith and the kids who have just sat down, so they get up and wait for the big table in the middle, and the two couples and their kids chat and laugh, as they have done so many times in the past.

Charlie keeps making googly eyes at Kit across the table, gesturing towards the toilets, and eventually Kit gets up and excuses herself, closely followed by Charlie.

'What's going on?' Charlie grins as soon as the door to the Ladies is safely closed.

'What do you mean? We just ran into Adam and the kids at the pumpkin patch and he asked us to join him for lunch. It's entirely innocent.'

'*Right.*'

'Not "*right*". God, Charlie. It is possible for divorced people to remain friends, you know.'

'I know. It's just that ... how come you never were before?'

'What do you mean? We've always been friendly.'

'You mean, always been friendly since you completely hated each other when you were going through the divorce?'

'Well, yes. Obviously, I mean since then.'

'Okay, it's true – once you got past the anger you have been friends.' Charlie frowns. 'But something's changed.'

She's right. Something has. There is a new-found ease between them, an acceptance, both of their divorce and of their right to lead separate lives, and also of the fact that they are both the parents of two children they love, and are standing by their decision to co-parent.

And because of that, there isn't a negative charge any more. No anger. No hurt. No pain. Just the ability to finally be friends.

'Nothing's changed.' Kit smiles. 'We're just in a good place. I think we've both truly moved on.'

'Really?' Charlie's eyes grow wide. 'I'd say the exact opposite. In fact, I'd go as far as saying that seeing you two together, today, seems ... I don't know ... right, I guess. Maybe I shouldn't say that, but it's true.'

'Oh Charlie. Of course you can say that, and I totally understand why you feel that. You and Keith were our best friends, and it's bound to feel great when the four of us get together. And time has a tendency to wipe out all the bad so you just remember the good. Honestly, sometimes I have a hard time remembering what was bad. But, Charlie, remember how lonely I was? Remember how we grew apart? How we ended up barely speaking to one another?'

'I do,' Charlie nods as she answers. 'I just wonder if you maybe didn't try hard enough to make it work. If maybe Adam had been willing to make changes, get another job, find something closer to home, maybe it could have worked, because seeing how well you two get on now just makes me sad.'

'It makes me sad too, but the thing is that Adam wasn't willing. He loves his job too much, is too defined by being a successful finance guy to ever give it up. I never cared about that stuff, and that was the biggest problem. That Adam cared too much.'

'Well, given the way the world is going, he may not have a choice. I thought Keith's career was going fantastically, and then – poof! The world changed. After Lehman and AIG went down, Keith was really worried, and now they've just fired seventy-five per cent of the department.'

'That's terrible! Is Keith's job okay? Why didn't you say something before?'

'It is terrible, but we're hoping that Keith is going to be okay. The worst thing is losing the stock. I know everyone says that you just have to leave alone whatever stock is left and that, although it may take years, it will come back again, but we're literally watching our savings dwindle away to nothing.'

Kit doesn't know what to say. She thinks of Charlie's large, beautiful house, her large, beautiful life. Everything you are supposed to have, living on Connecticut's Gold Coast, Charlie has.

It is everything Kit used to have too, but Kit has

learned to live without all the accoutrements, and is happier without.

She wonders if Charlie could do the same thing. Live in a small cottage, drive a third-hand Volvo wagon – nothing smart or sexy about it. Shop cautiously and sparingly in the sales, learn the price of milk, of eggs, and learn which grocery stores are cheaper, cutting out the coupons in the free magazines, remembering to bring them with her every time she needs groceries.

Charlie drives the obligatory black Range Rover, and Keith a BMW, 5 series. She shops at Rakers, the designer store in town, without thinking about it.

Kit knows that Charlie doesn't really care about all this, not deep down, but the problem with living in Highfield is that there are plenty of women who *do* care, and while Kit suspects Charlie would be perfectly happy living as Kit does, she would be judged by others if she had to give up these things, would be found wanting.

Already, since the collapse of Wall Street, everyone at the yoga centre is talking about it.

'Do you know anyone?' everyone is asking, meaning anyone who has lost their job, anyone who has lost their house, lost their life.

'There are foreclosures happening all over town,' Edie said yesterday. Now semi-retired, she is still keeping a close eye on what is going on. 'We're all being asked to go to conferences on short sales and fore-closures. Nothing whatsoever is moving, and everybody is waiting to see what's going to happen.'

Like vultures, the people in Highfield are waiting for someone in their circle to have their life circumstances changed, someone to feel sorry for, at the same time as having immense gratitude that they themselves are safe.

Nothing like a hint of Schadenfreude to make an insecure wealthy housewife feel better about herself.

'Come on.' Charlie smoothes her hair back in the mirror. 'They'll be wondering where we've got to.'

'Charlie –' Kit lays a hand on her arm to stop her just as they're about to walk over to the table – 'I want you to know that, whatever happens, I'm here to support you.'

'Thanks, Kit. I know. The only thing I'd ask is that you don't say anything to anyone. As it is we're having dinner with Tracy tonight because she's got some business opportunity she wants to talk to us about.'

'Business opportunity? She didn't say anything to me.'

'That's because she's looking for investors and she wants us to invest.'

'Oh well, I guess that's why she didn't come to me.' Kit laughs awkwardly.

'Yeah. I wouldn't take offence. Alice and Harry, from the Greenhouse, are coming too.'

'As investors?'

'Yeah. Apparently, Alice's ex is some super-big big shot on Wall Street and she got a big settlement in the divorce.'

'Really? Wow. That surprises me. I guess just because they seem so down-to-earth.'

Charlie nudges her. 'And I'm not?'

'Yes, you are. Very down to earth in your black Range Rover with your – how many carats are those diamond studs in your ears?' Kit laughs.

'As I've told you many times before, the Range Rover is practical for the flower deliveries, and I only wear the diamond studs because they're pretty. Three.'

'Three what?'

'Three carats each. Bigger than Melanie Colgan's. That's all I care about.'

They grin at each other, for Melanie Colgan is the girl who strives to be chair of all the charity galas, strives to be bigger and better, to have more than everyone else. Both Kit and Charlie try to stay as far away from her as possible.

When Melanie Colgan is in the front row of the yoga class, Kit and Charlie are in the back. When she is holding court on one side of the smoothie bar, Kit and Charlie are on the other.

As Charlie says, 'She's not a bad girl, she's just trying so goddamned hard.'

They go back to the table and pull out their chairs.

'Why is it,' Adam wonders, 'that when women go to the bathroom together they take four times as long as men?'

'Because we have to powder our noses to look pretty for our men,' Charlie says in a Southern accent. 'Don't flatter yourself thinking it's because we like to gossip about you, or anything like that.'

'Just checking.' Adam winks at Kit, and they signal for the bill.

*

'Has Charlie said anything to you about money?' Adam asks, as they reach their cars.

'Not much. Why?'

'It's just that Keith said things aren't looking good, and he's worried.'

'Charlie said they were hoping things would be okay. He still has his job, right?'

'Right, but they're doing another round of lay-offs in the next couple of weeks and Keith is pretty sure he's going to be among them.'

'She just said their stock was doing badly.'

Adam shakes his head. 'Tell me about it. He seems to think that Charlie doesn't understand how serious it is. Apparently, she bought herself a necklace at Rakers the other day, and that was just after Keith told her they had to rein it in.'

Kit grimaces. She's seen the necklace. It is beautiful. A Temple St Clair crystal globe encircled by a vine of tiny diamonds. It looks like it must have cost a fortune.

'I couldn't help it,' Charlie said to her. 'I've had my eye on it for months and I was feeling a bit low. It's just retail therapy, I know, but once I got over the guilt, I did start feeling better. I told Keith it could be an early anniversary gift.'

'That's some anniversary gift,' Kit said and laughed.

'Anyway, Rakers has never been so packed. All the news is doom and gloom, with people losing their jobs and their houses, but I swear, you'd never know it in Rakers.'

'I guess you're not the only one experiencing the power of retail therapy,' Kit said, and they both laughed.

Kit has never understood stocks and shares. There were times, during their marriage, when Adam would try to explain about the stock market, but Kit would reach a point in the conversation and just blank. She couldn't understand it, and didn't want to understand it.

As far as she is concerned, it is all smoke and mirrors. She wasn't the slightest bit surprised when the financial world collapsed because it all seemed to be a house of cards to her anyway.

When they went through the divorce, she wasn't interested in Adam's stocks and shares. Even when they were listed on the assets, she wasn't bothered, because she never thought of them as real money.

Every few months she tries to put a little money aside. Some into the SEP IRA that Adam started for her when they were first married, and some into what she thinks of as her nest egg, money for a rainy day.

The one place she never thinks to put her money is the stock market, and today she is grateful.

'What's happening with yours?'

'I've lost everything I had at Bear Sterns.' Adam had worked there for the first few years of his career, and his annual bonuses had been partly cash, and mostly stocks. 'And the rest of my portfolio has dropped about thirty per cent.'

'Oh well. Could be worse. Could be eighty per cent.'

'It might be soon. How about you? Are you okay?'

'I at least don't have to worry about my stocks disappearing, not having a portfolio.' Kit laughs.

It is not difficult for them to talk about money, as Adam never felt fleeced by Kit, and Kit has always been a little naive about money. Had she been more savvy, she would have got a tougher lawyer, and could certainly have had substantially more than she ended up getting. But she wanted to protect the children from a nasty divorce, wanted to be on as friendly terms as possible with Adam, so she ended up agreeing to a settlement that she knew was unfair, but that she believed ultimately saved them all from unnecessary pain, and helped assuage her guilt at the marriage breaking up.

And look at them now. How many divorced couples, even ones who had been through mediation, were able to put their differences aside and have lunch, together, with their children? How many were able to get on this well?

'But *are* you okay for money?' Adam says. 'You know you just have to ask if you need anything.'

'Thanks, Adam.' Kit smiles, knowing that her pride is too strong, that she would rather work three jobs than have to go to Adam to ask for money. 'We're fine.'

'You know, the kids and I were going to have a movie night tonight. Nothing fancy. We're going to Blockbuster, then doing pizza and popcorn. Why don't you join us?'

'I . . . can't. I have plans. But thank you. That's really kind of you to think of me.'

'Oh. Sure. A date?' Adam grins, but Kit is certain that it is only to hide some hurt, and she is sorry.

'Just a friend,' she lies. Why tell him? 'Thanks for lunch.'

They smile at one another, but Kit finds it awkward. She turns to call the kids over to say goodbye, still feeling odd as she and Edie climb into her car to drive home.

'Now *that* is a good man,' Edie says, as they pull onto the Post Road.

'He's a great father.' Kit nods. 'And yes, he is a good man.'

'Wasn't he a good husband?'

'In some ways. I know he loved me, but he loved his work more. He didn't pay any attention to me. I've never been so lonely. I know that seeing us together now, you can't understand how our marriage didn't work, but, I promise you, there were big problems. I was desperately unhappy.'

'And you're happier now that you're divorced?'

'God, Edie. You're so transparent!' Kit laughs. 'In some ways, of course I'm not happier. I'm a working single mother. It doesn't get much harder than that. There are some days when it's all I can do to keep my head above water. I adore my children, but it is just so damned exhausting being the only parent, making all the decisions, having to be all things to all people, with no one to ease the burden. But I get breaks. When the kids are with Adam I get to be me, the real me. I don't have to be someone's wife, or mother, or anything. I get to be selfish, and sometimes I think I deserve a little selfishness. I love my life today, and I love it because I created it. I painted the walls of my house, and I know where everything is, and if I don't want to do something, like entertain corporate clients yet again, I don't have to.'

Edie nods to show she understands before Kit continues.

'You know, Edie, when I was married to Adam, I did everything then. Sure, he paid the bills and did some of the weekend stuff, like Costco shops, but I did all the other chores because he was never around. In the beginning he was, that was when he was fun, the Adam you see today, but as he became more senior at work, we saw less and less of him. He'd get home after I was in bed, travel at weekends, not show any interest in me or the kids. When he was home he'd be stuck behind his computer in his office. It wasn't a marriage. It was two people barely co-existing.'

'You young people,' says Edie, shaking her head. 'You all think marriage is this great romantic fantasy, but a lot of the time that's all that marriage is. I loved my Monty, but did I like him all the time? Hell, no. There were times when I hated him, and some of those times lasted a couple of years, but it always passed. We'd made a commitment to one another and both of us knew we had to honour it.'

'Edie,' Kit says through gritted teeth, 'you weren't there. You don't know how awful it was.'

'You're right. I don't know. I'm sorry, sweetie. I didn't mean to upset you. It's just that I think there are so few truly good men out there, and Adam is one of them.'

'He is. And I'm sure that one day he'll make someone else very happy. It's just not going to be me.'

*

There is a message from Steve when Kit gets home, and she decides to call him back on her way to the grocery store. She checks her watch – yes, there's still time – before hauling the pumpkins from the car into Edie's house.

'Forgive me,' Edie says, as Kit is leaving. 'I truly didn't mean to upset you. I think of you as a daughter, Kit, and I only want to see you happy.'

'I know,' Kit says gently, reaching down to give Edie a reassuring hug. 'It's okay. I know you didn't mean it.'

'I still don't like that Steve fella,' Edie mutters into her ear, and Kit laughs.

'You will,' she says. 'And so will Rose. Wait and see.'

'Just checking in with you . . .'

Hearing Steve's voice spreads a warmth through her body, and she smiles as she fumbles for her ear piece – the last thing she needs is a fine for using her mobile phone while driving.

'You're not cancelling me, then?'

'Are you kidding? I wouldn't cancel for the world. I wanted to see if there was anything I could bring to dinner.'

'There's really nothing,' Kit says. 'Just yourself.'

'I'm not coming empty-handed,' he laughs, 'so how about wine? Red or white?'

'I think maybe red.'

'Great. Oh, and Kit?'

'Yes?'

'I can't wait to see you.'

Kit rushes back from Trader Joe's and dumps the paper bags on the counter – she has a trunk filled with recyclable shopping bags, but she always forgets to bring them in with her – then quickly unpacks and puts things away.

Steve mentioned the other night that he loved home-cooked food, and what could be lovelier than a home-cooked meal, a roaring log fire, and the soft, soothing sounds of Ray Lamontagne on the iPod?

She is making French onion soup, a provençale monkfish stew and an apple crisp, served with gourmet vanilla ice cream. Kit is a woman who recognizes the way to a man's heart is through his stomach, and the monkfish stew is something she ate at the Green-house last year and loved so much she begged Alice for the recipe.

'You should do a cookbook,' she told Alice at the time.

'I'd love to,' Alice said with a laugh. 'In another life-time when I have more than two free minutes a day …' But she had handed the recipe over and it has become one of Kit's favourites.

The onions have caramelized and are simmering in beef stock and red wine, with thyme and bay leaves, the baguette is already sliced, the Gruyère grated, waiting to melt sumptuously on the top.

The beans, olives, tomatoes and anchovies are cook-ing gently, the monkfish is washed and seasoned, ready to be roasted quickly at the end. The apple crisp, now prepared and in the fridge, will be placed in the oven just when Kit pulls out the monkfish.

The whole house smells delicious. She has scented candles, but nothing is quite so enticing as the buttery, garlicky scent wafting from the kitchen. Nevertheless, the candles are lit, as is the fire, and the music is coming from the iPod.

Kit is in the bathroom, getting ready. Tonight is probably the night, she realizes, thinking about their kiss. Tonight is the night she will go to bed with him. So many years since she has slept with anyone other than Adam. So many years that she has forgotten what this feels like, this anticipation, this cross between excitement and nerves.

And yet in a flash it all comes back, making her feel like a teenager again, her eyes alight, her skin glowing.

She has new underwear on, nothing too sexy – she is a woman in her forties, for God's sake, not a twenty-something – and her legs are newly shaved and moisturized with a lemon Jasmine moisturizer she uses only on special occasions.

The doorbell rings and she feels her heart catch in her mouth as she runs down the stairs to answer it. After all these years you would expect to feel less nervous, she thinks, feeling ever so slightly sick as she opens the door.

'Hi.' Steve, looking almost stupidly handsome, smiles at her.

'Hi. Come in.' She steps back, suddenly wishing she hadn't been quite so obvious in turning her home into a seduction set. Why did she have to go so overboard with the candles?

'Oh, this was on the mat outside the door.' He hands her an envelope with her name on it.

'Thanks.' She takes it and leads him into the kitchen. 'Can I get you some wine?'

He puts a bottle of red on the table. 'I brought some. God, it smells great in here. You must be some cook.'

'I try.' She is distracted as she looks at the hand-written envelope. 'Let me just look at this.'

As she reads, she frowns, deeper and deeper, then freezes, the colour draining from her face.

'What is it?' Steve asks, concerned.

'It's from a woman who says she needs to talk to me,' Kit says slowly.

'About what?'

'She says she's my sister.'

13

'I thought you didn't have any brothers or sisters.'

'I don't,' whispers Kit, as a photograph drops out of the envelope. She picks it up, in slow motion. It is the woman Kit saw out of the window, standing on the street this morning, looking at the house. She isn't surprised. It feels as if there is a part of her that has known, a part of her that knew there was more to her than met the eye.

Of course there is a sense of familiarity. This girl looks just like Ginny, Kit's mother. Granted, she isn't groomed, overly made-up, dressed in couture and climbing out of a town car, but look at her eyes. They are the same. The bone structure is the same. Her skin is much paler, but her mouth is the same as Kit's.

'Do you think she's lying?' Steve asks awkwardly, not knowing quite what to say.

'It doesn't look like it, does it?' Kit gives a short bark of laughter.

'What does she say?'

'Here.' She hands him the piece of paper while shaking her head. 'I need to sit down.'

Dear Kit,

*I landed in Highfield a few days ago, and have been trying
to work up the courage to contact you ever since, and now
I am taking the coward's way out and writing you a letter
instead of doing what I had planned and ringing your
doorbell.*

*I imagine you will have no idea who I am. My name is
Annabel Plowman, and I live in Hampstead, London. My
father lives around the corner from me. His name is John
Plowman. He runs a successful landscape business there in
London, but many years ago he worked as a full-time gardener
for Virginia Clayton (as she was then), just after you turned
twelve.*

*The way my father tells it, she was the love of his life. She
got pregnant, with me, and when her husband found out about
the affair, he demanded she give me up for adoption.*

*My father took me away, said I would be placed with a
family in London, but he was always going to keep me. He
was paid off handsomely to keep quiet, to make sure no one in
Virginia Clayton's life ever knew about me. He never cared
about the money, would have done anything to stay with our
mother, but he took it so he could raise me properly, not have
to worry about schools.*

*I've tried to get in touch with our mother many times.
My letters have gone unanswered, and the handful of times
I managed to reach her by phone, she wasn't the slightest
bit interested in talking to me.*

*My father tried to do everything right, but he never told
me, until very recently, that I had a sister. He thought that
I had had enough pain, being abandoned by my mother,*

that I shouldn't have to deal with losing a sister too.

I always wanted a sister. Someone to share everything with, someone to be my best friend. I cried when he told me, and I knew I had to meet you.

I'm staying at the Highfield Inn. Please, please, please contact me when you read this. I know it's probably a huge shock, but I so want to meet you, to get to know you.

Your sister,
Annabel Plowman

'Wow,' Steve says.

'I know. Wow indeed.'

'Shall I open this bottle of wine?'

Kit sighs. She was so ready for tonight, had the evening all planned, had been so looking forward to it, and now she can hardly think straight.

'Steve? I'm so sorry. I think maybe . . . I think maybe we should reschedule.'

'You do?'

'I just . . . I just can't concentrate. This is such a huge shock.'

'Let's talk about it,' Steve says, kindly. 'I totally get how you must be feeling. I'm here for you.'

'Thank you, Steve.' She smiles gratefully up at him. 'But I think I'm better off on my own. I feel like there's a ton of stuff I need to think about.'

'Are you sure?'

'I am. Maybe we can do it again this week.'

'I'd like that,' Steve says, not hiding his disappointment, but doing his best. Then, bending down to kiss her softly on the lips, he lets himself out of the house.

Kit opens the wine herself, pours a hefty glass, and goes to sit by the fire, the letter still in her hand. She rereads it, over and over, then stares in the fire, remembering.

There is a part of her that wants to believe this woman is a liar. But John Plowman. It is a name she remembers. A man she remembers. Well. Oh yes, Kit remembers, for he was one of the many who took pity on her when she went to stay with her mother, only to be largely ignored.

He was the head gardener at the estate in Bedford. A trained horticulturalist, with large, gentle hands, and a winning smile. He was sweet and kind, and spent hours with Kit every day, giving her small jobs to do, weeding, pruning, showing her how to pinch off the vegetables to encourage the fruit to grow.

It was the best summer she had ever had.

John Plowman. Kit remembers him well. She remembers him softening the hurt when her mother was yet again disinterested.

For that was the insanity. Each time Kit was flown out from her father's house in Concord, where she lived full-time, to visit her mother, she thought that this time it would be different, this would be the time that Ginny would pay attention to her, want to be with her, show her that she loved Kit.

Yet each time was the same. Not that she didn't

have fun, but it wasn't with her mother. Never with her mother. The temporary nannies, employed only for when Kit was staying, took her to shows, circuses, fairs. And John taught her about gardening, how to handle plants, telling her, in his singsong voice, stories of when he was a boy in Dorset.

She peers at the photo in her hand, and instantly remembers John Plowman's face. And then she picks up the phone.

'Mother? Hello? Can you hear me?' Kit is shouting over the crackle.

'What? Hello? Hello? I can't hear you. Who is it?'

'Mother? It's me! Kit.'

'Kit? Is that you?'

'Yes. Where are you? It's a terrible line.'

'Darling, I'm on a boat. Whoops!' She giggles. 'I keep getting in trouble. Apparently, it's a yacht, and we're in the south of France having the most marvellous time. I'm falling in love again and this time I think it's for keeps.'

Kit represses a sigh. How many times, exactly, has she heard almost the exact same words come from her mother's mouth?

'Mother, I need to ask you something. It's about a girl called Annabel Plowman.'

'What did you say? Darling, I can't hear you. Speak up.'

'Annabel Plowman. John Plowman's daughter. Your ...' She can barely say it. 'She says she's your daughter.'

There is a silence then, as Ginny allows herself to

remember. To remember John Plowman. To remember how he changed the course of her life.

Ginny was on husband three, or possibly four, it was so hard to keep track, and she was living at Summerhill, in Bedford, New York.

A grand old estate on three hundred acres, off Pea Pond Road, it had electric gates that swung open to reveal a majestic drive lined with centuries-old linden trees, leading you up to the low-slung, 1930s mansion.

It had been falling down before Mrs Virginia Clayton – as she had become – moved in, and Ginny had immediately phoned all her New York contacts – architects, designers, landscapers, to come and turn Summerhill into a house befitting the third wife of Jonathan Clayton IV.

Walls were ripped down, windows and roof replaced, plush fabrics re-covering the formerly threadbare sofas and chairs.

The top landscape architects in the country produced blueprint after blueprint of gardens inspired by the classic English designers – Capability Brown, Humphry Repton, Gertrude Jekyll.

By the time the renovation was complete – two years on – Jonathan Clayton had tired of living amid the noise and chaos, and spent Monday to Friday at their Park Avenue apartment with his mistress, Clara.

Ginny stayed in the guest cottage – itself a rather spectacular five-bedroomed manse – to oversee the renovations.

The staff that had looked after Summerhill for years

had to go. One creaky butler/houseman, a team of Guatemalan landscapers who, Ginny decided, didn't know their oak from their apple tree, and Jonathan's assistant, who was horribly indiscreet and loved nothing more than sitting down with anyone who would listen to gossip about the new and awful mistress of the house.

The team were replaced with staff from one of the New York domestic agencies. A butler fresh from butlering for an English CEO at his estate in Buckinghamshire, three Filipina maids who were so quiet as to be almost invisible, and two full-time gardeners, plus a head gardener to oversee them, a young man who had just graduated with a degree in horticulture and who was looking for work in America. John Plowman.

Ginny, left on her own all week, found there was nothing she loved more than walking around the gardens to see how they were coming along, chatting about the flowers and the plants with John Plowman.

It didn't hurt that he was so handsome. And charming. That accent! His easy smile and unaffected ways. Being around him made Ginny feel young.

His family, back in England, teased him about not having a girlfriend. There had certainly been plenty of girls, but when he was out with those local girls from his village, they just seemed so, well, girlish.

So unlike Mrs Clayton. Now there was a woman. Everything about her was perfect, from her perfectly painted-in eyebrows to the patent heels on her feet. And the fact that she was American added a touch of glamour and excitement to everything she did.

Her humour, her ability to tease him, her thirst for knowledge of everything to do with gardens.

He would bring her books on gardening and then be amazed when, a few days later, she would want to discuss them with him, pointing out that Gertrude Jekyll had done a specific colour planting in some garden or other, and she thought it would work here.

When he brought her a book on Triboli, a book filled with pictures of his masterpiece in Florence, the Boboli Gardens, she insisted they fly out to Italy, on a research trip.

He abandoned his hotel room on the first night, sweeping into her grand suite overlooking the Ponte Vecchio.

It was perhaps the most perfect four days of his life. They walked hand in hand through the cobbled streets, Ginny gasping at the beauty of his beloved Firenze, stopping every few steps to take more pictures while he laughed and teased her about being a typical American tourist, then gathered her in his arms and kissed her passionately, bystanders clapping and cheering them on.

'What are they saying?' Ginny blushed.

'*Brava! Amore!*' He grinned. 'I think – although Italian has never been my strongest point – but I think they're saying how wonderful it is to be in love.'

John Plowman knew his life was about to change for the better, and that Ginny would be the love of his life. Admittedly she wouldn't have the life she had had before, but this was the real Ginny; she would be happy in a small house, just as long as they could be together.

Kit came to stay in the house for two weeks one summer. John felt sorry for her, this pale little girl with the sad eyes, who barely spoke, and he took her under his wing, showing her the garden and getting her to help with small jobs, showing her how to deadhead, how to weed and prune.

He taught her with gentleness and sweetness, sorry only that Ginny seemed so uninterested in her daughter. She was her biological daughter, but couldn't have been less like her confident, outgoing mother.

Perhaps he could change Ginny, he thought. Perhaps when they were married Kit could come and live with them and they could be a big happy family.

'Oh darling,' Ginny said sadly, when he revealed his plans to her. 'I will always love you, but I'm not leaving my life.'

She didn't tell John she was pregnant for a few weeks. Didn't tell anyone. When he finally noticed her growing bump – she had taken to spending most nights during the week with John, in his small gardener's cottage – she cried.

'I don't know how to tell my husband,' she sobbed. Still, she refused to leave Jonathan and be with John.

There was no point telling Jonathan the baby was his – they hadn't slept together in almost a year – and an abortion was out of the question. It just wasn't something Ginny could do.

But neither did she want this child. There wasn't an ounce of maternal instinct in Ginny. Never had been, never would be. Her first marriage, which resulted in Kit, had been a mistake. It was Ginny trying to be the dutiful daughter, trying to lead the life her parents expected of her, rather than following her dreams. Life with a husband and baby proved impossible, hence her taking flight shortly after Kit was born. She had never wanted any more children and she had nothing but negative feelings for this baby from the moment she discovered she had conceived.

The pregnancy was more than an inconvenience, it was a disaster. She didn't delight in her changing body, she hated it; she wished she wasn't such a good Catholic girl, wished she could just go to see a doctor and have it taken care of, but there weren't enough Hail Marys in the world to take care of the guilt she knew she would have.

John was fired, and it was decided the baby would be put up for adoption. It was Ginny who contacted John, who asked him to find a family. Jonathan took the news of Ginny's affair in his stride, but it was one thing to find your wife was having an affair and quite another to raise someone else's child as your own.

Ginny went to London to have the child. In the Lindo wing of St Mary's Hospital, Paddington. No one knew her. No one thought to make a secret phone call to the gossip columnists on the papers in America.

While she was gone, her husband started thinking that it was time to replace Ginny with a younger, newer model. Not Clara – she wasn't wife material in the slightest – but he had been somewhat taken with a young socialite he had met at the ballet a handful of times, and there was definite chemistry between them.

And Ginny had already cost him more than his first

and second wife combined. It was definitely time for a change.

The divorce was quick, and relatively painless, made more so by yet another substantial financial settlement. She didn't see Jonathan again. And she didn't speak to John Plowman again for many, many years.

Ginny's voice is tense on the phone. 'How do you know about her?'

'She's here. In Highfield. She wants to meet me. She wrote me a letter and she's staying in a hotel here.' Kit takes a deep breath. 'It's true, then.'

'What's true?'

'She is my sister.' The words feel alien even as they leave her lips.

'Technically, yes. But honestly, darling, I don't know what she wants. She keeps trying to get hold of me too, and I just don't want to have anything to do with her.'

'Mother! How can you say that about your own flesh and blood? And how could you not have told me?' The fury comes out in her words, the little-girl hurt that she can't hide, even as an adult.

'You didn't need to know,' Ginny attempts.

'What?' Kit spits. 'This is my sister. How could you? How could you deny me a sister?' She is close to tears as she speaks, aware she is regressing, sounding like a nine-year-old, but the anger is such that she doesn't care.

'Kit, stop,' Ginny demands sternly. 'There's too much you don't know. I'll have to explain when I see you, and I'm sorry for your hurt, but ... there's more to this than meets the eye.'

'What do you mean?'

How can Ginny explain, how can she tell Kit that she has never wanted anything to do with Annabel because she has had nothing but negative feelings for her since before she was even born?

'Oh Kit. I've tried. Do you think I don't recognize that, despite all, she is still my daughter? I was a terrible mother to you, but I hope I'm making up for it somewhat now. I wish I could do the same for Annabel, but it isn't the same. Not just that I don't trust her, but that I don't have a bond with her. This is a baby I never even held, and a child who grew up to be a troubled and destructive woman.'

'I don't understand. You must feel *something* for her.'

'I have *tried* to feel something for her, but I don't, and I can't. She isn't someone who feels like my child. It isn't like you, Kit. I promise you it's not the same. And you must not trust her either. She wants money, and heaven knows her father was paid enough at the time.'

'So what if she wants money? She's your daughter.' And God knows you can afford it, she wants to say. But doesn't.

Kit hears Ginny sigh. 'Kit, I don't expect you to understand, but I have more than provided for her. Every time she has got into trouble over the years, I have been the one to bail her out, but don't you go telling her that. When she got into drugs as a teenager, who do you think paid for rehab? I paid her university fees, which was a waste of time because she dropped out halfway into her second year, and I have supplemented her life behind the scenes for many years.'

'You have?' Kit is shocked.

'Indeed I have. None of which she knows. This is a private arrangement between myself and John.'

Ginny doesn't want to explain to Kit that it was duty that made her provide for Annabel. Hers was a pregnancy that was not supposed to have happened, and Ginny paying for Annabel's mistakes comes from a sense of duty rather than any familial obligation you might expect a mother to feel.

'This child is not someone I owe anything to. She has spent years fighting drugs and alcohol, has never held a steady job as far as I know, and is obsessed with money. Her last serious boyfriend was a drug dealer, and she stayed with him because he kept her in cocaine and Rolexes. I know she's up to no good.'

'You've met her?'

'No. But John sends me pictures, and we talk regularly; he tells me about her. She never knew I was her mother until recently. Now she wants to meet me, and I know this is about money.'

'Mom, you're saying terrible things. I can't believe what I'm hearing. This is your daughter, a child you abandoned, and all she's asking for is to meet you. Her own mother.' Kit shakes her head in disgust.

'Don't call me Mom, Kit,' snaps Ginny. 'You know how I hate it. This is a girl with ulterior motives. Don't give her money – it will just go up her nose. Honestly, I'd say don't have anything to do with her.'

'I have to go,' Kit says, feeling dirty after this conversation. Sullied.

'Bye, darling,' Ginny says, and the connection is cut.

Kit tips the wine glass back and glugs the entire contents before refilling it and shaking her head, just as her phone buzzes from the kitchen, signalling that she has a text. It's from Charlie.

> How's yr evening? T is crazy. Doesn't seem to know finance world collapsing! Yr boss here too, being v. sexy and clever – I feel v. glam being out with r. mcclore! Hope u r misbehaving . . . C xxx

'Unbefuckinglievable,' Kit says, out loud, reading the text. 'Suddenly I have a sister who's not just greedy but a drug addict and alcoholic, and now one of my best friends is dating my boss and refusing to discuss it with me. Could it get any worse? Don't answer that!' She looks up at the ceiling, her way of communicating directly with God, curse words and all.

The Highfield Inn is not far. It is one of three hotels in town. There are the Berkshire Arms, an exclusive small boutique hotel with trendy restaurant attached, a Marriott that survives only because it provides conference facilities and is thus regularly packed by visiting business people, and the Highfield Inn.

Originally a Howard Johnson, it was not-so-sensitively restored a few years ago. It changes hands every few years, with every new owner vowing to turn it into something truly special, but it still looks like a motel, just a motel with some clapboard siding and a fresh coat of paint.

There is nothing luxurious about the Highfield Inn, and it is not a place anyone 'obsessed with money' would ever stay. It sounds like Ginny is making up stories.

Kit has had one glass of wine. Surely she'll be safe to drive. She could pick up the phone and call this Annabel Plowman, determine by the sound of her voice whether she sounds trustworthy, whether they should meet, but it would be easier still to jump in the car and zip over there, perhaps get a glimpse of her close up, just to get a sense of who exactly she is dealing with.

Kit won't have to meet her, not tonight. She can go in disguise, a baseball hat and glasses, her hair in a ponytail, a big scarf covering the lower part of her face. God knows it's cold enough, and what else does she have to do?

She goes upstairs to her closet to grab a hat, and less than five minutes later she's heading to the Highfield Inn, Annabel's letter lying next to her, on the passenger seat.

I4

A few blocks away from the Highfield Inn, Lotus, a trendy Asian fusion restaurant, is hosting Charlie and Keith, Alice and Harry, and Tracy, who, unexpectedly, brought with her Robert McClore.

The manager of the restaurant is fluttering around, quivering with excitement, for this is a first: not only does he have the owners of the hottest restaurant in Highfield in for dinner, but with them is the famous author, Robert McClore!

The waiters, who are mostly Korean, have no idea who Robert McClore is, but they are terrified of their manager, and are following instructions to bring out free tasters, and to provide the best service of their lives.

Alice chose Lotus. She chose it because while they eat at the Greenhouse every day, while they try to eat organic, local produce, no refined sugar, no white flour, nothing with any additives and preservatives, she can't resist the occasional cravings for spare ribs and sesame chicken, or a velvety chicken korma with sag paneer.

And they eat at their own restaurant so much, she didn't want to have the same food, didn't want to be interrupted every few minutes with questions from the staff, who, she knows, can handle everything perfectly well themselves when they don't have the option of asking her.

So when Tracy phoned and talked about meeting for dinner, she jumped in before Tracy mentioned the Greenhouse, and suggested the Lotus instead.

It takes a while for everyone to relax. These are, after all, people who don't know one another well, and Robert McClore is an unexpected guest, and it is hard to be normal, to not focus on the fact that there is a huge celebrity sitting at their table.

Do they ask him about his books, confess they are huge fans, or pretend that he is just like them?

It reminds Alice of the time she went to a party in London and Mick Jagger was there. He was the only celebrity in the room, and for most of the evening nobody spoke to him. It was Mick Jagger! Standing feet away from her, and every time she caught his eye, he smiled, looking desperately lonely, desperate to talk.

But no one wanted to be uncool, no one wanted to give away that they knew who he was, or that they were impressed, and so he stood, on his own, until one die-hard fan finally bit the bullet and went over to say he had been to every Stones concert in London in the seventies, and what was up with that playlist in 1982.

So very different, she thinks, to how Americans react to fame.

One night Oprah Winfrey had come to the Greenhouse for dinner. She had, it seems, been in the area to appear at a fund-raiser for Barack Obama, when he was campaigning for the presidency, and was staying with friends for a couple of days after the event.

They had walked into the Greenhouse for dinner on a Saturday night when the restaurant was packed, and

Alice had never seen anything like it. As Oprah walked in, it was as if an invisible spotlight shone upon her. A hush fell upon the diners, before a swell of excited whispering.

'Oh my God! It's Oprah! And Gayle!' Chatter, chatter, chatter. People made no bones about swivelling their heads to gaze, unabashed, as the group made their way through the restaurant, smiling and stopping to shake hands, to receive praise warmly and graciously.

'That,' Alice said, turning to Harry, 'is a true celebrity. Look at how good she makes people feel.'

'It's the gift of Oprah,' Harry said. 'That's why she is who she is.'

Tonight, at Lotus, Alice notes a similar effect, but on a far reduced scale. Everyone turns to watch them walk through the restaurant to their table, and Robert McClore is clearly recognized, but it dies down quickly, and no one comes up to say anything, to lavish praise upon him, perhaps because they know, from his reputation, how uncomfortable he would be.

It is not until their main courses are brought to the table – sesame-crusted tuna with pak choi and daikon salad, cilantro soy lime fish cakes, maple-glazed spare ribs, seared beef tataki with soy mustard sauce, wok-seared sesame chicken with papaya salad, udon noodles with lemongrass and kaffir lime – that they start to relax, start to enjoy themselves, aided somewhat by the constant refilling of the hot sake, and chilled white wine they are having with their meal.

'Okay, Tracy,' Charlie says, when silence descends again, the food having been passed around the table, everyone starting to dig into the mountains on their plates. 'Now tell us what this mysterious business venture is.'

'It's not mysterious.' Tracy laughs. 'It's just that I've found this building in South Norwalk that's unofficially for sale, and I've been to see it a few times, because I think it would be a great place for a branch of Namaste. I never expected Namaste to take off in the way that it has, but I'm realizing that yoga is becoming an integral part of people's lives. We're living in terrible times, times of stress and worry, and while the corporate world seems to be collapsing around us,' she pauses as Keith nods in agreement, 'the inner world, the world that embraces all things natural, green, organic . . .' she looks at Alice, then Harry, who nod, '. . . is thriving. People know that there's more to life than making money, and for many people, yoga is the first step.'

Tracy takes a deep breath before continuing.

'I always saw Namaste as being far more than a yoga studio. It's a *lifestyle*. I see it as a place where you can hang out all day, have lunch, have a smoothie, shop for organic products for your home. I want to be able to provide babysitting for children, to give classes on how to make your world a better place. It's more than yoga, it's a vision for the future.'

'It does sound amazing when you put it like that,' Charlie says. 'And I agree that more and more people are becoming interested in an alternative lifestyle.'

'That's just the thing!' Tracy says animatedly. 'It's not alternative any more. It's becoming the norm, and I want to capitalize on that.'

'So the world is moving away from making money, and you want to make money off the back of that?' Keith laughs, and Tracy pales.

'No!' Her voice is loud as she jumps on the defensive. 'That's too harsh. I want to provide a service to give people what they want. And if it becomes successful, well, great. Why not?'

'So tell us about the building you've found.' Charlie shoots a warning look at Keith, smoothes things over.

'It's a warehouse, just off Water Street. It's one of the old red-brick buildings that used to be an industrial warehouse. It's just under twenty thousand square feet, needs a ton of work, but could be the most amazing space for a yoga studio. I'm telling you, the energy in that place is wild!' Her eyes light up. 'It's like it's just been waiting for us to come in and take it over.'

There is a silence.

'Us?' Harry says, good-naturedly.

'Well, that's the thing. It isn't officially on the market. I happened to hear about it from a girl who comes to the yoga centre.'

'Who?' Charlie is curious.

'Oh she's not a regular. She's in some of my evening classes. You don't know her. But her husband works on Water Street, and this building is owned by a colleague of his. He was hoping to develop it into condos, but he'd leveraged himself to the hilt, and now that the market has collapsed all his investors have pulled out and the building's about to go into foreclosure, which means he's desperately looking for a firesale, but doesn't want to list it because he doesn't want word to get out about the trouble he's in.'

'Which means what?' Keith asks. 'Isn't the bank insisting he puts it on the market? And how much is he asking?'

'Apparently, he's done some kind of a deal with the bank, where they give him a break if he can sell it privately, and he wants six for it.'

'Six? Six what? Six hundred thousand?'

'Charlie! That seriously would be a bargain!' Tracy laughs. 'No. He wants six million, which is a pretty good deal. He was looking at developing it into eight luxury loft apartments, each of which was going to sell for around a million.'

'A million for a loft in Norwalk? Are you *sure*?' Alice is surprised. A million dollars would buy you a pretty wonderful house in Highfield, and Highfield is far more upmarket than Norwalk.

'South Norwalk has exploded over the last few years, and lofts there are becoming really desirable.'

'Well, not that desirable. Obviously,' Keith says.

'It's true, the market isn't what it was, but I have different plans. I'd see turning the entire building on the first floor into a fantastic yoga studio and restaurant, which is why I want to get you involved –' she looks at Alice and Harry – 'with a store, and conference rooms. That would take up about ten thousand square feet, and then we could still develop the second and third floors, still turn those into apartments, and we would market them as more than apartments because it's a different way of life – the key to alternative living.'

Tracy sits back, pleased with herself.

'So ... how much do you need to raise?'

'That's a good question. I'm glad you asked me.' She reaches down and pulls out some papers from her bag. 'I've prepared some numbers.' And, with a smile of encouragement from Robert McClore, she hands them round the table.

It feels like a very long walk from the car park to the Highfield Inn, and as she pushes open the door to the lobby, Kit suddenly asks herself what the hell she is doing. She's not at all sure she's ready for this, ready to meet this sister, and now that her mother has revealed all that she has, she wonders if she needs more time.

'Kit?'

Damn. She's barely through the door, and there she is, Annabel Plowman, sitting on the beige leather sofa in the window.

'Hi.' Kit falters, not sure what to do. The girl doesn't look like a drug addict and an alcoholic. She looks young and fresh and pretty. She looks exactly like the younger sister Kit has always wanted.

Kit walks over, and Annabel stands, both of them smiling awkwardly at one another.

'I don't quite know how to do this,' Kit says, realizing that she has welled up, the tears in her eyes mirroring those in Annabel's.

'Me neither.' Annabel smiles and holds out her arms, and the two women hug.

They pull apart, Kit not knowing what to say, until she spots the bar off the main entrance.

'Shall we go and get a drink?' she asks. 'Maybe find a quiet spot so we can talk?'

'I'd love to find a quiet spot,' Annabel says. 'But I don't drink. I'm nine months clean and sober.'

'Oh.' Kit doesn't know what to say. 'Congratulations.' So Ginny hasn't been lying. Or has she? She painted Annabel as an all-round evil person, and here she is, looking so innocent, yet admitting, instantly, that she has a problem with drink and drugs, but that it is behind her.

That is the problem with Ginny. Her own mother, yet Kit doesn't really know her well enough to know what to believe. She knows she is glamorous and wealthy and beautiful. She is fun and funny, and will light up a room as soon as she walks in.

She is also prone to exaggeration, to telling stories, to living in something of a fantasy world, and Kit honestly doesn't know how to separate fact from fiction. In another life, Ginny would have made a wonderful actress, another Joan Collins perhaps, a Grande Dame who would have shone on the silver screen.

So who is the real Annabel Plowman? She certainly doesn't seem to be the woman her mother described. She is only twenty-eight, has the freshness still of youth, a freshness that Kit herself once had, before marriage and children tired her out and took away her bloom.

'I know I shouldn't tell people immediately,' Annabel says with a smile, sensing Kit's discomfort. 'It's not called Narcotics *Anonymous* without reason, but I'd rather you knew the truth from the get-go. Can we maybe grab a coffee? There's a coffee shop through there. I think it's closed but they've been very sweet to me. I'm sure if I ask nicely they'll bring us a coffee and, obviously, a drink for you if you want one.'

She turns to look at Kit who is just staring at her. 'You're staring at me.'

'I am? Oh God.' Kit shakes her head, bringing herself back down to reality. 'I just didn't expect you to sound so ... English.'

'I'm a London girl, born and bred.' Annabel smiles. 'It's utterly weird for me to discover I have this whole American family I knew nothing about.'

'But you've known about my mother –' Kit stops and corrects herself – '*our* mother, for some time, haven't you?'

'A while, yes. She doesn't want to know me, though. I can't say I blame her entirely. I went a little off the rails for a bit, and it seems my dad was turning to Ginny for support, which means she's heard all of the bad stuff, and none of the good.'

'There is good, then?' Kit raises an eyebrow.

'Ah. I take it you've spoken to Ginny.'

'Not really. I tried to call her but you know how she is – she's off with some new man on a yacht in the south of France.'

'I don't know how she is,' Annabel says, a sadness suddenly in her eyes. 'I wish I did. My dad always says I have her eyes, that I look just like her.'

'You do. A younger, paler version. And you look like me.'

'I know. You look like me too.' Annabel grins. 'Isn't this weird?'

'The weirdest thing that's ever happened to me. Well, apart from being abandoned by my mother about three minutes after I was born.'

'If it helps, she isn't exactly overflowing with maternal warmth.'

'I kind of got that impression.'

'Put it like this: she didn't abandon me quite so definitively, but I only saw her for a couple of weeks a year, and when I say, "I saw her", I mean that quite literally. She would occasionally dress me up and parade me around, if she happened to be with friends who would approve of a perfectly quiet, well-behaved child, but most of the time whichever husband she was with didn't want children around, so I was entirely raised by my father as well.'

There is a silence, and Annabel's face slowly crumples.

'I'm so sorry,' she whispers, as tears trickle down her face. 'I had no idea. I had this fantasy that you had somehow sucked up all the love I didn't get. I thought you had the mother I always wanted.'

Kit reaches over and takes Annabel's hand, squeezes it tight. 'All my friends had the mothers I always wanted. Mothers who were there when they got home, who baked cookies for them, sat at the kitchen table and did their homework with them. I had a dad who loved me more than anything, but he was a single father who had to work, and he did the best job he could do, but he couldn't raise me in the way I wanted, couldn't give me the attention I wanted.'

Annabel laughs. 'I always say I was raised by wolves.'

'Me too!' Kit's eyes shine in delight.

'And there we both were, you in America and me in England, knowing nothing about one another. That's what I find so awful. I could have had a sister. We could have had each other.'

'We have each other now.' Kit doesn't let go of Annabel's hand. 'We're sisters. Flesh and blood. Which means neither of us needs to be alone again.'

'It's amazing!' Annabel smiles through the tears. 'Tell me everything. I want to know everything about you. Everything. Even if you think it's irrelevant or boring, I want to hear it all. I want to know about you now, and what you were like as a little girl. Is that handsome man I saw coming over your husband? . . . Oh. Shit. I sort of stalked you before I left you that note. Did you see me?' Kit nods and Annabel groans. 'I'm so sorry. But still, I want to know it all. What's it like being a mother? Tell me what it's like being you. Tell me.'

Kit laughs. 'Oh my God. Where do I start?'

In the car park outside the restaurant, Keith and Charlie are saying goodbye to Alice and Harry, all of them huddling by the cars, wrapping their arms around themselves to keep the night chill out as winter fast approaches.

'Am I being a bit dumb,' Keith says, 'or does Tracy not realize that the financial world is lying in ruins around our feet, and no one has the spare money to invest in anything right now?'

Tracy, who brought Robert, had parked in the car park across the street, and the others stand and wave them goodbye as her car pulls slowly past, both Robert and Tracy waving through the window.

'She is *so* going home to fuck him,' Charlie mutters to Alice.

'I know!' Alice breathes. 'I can't believe it. Although I guess if you are into older men, you probably can't do much better.'

'She's into older men and she's seriously set her sights on him.'

'Well, he's certainly attractive.'

'Not to mention desperately rich and famous. I don't know why she even bothered asking us for money. He could buy her the warehouse many times over.'

'I don't think he would, though. You know he has a reputation for being incredibly tight with money.'

'He does? Ha!' Charlie grins. 'Tracy will knock that out of him in a heartbeat.'

'Good luck to her,' Alice says.

Harry turns to look at Keith as their wives hug each other goodbye. 'It did feel a bit strange. Look, I'm a gardener, I've got no idea what those numbers meant, but I think she was asking us to give her all the money, without putting anything into it herself. Was that right? Because I'm thinking that can't be right.'

'Nope, you pretty much got it. She's asking us to put significant amounts of capital into a high-risk venture that's unlikely to profit in the short term, without putting any of her own capital in.'

'She did say she would if she could, but that her money was all tied up.'

'Right.' Keith laughs. 'That's what they all say.'

'So . . . what do you think?' Alice says.

'I think that even if we had that sort of money, I'd want to know a lot more information.'

'Are you going to ask her for that information?' Charlie asks.

'Sure. Why not? I don't think it's for us, but it doesn't hurt to have all the info.'

'Okay. Great. Well, let us know when you get it,' says Harry.

'I'll have her make a copy for you.'

And with that, they say goodbye.

'So are you the slightest bit interested?' Charlie asks as they climb into their car.

Keith turns to her slowly. 'Honey, right now we'll be lucky if we can pay the gas bill this winter.'

'What? You're joking, right? Right?'

'Charlie –' Keith looks away, and suddenly she knows things are serious, and she's not going to like what she's about to hear. 'Things are really not good at work. We need to talk.'

15

Tracy barely says a word as they leave the restaurant.

'I thought you were wonderful,' Robert attempts to appease her. 'Your presentation was thoughtful, professional and compelling.'

'So why was that goddamned Keith so dismissive?' Tracy turns to him. 'I felt like he was laughing at me all evening. What the hell was that about?'

'I have no idea. And I don't think he was laughing at you. If anything, he looked like a man who is worried about the way of the world. You did say he worked on Wall Street, and from what I hear, it isn't looking good.'

'So what? You also think I'm crazy, looking for investors in a new business in this market?'

'I didn't say that,' Robert says calmly. 'I believe that a good idea is a good idea, and it will work in any climate, it just might make funding a little harder.'

'Do you think it's a good idea?'

'Namaste? I think it's a great idea. I think you're absolutely right about people looking for something else, something other than the material lifestyle we've all led this past decade. And I think if it's supposed to be, it will be.'

Tracy stops herself from snorting in disgust. None of this was supposed to be. She was supposed to have been able to walk straight into any bank and be offered a ninety per cent mortgage, based on her assets, her income and her business plan.

It's not like she hasn't done this before, but how was she supposed to know there would be a mortgage crisis bigger than anyone had ever seen, and that the real estate market was going to come crashing down around their ears?

No one's giving mortgages now, and if they are, their demands are far higher. Two of her clients were recently offered mortgages with forty per cent down. Forty per cent! Who, particularly in these times, has that sort of money lying around?

Robert McClore, that's who.

Keith and Charlie, and Alice and Harry may have been reluctant, but their money has probably disappeared in the crashing house of cards. Robert McClore, on the other hand, has the kind of money that doesn't disappear, and the kind of income that isn't affected by Wall Street.

For when recession strikes, people turn to the most affordable forms of entertainment on offer: movies and books.

He has already mentioned his island in Maine. An island! In Maine! And he has a real-estate portfolio as well as being co-owner of a number of businesses, including a hugely popular radio station.

Robert McClore is the real deal. The Golden Goose. Too large a prize to blow it by asking for money at this stage of the game. She has done enough research to know that, with his reputation for stinginess and savvy business dealing, that would be the worst thing she could do.

Plus, the potential rewards are so much greater than just an investment in Namaste.

'How about a drink to calm you down?' Robert eyes Tracy warily. 'A nightcap. We could pop into the Horseshoe Tavern.'

Tracy takes a deep breath. This anger isn't appropriate. Not now. And not with Robert. She turns to look at him and smile. He is such a good man. So different to what she expected. So different to what she has waiting for her at home.

What she is dreading, when she gets back home.

Tracy thought Jed had disappeared. And as the years passed, the bad memories faded, and she started to remember some of the good. She remembered that she had never felt so attracted to anyone as she had to Jed. She remembered that when it was good, it was the best ever.

A fatal attraction.

She would Google him from time to time, see if she could find out what he was doing, where he was, whether he was married, had children, whether it would now seem that there was hope.

And then there he was, on Facebook. She sent him a message, telling herself she was just curious, that she wouldn't give him any information about herself, wouldn't let herself get sucked in.

She got sucked in.

He had changed. This time he had. He had been in

therapy for years. Had conquered his demons. Did she remember the early days? How wonderful it had been? How it had never been like that with anyone else, before or since?

He was flying in for business, he said. He'd love to see her. Just a quick drink.

For old times' sake.

He moved in with her two weeks later, in her dream little house in Highfield. Same old pattern. As fatally attractive as he always had been, he was loving, attentive, kind.

Until he wasn't.

When he strikes her these days, her mind goes somewhere else. She has a sanctuary in her head, a beach, a place she imagines to try to block out the pain.

He has learned his craft better, since the last time. He doesn't leave bruises where people can see. Not often. Vicious pinches. Twisted limbs. Slow and painful. There are no weeping apologies. Not any more. No promises that things will be different.

If she tells anyone, he says he will kill her.

And she knows this is true.

Robert McClore was Jed's idea. His grand scheme to get money. Seduce him into marriage, and over to California, where she will, on their divorce, be entitled to fifty per cent of his worth. In the beginning she complied because she was too frightened to say no.

But two things have changed. The first is that she is realizing Robert McClore is her ticket out. When she is with Robert, Jed can't touch her, and Robert is not some weakling that would be powerless over Jed. He's

184

Robert McClore. Jed would be no match for him. So now she has her own agenda, which is to work slowly towards getting away from Jed for good. She just hasn't figured out how and, for now, she needs to pretend to Jed that she is doing all this for him.

And the second is that slowly, quietly and without planning, she is starting to fall for Robert McClore.

She has seen him many times since they met at the book reading. Quick cups of tea that have stretched into hours. Dinners at quiet restaurants in neighbouring towns. Walks on the beach where they have shared their stories and bared their souls.

It is not the dangerous passion she once felt for Jed, but a feeling of warmth and safety when she is with him. A feeling of peace. When she looks up and sees him walk in the room, she finds herself smiling. It is entirely unexpected, and is throwing her.

And here he is, being so sweet, so solicitous, so caring when Jed's plan B didn't go ... well, didn't go according to plan. This isn't about Jed, she reminds herself. Forget about Jed. This is about Robert. And me.

Om Namah Shivaya, she says to herself in her head, over and over. *Om Namah Shivaya*.

'How about,' she says, turning to Robert, the blaze still in her eyes, but her voice soft and seductive now, 'how about going back to yours?'

Robert McClore doesn't remember the last time he was with a woman. He doesn't remember the last time he was as turned on by a woman as he is by this Tracy. There is something about her, and tonight, with jarring clarity, he realizes she reminds him of Penelope.

It was her anger that did it. The flash of fire in her eyes when she thought she was being dismissed by her friends. An anger that should have sent him running, particularly after the marriage he had; but it was an anger that was oh so familiar.

There are no coincidences in life. No coincidence that he should have been so drawn to Penelope, and no coincidence that tonight, when he saw Tracy's fury, he should have found himself more attracted than he had been, to anyone, in years.

For anger feels like home.

The son of a rageaholic, a mother who regularly saw red, screamed, shouted, threw things, Robert grew up in a permanent state of anxiety, trying to disappear, for fear of inadvertently setting her off.

And anything could set her off.

His conscious self would do anything to avoid people with a temper, but his subconscious kept trying to recreate home, kept bringing him back to people who recreated his childhood.

Tracy didn't expect it to be this easy. Robert is pouring her a Scotch, and she walks up behind him and puts her arms around his waist, leaning her head against his back. She feels the muscles in his back tense, then relax, and he turns slowly, crystal glass in one hand, decanter in the other, as she snakes her arms around his neck and pulls him close to kiss him.

Robert closes his eyes, every nerve on fire. He has forgotten it could be like this, and he picks her up, and carries her to the sofa, all thoughts forgotten, aware of nothing other than the woman in his arms.

An hour later, Robert is snoring softly on the sofa. Tracy covers him with a cashmere throw draped over a chair, and, very quietly, takes her mobile phone out of her bag. She types, quickly and silently.

am at rmc's. part 1 done. Spk ltr. X

She slips the phone back in her bag, and sits down on the sofa, gently shaking Robert awake.

'I should go,' she whispers as he opens his eyes, then she leans down and kisses him on the lips. She would rather stay. Would rather wake up in a huge soft king-size bed, watching the morning sun glint off the waters of Long Island Sound.

The anxiety and dread start to build as she approaches her house. She tries to breathe deeply, but it is always the same. Like playing Russian roulette, she never knows what awaits her.

Will Jed be in a good mood, will he be out, at some other woman's house, or will he be furious, waiting to take it out on her?

Tracy can no longer remember how it used to be during the good times with Jed, right at the beginning; she had forgotten, until Robert, that there is another way to be in a relationship, and she reminds herself that dealing with Jed is only for a short time, that soon she will get out of his clasp, and this time she will never go back.

*

'Just how bad is it?' Charlie perches on a stool at the kitchen counter as Keith opens the cupboard next to the fridge, pulls out a bottle of Jack Daniel's and pours himself a large glass.

Amanda, in sprayed-on navel-baring jeans and plunging glittery top, chooses that moment to totter in.

'Oh hi, Amanda.' Charlie smiles. 'Thanks for baby-sitting. I take it you're going out.'

'Yes. A bunch of us are meeting in town at the Tavern,' she says.

'At eleven o'clock?' Keith sits down next to Charlie.

'Why? That's early!' Amanda is surprised. 'Do you mind if you pay me now?'

'Sure.'

Charlie looks at Keith who pulls out his wallet, flicks through and grimaces. 'Charlie? Can you get this?'

But a look through Charlie's wallet reveals she is also out of cash.

'Can I give you a cheque?' Keith offers, seeing the disappointment in Amanda's eyes.

'No. I need the money for tonight. It was to pay for going out.'

'Keith, you'll have to go to the ATM,' Charlie says.

Keith looks hopefully at Amanda, willing her to tell him not to worry, that it can wait until tomorrow, but she doesn't. She thanks him, then sits down on the third stool, letting him know that she isn't going anywhere until she gets paid.

It isn't just that Keith doesn't want to go out again, on a night that is suddenly filled with winter chill, but that it has taken him days to work up the courage to be honest with Charlie about what's going on, and now that he's told her the beginning, he has to tell her the rest.

He wants to get it over with. Wants to ease his burden, because these last few days he has been sick with fear, trying to find a way to make it all okay; but there isn't a way, there just isn't a way to make this problem disappear.

Keith has lost his job. It hasn't been officially announced, but he has been pulled aside and warned that his group will be the next to go. When he was flush with cash, he would sit with friends and joke that most of the 'financial wizards' in this town were three pay cheques away from bankruptcy.

That included him, but he never thought of that at the time.

His pay cheques seemed so large, yet their lifestyle was so much larger. Their huge dream house, their large black SUVs, their kids being at Highfield Academy rather than at the public schools that most of their friends' kids went to.

But they have always had enough. Enough to pay the giant mortgage and the Home Equity Line. Enough to pay the $2,000 a month for the leases of the three cars – the Range Rover, the BMW and the Porsche Carrera.

They have had enough to take themselves to Pink Sands on Harbor Island for Christmas last year, and the Four Seasons at Palm Beach the year before.

They have had enough to shop at Rakers and, God knows, Charlie likes to shop. She needs the clothes for their dinners around town with friends, for their charity galas. And the charity galas are necessary for her work – half the time she does the flowers, and even if she doesn't, they are great opportunities to network.

So they have never quite managed to put anything away. They are only forty, after all, and his financial advisor said he has plenty of time to worry about that. They have small SEP IRAs, and of course he has had his stock over all these years.

The stock is their true retirement fund. The stock that has always been a large part of his annual bonus; the stock that can't yet be vested, but that is one day to carry them through.

Today that stock is worth almost nothing.

When panic threatens to overtake him, he tells himself that it will be okay, they still have the house. They bought it at the height of the market, for two and a half million dollars.

They have a mortgage of two million, and last year took out a Home Equity Line for four hundred thousand. Their neighbours, who live in an exact replica of their house, have had their house on the market for two years. It went on at three point two million – which everyone agreed was insane – and has been reduced, and reduced, and is now being offered at one point nine. There hasn't been an offer.

He has felt, these last few months, as if he were treading water. Surviving, but only just. And now he is almost certain he has lost his job – it is just a question of working out the leaving package – and there just isn't a way to keep funding this lifestyle.

He doesn't know how to tell Charlie. Doesn't know

what words to use. He has always prided himself on his work, loves working in finance, has never known any professional world other than Wall Street.

Half the hedge funds he dealt with on a daily basis have disappeared and, with them, the men who ran them. Just dropped out of sight. A few are attempting day-trading, and he has heard horror stories of men losing everything. He never thought he would be one of them. Or perhaps he did. He just refused to give those thoughts the room to breathe.

A failure, he thinks, as he pulls in the driveway, Amanda's babysitting money safely in hand. I am a failure. And feeling those familiar waves of nausea again, he trudges up the path to sit down with his wife and tell her exactly how bad it is.

Kit sees Adam through the sidelights of the front door. She never knows how she feels about him standing on the doorstep when he drops the kids off. Often, when she sees he is there, she is irritated. It feels like an intrusion. Often the kids call him inside, wanting to show him something in their room, or some homework they did, and he walks in, vaguely apologetic, leaving Kit simmering with resentment.

Other times, when he is not there, when he waves from the car as he reverses out of the driveway, she is saddened and wistful, wishing he had come in, wishing they had been able to have a chat.

Tonight she is happy to see him standing there. Her world suddenly seems upside down, and Adam's familiar face is like a port in a storm so as soon as she catches sight of him she feels a warmth, a feeling of safety, a sense of calm knowing that Adam will look after her.

'Hey, Mom!' Buckley rushes past her, ignoring her outstretched arms, and Tory flashes her a peace sign as she saunters up the stairs, her iPod plugged in.

'Good weekend?' Adam asks with a smile, dumping the backpacks and sweatshirts on the chair in the hallway.

'Hi.' They both turn to see Annabel, in jeans and one of Kit's old shirts, walking out of the kitchen, munching on an apple. 'You must be Adam.'

'I am.' Adam is cautious. 'And you are?'

'I'm Annabel.' She extends a hand. 'How do you do?'

Adam grins, shooting a look at Kit, and she knows he is wondering who the hell this posh English girl is, and what the hell she is doing here.

'I'm just great, thank you,' he says. 'Are you … a friend from England?'

'Not exactly.' Annabel raises her eyebrows. 'Kit? How do we explain?'

Kit smiles back. 'It's totally weird, and you won't believe me.'

'Try me.'

'Annabel's my sister.'

'You haven't got a sister.'

'Wrong. I didn't know I had a sister.'

'You're shitting me.'

'I shit you not.'

'She shits you not,' Annabel adds, smiling.

'Wow. I mean, that's awesome! You know what? I

192

see it. Jesus. I do. You look like Ginny, but with Kit's mouth. You really *are* sisters. How in the hell did this happen?'

'It's a long story,' Kit says. 'Yet another one of my mother's dark secrets from her mysterious past.'

'Not so much of the dark, please,' says Annabel.

'Do you want to come in? Somehow, I've got to explain it to the children.'

'Do you want me to stay?'

'If you want to.'

'I will if you want me to.'

'Only if you want to.'

'Oh for God's sake!' Annabel steps forward to grab Adam by the arm and drag him into the living room. 'Will you just *stay*?'

It has been a crazy day. Crazy and wonderful, in equal measure. Kit couldn't let Annabel stay at the Highfield Inn. Not only is the place a dump, as she explained, she wanted to get to know her. God knows they had enough to talk about, and she has a perfectly good sofa bed in her study at home.

They talked long into the night on Saturday. Annabel was honest and funny and charming. She talked of the pain of not having a mother, of her insecurities, her neediness, her tendencies to get involved in bad relationships, because she didn't think she deserved better.

Which explained the drugs and alcohol. 'I was trying to make it all go away,' she told Kit. 'Those feelings of worthlessness, of not being good enough.'

'I feel that too.' Kit had listened, shocked at how similar they were, even though she has never felt the need to turn to the same substances. Perhaps because she married so young ... perhaps Adam had been her saviour. Possibly, had she not met him, had her first child by the time she was the same age as Annabel is now, she would have gone down a very different path.

'I wish I had this,' Annabel said, gesturing around her.

'What?' Kit laughed. 'You wish you had a tiny little house and were a single mother to two kids, struggling to keep your head above water?'

'That's not how I see it,' Annabel said. 'Your house is beautiful. Small, but perfect. When you talk about your family I can see how much you love them. Your kids sound great. You even have an ex-husband who sounds really nice. You *have* a family. That's what I meant.'

'I'm not sure my ex counts as my family any more.'

'I think he does. I think once you're family, you're always family. But this is what I always wanted. Kids. A home that feels like this. Hopefully, a husband.'

Kit smiled indulgently. 'You're only twenty-eight. You have plenty of time. I think one of my greatest mistakes was marrying too young. Neither of us had lived. Neither of us knew what we wanted, or who we were going to become.'

'And who did you become?'

Kit laughed. 'He became a big-shot banker, and I became a mom who didn't want to have this marriage where I never saw my husband, who was lonelier in my marriage than I have ever been since.'

'That's hard. I understand the loneliness. I've been lonely my entire life.' Annabel's voice softened as her eyes welled up.

'You don't have to be lonely any more.' Kit reached over and lay a hand gently on her arm. 'You have a family now.'

Kit had been drinking; Annabel had not, sticking to cranberry juice and soda. Some time around midnight the two of them found themselves riffling through Kit's closet, with Annabel trying on Kit's clothes, Kit trying on her own clothes, showing off her wedding dress (still kept just in case Tory should ever decide to wear it for her own wedding day).

They got the giggles at one point, both of them laughing in exactly the same way, doubled over as if in pain, eyes scrunched shut while tears poured down their faces; and realizing they both laughed in exactly the same way only made them laugh more.

'This is what I always wanted,' Annabel said, lying on Kit's bed long after midnight, next to a pile of clothes Kit insisted on giving her, both of them still chattering away, so excited to have found one another. 'A sister.'

'I know.' Kit smiled, as emotion threatened to overwhelm her. 'Me too.'

They stayed up until the early hours of the morning. Kit couldn't remember the last time she had done that. Maybe an election night one time? But she remembered it hadn't been fun. This was fun. More than fun. Exciting. Exhilarating. It felt as if she had found a limb she never realized was missing.

That's what it is, she thought with a start. She makes me feel whole.

'Kids? Buck? Tory?' she yells up the stairs.

'I hate her yelling up the stairs,' Adam says, turning to Annabel. 'She used to do it when we were married and I kept telling her it drove me nuts.'

'Well, luckily for me I'm not married to you any more and I don't have to listen to you. Buck? Tory?' Kit yells even louder up the stairs and Adam groans and covers his ears.

'What is it, Mom?' Buckley yells back. 'I'm on YouTube. Can't it wait?'

'No it can't. I need you both down here. There's someone I want you to meet.'

'Oh God,' they all hear Tory mutter with a groan as she emerges from her bedroom in a sulk. 'Probably Mom's new boyfriend.'

'Wrong guess,' Annabel says brightly from the bottom of the stairs, and Tory's interest is instantly piqued.

She peers down the stairs at this young pretty woman who sounds like Hermione Granger in the *Harry Potter* movies.

'Who are you?' Tory says.

'This,' Kit says, 'is your aunt.'

16

'What do you mean, we have an aunt?' Tory looks utterly confused, while Buckley looks like he couldn't care less and just wants to get back to his computer.

'It's a very long story,' Annabel says. 'Kit? Do you want to start?'

'Come on, guys,' says Kit, ushering them into the living room, 'let's sit down.'

'Aw, Mom,' Buckley whines. 'I'm in the middle of something cool. That's great that we have an aunt. Seriously.' He turns to Annabel. 'Welcome to the family. Now can I go?'

'Buckley!' Adam reprimands him. 'Don't speak to your mother like that.'

'Like what?'

'With that attitude. Enough. Sit down.'

'Thanks, Adam, but it's okay,' Kit says. 'You can get back to your computer when we've finished.' She is momentarily thrown, because it is so nice to have someone tell her son to behave, so nice to not be the only one dealing with the kids, attempting to teach them manners, reprimanding them. It is so nice not to be the bad cop all the time.

'Okay, so I know you love Gigi, and I also know that you both know that Gigi wasn't exactly . . .'

'Who's Gigi?' Annabel leans forward.

'Ginny.'

'Yeah. She refused to be called Grandma,' Tory explains. 'So she decided it would be Gigi, as in GG, for Gorgeous Grandma.'

'Figures.' Annabel snorts.

Adam laughs. 'Yeah, no surprises there.'

'So, kids, Gigi wasn't the greatest mother to me, and I know you –'

'Yeah, Mom, we know. Just because she wasn't the greatest mother, doesn't mean she can't be a great grandmother ...' Buckley is clearly itching to get back to his computer.

'... Even though,' adds Tory, 'we hardly ever see her.'

'Yeah, but she sends great gifts.'

'That's why we love her,' Tory says, grinning.

'Can you just let me get to the point? So, long after I was born, Gigi, it seems, had another baby.'

'That would be me.' Annabel raises a hand.

'Right, and neither of us knew about the other. Annabel was raised by her dad in England, and hasn't even met Gigi, and, well, you know about me.'

Tory's eyes grow big. 'Wow! That is so cool. So how did you find out about one another?'

'My father just told me. I didn't know anything. I didn't even know who Ginny was until recently, and when I Googled her, I found your mum's wedding announcement in the *Times*, where it said she was Ginny's daughter, so then I had to track down your mum.'

'So did you really come all the way from England to find us?'

'That's right.' Annabel nods. 'Virgin Economy all the way.'

'Pity you couldn't get upgraded to Upper Class.' Adam grins. 'It's really something.'

'Tell me about it. I tried. I was standing in line waiting for the cute guy to call me over, so I could tell him my story and charm him into an upgrade, and instead I get the battleaxe who barely even looks at me. I didn't bother trying.'

'So then how exactly did you find my mom?' Tory is transfixed.

'Well, first I tried to contact Gin – Gigi, but her maternal instincts weren't kicking in that day. Or any other day. She didn't want to know, so I turned to the Internet. I found something about Robert McClore giving a talk at a local bookstore, and they printed the press release online. They said for further information to contact Kit Hargrove. I thought, how many Kit Hargroves can there be? So then I had the town, and I already had your dad's name from the wedding announcement, so I Googled him and when I found he lived in Highfield too, I knew I had the right person.'

'That is so awesome!' Tory breathes.

'It is kinda cool,' Buckley grudgingly concedes.

'Don't you think Annabel looks like your mom?' Adam asks, looking from one to the other.

'No!' Tory is adamant. 'Annabel's beautiful! Oh my God! I'm sorry, Mom, it's just that you're – well, you're Mom. You just look like you. Anyway, Annabel has make-up and highlights, and she's wearing clothes that a mom would never wear. She's cool.'

'As it happens,' Kit says, 'the shirt she's wearing is mine.'

'Oh. Well, it doesn't look as good on you, then.'

'Great.' Kit attempts a laugh. 'Any more criticisms before I kill myself?'

'I think you're beautiful.' Buckley shoots Tory a killer glance before getting up and giving his mom a kiss.

Once a mother's boy, always a mother's boy, thinks Kit, trying not to focus on the fact that Tory is right.

Look at Annabel. She is gorgeous – no two ways about it. Admittedly, she is twenty-eight, has had no children, has not been ravaged by the stresses and strains of marriage and motherhood. But even at twenty-eight, Kit did not look like this.

Annabel's hair is long and wild, with copper and auburn highlights that whisper expensive hairdressers. Her make-up is subtle and understated; there is just enough chocolatey eyeliner to emphasize her large hazel eyes, just enough shimmery blush to bring out her cheekbones, just enough plummy gloss to show off her full, wide lips.

She is slim and tall. Tight dark jeans flare over beaten-up tan leather boots, stacked heels giving her even more height than she has already. A shirt of Kit's, which always looked awful on Kit, looks amazing on Annabel, half tucked in, with a cluster of bohemian beaded necklaces around her neck. It is a style that is mismatched, but ineffably cool. And the accent! That cut-glass proper British accent! No wonder Tory is so mesmerized.

Kit has never looked this good in her whole life.

Even Adam can't seem to take his eyes off her, which, Kit tells herself, only bothers her because Annabel's twenty-eight. Twenty-eight, for God's sake! At forty-two, Adam is almost old enough to be her father.

'I think you're beautiful too,' Adam says quietly, and as Kit looks up, feeling as if she may be about to cry, she realizes he's saying it to her.

'Thank you.' She smiles, and this time it's genuine.

Later on, when Adam has left and the children are watching TV, Kit and Annabel clear up the plates after dinner, chatting quietly.

'I don't blame Ginny – Mum – whatever it is I'm supposed to call her,' Annabel says. 'Dad says he kept in touch with her, would keep her updated as to what I was doing; and let me tell you, for a long time what I was doing wasn't pretty.'

'What do you mean?' Kit puts down the sponge, takes the kettle off the stove and pours hot water into two mugs, letting the camomile tea bags steep while she goes to sit at the table.

'I had a rough few years. I fell in with a bad crowd after university, and there were a lot of drugs, a lot of bad stuff.'

'What kind of drugs?'

'You name it, I did it.'

'Heroin?' Kit breathes, hoping the answer is no.

'Among other things. Don't worry –' she pushes up her sleeves and shows off her arms – 'no track marks. I didn't inject. Mostly, it was crack. Smoking it. I know it's hard to imagine this, looking at me today, but for a long time I looked like Amy Winehouse. But without the beehive, obviously.'

'Ouch. That's not good.'

'No. It wasn't. Dad paid for rehab twice, but I didn't want to be there, didn't have any willingness, didn't want to change; and unless you want it badly enough, it doesn't work. I hadn't reached my bottom.'

'What does that mean?'

Annabel laughs. 'It's a recovery term. It means you're not ready to get better until you've reached rock bottom.'

'Okay.' Kit is awkward. 'I'm sorry, I don't know anything about . . . well . . . drugs and alcohol, or . . . AA, I guess. This is all new for me.'

'And I know so much about it that I assume everyone is as familiar with the terminology as I am,' she explains.

'So what was your rock bottom?'

'An overdose.' Annabel shrugs, as if she was saying, a headache. 'They found me overdosed on a park bench on Primrose Hill.'

'They?'

'Someone walking their dog. I'd been there all night. I know I'd been in Camden, scoring, and I don't remember much else. I was rushed to hospital, and something changed for me: I knew that I was going to die if I carried on, and all of a sudden I didn't want to die.'

There is silence as Kit digests what Annabel is saying.

'It's odd,' Annabel says, looking at Kit curiously. 'You don't have the addict gene. I can tell.'

'What do you mean?'

'I think we are either born addicts, or not. I don't think my upbringing led me to that life – God knows my father did an amazing job – but I would have fallen into alcohol or drugs, or both, no matter what my family life had been. That was probably the biggest lesson I learned in rehab. I'd spent my whole life being a victim, thinking that if I'd had a mother, a normal family, I wouldn't be the person I was, wouldn't need to drink or do drugs to numb the pain, but rehab taught me that it has nothing to do with anyone else, that sitting on the pity pot just leads to more abusive behaviours. The only person who can take responsibility for my own life is me.'

'So what did you mean about the addict gene?'

'That you don't have it. But I bet our mum does.'

'Why?'

Annabel shrugs. 'It tends to run in families. Addicts beget addicts, all that stuff. My dad doesn't have it, so my guess would be Ginny does. Even if she hasn't ever acted out, she's still got the gene.'

'Okay, so it's not like I've spent a ton of time with her, but I would have noticed if she were drinking a lot, or,' Kit splutters into laughter at the thought, 'snorting cocaine.'

Annabel smiles. 'It doesn't have to be drugs or alcohol. Addicts can be addictive, or compulsive, around pretty much anything. A lot of recovering alcoholics turn to sugar once they give up alcohol, using sugar in exactly the same way, to numb the pain.'

'Yeah. Not so much. Mom's been a size two ever since I can remember. She's totally obsessed with her figure and eats almost nothing. And she exercises like a crazy woman.'

'That's something. They call it exercise bulimia. It's when you use exercise as a form of control. That could absolutely be her addiction. It can also be sex ...'

'She *has* gone through five husbands. And I think she's found her sixth. Do you think that counts?'

'You *think*?' Annabel laughs. 'And of course there is my favourite addiction of all. Shopping.'

'Aha! Now I think you've got it. That's our mother all over.'

'Figures. I haven't met her, but in every picture I've ever seen of her, and God knows there are enough of them all over the Internet, she looks like she's seriously high-maintenance.'

'It's true. She uses Chanel like I use Old Navy.'

'That's what it looked like from the photos. Some of those diamonds are so huge I thought they must be fake. But they're not, are they?'

'Fake? On Mother? Good Lord, no!' Kit's hand flies to her chest, feigning horror. 'Seriously, I look in the mirror and wonder how on earth she could have had me. No wonder she didn't want anything to do with me. The very fact of my naturally curly hair was probably enough to send her running.'

'Oh God!' Annabel giggles. 'I know this is awful, but it's so nice to be able to talk about these things, and with you! Someone who's been through exactly the same thing. Anyway, I love your hair.'

'Right. Because you'd just love to trade your fantastic mane for my untamed mess.'

'You should let me dry it for you,' Annabel says. 'I'm an ace at straightening.'

'Maybe I will.'

And maybe she should. Maybe this is what she needs, a breath of fresh air, someone who can take her in hand and help her realize her full potential. Not that she's ever wanted to do this before, but she saw the way Adam looked at Annabel, knows that if she put just a little bit of effort into her appearance, if she could actually be bothered to do more than tug a brush through her hair before shoving it back in a ponytail, it might be . . . fun.

The phone rings, disturbing Kit's inner fantasy of a Cinderella-like transformation.

'It's me.'

'Charlie? What's the matter? You sound awful.'

'I . . .' and Charlie breaks into tears.

'Charlie? What is it? What's going on?' Kit's heart leaps into her chest. 'Is it the kids? Has something happened?'

'No! Everything's fine. I mean, the kids are fine. Keith is fine. Kit, we've lost everything.'

'What do you mean? What are you talking about?'

'Keith's lost his job. We're in serious debt, and the bank is about to foreclose on the house.'

'Oh shit.'

There's silence as Charlie breaks into a fresh round of tears.

'Can I come over?' she asks eventually, when she has gathered herself.

'Come over right now.'

Annabel looks at Kit with concern. 'Is everything okay?'

'Doesn't sound like it. That was Charlie, my best friend.' She notes Annabel's raised eyebrow and adds, 'It's a she. Charlie's short for Charlotte. Her husband works in finance. Or . . . did.'

'Oh dear. A Wall Street casualty?'

'It seems so. God, I feel awful. You keep waiting to hear of someone who's been affected, but you don't think it's going to happen to your best friend.'

'Is it really bad?'

'I don't know. She says he's lost his job and they're about to lose their house.'

'Oh God.'

'She's coming over. I guess we'll find out more soon.'

The back door swings open. 'Hello?'

'Who's that?'

'It's Edie. My neighbour. Hi, Edie!' she shouts. 'We're in here.'

Edie walks in, spying Annabel. 'Oh good. I thought for a moment "we" meant that man you've been seeing.'

'You're seeing someone? You didn't say anything! Aha! It's that handsome man from yesterday morning – I forgot all about him.'

'We've kind of had a lot of ground to cover,' Kit says, laughing. 'Annabel, this is Edie. Edie, this is Annabel. My sister.'

'Your sister? I thought you were an only child.'

'Long story,' they both say in unison, breaking into peals of identical laughter.

*

Charlie stops short as she walks in the front door, her face tear-stained, her eyes bloodshot and puffy.

'Who's here?' she whispers. 'Oh God, it's like Grand Central Station. I didn't know you had people over.'

'It's not people. It's just Edie, and Annabel, my long-lost sister who I didn't know existed before yesterday.'

'Are you serious?'

'Completely.'

'Oh God, Kit. I'm so sorry. You should have told me. I don't want to intrude.'

'You're not intruding. I can send Edie home and Annabel can go upstairs. We can talk for as long as you want.'

'Don't send Edie home. Perhaps she'll have some words of wisdom for me. And ... Annabel? That's fine. She can stay. I feel like I need all the support I can get right now.'

'Do you want a glass of wine?'

'Do you have any vodka?'

'Go in and sit down. I'll see what I can find.'

'Well, young lady,' Edie says, pushing her glasses back firmly on her nose. 'It sounds like you are going to be making some changes in your life, but that is not necessarily a bad thing. I am far older and wiser than you, and I have found that what feels like a hardship at the time usually contains some wonderful lessons, and many that you are all the better for learning.'

'But I'm losing my home,' Charlie says plaintively. 'Everything we've worked for. And I'm so embar-rassed.' She groans. '*We're* going to be the people everyone talks about. Everyone's going to be whispering about *us*. It's the most humiliating thing that's ever happened to me.'

'Nonsense.' Edie's voice is sharp. 'It's only humiliating if you allow it to be. Look at this one over here —' She gestures to Kit. 'She lived in a big house with all the bells and whistles, and now she lives here, and it hasn't done her any harm.'

'But that's different. Kit chose it. She didn't have her life pulled out from under her feet.'

'It doesn't matter. The end result is the same: we learn to accept what is given us, and move forward with grace. If you're worried about what your friends will think, I'd suggest you look at who you're calling a friend. Kit, would you judge Charlie because her husband has lost his job, would you gossip about her with anyone?'

'No!'

'Exactly. This might be the time when you find yourself re-evaluating your friendships. Anyone who chooses to whisper about you, or spreads rumours, isn't that good a friend, I should say.'

There is silence, as Charlie contemplates her friends. It is true, her friends would never say anything bad about her; but it isn't her friends she is worried about. It is the women in the Highfield League of Young Ladies, the women at the charity galas and events she attends so frequently, although, at an average of $250 per person, per ticket, it looks like she won't be continuing to attend.

It is the mothers at Highfield Academy, whose

smiles and highlights, diamonds and designer hand-bags are all testament to their happiness at all being members of the same, exclusive, club.

Then again, the school fees are thirty thousand dollars a year. Although Emma's pre-school fee is the bargain basement price of just under ten. And that doesn't take into account the horse riding lessons, the Hunt Club fees, the piano lessons, the ballet, the every-thing else that contributes towards the cost of raising what is considered to be a well-rounded child on Connecticut's Gold Coast.

None of which they can afford any more. Oh God. The children. Awful for Charlie, but how will the children react? How will they feel, having to leave Highfield Academy, all their friends, the public schools. The lessons will have to stop, the $125 AG kids' jeans for Emma, the weekly mani/pedis for Paige.

Her friends won't judge her, but it isn't her friends she is worried about. It's everybody else. How will she ever be able to hold her head high in this town again?

17

Adam lies in bed in his boxer shorts, one arm behind his head, one arm holding the remote control, endlessly flicking up and down the channels.

Eventually, he settles on MSNBC, but he's restless tonight, can't focus on what Rachel Maddow has to say, so gets up after a while, goes downstairs and pours himself a hefty Scotch.

He is bothered by this evening. Bothered by Annabel. Bothered because he couldn't take his eyes off her. Couldn't help but imagine what she would look like naked, on all fours in front of him, whispering encouragement as he drove himself into her.

Oh fuck. This he doesn't need. This is his ex-wife's sister. This is definitely not going to happen.

So why can't he stop thinking about her?

Until Adam and Kit were separated, Adam hadn't realized quite how much he had missed sex.

As a young man, he remembered his friends joking about how married people never had sex, but he knew that wouldn't happen with him and Kit, their sex life, after all, was the one area in their marriage that was always explosive.

But it had changed. Almost overnight. As soon as Tory was born. Kit just wasn't interested any more. At first she said she was too tired, that all she could think about when she crawled into bed was sleep, that it was to be expected with a newborn.

The newborn became a toddler. Who became a child. And still, they never seemed to recover their intimacy; or rather, Kit never seemed to recover her libido. Three, four, five times a week became, swiftly, once, and then not even that.

He hadn't changed. Kit may have been exhausted, or uninterested, but his needs were the same as ever, so what was he supposed to do? He would wake up early and masturbate quietly in the shower, so as not to disturb Kit, desperate for some relief, but, even more, desperate for some affection, some intimacy.

He had been tempted, but only peripherally. Adam was not a man who would be unfaithful, of this he was sure. He was simply a man who wanted more sex *with his wife*, who couldn't understand why she wasn't able to give it to him.

Every night was the same. He would lie in bed, watching television, listening to Kit getting undressed in the bathroom. Sometimes he would remember the early days, when she bought frothy, silly underwear from Victoria's Secret, underwear he would peel off with his teeth.

Now, or at least during those last few years, she wore an unattractive shade of *greige*. Nude, he thinks it is called. Flesh-coloured bras and panties, not a hint of lace or frill or sensuality.

She would walk into the bedroom, face freshly scrubbed, in a long, brushed-flannel nightgown, equally unsexy, climb into bed with a book, and sit back against the pillows, asking him to turn the volume down.

He would reach out, stroke her thigh, and she would give him an affectionate smile, pick his hand up, kiss it, and place it firmly back on his side of the bed.

Occasionally, he was persistent and, occasionally, it paid off. But he always felt she was doing him a favour, fulfilling her duty, her conjugal rights.

It wasn't that she didn't like sex, she would say. She loved it once they started; it was just that she could never be bothered. She has a theory, she would say, that women are genetically engineered to be voracious to get their man, genetically engineered to have a high libido in order to procreate, then, once the children are born, their libidos are genetically engineered to shrink to nothing.

He supposed it might be true, yet couldn't help but feel rejected. He didn't just *want* sex, he *needed* sex. In the same way that he needed to use the bathroom, and eat, and sleep, he needed to have sex. And he needed to have it with his wife.

When they first separated, he was numb with shock. It lasted for months, and he threw himself into his work, the only bright spots being the times he spent with his children.

He knew how far he and Kit had drifted apart, but somehow he never thought it would end, never realized just how unhappy she was. He knew, on some level, she hated who they had to be for his job, but she always did it, dressed up, hosted dinner parties, kept a beautiful home, and he thought they were just words.

Once the shock wore off, he realized that this was

now his life: the farmhouse by the railway station, empty every night when he came home; the lone trips to Whole Foods in an attempt to keep his fridge stocked, although most of the time he would eat out, unless the kids were with him, and then he would try to create a stable home, would attempt to cook simple meals, chicken, mac and cheese, pasta.

No wife waiting to greet him, making him dinner, no kids to kiss goodbye when he left them, still fast asleep, to catch the 'death train' in the morning. No dinners out at good restaurants in town, no charity galas with Keith and Charlie, no ... fun.

It was as if the fun had been sucked out of his life, without his permission, in one fell swoop.

Six months passed, and he found himself at a work dinner. His team had taken a table at a charity benefit, and some clients were coming. Adam found himself sitting next to Elysse, a single girl, who made it quite clear, quite early on, that she was interested.

Later on, after copious amounts of alcohol, he went back to Elysse's apartment, stunned at how easy this was, stunned that the modern woman would fuck him on the night of meeting him, then wave him off without even giving him her phone number.

It was a wake-up call. He worked, and had the ability to socialize, in a city where the women outnumbered men to such an extent there was never any shortage of interested parties. Everywhere he went, he suddenly realized, he saw gorgeous women with not-so-gorgeous men, and if they could do it, well he, in his early forties and still in great shape, could certainly do it too.

It was as if he was a child let loose in a candy store. Never had he known women so forward, so direct, so willing. And adventurous! Those years of sporadic, vanilla sex with Kit disappeared as he indulged every fantasy he had ever had.

His work colleagues would tease him about his voracious appetite, but after all those years of being in the desert, he deserved a little fun. He was, he realizes now, more than a little manic, although a couple of divorced men he knew said they went through the same thing.

'Got to get it out of your system,' one said, slapping him on the back approvingly. 'And God knows we deserve it after the wives we had.'

Now, finally, he has got it out of his system. He has a peace that he hadn't enjoyed for a long time, and is starting to actually date, rather than just take women out for dinner in order to have sex with them later.

He has been seeing a girl in the city for a few weeks. She is cute, but she doesn't really do it for him, doesn't really turn him on.

Not in the way that Annabel has turned him on, in the space of just – what? An hour?

Oh God, he groans, please let me forget about her. And sinking his Scotch in one gulp, he trudges up the quiet stairs, back to bed.

'You look happy.' Robert McClore eyes Kit as she comes into his study to say good morning.

'I am,' she says. 'It's been an extraordinary weekend.'

'Oh yes?'

She is tempted to tell him the story, but won't, for two reasons. The first is that she is well aware of the number of people who offer to tell Robert their stories: 'You should write a book about it,' they say. 'Have *I* got some stories for you?' Robert always smiles, and listens graciously, but as he's said to Kit many a time, the stories he tells are his own. Not those of other people.

And the second reason is that telling him about Annabel would be a transgression, somehow. She likes the fact that she and Robert are not friends, that they are able to chat and there is a comfort between them, but neither of them shares the intimate details of their own life.

Although now, given Tracy's burgeoning friendship with him, it is starting to feel a little awkward.

'Just . . . life,' she explains with a smile. 'But good.'

'Excellent,' he says. 'And getting better, I suspect. Something arrived for you.'

'For me? Here?'

'Yes. It's on your desk.'

Kit leaves and goes into her own office, and on her desk is a huge bouquet of creamy white roses. She gasps, in delight, and pulls out the card.

Thinking of you, and hoping your weekend went well. I'd love to rearrange . . . Steve

Steve. So much has happened in such a short space of time, she has forgotten about Steve entirely, forgotten that just days ago she was planning to seduce him, but that was before she discovered her sister, before her life changed immeasurably.

A warm glow spreads through her as she sits down in the chair and studies the note. How lovely. And how long has it been since anyone has thought to send her flowers?

She picks up the phone and calls Charlie.

'I am sitting at my desk with the most beautiful bouquet of roses that you clearly made for me, from Steve.'

'I'm so glad you like them! He asked me if I knew your favourites.'

'How did he even know to call you?'

'He asked Tracy if she knew of any good florists.'

'Well, they're beautiful. Thank you.'

'You're welcome. He sounds sexy.'

'I haven't even thought about him, it's been so crazy these last few days. But I'm thinking about him now.' Kit laughs, then recovers quickly. 'But you. How are you? How are you feeling today?'

'Terrible.' Charlie sighs. 'And Keith's a mess. He seems to be paralysed with fear, so not only am I working and running the floral business, I'm now trying desperately to salvage whatever's left.'

'There is something left, then?'

'No. Not really. But I've left messages with the bank. I've heard that banks will consider doing deals, writing off some of the loan if you can just get the house sold. To be honest, Kit, I'm just trying to avoid a foreclosure. I realize we're walking away with nothing and I don't know what the hell we're going to do, but to have our credit destroyed will make it all so much worse.'

'I wish there was something I could do.'

'Me too. Right now I'm just making phone calls and praying to God. Not necessarily in that order.'

'Do the kids know?'

'No. I don't want to tell them anything until I have to.'

'But ... if there really is nothing left, where will you go?'

'We'll have to move in with my parents, I guess. Or Keith's, although, to be honest, I'd rather stick needles in my eyes. But what choice do we have? I'll have to give up my own business, because I can't afford a space, so I'll have to find a job, and so will Keith.'

'But ... your parents are in New Jersey,' Kit gasps. 'You'd leave Highfield?'

'Not unless we have to, but, Kit, right now there doesn't seem to be a choice, and I'm just grateful my parents are still around and there'd be room for us.'

'Oh Jesus, Charlie,' Kit says. 'It's just awful.'

'I know. I feel like everyone knows, too.'

'But they don't. How can they?'

'The financial world is very small. Everyone knows everyone. Someone already asked me, at yoga, if everything was okay because they'd heard Keith's company was in trouble.'

'That doesn't mean they know anything.'

'I guess. You know what else was weird?'

'What?'

'Tracy. I don't know whether this was because Keith was obviously not interested in investing in her business idea, but she was really weird with me today.'

'Really? Weird, how?'

'Just . . . off. I tried asking her about Robert and what was going on, and, I swear, she just cut me off. Also, she had a black eye.'

'*What?* How did she get a black eye?'

'She said she walked into a closet door when she was going to the bathroom in the middle of the night.'

'Have you ever walked into a closet door, at night-time or any other time?'

'No.'

'Me either. Did you think she was telling the truth?'

'No. It totally felt like she was hiding something.'

'But what? How the hell could she have got a black eye? You're right. That is weird.'

'Damn. That's my other line. Listen, Kit, promise me you won't say anything to anyone about our financial stuff.'

'Of course! I wouldn't ever do that.'

'I know. Thank you, sweetie. I love you and I'll talk to you later. Gotta go.'

Charlie clicks over to the other line. 'Hello?'

'Charlie? It's Alice.' Her clipped English accent is unmistakable.

'Hi! How are you?'

'I'm fine, thank you. How are you?'

'Okay.'

'Listen, I hope this isn't inappropriate to call you, but I was wondering what your take is on Saturday night.'

'What do you mean?'

'Just ... I don't know. Harry and I were talking afterwards and we just thought it was, well, a little uncomfortable. Look, the restaurant is doing okay. Not great, not like it was a few months ago, but good enough. We're very lucky, but everybody is suffering somewhat in these terrible times, and it seemed bizarre that she would think any of us would be in a position to give her what sounded like a rather vast amount of money.'

'I agree, it was a bit odd.'

'And more than that, she seemed resentful when none of us said yes absolutely. I just felt there was a strange energy from her, and it made me slightly uncomfortable. I don't want to get into gossip, but Harry and I won't be investing, and I have no idea what you and Keith are thinking, and I so hope I'm not overstepping the mark here, but I wanted to say that I'm not sure it's a good idea.'

'Alice, you are totally not overstepping the mark, and don't you worry, Keith and I aren't going to be investing either.' For a minute, Charlie wonders whether to tell Alice. They are friends, after all, and it seems duplicitous to not mention something so big, but the mere thought of saying it fills her with shame.

It was one thing telling Kit, her best friend, who she knows won't judge, but quite another to tell anyone else, particularly those who think you are fine. If it wasn't so depressing, she would almost laugh.

Charlie continues, 'But interesting that you sensed there was a weird energy from her. I kind of felt the same thing this morning.'

'Oh God,' Alice groans. 'I wasn't going to gossip . . . Look, I barely know her, but I do know to trust my instincts, and there's something that doesn't smell quite right, and I do kind of wonder whether she's after Robert McClore for his money. I mean, God, I so should not be saying this, but they seem such an unlikely match.'

'Ya think?' Charlie bursts into laughter, the first genuine laughter in the last few hours. 'I think Robert McClore is probably far wiser than we realize, but I'll talk to Kit, just make sure she watches out for him.'

She puts the phone down, shaking her head, thinking about Tracy, wondering how it is you can be good friends with someone, or at least think you are good friends with someone, and realize suddenly that you don't know them at all.

Kit arrives home, and stares at her house in disbelief as she pulls into the driveway. There, on the front doorstep, is another giant bouquet of roses.

I wanted to make sure I didn't miss you. Steve

Buckley is riding round the neighbourhood on his bike with friends, and Tory is upstairs, ostensibly doing homework, but Kit knows she is probably sitting in front of the computer instant messaging all her friends.

She doesn't get beyond the hallway, a huge smile on her face, before she pulls out her address book, picking up the phone to call him.

'Hi, it's Kit.'

'Hey.'

'Did I wake you?' She is confused, it is mid afternoon but he sounds as if he has been asleep. 'Are you at work?'

'I had a meeting locally at lunchtime and I came home to get some stuff done, and I fell asleep on the couch.'

'I'm so sorry. Listen, we can talk later. Go back to sleep.'

'Wait, I've been thinking about you. How did everything go with your sister?'

'It's a very long story but it's all good. I'll tell you when I see you.'

'When can I see you? I'm missing you.'

'And I . . . I miss you too.'

'Really? Well . . . could we do something on Thursday?'

'Perfect. I'll see you on Thursday. I can't wait.'

The kids will be with their dad on Thursday night – since the divorce he has been forced to be home earlier to look after the children – which leaves just her . . . and Annabel. Damn. But surely Annabel won't mind going out for the evening so she can have a quiet dinner?

'Annabel?' she calls up the stairs. 'I'm home.'

'Hi! I'll be right down. I'm just borrowing your computer.'

'Sure,' Kit says, fighting a smidgen of irritation, then realizing how ridiculous it is to be territorial, to wish that she had been asked first. She has become more selfish, she knows, since living on her own with the kids. She is used to having everything done her way, is used to her stuff being her own (or at least *was*, before Tory turned thirteen and decided that what was her mother's was also hers).

And so what if Annabel didn't ask to use the computer? This is her *sister*, for God's sake.

In the kitchen she is momentarily dismayed to see a dirty dish and three dirty mugs piled haphazardly by the side of the sink. She sighs. She will have to tell Annabel that she has to clear up, and clean up, after herself. There are rules in this house, and she has to abide by them.

'Hi!' Annabel bounds into the room and gives Kit a huge hug, and everything is instantly forgiven. 'How was work?'

'It was good,' Kit says. 'What did you do today?'

'I made us supper,' Annabel says. 'Fish pie.'

'You did?'

'Look!' Annabel opens the oven to reveal a golden, cheese and potato-crusted pie bubbling away. 'I thought it was time someone looked after you.'

'This is so nice!' Kit beams. 'I feel like I'm coming home to a wife.'

'Wife, sister. I don't mind which it is. It's just lovely to be here, and to be part of your family. Speaking of which, I still don't understand why you let that handsome husband of yours go.'

'Adam? Handsome?' Kit laughs.

'Well, okay, so he's not my type, but he is obviously a good guy. And you seem, I don't know, *right* together. There's still unresolved business, I think. Would you try again?'

Kit shakes her head sadly. 'I've thought about it, from time to time, but it would feel like going backwards. Anyway, see those gorgeous flowers over there?'

'Oh wow! Those *are* gorgeous.'

'Yes, well, they're from Steve, who you might meet on Thursday. I need to keep moving forward, not turn back to the past. And I wanted to ask you: is it okay if I have the house to myself on Thursday?'

'Oh . . . sure. I can go to the movies or something.'

'You could go out with Edie, maybe? Or Charlie? I'm just planning a date here.'

'Aha!' Annabel grins. 'In that case, of course I'll make myself scarce. You deserve it.'

'Thank you.' Kit lays a hand on her arm. 'I knew you'd understand.'

18

Tracy peers at her eye in the mirror and sighs, opening her make-up drawer and digging out the Dermablend.

She had iced her eye, slathered arnica on it, but it has been difficult to hide the discoloration, although by now you would think she had had enough practice at hiding the bumps and bruises.

When she was a little girl, she dreamed of a knight in shining armour, her Prince Charming who would carry her off and rescue her from her nightmarish family. She always knew that she would do better, that she would never put up with what her mother put up with, that if anyone ever treated her the way her dad treated her mother, she would leave.

'Why don't you divorce him?' she used to hiss at her mother, as her mother tiptoed round the house, telling Tracy to ignore him, to stay out of the way, making sure everything was perfect before her father came back from one of his business trips, terrified to give him any excuse, any reason to lose his temper.

'He said he wouldn't do it again,' her mother would say; but then he would, and she would ice her own face, wiping the tears, telling Tracy that she would leave, they would run away together ... And her father would come back later, arms filled with flowers, contrite, desperate, falling on his knees in floods of tears, swearing he would never raise a hand to her again, and they would stay. And on it went.

She never dreamed she would end up where her mother was. Too frightened to leave, too frightened to stay. She thought, when she married Richard Stonehill, that it was finally over, and when she thinks that *she* was the one who Facebooked Jed, *she* was the one who went back, she almost vomits.

Jed has a plan. Tracy is part of that plan. And right now she's trying to figure out a way to continue with the plan, but without him. It will take time to think of just the right way to get rid of him, but this time she really wants to leave for ever. This time she really wants it to be different.

Because now there is Robert McClore, the single bright spot in her life, the one joy that is slowly enabling her to detach from the fear, from the rest of her life that is so dark.

Tonight, Robert is taking her to Stonehenge for dinner. It is a tiny, romantic inn in Ridgefield, and he mentioned she should bring an overnight bag in case they feel like staying – he has booked a room, but doesn't want to seem forward, is leaving the decision in her hands.

And she knows what her decision will be.

This time, for the first time, she thinks she may have fallen in love.

On the other side of town, Robert McClore leans back in his chair, sips his cappuccino and smiles to himself with satisfaction.

Chapter four. Already! Never has a book been easier to write. It is as if he is writing on auto-pilot, the words flowing from his fingertips in a way they haven't since – well, probably since his first novel.

Writing was so creative back then, but of late it has felt more and more like a business. He has contracts to fulfil, books to write: one book a year, whether inspiration strikes or not.

It has become a job, and one that he is starting to find dull.

The business of outlining, of researching, of sifting through to decide which bits are relevant and which bits are not, used to light him up with passion.

The moment when characters you thought were pivotal suddenly become irrelevant, when others, supposed to have been bit parts, end up driving the plot, taking over the book, filled him with pleasure.

Everything about being a writer used to excite him, but these past few books have felt mechanical, as if he is just going through the motions.

Something has to change. This he knows, as much as he knows that the creative process is all *about* change.

He always starts a book with an outline, but has to be fluid, malleable, has to accept that the characters will take over, and that it's quite possible the finished book will be nothing like the book he had in mind.

This is why he couldn't ever do as his agent wants him to do, and take on ghost writers, employ a team, others to write his words.

Oh he knows others do it, knows it is the Warhol Factory mentality that would thrill his audience, those who want instant gratification, who email him daily demanding he produce more, telling him they can't bear the wait for a new McClore book, but he can't.

His agent, his publisher, suggested a ghost writer for a series of mysteries, but this book is so easy to write that he will be finished in a matter of weeks, doesn't need a ghost writer. How could a ghost writer possibly tell his story, how could a ghost writer have really known what it was like being married to Penelope, the affairs, the anger, the volatility?

How could he possibly entrust that to someone else?

He started off with pseudonyms for everyone, started off writing in the third person, but halfway through the first chapter he wrote it as it was, in the first person, just as he experienced it at the time.

He can change the names later, will *definitely* change the names later. But right now, Penelope is Penelope, he is Robert, and everything is just as it was. The clubs, the restaurants, the parties, the celebrities. They will be changed, names will be made up, because this is a work of fiction, at least as far as everyone else is concerned.

The only person who knows is Tracy. And she doesn't actually know anything, but it was her idea, and he said it was an interesting one. She doesn't know how close the story is, though. He wouldn't tell her that. Even Kit, whom he has come to trust implicitly, doesn't know. He has his own computer in his study, password-protected, and is not printing out each chapter, as he usually does, to give it to Kit to proof-read; he is just writing, and will wait until the end before printing it out.

In many ways, this is the easiest book he has ever written. It does truly feel, as Tracy suggested, that this is the one story he has always been destined to write, a story that is, as a consequence, remarkably easy to tell.

He thinks of all the women's fiction that peppers the shelves of the local library, the local bookstores, fiction that depicts women's legs, or cartoon drawings of handbags, all in shocking shades of pastel and pink.

He flicked through some of those books. Tales of twenty-something single girls looking for Mr Right while tripping through city streets in fabulous designer heels, or, as they get older, tales of divorces, of adultery, of women miserable in the suburbs, trying to make sense of unhappy marriages, or moving ahead with new-found romances.

'Chick lit,' he said, sniffing derisively, privately thinking it wasn't writing, it was *journaling* – the women getting out their angst, their frustration with their relationships, their dissatisfaction with their lives in the form of a novel.

Where was the fiction, he wondered. Where was the story-telling? The art? But now he sees the ease in writing about your life. It's true that it doesn't feel like the same discipline, but it is a discipline nevertheless, a craft: to draw upon your memory, to analyse the emotions, to paint the pictures in a way that is so authentic, it cannot help but resonate with your readers.

And it is extraordinarily cathartic. In many ways it enables him to process his relationship with Penelope, his relationships with all of those people, in a way he never thought possible. He sees them all in a new light, is able to see Penelope as a hurt child, a child in a woman's body, who struck out because she was scared.

She wasn't the villain he thought she was at the time. And this, perhaps, is the most extraordinary thing of all – that in writing this book, writing about Penelope for the first time in his life, he finds that his own anger has gone, and it gives his writing an honesty and a clarity that his fans won't recognize as coming from Robert McClore.

It is Tracy he has to thank. Tracy with her easy smile, her wisdom. He hasn't had a muse in many years, not since Penelope, but it feels as though Tracy has come into his life at just the right time. It is time for a muse. Time for him to move on.

He checks his watch. Good Lord, it is four o'clock. He has written for eight hours solidly. Eight hours! That is unheard of. A good writing day is anywhere between three and five hours, but eight hours have passed in a flash; and he knows this is good, knows, in fact, this may be the best thing he has ever written.

He stands up and stretches, then shuts off his computer, thinking about Tracy. He is picking her up at half past six, and he feels a flutter of anticipation and excitement as he walks up the stairs. It is the first time he has been this excited about a woman since Penelope, who is vivid again after all these years when she was supposed to have died.

'I'm not sure about those roses,' Edie says, suspicion in her eyes as she reads the card again. 'I still think he has an ulterior motive.'

'Oh Edie,' Annabel says with a laugh. 'Don't be such a killjoy. I think it's romantic.'

'It would be romantic if he'd left one small posy. But two enormous bouquets of roses? That feels like manipulation.'

'Manipulation?' Now it's Kit's turn to laugh. 'Why? Do you think he's after my secret millions?'

'Do you have secret millions?' Annabel's eyes light up.

'Sadly, if I do, they're so secret even I don't know about them.'

'Bugger. I guess I'll just fly home, then.'

'Thanks.' They smile at each other, already comfortable in their teasing, in starting to know what it is like to have a sister.

'Stay for dinner, Edie,' Annabel says. 'I've made enough for an army.'

'Well, I will,' grumbles Edie, 'but you two are terrifically naive. You just wait and see. I'm telling you he's not to be trusted. He's too charming and too good-looking, and I'm old enough to know that my instincts are always right.'

Annabel grins at Edie. 'I think you're just jealous. I bet you wish someone would send you some white roses and whisk you out for sumptuous, dinners.'

'At my age? Girls, you're ridiculous,' Edie says, but she can't help a small smile.

'Well, you did say tennis this weekend,' Kit reminds her. 'You and Rose will have to check him out properly.'

'Especially his thighs,' Annabel adds. 'Anyway, I

think he sounds lovely, and I admit, it might have been a bit ... naff ... if he'd sent red roses, but white? I still think it's romantic.'

'So what about you, young lady?' Edie asks curiously. 'Do you have a special somebody back home in England?'

'I wish.' Annabel sighs. 'Unfortunately, I have a penchant for bad boys, and after the last one I've decided to swear off men for a while.'

'How bad is bad?' Kit wants to know.

'*Really* bad.' Annabel shoots a warning look at Kit, not wanting to divulge too much in front of Edie. 'Drink, drugs, tattoos, violence ...' She shakes her head. 'Put it like this: show me a man who knows how to treat a woman like dirt, and I will faint with delight at his feet and allow him to treat me like the doormat he so clearly wants me to be.'

Kit laughs. 'Annabel, you're too much. I don't believe you.'

'I know. No one does. When I'm single, I'm this fabulous, independent, confident woman, and then I get involved with one disastrous man after another and I turn into this needy, insecure, fearful girl who becomes frightened of her own shadow. I'm telling you, I may become a lesbian after the last one.'

'I tried that, and I wouldn't recommend it either,' Edie says nonchalantly. 'Women are much too high-maintenance. All that drama! It was exhausting.'

'Edie!' Annabel's mouth falls open in shock.

'This is why we love her.' Kit puts an arm around Edie and plants a kiss on her cheek. 'Because she has lived more lifetimes than you and I could ever even dream about.'

Annabel is rapt. 'Tell us all about it. I want to know everything.'

'Her name was Monika.' Edie takes off her glasses and smiles at the memory. 'I was nineteen, in my second year at Yale, and she was a German exchange student, studying in America for a year.'

'What did she look like?' Annabel asks, as Edie drifts off into the memories.

'I have a photograph somewhere in a drawer. Would you like me to get it?' Edie gets up and disappears through the back door.

'Edie in a lesbian love drama!' Kit breathes to Annabel. 'Who would have thought?'

'I know! I guess everyone has their secrets,' Annabel says. 'Even Edie.'

The room at Stonehenge is dark, candlelit, romantic. Tracy looks at Robert, her heart softening, as he reaches out and strokes her hand, both of them smiling as the waiter silently refills her glass of champagne.

'That was a wonderful night the other night,' he says.

'It was,' she echoes, 'and more than that, it was special. *You're* special. I think you're an extraordinary man.' Robert beams in the face of her compliment.

How ironic, she thinks. That it has taken her forty-one years to discover what love is, and that it has come when she least expected it, when she wasn't looking, when, in fact, her plans were far more devious.

She had married Richard Stonehill because he felt safe, because she'd had enough pain to last her a life-time, and because although Richard had many faults, and faults she was aware of before she married him, she knew he wouldn't hurt her.

She knew because there was no passion, and the only time she had felt passion, it had come with a price.

When she agreed to Jed's plan, and realized that she could use Robert to get away from Jed, she thought she was being given a second chance. Not at happi-ness – that would have been too much to ask – but at a lifestyle she would never, could never have on her own.

She could have diamonds and pearls and holidays and clothes and a huge house, and be Mrs Robert McClore!

She could go to movie premieres, and parties, and be friends with the right people, and perhaps then she would be happy, perhaps then she would fit in.

Robert McClore was offering safety. He was many things, but he was not a man who had a temper, of this she was certain. He was old school, a man who knew how to take care of a woman, who opened doors, treated women with respect, and charm. He was offer-ing her a chance, a chance of security she didn't think would come around again.

But sitting here tonight, at the tiny corner table lit up with candlelight and love, Tracy knows there is so much more than this.

'I love you,' she whispers.

They are words she has never volunteered before,

always too frightened to say them first, and Robert's eyes fill with tears as he leans over and gathers her in his arms.

19

'You are just totally cool,' Tory breathes, as she and Annabel sit in a booth at the old-fashioned diner, sharing a chocolate milkshake. 'Seriously, I can't believe that you're related to my mom, and I can't believe you're my *aunt*!'

'Well, thank you.' Annabel pours the rest of the pitcher equally between their two tall glasses. 'And I have to say *this* is totally cool. I love this place. I feel like I've stepped back in time to the nineteen fifties. Do you have any idea how lucky you are to live here?'

Tory shrugs. 'I guess.'

'And your school! All those cute boys you get to go to school with. So which one do you like?'

Tory flushes.

'Oh come on. When we just passed that big bunch of your friends on Main Street, there were some truly good-looking boys. I'd be a disaster if I were in your place. I went to an all-girls' school, super-strict, with uniforms, and the only boys we ever saw were the boys at UCS, and even the sight of a black and maroon striped blazer was enough to have me salivating. If they'd been in class with me I'd never have got anything done.'

Tory laughs.

'It's true,' Annabel says. 'I would never have done

work if there'd been boys to pass notes to. I was utterly boy-crazy. So, if you're not going to tell me, I'm just going to have to guess. If I were a thirteen-year-old girl, I would probably like the boy who had the red checked shirt on. He was handsome.'

Tory blushes a bright red.

'I *knew* it! You like him.'

'No! I don't.'

'Oh, come on. I'm your aunt. You're supposed to tell me these things, and especially if you think I'm cool.'

'You swear you won't tell Mom?'

Annabel grins and raises her right hand. 'Brownie swear.'

'You were a Brownie?'

'God, no!' Annabel laughs. 'I was far too naughty. So, go on, I'm right, aren't I? What's the story?'

'I do kind of like him, and then my friend Liv said he'd asked her if I was going to this bar-mitzvah party on Saturday night, and she thinks he likes me too.'

'Well, he was kind of gazing at you.'

'He was?' Her eyes light up with pleasure.

'Absolutely. So, a party on Saturday night. What are you going to wear?'

'I don't know.' Tory's face falls. 'Mom says she can't afford to buy me anything new, and Dad always says he will, but he forgets. I guess I'll just wear the black dress I always wear.'

'Hmm. You know one of the jobs of an aunt?'

'What?'

'To spoil her nieces and nephews. Which means I think we should go shopping.'

'Are you serious?'

'Of course! Where should we go first?'

'Can we go to Kool Klothes? Please? It's kind of expensive but they have a huge sale on and I love almost everything in there.'

'Okay.'

'And then can we go to Claire's? Because they have these earrings that are totally cute and they're only about five dollars, and they're amazing, and Maxi and Annie and Natalie have them and I'm the only one who doesn't and –'

'Woah!' Annabel puts her hand up, laughing. 'Slow down. The answer is yes.'

A phone starts to ring, and as Tory reaches into her backpack Annabel looks at her in surprise.

'You have a phone?'

'Yeah. Everyone has them. We use them to text, though, not for the phone. This is probably Mom or Dad.' She riffles around her backpack, eventually pulling out the phone and flipping it open.

'Hey, Dad. Guess what? I'm in the Beachside Diner with Aunt Annabel.'

Annabel hides a surreptitious smile when she hears this, the first time Tory has called her Aunt Annabel. Oh the power that shopping will give her . . .

'So she said she's going to take me shopping, and she has Mom's car, so you don't have to pick me up, she can drop me at yours . . . uh huh . . . uh huh. Okay, hang on,' and she passes the phone over to Annabel.

'I hope my daughter isn't being too demanding?' Adam's voice is familiar, after just one meeting.

'Not at all. We're having a gorgeous time and now I'm about to take her out and spoil her.'

'I don't even know how to thank you, but you clearly know the way to a thirteen-year-old girl's heart.'

'Well, I would hope so, having, once upon a time, been a thirteen-year-old girl myself.'

'Listen, why don't you join us tonight? I was planning on taking the kids out to Gino's. It's a crazy Italian restaurant on the edge of town, family style, completely casual but fun. It's the kids' favourite place. I know they'd be thrilled if you came.'

Annabel doesn't have to think. Tonight is the night she has been banished from the house, and all she has planned are the movies, trying to sneak early peeks at the movies that won't be out in England for months.

'I'd love it.'

'Great! We should probably meet there. Do you need me to give you directions?'

'I don't know. Let me ask Tory. Do you know the way to Gino's?'

'Yes.'

'Good, because we're going to Gino's for dinner.'

'We are? Oh my God! This is turning into the best day ever.' Tory reaches over and grabs the phone. 'Bye, Dad — we're going shopping now and I love you *so* much!'

Adam laughs when he sees Annabel and Tory walk in, laden down with shopping bags.

'My God!' he says. 'Did you buy *everything* in town?'

'Almost!' Tory is giddy with delight. 'We even got

238

something for you, Buckley.' And she reaches into a bag and pulls out a *Star Wars* Transformer.

'Woah, cool!' Buckley grins.

'What do you say?'

'What?'

Adam looks sternly at Buckley. 'How about "thank you"?'

'Um, yeah. Thank you!'

'They have a table for us in the front room,' Adam says. 'I hope that's okay. It's kind of loud and crazy but the kids love it.'

'Yeah, the back room is totally boring,' Buckley says. 'And you have to shout in the front room.'

'He's right.' Adam stands up from the bar stool and extends an arm to guide Annabel through the restaurant. 'There won't be any getting-to-know-you soft conversation tonight.'

Tory gives her dad a strange look, then looks at Annabel, who shrugs, as if she has no idea what Adam is talking about, but she felt it too, a hint of flirtation in the comment, a frisson of . . . something.

The restaurant is mobbed, and it feels, dodging the waiters bustling around with huge trays of food held high over their heads, as if everyone sitting there is smiling, laughing, having a great time.

'This is amazing!' Annabel shouts to Tory, who is suddenly quiet. 'I see why you love it.'

Tory doesn't say anything.

'So what does "family style" mean?' Annabel asks, and Adam explains they will all share from large platters of food in the centre of the table.

A round, smiling brunette appears, order pad poised. 'Good evening, everyone, my name is Maria and I'll be your server for the night. What can I get you folks to drink?'

'Kids?'

'I'll have a Coke,' Tory says.

Adam raises an eyebrow. 'Oh no, you won't. You can have seltzer.'

Tory tuts loudly, and for the first time Annabel sees a hint of teen angst, of Tory being not quite the perfect girl she had presumed.

'Fine,' she huffs. 'Cranberry juice and seltzer.'

'Me too,' says Buckley.

'And how about Mom?' says Maria pleasantly, waiting for Annabel.

'She's not our mom!' Tory says quickly, and is it Annabel's imagination, or is there a slight glare in her eye as Tory looks at her.

'Nope,' Annabel says. 'I'm their aunt. That's why there's a family resemblance.'

'Well, I was close! So how about you, Aunt? What can I get you?'

'Cranberry juice and seltzer sounds great.'

The food comes, Annabel is forgiven for whatever transgression she unknowingly made, and even though she barely speaks to Adam, she knows he is watching her, can feel his eyes upon her all the time.

She is not unused to this, but not from her new-found sister's former-and-probably-from-what-she-can-tell-shouldn't-be ex-husband. This is one complication she doesn't need. It's not even as if he's her type. He's far too nice a guy for Annabel to be attracted to. Sure, he's decent-looking, and his body seems in pretty good shape for a guy in his early forties, but nice guys like this have been chasing Annabel for years, and she's never been the slightest bit interested.

What he does have, however, is something Annabel has always wanted.

He has a family.

He and she and Tory and Buckley do indeed look like the perfect family. Sure, she's a little young to be a mother to Tory, but not too young, it would seem from the waitress's comment.

A family. As a little girl, she had wanted to have a mother and a father, to have siblings; and now, as an adult, being here with Adam and the kids, she wants this.

To sit, as a perfect nuclear family, in a restaurant such as this, laughing and talking about nothing very much, even telling the children to stop fighting – this is all part of a happy family life she wants. Very, very much.

'What?' She realizes Adam is saying something to her. 'I can't hear you.'

'I said I saw a piece you'd written on how your life changes when your friends start having kids. I thought it was really interesting.'

'Oh. Right. Thanks.' Annabel is stunned. She has flitted from career to career, and for a brief while, between rehab stints, fancied herself a journalist. She met a guy at a club, one of the nice guys, who was an editor, and part of his wooing process involved commissioning Annabel to write pieces she really had no business writing.

The piece to which Adam is referring was written one night in a drug-induced haze. She recalls rambling on and on, venting her rage at one of her friends who had, she felt, abandoned her once her baby came.

It was only after her final successful stay in rehab that she was able to take responsibility, to accept that the friend had abandoned her because she couldn't deal with Annabel's erratic behaviour and unreliability any more.

It was a piece published years ago, in a crappy magazine in England. The only way Adam could have found it would have been online, and even then it would never be something he just stumbled across.

Which means he has been Googling her.

Which means she is right, has not imagined him gazing at her with puppy-dog eyes.

Her sister's husband has a definite crush on her.

Kit's living room is once again set for seduction, and this time there will be no last-minute changes.

The plates are sitting in the sink, waiting to be stacked in the dishwasher at an opportune moment, the fire is crackling softly, and the candles are slowly burning down. The iPod playlist ran out a long time ago, and the only sounds are soft murmurs and gentle laughter, the occasional sigh of pleasure.

Steve is lying on the sofa, holding Kit in his arms and planting soft kisses on her forehead. She is closing her eyes in sheer bliss, for this is what she has missed more than anything.

Not the sex, but the affection. Affection she hadn't had from Adam for years. Lying on a sofa and being held, being told you are beautiful, *feeling* beautiful.

When was the last time she felt beautiful?

Not for years.

Not like this.

Adam's body had become as familiar to her as her own. There was comfort in knowing every curve, every bump, every groove, but there wasn't the anticipation, the sheer heart-stopping thrill of discovering a new body.

Their sex life had become, as with so many married couples, routine. Quick, familiar. Kit wanted nothing more than to close her eyes and go to sleep at the end of the day. Lovely, loving, once they started, but it was the same moves, the same positions, each of them going through the motions until sleep claimed them both.

And here was Steve, so different from Adam, his skin so tan, the hair on his arms dark, his body strong and yet soft, waking her up from a deep sleep with every anticipatory stroke.

She remembers once, standing in her bathroom, peering into the mirror, her chin thrust forward, tweezers poised to seek out and kill the two stray whiskers that had shockingly appeared underneath her chin just before her thirty-fourth birthday.

'That's sexy,' Adam said, laughing at her, as he passed the open door on the way to shave in his own bathroom.

'Could be worse,' she said, moving her face from side to side to check that no more had appeared. 'I could be shaving.'

'Oh God,' he groaned, and they both laughed.

'But seriously,' she said, finishing her plucking and raising her leg on the bathroom sink to shave from the knee down, 'don't you ever feel it would be impossible to start again?'

'What do you mean, start again?'

'I mean, here we are, we've been together for years, and we know all each other's disgusting habits. I could never get divorced and be with another man. Actually, I'd never find another man who would put up with me.'

'I hope you *don't* find another man.' Adam shot her a strange look, but he was used to her musings.

'Yeah, don't worry about it,' Kit muttered, contorting her body to shave up the back of her legs. 'Two children later, with my saggy boobs and varicose veins, not to mention my whiskers, who'd have me?'

'Ah, my lovely furry wife –' Adam blew her a kiss – '*I'd* have you.'

'Damn good job.'

But it was true, once they had actually got divorced Kit did wonder who would possibly find her attractive again. When she met Adam she'd been young, hard-bodied, not a hint of cellulite or middle-aged spread.

Now, even with yoga, she has a pot belly she'll never get rid of, lumpy veins in her legs that she blames her father for, and orange-peel skin on her thighs, which no amount of anti-cellulite cream seems to remove.

Not that she cares particularly. In a community

where looks and youth are so prized that the house-wives all indulge in Botox, Restylane, laser resurfacing treatments to continue looking good for their wealthy husbands, Kit doesn't bother.

Yoga is less about keeping her fit, and more about keeping her calm. As for joining a gym and leaping around doing circuit training, or – God forbid – having a personal trainer come to the house once a week, she just can't be bothered.

One benefit of the divorce was unexpectedly losing weight (she can even fit into her wedding dress again), but as for firming and toning, forget it.

Until now.

Steve unbuttons her shirt and, as a reflex, she pulls her stomach in and stretches out to try to elongate her body.

'You're beautiful,' he whispers, moving up to kiss her on the lips, before disappearing down her body. 'Relax.'

And she does, forgetting about her belly, her cellulite, her sag, not thinking about anything, just feeling Steve's lips on her skin.

'Will you stay?' she says later, much later, when they are cuddled up by the dying fire.

'I wish I could.' He smiles at her and kisses her on the nose. 'I have conference calls to Europe at five o'clock in the morning. Next time. What are your plans tomorrow?'

'Tomorrow?' Does he mean day or night, she wonders. Does he want to see her tomorrow? 'Nothing much. Just work.'

'Ah yes. Assistant to the famous author. I'd forgot-ten. Do you like it?'

'I love it. Why?'

'No ... I – I just see you as something more than an assistant.'

Kit sits up, startled. 'It's not demeaning. It's wonder-ful. I love it. What do you mean?'

'Oh God, not that it's demeaning. I didn't mean that at all. I just meant I saw you as running your own business. I don't know ... something that's all yours.'

Kit smiles. 'Funny, I always wanted to own a clothes store.'

'You did?'

'I know. Weird. Especially since I'm not exactly the fashion queen, but I always saw myself as having this great little independent store, with inexpensive com-fortable chic clothing, and a great bunch of loyal customers. I had visions of a cappuccino machine in the corner, and building a community of wonderful people.'

'I think it's a great dream. Maybe you should start thinking about how to turn that dream into a reality.'

'Now? I don't think anyone's able to turn business dreams into a reality in these times. Tracy's trying to open another branch, and I think she's having a horrible time raising money.'

'Tracy?'

'Who runs Namaste? You know. She's always in the front. Tall gorgeous blonde? Don't tell me you don't remember her. She's the one who told me about you!'

'Of course.' He smiles and draws her closer to kiss her. 'Isn't she dating someone?'

Kit laughs. 'You've obviously been listening to too much yoga centre gossip. She's kind of seeing my boss, I think. I've barely seen her. I don't know what's going on but it feels like she's avoiding me. Which is awful.'

'That's rough. I'm sorry,' Steve says. 'You should sit her down and talk to her, tell her how you feel. So much of the time these tiny things blow up into something huge because people just don't know how to communicate. Tell her. I bet she has no idea you feel she's avoiding you.'

Kit smiles gratefully. 'You're so right. Thank you.'

'Listen, if I don't see you tomorrow, if this work thing takes over – which it might – will you come on Saturday? Your neighbour Edie has already phoned to confirm that I'm in for tennis,' he says, and groans. 'Will you come and cheer me on?'

'I'm so sorry. Of course I'll come and cheer you on. I wouldn't miss it for the world,' Kit says, then covers his face with kisses.

20

Charlie pretends to be busy with the children, so intensely focused on them that she doesn't have time to look at her husband. A distracted goodbye with no eye contact being about the best she can manage these days.

Her resentment is huge. How could he have let them get to this stage? How could he have pulled the wool so firmly not just over the eyes of everyone they know but, far more worryingly, over her eyes, his own wife?

For there had been times, over the years, so many times, when she had asked him if they could afford it.

'Can we really afford this house?' Her eyes, she recalled, had been large when they had first seen it, when Keith had been so determined to make an offer. It had been the biggest house of any she knew, a fairy-tale, a house that would instantly make her the envy of all their peers.

'Of course we can,' Keith said, explaining about leveraging and interest rates, and how their money, put to use elsewhere, was working harder; and she didn't think to ask what money, because Keith was, after all, a banker. He was supposed to know about such things.

'I make more money than ninety-nine per cent of this country,' he would say, defensively, if she ever questioned how his salary, while substantial, could possibly be enough to carry their ever more elaborate lifestyle.

'I'm on track for a million-dollar bonus,' he would say, to allay her fears, and then come up with an excuse when the cash bonus never materialized, and what he got instead was almost entirely in company stock. The stock that is worth nothing today.

'You should have a Range Rover,' he said, indulgently, a couple of years ago, standing in the Land Rover showroom and riffling through the papers, waiting to sign the lease. 'It's what you deserve.'

And because Keith always said they could afford it, she believed him; and because he always said they had the money, she continued to spend. And now that he says there is nothing left, she is filled with nothing but burning resentment.

There is nothing left.

The bank has agreed to the deal. Which only means that they will accept a sale price of less than the mortgage. In this market, it means nothing. The only houses still selling in Highfield are the ones by the beach, or overlooking the harbour, with water views.

And even those aren't selling like they used to. In the old days, you couldn't buy at the beach, for love nor money. The houses tended to sell off-market, and if they ever did hit the open market they would be gone in days to the highest sealed bid. Now, even the beach area is littered with For Sale signs.

The realtor came yesterday, with a list of directions of what Charlie has to do in order to expedite the sale of the house. She has to clear out the basement, tidy up the clutter, apply a fresh coat of paint in the playroom where Emma has been overenthusiastic with the finger paints.

'It's adorable,' the realtor said, 'but someone coming in may not find it quite so lovely. We want it clean and fresh so they can put their stamp on it.'

'Do you think it will sell?'

'At this price? One point eight? Under normal circumstances it would be snapped up, but ... these aren't normal circumstances. Still, I think it will move. Particularly when you have an identical house on the street at one point nine, and this has a better yard. Even now, even in these times, people still need to move house, and there's a huge relocation starting, a company from Boston relocating to Norwalk, and a lot of their employees are liking Highfield because of the school systems. Are you sure you don't want to put it on for higher? I think you can afford to give it a few weeks at two, or even two point one, before dropping the price.'

That's just it, Charlie thought. We *can't* afford it.

She is now waiting for the photographer to arrive. The listing has already gone up on the website, with the old exterior shot from when they bought the house. Which means the word will be out, because the wealthy Highfield housewife knows everything about the real-estate market, spends Sundays popping into Open Houses, knows all about who's moving, why and where, as soon as it happens.

She can hear the game of telephone now. 'Do you know Charlie Warren has her house on the market?' 'But they just finished decorating!' 'They must be in trouble!' 'And you know their nanny, Amanda, is looking for a job – they had to let her go!' 'Isn't it awful?' It is, but they are excited at the gossip, and relieved it isn't them.

Keith spoke to his parents yesterday. She is speaking to hers today. She still doesn't know what to do, only that something has to be done.

Going to her parents, whom she adores, means New Jersey. Leaving everything she knows, everything she has built here, and she just doesn't think she has the energy to start again, not to mention traumatizing the children even more.

Keith's parents live in Highfield. The children could stay in their drama classes, their Little League teams, they could keep their friends, particularly Paige, who, at thirteen, may never recover from being pulled out of her life if they moved to New Jersey.

And yet, staying in Highfield would mean having to deal with everyone knowing, being the centre of the gossip, walking into rooms full of people in the certain knowledge that she is the reason for the sudden hush.

How is it possible to go from having everything, to suddenly having nothing? These last few days, more and more has emerged. They were, indeed, living the American Dream, but a dream created by smoke and mirrors, created by the people willing to lend them money, far more than they could afford, far more than they had a right to expect, merely because Keith worked in finance so the potential for gold seemed endless.

Almost nothing they have is theirs. The house is owned by the bank, the cars are leased. The stock is worth nothing, and so they are left with possessions.

Charlie has been making lists. The Persian rugs in the family room – the antique, signed Persian rugs that they bought for seventy-five thousand dollars, thinking they were a steal because they bought them with valuations of one hundred and fifty thousand dollars – might be worth, she guesses, fifteen thousand each. If they are lucky.

For who is buying rugs in a market such as this?

The baby grand piano, a William Knabe that cost ten thousand to restore, might be worth – what? Five? Ten? Certainly not the thirty to forty thousand the restorer had said they could expect when they had the work done three years ago.

Her clothes. Her jewels. The huge diamond studs that cost so much, yet would resell for so little.

This morning she went onto eBay, but not, as she has done so many times before, to scout out a bargain, to look for a piece of furniture for the living room, an antique desk, a Swedish table, but to list items to sell.

She is being methodical because it is keeping her calm. Making lists, keeping herself busy, is stopping her from breaking down and screaming.

This morning, the *New York Times* had an article listing wealthy towns that were suffering. Highfield was close to the top of the list. Stores, upmarket designer stores, were receiving countless cheques that were bouncing, from people the stores assumed had more money than God.

It should be some consolation that Charlie isn't

alone, but it isn't. Just keep moving, she tells herself. One foot in front of the other. But right now, while she's moving, she can't forgive Keith, can't do anything other than sit at the kitchen table once the kids have gone to bed and ask him, coldly, what else she needs to know.

He has cried, confessed his idiocy, says he didn't know how to tell her things were going wrong, didn't want to hurt her, was trying to protect her, but Charlie is not swayed by his tears.

And then he jumped on the defensive, again. This wasn't his fault. The world was collapsing around them, thousands of families were in the same boat, how was he supposed to know this would happen? Nobody could have predicted this. *Nobody.*

'You weren't supposed to know this would happen, but you were supposed to have been more sensible. You were supposed to have taken out a mortgage we could afford. Jesus. I didn't even know about the Home Equity Line. What the hell was that all about?'

'We needed the money, and you *did* know. You signed it.'

'Of course I signed it. I signed everything you put in front of me, telling me this was a wise financial move. You know I'm hopeless with money, I don't understand it. I trusted you to take care of it.'

'You never stopped me.' Keith felt resentment too, and fear at having to shoulder this burden alone. 'You could have read it, but you were never interested. Every time I tried to sit down with you and talk about money, you shut off.'

'Oh I see. So it's my fault? Great. Thanks a lot.'

He is a banker. He was supposed to invest their money wisely. Isn't diversification the name of the game? Hell, even Charlie knows about diversification, and she's just about the worst person with money she's ever known.

As Keith is now pointing out.

He is sleeping in the spare room. And she is making lists. Wandering round the house at night, scribbling guesstimates of their furniture. Sitting in her closet, wondering what designer consignments will get, and whether she can talk them into taking fifteen per cent rather than their usual forty.

Nothing they have is really worth anything. Not in the grand scheme of things. Keith isn't working, and thinks it's unlikely he will find another job for a while, and Charlie's business is fun, but doesn't even begin to fund their lifestyle, not to mention that flowers are a luxury that people can now ill-afford.

If they are lucky, they may be able to scrabble together a hundred thousand from selling their possessions. A hundred thousand which will last them a while, once their children are out of school.

Oh God. Highfield Academy. There is always the possibility of financial aid. With a huge swallow, Charlie picks up the phone and dials the familiar number of the Academy.

'Hi, this is Charlie Warren. I'd like to make an appointment to see the headmaster.'

*

Tracy tries telling Kit she doesn't have time to meet them, but Charlie arrives and won't take no for an answer.

'We miss you and we're not accepting no.' Charlie plants herself in front of the desk in Tracy's office and refuses to move. 'You're coming upstairs to the smoothie bar even if we have to drag you ourselves.'

'You wouldn't.'

Charlie puts her hands on her hips. 'Try me.'

'Okay, okay!' Tracy throws her hands up in submission. 'I'm coming.'

Kit glances at Charlie, who shrugs, for although Tracy is coming, there is little joy in her voice, and little energy in her step as she trudges up the stairs in front of them.

'So what's going on?' Charlie goes first. 'We're worried about you.'

'Worried about me? I'm fine. Why are you worried about me?'

'Because you've barely spoken to me since that night we went out for dinner with Alice and Harry, and Kit says you've barely spoken to her, and we're worried about you.'

Kit reaches over and places a gentle hand on her arm. 'We love you, Tracy. That's why we're here. We're your friends, and if there's something bad happening in your life, we want to help.'

'Let me tell you, there are bad things happening in my life, and right now I'm looking for all the help I can get; and as embarrassed as I am, I'm not afraid to accept it.' Charlie swallows. 'And you shouldn't be either.'

Tracy is aghast. 'What kind of things?'

'Let's just say the current financial crisis is affecting me deeply.'

'How deeply?'

Charlie shrugs, as if it is something inconsequential. 'There's nothing left. That's why Keith was so antsy when you were asking him for money. Turns out – tah dah! – we haven't got any.'

'Are you serious?'

'I wish to God I was joking, but no. Sadly, I am serious.'

'So what are you going to do?'

'Sell the house, sell everything I have, pull the kids out of the private schools unless they agree to grant us financial aid, and either move in with my parents in New Jersey, or, God forbid, although it's looking more likely, move in with Keith's parents here in Highfield.'

'But you hate Keith's parents,' Kit says.

'I know. Everything else I can just about deal with but that may just push me over the edge.'

Tracy just sits, looking at her open-mouthed. 'Oh my God,' she says, tears welling up in her eyes. 'I am so sorry. I had no idea.'

'It's only money.' Charlie feigns an insouciance she doesn't feel, scared that if she reveals her true fears, she will start crying and will never be able to stop.

'Oh Charlie,' she says. 'I've been so selfish.'

'No, you haven't. I'm fine. And anyway, we're not

here to talk about me, we're here to talk about you. What's going on with you?'

'I've just been working hard.' Tracy recovers her composure. 'The holiday season is starting and it seems to be a crazy time of year. I just haven't stopped, but I realize I've been a really bad friend. I'm sorry.' She looks first at Charlie then at Kit.

'So you really are okay?' Kit asks, dubiously, for Charlie was right: Tracy does look pretty terrible, and that's definitely a black eye.

'This?' Tracy touches her eye. 'A rogue closet door in my house, can you stand it? Everyone thinks I've been secretly beaten up by someone.'

'Robert McClore?' Charlie raises an eyebrow.

'Probably.'

'So, how are things with you and Robert?'

'What things? We just . . . had dinner.'

'Oh right,' Charlie splutters. 'He could barely take his eyes off you.'

'Well, he's a wonderful man. Really interesting. But Kit knows that.'

'It's true.' Kit still feels weird, still feels that Tracy is hiding something.

'Speaking of wonderful men,' Tracy deflects the subject smoothly, 'are you still seeing that good-looking guy who came in here?'

'Steve?' Kit grins. 'I guess you could say that. Well, I did see quite a lot more than I expected to last night.'

'Oh my God!' Charlie's eyes widen. 'Do you mean to say you lost your post-divorce virginity last night and you didn't even tell us?'

'We had other things to talk about.'

'Listen, girlfriend. When it comes to sex with a new man, there *is* nothing else to talk about. Hell, the way things are going with Keith and me right now, I might be on the market myself shortly, so you're going to have to tell us everything.'

'Everything like what?'

'Like was it totally weird, being with someone other than Adam?'

Kit shrugs, not sure how much to say. 'It was weird, but it was lovely. It's like, when you're married, you completely forget what that feeling of true lust is like after a while. And let me tell you, he does have a body worth lusting after.'

'So you actually *did* sleep with him?' Tracy is transfixed.

'I did! Can you believe it? Me, Miss Goody Two Shoes, who has only had two lovers her entire life, and now I know what it's like to be a slut!' Kit laughs.

'Hardly a slut with three lovers,' Charlie points out.

'But you're surprised, aren't you?' Kit says gleefully. 'I know you guys think I'm prissy. You never expected me to jump into bed with him.'

'You're right. I didn't,' Charlie says.

'Me either. Listen, guys –' Tracy looks at her watch then stands – 'I'd love to stay and chat, and I'm so glad we had a bit of time together, but I have a really big phone call coming in soon from some potential investors, and I have to prepare.'

'Oh God,' Charlie says. 'I never even said sorry for that night. I had no idea what deep trouble we were in, and Keith was being difficult because he knew and he didn't know how to deal with it. Tell me you don't hate him.'

'I thought *you* were the one who hated him?' Kit raises an eyebrow at Charlie.

'Well, yeah, right now I do, but it won't last, and just because I'm allowed to hate him doesn't mean my friends are.'

'Good point.'

'I don't hate him,' Tracy says with a smile, then disappears.

'You see,' Charlie leans forward and hisses to Kit. 'She *is* weird, isn't she?'

'What do you mean, I see? I was the one who was saying it. I felt like she couldn't wait to get away from us.'

'It's just weird. What do you think's going on?'

'I honestly don't know. And I don't even know how we find out. It feels like she has some sort of secret life.'

Charlie starts to laugh. 'Wow. Working for Robert McClore must be rubbing off on you. This is sounding more and more like one of his thrillers.'

'No, but seriously? Think about it. She moved here a couple of years ago, didn't know anyone, no one knew her. We all take people at face value, assume that everyone's as decent and honest as we are, but not everyone is.'

'You realize we could be talking about Annabel here?' Charlie interjects.

'Well, yes. I guess we could be. The point is, back to Tracy, that we really know nothing about Tracy. I thought we did. I mean, I've considered her one of my closest friends, but we only really know what she's chosen to tell us. Annabel at least is related, at least according to my mother. I say that maybe we should try to find out a bit about Tracy. And not because I think there's anything weird to discover, but because I'm worried about her. It feels like there's something she's not telling us, and we may find some information that will help us.'

Charlie looks uncharacteristically upset, and Kit realizes how much this is bothering her.

Kit takes a deep breath. 'Okay, so I wasn't going to tell you because I thought it would freak you out, but I Googled her.'

'You did? See! I'm not the only one who thinks she's being strange.'

'I thought that whole scenario on Saturday night, when she was asking you for money, was out of character, and I think it's really bizarre that she seems to be dating my boss but won't talk about it. And you're right – on top of her acting like she can't wait to get away from us, she also looks terrible.'

'So, did you find anything?'

'Not really on her. I mean, a bit. I found pictures of her when she was married to Richard Stonehill, which were freaky because she looked completely different. She was a blazing redhead. I swear, you'd never recognize her. But I did find something else that was ... odd. You remember how she mentioned a first husband? Jed? I found him. Jed Halstead. And he has a criminal record.'

'Are you serious?' Charlie is shocked.

'I know. I felt the same way.'

'But what does that mean, criminal record? What for?'

'Larceny and credit card fraud. That was all I could find. God knows what else there is.'

'Oh Jesus.' Charlie whistles. 'And what about Tracy? Nothing on her?'

'Not that I could find. Just an old story which linked her to him, but she was never implicated.'

'God. I knew my instincts were good. So what now?'

They sit in silence for a while.

'It's just so strange. What do you think the story is?'

'I have no idea,' Charlie says. 'But I'm pretty certain there is a story. Hey, why don't you ask Robert McClore? He's the expert on mysteries.'

'Oh right. Hey, Robert, don't you think there's something totally weird about your new girlfriend? How do we find out more? That would be one sure-fire way to get myself fired.'

'Don't tell him it's about Tracy. Say . . . say it's about Annabel.'

'You know what?' A smile spreads on Kit's face. 'That, as Annabel would say, is sheer bloody genius.'

Edie swings into Rose's driveway, pulls out her tennis racket and marches up the steps and into the house.

She has been friends with Rose for almost fifty years and has been coming to this house for swimming and tennis and parties for all that time. In almost five decades nothing has changed. The house, a stucco contemporary that was featured in all the architectural magazines of the time, was once the biggest and grandest house on the street, but it is now dwarfed by the huge shingle houses that surround it.

Many an offer has been made, because the plot is worth a fortune. Rose is used to going out to the mailbox to find a handwritten envelope.

'We love your house,' they all say. 'It would be a dream house for our growing family, and we'd love to talk to you if you ever decide to sell.'

Some have been more forward, some even asking her to name her price. A couple of times, hedge fund boys, at the height of the boom, threw ridiculous numbers at her and were aghast that she wouldn't accept, not understanding that this wasn't about money, this was about her *home*.

And she isn't stupid. However many times the letters tell her how much people love the house, she knows that in their eyes they see a demolition. The thought of the bulldozers coming in and razing all that she has built, loved, shared with her husband before he passed away, is inconceivable. She will not allow it to happen.

They would all love to buy Rose's house because hers occupies a double plot, almost four acres, and is perched on a hill, with magnificent views over the harbour, but Rose has often said that the day she leaves, she will be carried out in a coffin.

She has a tennis court, a pool, even – heaven forbid in these days when safety is paramount – a waterslide, and opens her house regularly to all the neighbourhood kids, who are thrilled to tumble down a slippery slide into an icy-cold swimming pool, for she does not believe in heating a pool when there are far more important priorities.

The house is filled with paintings and sculptures, either works by friends of Rose, a painter herself, or those bought while she was married, when she and her husband travelled all over the world.

There are books lining the walls, and these are not books for display but books that have been lovingly held and read and reread, their pages well-thumbed, their spines sometimes split.

Blown glass animals from Murano, huge lumps of amethyst and rose quartz, porcelain pill boxes that were her mother's – it is a house that has only been added to over the years, with nothing ever taken away.

The cream of Highfield high society has always been found in the living room of Rose's house, or sipping cocktails on the terrace. Not the people who consider themselves high society today, the hedge fund husbands and their gala-giving wives, but old Highfield, the people who founded this town, who moved up from Manhattan. The artists, the writers, the actors, together with the handful of old-money names whose families, in some cases, are traceable back to the *Mayflower*.

This Saturday morning tennis game has been going on for twenty years. Back when they both had living husbands it was a foursome, and now they have revolving spots, different people coming every week, Rose making sure that whoever is invited is interesting, for she always has a luncheon afterwards, with more people dropping in, and there is nothing Rose loves more than bringing people together.

For twenty years, Rose and Edie have been bickering like an old married couple themselves. They try not to partner one another, for Rose spends the entire time muttering that Edie is as slow as molasses, and Edie complains that Rose spends too much time at the net and has a horrible backhand.

Newcomers are always horrified at the way they talk, but the regulars have learned to ignore it. As soon as the games are over, Edie and Rose are back to being best friends, and by the time they all sit down to lunch, you would have no idea that just minutes before they were shrieking at each other.

'Rose!' Edie calls up the stairs.

'Come up!' Rose calls down. 'I'm in my dressing room. Anyone else here?'

'Don't think so.' Edie pushes open the door. 'What are you getting so dolled up for? It's only tennis.'

'This isn't dolled up. It's lipstick. That's tantamount to brushing my hair. So who's this fellow you invited?'

'Steve Halladay. He's attempting to woo the lovely Kit, and I don't trust him. And I know you're a rather wonderful judge of character, so I thought I'd invite him to join and see what you think of him.'

'I don't care about his character,' Rose says. 'How's his tennis game?'

'No idea. Consider this one a favour for me.'

'Of course.' Rose smiles tenderly at Edie, who thinks once again that despite the bristle, Rose is more kind-hearted than anyone she has ever known.

'Who's your contribution?'

'Lovely fellow. Bobbie Bhogal. He's some sort of hugely successful entrepreneur, lots of businesses in England, and the most delicious English accent. You know how I love an Englishman.'

'So how's his game?'

Rose laughs. 'I don't really care either. He's here for a few days on business. He has all these Internet websites, and I thought it would be nice to invite him. If he's hopeless I'll just have him sit on the side and tell us stories. Honestly, I could listen to him talk for hours.'

'Why, Rose! You sound like you have a soft spot for him!' Edie looks at her slyly.

'Well, I do. Or at least I would, if he was forty years older, or I was forty years younger. Plus he has a beautiful wife and a set of twins. Sadly, it is not meant to be.'

'So how do you know him?'

'George Sullivan told him to look me up if he was ever in New York. He was in New York last week, and he phoned. I took him for dinner.'

'You old flirt.'

'I know! But isn't it fun? And George says he's a good man, so at least we know we won't have two bad seeds. Oh, isn't that the doorbell?'

'I'll go,' Edie says. 'You stay and finish trowelling on your make-up.'

'Yay, Steve!' Kit claps and roars from the sidelines, Annabel at her side. 'You've got to admit,' she mutters out of the corner of her mouth, 'he's pretty damn gorgeous.'

'I will say that although he's an "older man" –' Annabel makes quote marks with her fingers – 'he's a damn fine-looking one.'

Kit turns to look at her with a grin. 'I keep forgetting you're twenty-eight. Let me tell you, by the time you hit the ripe old age of forty, men like that are better than damn fine specimens, they're a dying breed.'

'Aren't they just a little bit saggy and wrinkly?'

'No more saggy and wrinkly than me. Actually, I'd say Steve's in pretty fantastic shape. Look at his leg muscles when he runs.'

'Granted, he is pretty fit.'

'So, what did you think of him?'

Annabel laughs. 'We only said hello. I didn't have much of a chance to form an opinion. Anyway, it's not my opinion you have to worry about, is it? What Rose thinks of him, that's the million-dollar question.'

'I'm not sure she's focusing on him.' Kit glances over at Rose. 'She's too busy making googly eyes at Bobbie Bhogal.'

'So what line of business are you in?' George, a native New Yorker who makes no bones about it, turns to Steve as Bobbie pulls up a chair and joins them at the table.

'I'm in computers,' Steve says. 'How about you?'

'Well, I'm a journalist, but Bobbie knows an awful lot about computers, don't you, Bobbie? What kind of work in computers?'

'Mostly software design,' Steve says, then asks Bobbie, 'What do you do?'

'My business is really retail, but we've taken huge advantage of the Internet opportunities and have a number of successful websites right now. Do you do website design?'

'Not really. Programs for businesses, that kind of thing.'

'Would I have heard of any of them?' George is persistent.

'Unfortunately not,' Steve says, changing the subject. 'But I'm working on it. So, George, how long have you been in Highfield?'

Kit, sitting to Steve's right, smiles. She understands him not wanting to reveal everything about himself. God knows there have been enough times when she has faced a barrage of questions, and she hasn't been in the mood to talk.

Under the table Steve rests his hand lightly on her

thigh. She moves her leg closer to him and he looks over at her and winks.

'George, stop monopolizing these handsome young men,' says Rose, as she sails over with a plate of salad in her hand and sits down at the table. 'It's my turn. Steve, I want to know everything about you.'

And Steve, removing his hand, has no choice but to turn to Rose and answer her questions.

'So?' Edie corners Rose in the kitchen. She knows she ought to wait until everyone has left, but she can't, she has to know now what Rose thought of Steve.

'Well, he's fifteen flavours of delicious, isn't he?' Rose says dreamily.

'Oh Rose, I wasn't asking about your loins. What does your head think of him? Don't you think he's a little smarmy?'

'Smarmy? Good Lord, Edie. No. I think he's perfectly charming, although he's so unbelievably handsome I'm not sure I care too much what his personality is like. The fact that he is charming and funny and, by the way, extremely interested in me, is only an added bonus.' She peers at Edie. 'Edie Dutton! If I didn't know better I'd say you were jealous.'

'Jealous?' Edie splutters with indignation. 'Jealous of what?'

'Jealous because Kit is the daughter you never had, and you love having her all to yourself. I think you're scared because this Steve is delightful, and if she falls in love with him and ends up – oh, I don't know – *marrying* him, Kit won't have any time left for you, and you'll be back to being all on your own again.'

'Rose, that's ridiculous.' Edie sniffs.

'It may be, but I'm right. I know I am. Don't worry, my dear,' she says, patting her arm, 'whatever will be, will be, and you and I will always have each other, so you don't have to worry about being lonely. You could always move in here, you know that.'

'If I moved in here I'd end up going to prison for murder,' Edie grumbles, and she turns and walks out of the room. She is irritated, because while she doesn't trust Steve, doesn't like him at all, she also knows that however much she may not want to admit it, there is a grain of truth in what Rose said.

Perhaps more than a grain. Perhaps a whole barrelful.

Kit sails through Saturday with a large smile on her face. From tennis in the morning, to lunch, then the evening, when Annabel offers to babysit and Kit is able to run out and meet Steve for a quick drink.

They sit at the bar of the Driftwood Inn, knees intertwined, holding hands and – oh how teenage is this! – even making out, ignoring the comments all around, sheepishly smiling at the cheering patrons when they break apart.

Kit feels giddy with excitement. This is like being sixteen again. She hasn't felt this young, this energized, this excited about life, for years, and didn't think she would ever feel this way again.

She assumed that this heady feeling came with youth, disappeared as you trudged your way into middle age, never thinking that she would get a second chance at it, never thinking that it would feel so good, would be as stimulating and addictive as a drug.

Kit can feel the electricity when his leg touches hers. She wants to rip his clothes off here and now. If I had a spoon, she keeps thinking, I would eat you up whole.

She wants to kiss him, lick him, inhale him. It is as if she has woken from the deep coma of her almost sexless marriage – at least that was what it was in the latter days – to find that her libido has been quietly and secretly welling up somewhere, leaving her with an appetite that is terrifying in its voraciousness.

'Can we go back to your place?' she whispers, knowing that it is too soon to bring him into the house when the kids are there. *That*, she isn't ready for.

'I wish we could,' he says, nuzzling her neck and groaning in disappointment. 'I've had painters in all day and it's the most God-awful mess, plus it stinks. Sheets covering everything up, dust everywhere from where they sanded. I don't even know how *I'm* going to stay there tonight.'

Kit tries to hide her disappointment, but, like a child with a view of candy, she doesn't want to wait, doesn't know how to wait. 'Damn.'

'Soon, my darling.' Steve smiles, and placing his fingers underneath her chin he lifts her face, kissing her frown away. 'What are your days without the kids this week?'

'Wednesday and Thursday. And next weekend I have no kids.'

'So how about on Wednesday I cook you dinner? At your place? And then maybe on the weekend we could go away somewhere? I keep hearing that there are all these romantic inns dotted around the Connecticut shoreline, and I've barely been out of Highfield.'

'Are you serious? I'd love that! Oh God! An inn! That would be so romantic!'

'We'll bring boots and do some hiking, and we'll find somewhere that has roaring log fires in the bedroom. Lots of books, and – hey, if we feel like it, we can always forego the hike and stay in bed all weekend. Maybe we could even go up Friday.'

Kit frowns again. 'I work on Fridays, remember?'

'Oh. Yes. I forgot. Don't you think he'd give you the day off?'

'I don't really like asking him. He's not great with change.'

Steve shakes his head. 'I don't know why you work there. I still think it's too lowly for you, an assistant.'

Kit laughs in disbelief. 'Lowly? You're kidding, right? It's an amazing job!'

'I don't think it's lowly, God no. I'm just wondering what other people think.'

'What do you mean?'

'Well, being an assistant is just … I don't know … I just see you as being the boss, I guess.'

'But it isn't like that. At all. I'm not inferior to him, not in his eyes and not in mine.'

'I shouldn't have said anything. I'm sorry.'

'That's okay,' Kit says, but there is a small seed of doubt. Do people think the job is below her? Is it? But that's ridiculous. It's a job she's proud of and, more than that, a job she loves. She shakes her head, unable to dislodge the discomfort, but she comes back to the present to hear Steve talking.

'... so on Wednesday we'll do dinner. It's not long to wait. And you know what they say, absence makes the heart grow fonder.'

'What? You mean I'm not going to see you until Wednesday?' Kit's face falls.

'No, I meant we wouldn't be able to spend the night together until Wednesday. I want to see you every day, all day if I could.'

'I think my children might have a thing or two to say about that. Not to mention my ...' she is going to say 'boss', but doesn't: '... Robert.'

'I'd love to meet him,' Steve says. 'I know it sounds cheesy, but I really am a huge fan.'

'You'll meet him soon,' she says. 'Promise.' For a minute she is tempted to invite him to come and collect her one day, to casually introduce them, and bathe in the glory of being the one to facilitate the introduction.

But Robert is so private, and she doesn't know how he will feel, having a relative stranger coming to the house. Something in her gut tells her he would not be pleased, that Robert is only ever ready and willing to meet new people on his terms.

She will tell Robert that Steve is a fan, and perhaps then Robert will issue an invitation himself. That would be better.

*

Robert has not been himself of late. He is always in his study, their friendly chats over coffee now seemingly a thing of the past.

'Forgive me,' he said yesterday. 'I am writing, and it is intense. I find I cannot think of anything else. We will resume our usual routine when this book is done, but for now I need to shut myself away and get the words on the page. Will you continue answering the fan mail, making the appointments I email you about?'

'Absolutely,' she said, relieved it had nothing to do with her, for she had instantly feared she had done something wrong.

It would be hard, right now, to ask him about background checks. When they chat, it is easy to ask him about anything, but when she sees him these days it is as if his head is in the clouds, so distracted is he.

This morning, this sunny Wednesday morning, Kit goes into the kitchen, as she so often does when she gets there in the morning, to make herself a cappuccino to take into the office, and sitting at the computer on the little desk to one side of the kitchen, wearing a long white waffle robe and looking very much the lady of the house, is Tracy.

Kit starts. Is about to back out of the room. She should be delighted to see Tracy, but it feels all wrong. She can't back out. What if Tracy looks up and sees her? And it's not as if Tracy doesn't know about her, for heaven's sake. It's not as if Kit is the other woman.

'Hey, Tracy!' Kit musters a warmth she doesn't feel, for suddenly she is territorial over Robert. Robert is hers. Not Tracy's. And as childish as this makes her, she knows she didn't want to share him. Not even with one of her best friends.

This is the first thing that is entirely hers. For over fifteen years she has been doing things for other people. As a wife first, then a mother, everything she did was to make other people happy.

And here, finally, is something that is just hers. It is like a precious gem in her busy chaotic life, this quiet time she carves out as Robert McClore's assistant, all the more precious because it is so removed from her other life.

This is what is so unsettling. That her two lives are merging. With Tracy becoming involved with Robert, it makes him belong to all of them. And Kit doesn't like that. Not one bit.

'Oh! Kit.' Tracy's voice isn't nearly as warm as Kit's, and she quickly exits out of whatever she was looking at.

'I guess I shouldn't ask what you're doing here?' Kit attempts a teasing smile, which comes out as more of a grimace.

'Right.' Tracy is distracted. 'I'll get out of your way in a second. I was just looking something up.' She shuts down the computer. 'Robert asked for you to bring him a cappuccino.'

Kit stands still, a fury rising up in her. How dare Tracy treat her like a servant? Who the hell does she think she is?

'The cappuccino machine is over there,' she says, through gritted teeth. 'I'm sure you can manage it.'

Tracy looks at Kit. 'Is everything okay?'

Kit hates confrontation, of any sort, but this time she has had enough. She does not want to do what she would always have done in the past, which would be to say, 'Everything's fine. It's nothing,' or 'I'm just having a bad day,' and walk off steaming, resentment oozing out of every pore.

Not any more. This time she needs to speak up.

'I felt like a servant when you just spoke to me that way.'

'What?' Tracy looks up, exasperated. 'Oh for God's sake, Kit. That's ridiculous.'

Kit's anger now boils over, the mixture of invalidation, belittling and dismissing altogether too much for her. It reminds her of her mother. Of her childhood.

'Who do you think you are? I thought I knew you, I thought you were a friend, but not only do I not know you, I don't like who you're becoming. Ever since you started ... hanging out ... with Robert, you've been distant, and barely speak to us. We call you and you don't return the calls. You seem to resent us coming into the yoga centre.'

Kit finds that now she has started, she cannot stop.

'And just now, asking me to get something that you could get perfectly well yourself, you were imperious and rude. I will not have you treating me like I'm one of your staff. I don't know what's going on in your life, but if you want to have any friends at all left in Highfield, you're going to have to stop this behaviour and start treating people with respect.'

Kit doesn't stay to let Tracy rebuff her. She turns on her heel and storms out of the room, her face flushed with anger, her heart pounding. She closes the door of her office and sits down at her desk, burying her head in her hands.

Oh God. Perhaps she shouldn't have said all that. She hadn't planned to, but she just saw red.

What she doesn't see is Tracy, also shocked, bursting into tears. Leading three different lives is taking its toll. The secrecy, the lies, the constantly having to keep her defences up, are proving overwhelming. Kit and Charlie are the women she has found friendship with, but backing away from them has been the only way she has known to stop them finding out, and her sadness at this huge loss comes pouring out as she sits in Robert McClore's kitchen.

She never meant to hurt anyone. She just wants all this to be over.

And as for thinking she's better than Kit? If she wasn't so upset, she'd be laughing, for she knows, has always known, she is so much worse.

22

Kit is still shaking from her altercation with Tracy, but today is not the time to tell Charlie about it. She walks gingerly through Charlie's hallway, and is astonished at the disarray, the boxes scattered around, the packing materials strewn all over the floor.

'But why are you packing stuff up now?' she asks. 'Surely you want people to see the house furnished?'

'We do, and this isn't packing. This is selling. Christie's are coming to get the rugs and the piano, and I'm putting a ton of other stuff into the Silk Purse in New Canaan to see if we can consign it. I'd much rather leave it here too, but we need every penny we can get right now.'

'Oh God, Charlie. This is just awful.' Kit perches on a stool in the kitchen and puts her tomato tart on the table. For a long time they have been meeting at the local sushi joint for lunch, Kit and Charlie, often Tracy, and a revolving assortment of acquaintances and friends.

It feels clean, healthy, and they've never thought about the expense, until now. Without thinking, Kit suggested Ikusan for lunch, and there was a silence from Charlie.

'Just come to me,' Charlie said. 'I'll make lunch,' and instantly, Kit heard her humiliation.

Charlie has made minestrone and salad, and Kit has brought a roasted garlic, tomato and parmigiano tart, picked up from the local gourmet foodstore on the way over here.

'It just feels so real, seeing everything ready to go.'

'Tell me about it.' Charlie attempts a smile. 'It's a hell of a lot worse for me.'

'Do the kids know?'

Charlie shrugs. 'They know Keith's lost his job and we're moving. We didn't spell it out for them, but with Paige we didn't have to. She went storming up to her room and slammed the door, and now she's ignoring me.' She sighs. 'I get it. I wish I could slam the door to my room and pretend it's not happening, and I understand how ashamed she is. I'm ashamed myself. Dropping the kids at school is hell, and I swear everyone's staring at me with sympathy in their eyes.'

'You really think they all know?'

'Yes. I do. We live in a very small town and, because of that, gossip is rife. All it takes is one person to know, and then the whole town knows.'

'So have you decided where you're going?'

'Yes. For now, we're moving in with Keith's parents.'

'You *are*? God! I mean, I'm thrilled, because you're staying here, but are you sure you can deal with them?'

'Actually, they've been amazing. Turns out they've been totally worrying about how we were living, and Keith's dad got them into the same kind of trouble when they were about our age, so his mom has been nothing but sympathetic. Funnily enough, it's been a bonding experience for us.'

'Well, at least that's one good thing to come out of it.'

'It is, but it's also been hard. I always thought Keith would look after us, and I always trusted him with money, assumed he knew what he was doing. But his mum said he's just like his father – it disappears through his fingers like sand.'

'What do you mean?'

'She said Keith's dad was the same. It was all about show, and having to live in a big house, and needing everyone to think he was important, when he really couldn't afford to fund their lifestyle. She said that even when he was making money, he never seemed to hold on to it. She told me this story of when Keith was a kid, in third grade, I think she said. They were playing Monopoly, and Keith, who was acting as if he was winning and completely knew what he was doing, turned out to have one property at the end of the game and no money, and no one could understand how his money had all disappeared. She said she knew, instantly, that Keith was going to be just like his dad. They can't help it, she said; they just can't seem to keep money.'

'Bet you wish you'd known that before you married him,' Kit says.

'Tell me about it,' sighs Charlie. 'You know, I always thought she was rude and dismissive about our lifestyle. Actually, I guess I always thought she was kind of jealous. But it turns out she was worried, because she could see us falling into exactly the same trap they fell into. Apparently, every time she tried to talk to Keith about it, he'd just tell her not to worry, that business was great; and then he'd say his usual crap about being in the top ninety-nine per cent of earners in the country, as if that justified everything.'

'Nothing can justify living beyond your means.'

'Now you're telling me. Anyway, the bottom line is that she's been amazing. She also said that after they lost everything she took control of the finances, and she advised me to do the same.'

'I thought you hated anything to do with money.'

'I do, I don't have the patience. But before I got married, I always lived within my means, and even though I don't understand stocks and shares and leveraging, and all the stuff that got us into trouble, I understand how to live within a budget, so that's what I've been working on.'

'And how does Keith feel about it?'

'He doesn't have a choice. His mum actually sat him down and told him that if he wanted to save this marriage, he would have to let me be in charge of the chequebook and all the accounts.'

'Wow! And he listened?'

'Yes.'

'So are things any better between you two?'

'Honestly? No. Right now I hate him.'

Kit takes a sharp intake of breath. 'Are you serious?'

'Pretty much. Most of the time I can barely talk to him.'

'Do you think … I mean … are you going to …'

'What? Get divorced?'

Kit nods.

'I don't know. I'm not thinking that far ahead. Things are about as bad as they've ever been, and if we didn't have the kids, it might be a very different story. But I also hope that this anger I feel will pass, and we can find our way through. I just . . . I guess the hardest thing has been realizing that Keith isn't who I thought he was. He isn't a financial whizz-kid; he's been completely irresponsible, and inept, at least as far as finances go.'

'You really think he's that bad? This is the worst financial crisis we've ever known, surely you can't blame him entirely.'

'Yes and no. I agree that these are terrible times, but we just couldn't afford our life, and that's what I have a problem with. You look at his salary and his bonus, and my salary, and you look at our monthly expenditure, and it just doesn't add up. I take full responsibility for the consequences of not being interested, because if I'd known, I would never have let it happen. I was stupid and naive, and passed on all responsibility to Keith, and I wish I hadn't. I can't help but resent him for constantly saying it was fine, that we could afford it, when we so clearly couldn't. Even without this crash, we were living on borrowed money, which is fine if you have a fortune in savings that are earning better interest elsewhere, but we didn't. We had nothing.'

'I can't even imagine,' Kit says. 'It's just awful, for both of you.'

'And for the kids. We went to see the headmaster to talk about financial aid, and even then Keith was trying to pretend it wasn't so bad, because he didn't want anyone to see him as a failure, and meanwhile we have to show exactly how bad it is in order to qualify.'

'So did you get it?'

'We don't know yet, but I don't think it's good. The headmaster was fine, and he said they would meet with the board and discuss it, but they're only ever interested in the wealthy parents, so I can't imagine they'll be the slightest bit interested in us now that the money's gone.'

'No! That sounds so mercenary.'

'I know. It's one of the things I've always struggled with, that Highfield Academy is such a status symbol, but I guess when you're part of the club, you don't think about it. I've always known that they treat the famous and the wealthiest parents differently, but I think they always saw us as among the wealthiest, so we took it for granted.'

She sighs before continuing.

'I've met people who went to the Academy for interviews and hated it because they felt it was so elitist, and I always felt I had to defend my children going there, but already I feel like an outsider, and I suddenly realize exactly what everyone is talking about.'

'You can't seriously mean you're being treated differently.'

'Oh I do. There was a dinner party last weekend with a group of parents in Paige's grade, and we've always been included. I mean, it's like a regular dinner club, and we're friends with these people, we're part of this group. We weren't invited.'

'Jesus! That's horrible!' Kit is shocked.

'I know. If it hadn't happened to me, I wouldn't have believed it.'

'Are you sure there isn't some other explanation?'

'Put it like this: I wasn't supposed to find out, and one of the moms asked me what I was bringing, and was mortified when I said I knew nothing about it. So then the woman who's hosting rang and left some stupid message saying they were having some work done in the house, and they had to keep it very small as they didn't have access to their dining room, and she hoped I wasn't offended.'

'That sounds reasonably plausible, no?'

'Yes, except the next day she had a holiday gift show. In her dining room.'

'Oh my God! So she lied completely.'

'Yes.'

'Did you call her on it?'

'I couldn't be bothered. I just want to stay as far away from those people as possible. The truth is, I liked them, but they were never my real friends. I would never call up a single one of those mothers if I was in a crisis, and isn't that, after all, the definition of a friend?'

Kit smiles. 'It's part of it. Trusting someone, being able to be yourself and feeling safe. Those are all parts of it too.'

'Well, thank God for you.' Charlie raises her Diet Coke in a silent toast to Kit, and Kit, with tears in her eyes, raises her can in return.

*

Later that day, Edie puts mint leaves from her garden into the pot and pours hot water over them.

'I love your kitchen,' Kit says, looking around happily. 'It's so ... cosy.'

'You mean cramped.' Edie barks with laughter, placing a steaming mug in front of Kit. 'Don't worry. I love it too. I can stand at the sink and everything is within about three steps.'

'I didn't mean the size. I meant the way you've done it. I love that it's so retro.'

'This isn't retro, my dear girl. This is original. These closets were installed in 1958.'

'That's what I meant.' Kit grins. 'Now, Edie, I know you don't want to talk about it and you're doing everything you can to avoid it, but your friend Rose gave Steve the all-clear, didn't she?'

'Yes, but that doesn't mean she's right.'

'You said Rose is always right.'

'Not always. She's an excellent judge of character, but I'd forgotten how much she is swayed by a handsome face and a full head of hair.'

Kit starts giggling. 'Oh Edie, just admit it. You might be wrong.'

'I hope I am wrong about your young man,' Edie says and frowns. 'For your sake.'

'Well, I like him, and I'm happy,' Kit says. 'Isn't that enough?'

'Maybe for now. I would say be careful, but I'm old enough to know, from the look on your face, that it's far too late for that.'

'It is a bit.' Kit sighs. 'And if it makes you feel better,

he's lovely to me. I feel thoroughly spoiled, and no one has treated me quite this well for ages. He's sending flowers every day.'

'I can tell. Your house looks like a florist has set up shop.'

'And yesterday a bottle of French perfume arrived! Smell!' And Kit extends her wrist.

'Very nice.'

'You just hate being wrong.'

'I do, it's true. But I hope I am. Where's that sister of yours tonight?'

'Going to a movie. She planned to go the other night but Tory sweet-talked her into having dinner with them and their dad, so she's off tonight.'

'And how's it going with her?'

'Great,' Kit lies, not ready to voice her irritation at Annabel constantly helping herself to Kit's clothes, her make-up, the mess Annabel leaves around everywhere; her unease at the way Annabel is making herself such a huge part of Kit's life that she can't possibly be ignored.

It's amazing how much Annabel is getting on Kit's nerves, particularly as she's taken to disappearing for hours. Most of the time she's not even there that much, but when she is, boy, does she make her presence known.

Kit should be grateful, should stop being so petty. It must be because she's used to living on her own, she thinks, just her and the kids, who are used to one another's habits.

For the first few days, it was lovely having the company, but now it seems that when Annabel is around, all she wants to do is talk. Just the other afternoon Kit found herself looking up from her book and thinking, 'Do you ever shut up?' She instantly felt guilty at the thought, then resentful of Annabel curling up next to her and chatting about some inane thing.

She helps herself to food, but hasn't offered to contribute a penny, nor lifts a finger to do the washing-up or put anything away.

Kit comes home regularly to find Annabel in her clothes, then is annoyed at herself for being angry as Annabel lays her head on Kit's shoulder and says she always wanted a sister, and isn't this fun, to swap clothes.

Kit has yet to wear anything of Annabel's.

It's like having another teenage daughter. Tory and Annabel both help themselves to Kit's things, but she can yell at Tory, remove privileges – hell, she can ground her if she has to.

What is she supposed to do about Annabel?

I have to love her, she keeps telling herself. I must not be irritated. She is the sister I always wanted. She is family.

And no, she is not taking me for granted, even though that is exactly how it feels. She is not exploiting my kindness or taking advantage, and I will not think about the fact that I am the one working hard, clearing up, making her breakfast, lunch and dinner every day. The only thing she seems to do is make endless cups of English tea, and I don't even drink English bloody tea, as Annabel would say.

I am just being grouchy, Kit tells herself. I must

breathe. Do more yoga. Meditate. Find my inner peace because she is my sister and she is not going anywhere, and anyway, isn't this what I always wanted?

Surely two grown women living under the same roof, in such a small space, is always hard work. Surely this will pass. And how long is she damn well staying anyway? I mean, when, exactly, does her visa expire?

Kit lets herself into her house and trips over Annabel's boots in the hallway. Sighing, she picks them up and takes them out to the mudroom, where all the boots are kept, lining them up neatly on the boot rack.

Back in the living room she picks up Annabel's coat, draped over a chair, and hangs it up in the closet, then hears a crash and a muttered 'Bugger!' from upstairs.

'Hello?' Kit calls up the stairs. 'Annabel?'

'Oh . . . hi, Kit. I'll be down in a minute.'

Kit starts to walk up the stairs. 'I thought you were going out tonight?'

'I am. I'm just getting ready. Hang on. I'll be down in a sec.'

Kit heads towards her voice. Coming from Kit's bathroom. She walks in and finds Annabel, on her knees, frantically clearing up a mess of cream and broken glass on the floor.

It is Kit's favourite moisturizer. Designer, desperately expensive. She rarely buys it any more, but Adam gave it to her on her birthday last year.

It shouldn't matter. Kit knows it shouldn't matter, but she's stressed and tired and emotionally fragile after her confrontation with Tracy, and seeing Charlie packing up her house, and she just stands there and starts to cry.

'Oh God, Kit, I'm so sorry.' Annabel's face falls as she stands up and attempts to put her arms around Kit.

'Please don't.' Kit pushes her away.

'I'll buy you another one. Just tell me where to get it and I'll buy you another one tomorrow.'

'It's not the damn cream,' Kit says. 'It's everything. You're standing here in my bathroom, wearing my robe, and helping yourself to my cream and my make-up without asking. Did you ever think of just asking? My God. It's like having another teenager but it's worse because I don't want to upset you by saying anything.'

Annabel's face hardens. 'I didn't think you'd mind. You kept saying I should help myself. I thought that's what sisters do.'

'Maybe they do if they've grown up together, but we've just met and I feel like my house has been taken over, and I need some help. Just now I came in and put your boots away and hung your coat up, and I feel like I shouldn't have to ask. I shouldn't have to ask you to do these basic things when you hear me telling my kids to do it every day.'

'But why didn't you just ask? How was I supposed to know?'

'I don't have a housekeeper, Annabel. When you make yourself lunch and leave everything out, and dirty dishes in the sink, and food on the counter, who do you think puts it away? Who do you think washes up? And I'm tired. And I'm tired of doing everything myself.'

'Fine. I'm going to get my stuff together.' Annabel turns to walk out of the room.

'What?' Kit is shocked. She didn't expect a reaction like this.

'I know when I'm not wanted.'

'I didn't say that! I just want to be asked before you borrow my stuff, and I want you to help. I don't want you to go.'

Annabel turns, looking so like a little girl lost that Kit almost feels her heart breaking.

'I'm sorry, okay?' Kit says, moving towards Annabel and putting her arms around her. 'I'm just tired. I didn't mean to upset you.'

'I'm sorry too,' Annabel says. 'And I'm leaving soon anyway, but I'll try to be better.'

'You're leaving?' Kit pulls away. 'When?'

'My visa's up in three weeks.'

'Oh.' Kit's heart sinks. She was hoping she'd say three days.

'So can I ask you something?'

'Sure.'

'Would you mind if I borrowed your black sweater tonight? I'll be incredibly careful with it. Promise.'

Kit smiles. 'Okay. And thank you for asking.'

Annabel rings the doorbell, still not quite sure whether this is the right thing to do, but guessing, by the twitchy feeling in her stomach, that it probably isn't. She just doesn't know how to say no; not to mention that this is something she wants.

Love. Family. Security.

These last few days, as she and Adam exchanged funny, and slightly flirtatious, texts, she has begun to realize that it isn't as innocent as it seems.

She thinks Adam isn't her type, being far too old, far too nice for her, even if he is attractive, even if he does quite obviously think she is the bee's knees.

Annabel is used to being adored, but has never been interested in being adored. If you want Annabel to fall in love with you, treat her like a doormat, ignore her, pique her interest by being completely uninterested.

But Adam is different. There is a familiarity about him, a safety. Not a father figure, that would be too unhealthy, but certainly a caretaker; and finding herself in such unfamiliar surroundings, having her life change so much, Annabel has a craving to be taken care of, a craving to be part of a family.

Still. She isn't planning on hurting Kit. Knows she is playing with fire, and is only here tonight because Adam asked her if she thought they should plan a surprise party for Kit for her birthday.

How odd, she thought, that Kit's ex-husband should be so involved in her life, still present at family cele-brations, still welcome in their home; but she can see how much healthier this is for the children, and his request seemed reasonable, given their relationship.

She texted: 'Should we meet in Starbucks?'

'Come over,' he replied. 'If you're lucky I may even make dinner.'

She didn't say anything after that.

And now here she is. She is wearing Kit's black sweater. It looks fantastic with her chunky crystal beads and the large beaded hoops she picked up a couple of years ago in Goa.

She was going to wear Kit's cashmere wrap cardigan, but she wore it yesterday and caught the sleeve on a piece of jagged wood, and now there's a bloody great hole.

She's not sure how to tell Kit, particularly after their conversation tonight, so until she figures out what to do with it she has thrown it in the back of the closet. She hopes Kit will forget about it for a while, so she has a chance to find someone to mend it, although the hole is so big it looks a little beyond repair.

Oh well. It's only a cardigan, and Annabel can always hide it until she goes, then if Kit decides to have another freak-out like the one earlier, Annabel will be on the other side of the Atlantic.

In fact, she's been trying to get hold of her dad to send her some more money because she's been spending it like water since she got here, and the money he gave her to last her the trip is pretty much gone.

He's been really difficult to get hold of, which is unlike him. He has always been there for her, has sacrificed so much to be the most wonderful father she could have imagined, always helping her, always bailing her out when she got into trouble. He looked after her financially during all those stints in rehab, and he still supports her now as she attempts to find her true path, this time, she hopes, as an actress.

She doesn't know what she'd do without him. Sure, there have been boyfriends in the past but they have been terrible and abusive, treating her like dirt. No, the only man she has ever been able to truly rely on is her dad.

She has always been able to count on him. Which is why it's so odd that he hasn't returned her calls. She hopes he is okay, but as Adam opens the door, a mixture of happiness, expectation and nervousness in his eyes, she forgets all about her father and steps into the house.

23

'Wine?' Adam leads Annabel into the kitchen, unable to stop smiling, knowing he has an ulterior motive, and happy just to be in her company.

'No thank you. I don't drink.'

His face falls. He has been out this afternoon and stocked up on everything he will need for tonight. Wine, vodka, cranberry juice. Salmon, spinach, shallots. The *Joy of Cooking* lies open on the counter, and the salmon is poaching gently in white wine and butter. He has forgotten she didn't drink.

'Oh. Cranberry juice?' He opens the fridge.

'Don't worry. I'm fine with water.'

'Are you sure?' He squints into the fridge, his heart sinking. 'I have . . . lemonade? Or chocolate milk?'

Annabel laughs. 'As tempting as the chocolate milk may be, I'll stick with water.' She walks over to the stove, and lifts up the lid of one of the pots, leaning down to smell. Adam watches her hold her hair out of the way, and aches to touch her.

She looks up. 'Something smells *amazing*.'

'I hope it is. It's salmon poached in white wine . . . Oh shit. Wine. You don't drink. Do you *eat* alcohol?' He attempts a laugh.

'No. Oh God. Now I'm sorry. You've clearly gone to

so much trouble, and I had no idea. Honestly, though, I'm not that hungry.'

'I have some more salmon in the fridge. Why don't I cook that one separately for you? I can just grill it.'

'Are you sure?'

'Absolutely. And I promise you there isn't a drop of alcohol in the soup.'

Annabel laughs. 'Thank you for being so understanding. I wish I could eat that salmon but one sip of alcohol and you'll probably find me rolling around underneath a skip within a few hours.'

'Skip?'

'Dumpster.' She laughs.

'You were that bad?'

'I wasn't *good*. Although I will say I never actually did end up under a dumpster. Close, though.' She smiles, and Adam can't tell if she's joking or not. 'But I'm not here to talk about me,' she says. 'I'm here because I'm intrigued.'

Adam's heart skips a beat. 'You are? By what, may I ask?'

'By your idea to throw a surprise party for Kit. I think it's a wonderful idea, and I love that her ex-husband would do that for her. I think the two of you set such an amazing example for the children.'

'Thank you.' Adam manages to hide his disappointment.

'So,' Annabel perches on a stool at the counter and Adam places a tall glass of iced water in front of her, 'what are you thinking of doing?'

*

294

Robert McClore snores loudly as Tracy shakes him gently, but there is no waking him tonight.

She sighs, and moves back to her side of the bed. She wants to tell him. Tell him about Jed. Tell him about Jed's plan, and why she went along with it, and how she never expected to fall in love with Robert.

She needs to confess, so he can help her, because releasing herself from Jed's clutches, while falling in love with Robert, is proving too overwhelming for her to handle by herself.

As she lies there, watching him, she leans in and inhales between his shoulder and chin. She loves smelling him exactly there, absorbing the faded cologne, the unmistakable scent of Robert that always makes her feel safe.

She thinks about shaking him harder, ensuring he wakes up so she can finally rid herself of the burden of knowledge she has carried alone, but she hesitates. What if he doesn't believe her? What if he feels betrayed and ends it? What if he never wants to see her again?

She climbs out of bed and curls up on the sofa in the bay window, wrapping herself in the cashmere blanket draped over the back, as she looks out over the water and waits for the sun to come up.

On nights like this, she knows she won't go back to sleep. On nights like this, the only thing to do is wait until morning and carry on as if everything is fine.

Robert is fast asleep, dreaming the dreams of the drugged, blissfully unaware that the woman he is becoming increasingly dependent on, the woman he is finding he adores, has secrets she is struggling with.

Robert is wary. He feels with Tracy, much as he did with Penelope, that there are secrets there, a hidden well that he is determined to tap into. As a writer, he creates stories around everyone he comes across, but with Tracy it has been almost impossible. She will tell him she is being open with him, but he cannot help feeling that there is far more there than meets the eye.

He wonders what it is that she is not telling him, and hopes she reveals whatever it is soon, for he didn't expect to fall in love at this stage of the game, and wants to protect himself from any hurt.

He was not looking for anyone, but had he been, he might have looked for a companion perhaps, someone to keep him company as they grew old together, someone with whom to share these golden years, rather than a passionate, obsessive love that he really ought to have grown out of.

And yet there is something so invigorating about feeling these feelings again.

Tracy has become his muse, has inspired him to write as he has never written before. He has told his story, and it has been the easiest and most cathartic book he has ever written.

Of course he has to make changes, needs to make some serious edits before anyone ever sees it, but he has written this book with a passion and verve he hasn't felt for years.

Tracy has turned writing back into a creative process. For so many years it has just been a business, a treadmill, turning out thriller after thriller, engaging research assistants, writing as painting-by-numbers, fitting the formula, keeping his readers happy.

He hasn't written like this since he was a young man. Perhaps it was easier because he was writing something he had actually lived, didn't need to weave in facts and figures supplied by his assistant, but he is certain he has been inspired by Tracy, and he wakes up every morning, glad to be alive, looking forward to writing, and looking forward to being with his muse.

Annabel may not have had anything to drink, but Adam has. Not so much that he is drunk, but certainly enough to have made him relaxed and open in his admiration for Annabel.

They started the evening in a stilted manner, focusing on the party, writing lists, using their shared goal to bandage any awkwardness there was, but by the time they sat down to eat, they had started talking properly, Adam asking Annabel about her father, about her childhood, fascinated by everything she said in her musical, clipped English accent. He could have listened to her all day.

Or all night, as the case may have been.

'So how long are you planning on staying?' he asks, making her a camomile tea.

'My visa is six weeks, and I've been here three, so not much longer.' Her face falls. 'I can't believe how quickly it's gone, and I can't believe I have to leave.'

'You like it here?'

'More than like. I love it. I wish I could stay. I was

thinking that if I went back home, I could just shoot back for another three months.'

'You know, if Ginny is your mother, aren't you eligible for dual citizenship?'

'I am, but right now she refuses to recognize me as her daughter, and I need her to petition me. She won't even take my calls. I don't want anything from her, except the right to be recognized as half American.'

'I would have thought she'd do it. She's a tough old broad, but I've always got on with her really well.'

'Maybe you can have a word with her? God knows she refuses to talk to me.'

'I will. If you want me to. Hopefully, she'll make it for the party, and I can pick her up from the airport and talk to her then.'

'Really? That would be amazing!'

'I don't mind at all.'

Annabel beams with delight at Adam, and then, without planning it, without even truly thinking about it, she leans across the table, and kisses him.

Lightly at first, a thank-you peck on the lips, pulling away to see Adam, his eyes closed, his lips parted slightly, then going back in to kiss him again, this time longer, sweeter, and the next, sweeter still.

'Oh God,' Adam groans, as they finally disengage. 'We shouldn't be doing this.'

'I know,' Annabel says. 'Should I go?'

'God, no!' he says, and pulls her over to sit on his lap.

She could stay. She shouldn't stay, but she could. And she wants to. But Kit is expecting her home, and how could she explain it? And isn't this bad enough?

They move from the kitchen table to the living-room sofa, grappling around like lust-filled teenagers, clothes being torn off and thrown across the room.

'I'm not going to sleep with you,' Annabel says, as Adam licks his way down her body.

'I don't think you should.' Adam stops to grin up at her. 'Who said anything about sleeping?'

'For an old man,' she says as she lies in his arms, still on the sofa, one leg draped over his, 'you've got a pretty impressive amount of energy.'

'Old man?' Adam laughs, exhausted, sated, happy. 'Who are you calling an old man?'

'You're almost fifteen years older than me!' Annabel says, and Adam shivers with horror.

'That's awful. Can you just stop already?' he says, no longer smiling.

'I'm sorry. I didn't mean it. I think you're gorgeous.'

'You do?'

'I do.'

And Adam's ego swells, for while he has made many conquests since splitting up with Kit, none has been quite so young, nor quite so beautiful, as Annabel.

Nor have any of them been quite so forbidden, but that is something he is trying hard not to think about. She'll be gone soon, and this can never be anything more than a fling. They just have to keep it a secret for another three weeks.

And after the party no one will question the fact that they spent time together – people will assume they were spending hours planning the surprise.

It's the perfect excuse.

Annabel leans over and fishes her BlackBerry out of her bag, quickly checking for messages.

'Am I boring you?' Adam laughs, conscious of his own addiction, but his BlackBerry is safely upstairs, charging on his bedside table, and he cannot be bothered to go upstairs and check it.

'No.' Annabel kisses him gently. 'Never. I was just seeing if Dad had called me back. I've left masses of messages and I'm starting to get worried. I really need to talk to him.'

'Is everything okay?'

'Well, yes, everything's fine, but I wanted him to send me some money. I didn't expect everything to cost as much as it does, and I'm almost all out, so he's going to have to wire me something pretty quickly or I'll be completely stuck.'

'You mustn't worry about that.' Adam smiles indulgently. 'I can help you.'

'Really?' She sits up. 'Are you sure? I mean, I wouldn't want you to feel uncomfortable, and that's not why I said anything. I was going to ask Kit ...' She stops, uneasy at bringing up Kit's name so soon after she slept with her ex-husband.

'I can afford it, and I don't want you to worry. How much do you need?'

'I ... look, I honestly don't know when I can pay you back. I need to find some work and I feel awful about –'

'Don't feel awful!' Adam interrupts her. 'I can afford it, and it would be my pleasure. Think of this as a gift. If you can pay me back at some point, that's fine, and if not, that's also fine. What do you need?'

'I don't know. A thousand, maybe?'

'Why don't I give you three? That should cover you for a while, and it enables you to feel safe. Think of the additional money as a safety net, and you can always give back what you don't use.'

'Oh my God!' Annabel throws her arms around him. 'I don't know what to say! You're amazing! How can I thank you?'

He pushes her back gently, with a small smile. 'I have a pretty good idea.'

And after that, they don't say anything at all for a very long time.

24

These past few days, Annabel's behaviour has become increasingly mysterious. Kit suspects she has a boyfriend, but every time she asks Annabel clams up, which is so out of character, even from the little Kit knows of her, that she doesn't quite know how to pursue the topic.

She is out more and more, although less so when the kids are with their dad. Kit imagines Annabel feels guilty about leaving Kit on her own to do whatever she has been doing, although Kit loves nothing more than having the house to herself and is slightly resentful of not getting that time alone.

She wishes she could be more forthright. Wishes she were the type of person who could draw Annabel aside and say, kindly, 'I really need to be on my own tonight.' But she could never do that; she is too worried about offending, of being disliked, too caught up, even at this age, with being a 'good girl', too fearful of a confrontation of any kind.

The problem with Annabel being there, is that she's so clearly *there*. There is no fading into the background with Annabel, and Kit is torn between loving the company, and resenting the intrusion.

And the kids adore her. Tory is all moon-faced and pie-eyed when Annabel is around. She's the fairy godmother Tory has always wanted, dressing Tory up in her clothes, doing her hair and make-up, seducing her with her dulcet English tones.

Even Buckley is keen. He is more reticent than Tory, certainly, but Annabel's willingness to go outside, whatever the weather, and play baseball – Buckley is attempting to teach her the game – has won him over, and while he would never admit to out-and-out adoration, when he is not on his computer or outside playing baseball (more challenging now that winter is truly setting in), he is usually getting Annabel to play Star Wars with him on the Wii in the family room.

But it is more than the disappearances that are making Kit uncomfortable. Annabel has started buying her gifts. Flowers for no reason, a scarf she saw and thought of Kit, a new lipstick she thinks Kit absolutely has to have.

Small things, but Kit cannot help the feeling that these gifts are loaded; that, as bizarre as it may sound, there is something about the gift-giving that feels like a guilty husband suddenly surprising his wife with flowers, or beautiful underwear, after he has left his mistress.

Kit knows she is being ridiculous. What, after all, could Annabel possibly have to feel guilty about?

Kit pats the concealer under her eyes, wishing there was a magic cure for the shadows there, shadows that are all she sees these days when she looks in the mirror.

But for forty-one, she isn't bad. She remembers when her father turned forty and the two of them went out for dinner, Kit dressing up, loving being taken to a proper grown-up restaurant, loving pretending to be the wife. And her father seemed so old. When did forty stop being middle-aged, for Kit doesn't feel the slightest bit middle-aged?

If anything, since her divorce, she feels as though she is regressing. During her marriage she noticed she had become a 'maam' at some point. She didn't mind in the slightest, but after her divorce people started calling her 'miss' again.

She knew it didn't have to do with a wedding band, for she chose to continue wearing a ring on her wedding finger. Not her wedding or engagement ring, or the eternity band Adam had bought her after she gave birth to Tory, but a hammered white gold ring with an emerald. It was a gift she bought herself on the day she divorced. A ring she had been admiring, and finally treated herself to, to celebrate the start of a new life.

'You can't buy yourself an emerald,' Charlie gasped, when Kit turned up at her house to show off her latest purchase. 'They're bad luck.'

'Not this one,' Kit said instantly, and confidently. 'This one will bring me luck. You wait and see.' And she was right. It has.

It doesn't look like a traditional wedding band, and nothing like the large pear-shaped diamond she wore all those years, but people were less traditional these days, and it could certainly pass as a wedding band; yet still, people were calling her 'miss'.

'You *look* younger,' Charlie said once, when they were discussing it. 'You look, well, *real*. Like a real person. When you were married you looked like the wife of a hot-shot banker.'

Kit laughed. 'That would be because I was the wife of a hot-shot banker.'

'That's the point. You looked it.'

'Do I really look that different?'

'Yes. You do.'

Occasionally, Kit looks at old photos of herself. She didn't particularly want to keep the albums from her marriage, except for the ones with the children, but now that there is little negative charge around Adam, she is able to look at them without feeling anything other than amazement: this was her life, this is who she used to be.

Kit, like so many women, is a consummate chameleon, or at least was, before her divorce. In those days she wasn't at all sure of who she really was, and so she tried to fit in with what she thought people wanted her to be.

With Adam, that meant being a perfect hostess, a perfect wife. Dressing up, looking glamorous and elegant, in an attempt to present themselves as the perfect couple.

But designer suits and high heels just weren't Kit. She knew how to do them, knew how to pull off the look – with a mother like Ginny, how could she possibly not know? – but she always felt like a poor facsimile of her mother, who was, she suspected, the type of person Adam really wanted her to be.

And because she was so much happier in jeans, with no make-up, her feet in Dansko clogs or Uggs, she was never able to relax in those formal clothes, never able to be herself, always felt as if, at any moment, the façade would slip and Adam's colleagues or business partners or friends, would see that she was not the person she was pretending to be, and that Kit Hargrove, plain old Kit Hargrove without all the accoutrements, was no one.

There had been a time – Kit must have been around eleven – when she was staying with her mother during the summer, and Ginny had been ill. Kit had tiptoed in to see her early one morning while Ginny was asleep, and Kit had been entirely shocked. Ginny's face was scrubbed bare, her hair wispy and thin around her face, her mouth hanging slack as she snored lightly.

This wasn't the woman Kit knew as her mother. This was an old woman. A stranger. And often, as Kit set about turning herself into a glamourpuss for Adam, she thought of her mother, of how she too wore her clothes, her make-up, her jewels, as a costume.

They certainly worked as armour. Kit *felt* reserved with them on. She could be someone else: gracious, elegant, charming. What she couldn't do was what she does all the time at home these days, now she doesn't have to pretend to be someone else: curl up on the sofa, or slouch at the kitchen table drinking coffee.

She did what all the other women did, what she thought she had to do in order to be accepted. She spent her days going to ladies' lunches, or sitting primly at the local theatre, or attending book group meetings where everyone strived to show off their intellectual prowess.

She dressed her children in the requisite French

designer clothes, put them in class after class after class, because she was trying so hard to be like all the others, to be good enough, to be liked.

But since the divorce, she has changed immeasurably. Since the divorce, she has remembered who she is. Not a meek replica of all the other wealthy wives in Highfield, not someone who follows the pack, but someone who is in full charge of her life, who doesn't have to prove anything to anyone else, who never feels the need to play a role, or try to be someone else.

These days she has taken to wearing little or no make-up, choosing clothes for practicality and function, not to impress, and as a result she moves differently, with a grace and comfort in her skin that is surprising to those who only knew her during the marriage.

She doesn't blame Adam. She blames herself. She thinks that both she and Adam were trying to play a part, being who they thought they were supposed to be: a successful couple living in Highfield, being seen at all the smartest restaurants and parties in town.

It wasn't so much pressure that Adam put on her, as pressure she put on herself. She didn't want to let him down, wanted to fit in. She wanted, so very much, to be the woman she thought he wanted her to be.

Today, she is back to being 'miss', because, she suspects, she is lighter. The make-up, far from keeping her youthful, aged her, and the hairstyle was really too severe for a woman of her age.

But still. The lines, the shadows under her eyes she can do nothing about, even if, more generally, for forty-one she's in pretty good shape.

Charlie is taking her out for her birthday tonight, which is a lovely surprise, particularly given that Charlie really can't afford it, but she has insisted. Kit was hoping Steve would be around, but he has a business trip. However, he said he has a special gift to give her tomorrow.

Things are going well. Kit is happy, and starting to trust in the possibility of a relationship again. Steve seems to be going full speed ahead though, which, at times, makes Kit nervous.

Just the other night, they were out at dinner, and Steve moved the bottle of wine out of the way so he could gaze into Kit's eyes. It made her feel ever so slightly awkward, not to mention that her palms were a bit sweaty, hence her embarrassment when he reached over for her hand.

'I know this is very soon,' he said, 'but I ... I think I'm falling in love with you.'

'You are?' She didn't know what to say. Part delighted, part appalled. How could he possibly be in love with her after a handful of dates? Sure, men had told her this before after an equally short time, but not since she was around twenty.

Steve sat and waited for her reaction, but she couldn't give him one. She was flattered, but nervous. This seemed a little ... much.

'I ... I love being with you,' she said awkwardly, knowing she couldn't possibly say she loved him too.

'That's okay.' He smiled. 'I know you're not ready, but you will be. Honestly, Kit, I've never felt this way about anyone before.'

'But ... you hardly know me,' she said eventually, trying to push her discomfort away.

'I know enough to know you're an amazing person,' he said. 'You're beautiful and smart and funny, and you make me feel like the best person I can be when I'm around you.'

Christ, she thought. This sounds like a line from a very bad chick flick. But she didn't say anything. She just smiled.

Later that night, in her bed, when he rolled off her and pulled her close, kissing the top of her head and squeezing her, she told herself she was being ridiculous to have reservations. Look at this amazing man! Who wouldn't want a man like this falling madly in love with her!

Perhaps her cynicism was unnecessary. Just because she didn't believe in love at first sight, that didn't mean it didn't exist, and maybe Steve genuinely did feel all that he said he felt. Maybe she was just wary because she'd been through a divorce, was wary of being burned, of giving herself too easily, too fast.

She should count her lucky stars, she knows. There are dozens of divorced women in this town, and post-divorce life is lonely for so many. How lucky to have found a wonderful man, good-looking, successful, unattached and, most importantly, *in love with her*.

Tonight, though, he is away, and she will confess to missing him, to wishing he was here on her birthday. He can't help it, she knows, but it seems so sad, to be celebrating her birthday with just Charlie.

They are going to the Greenhouse, and Kit knows

Charlie will have organized a cake, will have done something to make it special, but she sees Charlie all the time and she wishes others were coming, to make it feel more of a celebration.

Tracy is busy. Alice is working. Annabel said she has a date, with a guy she met at the grocery store.

'We'll celebrate with them another time,' Charlie said. 'Tonight it's just you and me.'

Kit finishes her make-up, flips her head upside down and runs her fingers through her hair, then sprays it smooth to make sure it stays that way.

She slips into her black dress, and grabs a bag, glancing in the mirror and thinking what a shame it is she looks so nice when it is only Charlie who will appreciate it. Then she goes out through the door, shutting it firmly behind her.

'SURPRISE!'

Kit's eyes widen in shock, and delight. Charlie, Keith, Steve, Adam, Annabel, Tracy, Robert, Edie, Tory and Buckley are all crowding round, hugging and kissing her, in the private room at the Greenhouse.

'Oh my God!' She is shaking. 'I can't believe this!'

'We can't believe we kept it a secret!' Annabel flings her arms around her. 'I've been skulking around trying to organize it, and I was convinced you'd know what I was doing.'

'No! I thought you were skulking around having a secret affair!' Kit laughs.

Annabel blanches, ever so slightly. 'As if!' she says, relieved when Kit turns to hug the other guests.

'Your business trip?' she says to Steve, who gathers her in his arms and kisses her hard on the mouth.

'I wouldn't abandon my favourite girl on her birthday,' he says with a big grin, and Kit feels tears well up in her eyes.

Adam watches her, feeling strange. Strange, perhaps, because for the first time since the divorce he doesn't have feelings.

He loves Kit, will always love her, and can now admit to himself that he has been harbouring a secret desire for them to get back together. Or at least he had, until he met Annabel.

Now, with sudden clarity, he can see that he and Kit could not get back together. They have both moved too far without one another, and trying again would be, for both of them, taking giant steps backwards.

Annabel.

He didn't believe in love at first sight either. Until he met Annabel. Or is it lust? Whatever it is, he cannot stop thinking about her. Counts the hours until he can see her. Has taken time off work to be with her. He loves the way she makes him feel when he's with her: young, energized, excited, as if his life is just starting and all the possibility is in the future.

Of course he has got over Kit. Who wouldn't, with someone as gorgeous as Annabel in his bed? As for the fact of Annabel being Kit's sister, surely in time that will all work itself out. Annabel has to go back soon, but he has started making calls to immigration lawyers, started trying to figure out how she can stay, because now that he has found her, he does not want to let her go.

It couldn't be more perfect. Kit has a man herself, and he has Annabel, and the kids adore her. Sure, there were those few times when Tory clearly suspected something was going on – he must remember that she is not a child any more, that they have to be discreet, careful – and Tory narrowed her eyes at Annabel, protecting her father, he imagines.

And it's quite possible, *probable*, in fact, that Tory will have some difficulty, but that's less to do with Annabel being her aunt, and more to do with her father having a serious girlfriend.

Time will iron everything out. Tory adores her, and even if she gives her a hard time at first, Adam can absolutely see how they will all live happily ever after, because how could they not, when life is so un-believably exciting, so filled with opportunity and possibility?

Tracy comes forward to hug Kit. She doesn't want to be here, has found that the handful of times she has seen Kit since they had that argument at Robert's house have been deeply uncomfortable.

But how can she not be here? How could she possibly have said no, even if Kit is as reluctant as she is? She is acting 'as if', pretending that everything is fine. She flashes a bright smile, a smile that doesn't reach her eyes, although no one sees that, except for Steve, who happens to be looking.

'Happy birthday, my darling,' Tracy says, pulling her in, affecting an intimacy she doesn't feel, not any more.

'I'm so happy you're here,' Kit says, her smile equally false, for she is finding Tracy more and more distant, is hurt by the loss of their friendship, by what she sees as Tracy's rejection.

'Hey, Mom.' Buckley allows himself to be pulled in for a bear hug, and Kit covers him with kisses.

Only then does her emotion threaten to run over, and tears fill her eyes.

'I can't believe you guys,' she says, pulling Tory in for a group hug. 'Did you know about this all along?'

'Yeah.' Tory smiles sheepishly. 'We helped organize it with Dad.'

'I chose the cake,' Buckley says, looking up. 'I wanted an Indiana Jones ice-cream cake from Carvel but Dad said no.'

Kit looks at Adam and laughs. 'I'm glad to hear it. Adam, are you behind all this?'

'Well, not just me. Everyone helped.' Adam smiles.

'Especially Aunt Annabel,' Tory says.

'Thank you.' Kit continues looking at Adam, the smile in her eyes genuine. 'I don't know what to say. Thank you.'

And with that, everyone sits down to eat.

25

It should, perhaps, feel more strange than it does, sitting at a table to celebrate her birthday with her ex-husband and her new boyfriend, but in fact Kit is perfectly comfortable, and thrilled that so many people have gathered together in her honour.

The thought that went into this quite blows her away.

Particularly, that this was clearly Adam's idea. Steve is holding her hand under the table, but she is watching Adam, sitting next to Annabel at the far end, and with clarity she realizes Adam is indeed quite smitten with her. She recognizes his behaviour, from those very early days when Adam was smitten with Kit.

His ready laugh, his enthusiasm, his witty banter. He is very much 'on', and Adam is only 'on' when there are clients, or, it seems, women, to impress.

She thinks of Annabel's comments about Steve being an 'older man' at the tennis match, and hopes Adam doesn't embarrass himself too much, flirting so obviously with someone so young.

There are close to fifteen years between them. Adam is almost, but not quite, old enough to be her father. Kit remembers when a friend got her first au pair, a gorgeous eighteen-year-old called Anna, from Sweden.

Everyone teased the husband and told the wife to

watch out, that the husband would disappear with the au pair. But Anna was such a child, it was inconceivable that the husband, or indeed anyone their age, would ever seriously consider it.

Of course it happened to other people, with these young girls working for them, but Kit had never understood it. Youthful glow, long, burnished limbs aside, what could they possibly have to talk about? Were those men really that shallow?

There *was* a woman in town whose husband left her for a nanny known, to this day, as the Brazilian Bombshell. Kit had heard about him for months before actually meeting him a year ago, at a birthday party for one of Buckley's friends.

Someone pointed the father out, whispering that he was the one with the Brazilian Bombshell, and she was entirely unsurprised, for the father had clearly been giving her the eye for the past hour. She wasn't sure if this was because he knew she was divorced, or because he was sleazy, slimy and a serial philanderer. She suspected it was the latter, and that had she given him the slightest sign of encouragement he would have jumped at the opportunity.

No wonder the Brazilian Bombshell was taken in by him. Anyone with an ounce of maturity would have spotted him instantly for the slimeball he was.

And okay, Annabel isn't exactly eighteen, but she is only twenty-eight, and Kit doesn't want Adam to embarrass Annabel, never mind embarrass himself.

'You're staring,' Charlie mutters under her breath.

'Oh God? Am I?' Kit turns to her.

'Yup. Am I going crazy or do you still have the hots for your ex-husband?'

'What?' Kit attempts to splutter with laughter, except it doesn't quite come out like that.

'So why are you staring, then?' Charlie leans forward, whispering conspiratorially, close to her ear. 'You haven't been able to take your eyes off him for the past hour, and that's despite having the new boyfriend sitting on your other side.'

'Actually, I was just wondering if he was flirting with Annabel. I was hoping he wouldn't embarrass himself because, let's face it, she could practically be his daughter.'

'Well, only just. And Annabel's a big girl. From everything you've told me – rehab, drugs, and so on, and so on – I'm pretty certain she knows how to take care of herself. Anyway, she doesn't look like she's having a bad time.'

'Do you think she's flirting back?'

'Why? Are you jealous?'

'No!'

'Sure?'

'Sure I'm sure. Just curious.'

'Well, I have to admit it would be more than a little weird for your ex-husband to have a thing with your sister.'

'It would be horrible.'

'It would be. Even though it's not like you grew up together and have a strong family relationship. It's like those awful stories of people who meet, fall in love and get married, and then discover they are brother and sister, separated at birth.'

'It's not actually like that at all.'

Charlie cracks up laughing, and Kit realizes, with a start, that Charlie is very, very drunk. 'You're right. It's nothing like that. I've had too much to drink. Alice?' She calls over to the other end of the table, where Alice has managed to sit down for a quick celebratory drink.

'Yes, Charlie?'

'I just want to say I love this place and I hope you don't suffer at all in the recession.'

A silence falls over the table.

'No, I'm serious. I know it's quiet, and God knows I've never seen the place so empty on a Saturday night, but I think it's still the best food in town, and if you ever needed any additional investors, I'd invest.'

Kit nudges her sharply under the table, to shut her up, but Charlie, it seems, is drunk, and on a roll.

'Actually, I take that back. I can't invest. We haven't got any money because my husband lost it all and, at the age of forty, I'm moving in with his parents.'

'Charlie! Shut the fuck up!' Keith is in a fury as he stands up and abruptly shoots his chair back.

Kit wants to reprimand him about the language, for Tory and Buckley are both at the table, but there are no words in the face of Keith's anger, and she just sits quietly, wishing they would both calm down, hoping this won't ruin what has been, so far, a lovely evening.

'DARLING!'

They all turn at the shriek from the entrance, relieved

there is a break in the awkwardness, to see a tiny blonde woman stalk regally towards the table, her over-made-up eyes on Kit. She is in a black and white bouclé suit, large gold and pearl earrings, a fur collar and a cashmere cape, her age indeterminate, thanks to her wonderful plastic surgeon, her hair expertly blown out this morning, as it is every morning, by her personal hairdresser.

'Oh my God!' Annabel whispers, turning to Adam. 'She came?'

'Mother!' Kit masks her surprise, and stands up to greet her.

Ginny throws her arms extravagantly around Kit, before spying Tory and Buckley, and throwing her arms around them.

'Who *is* that?' Tracy asks Robert. 'She certainly knows how to create a scene.'

Robert watches Ginny. 'I'm guessing – this is only a guess, mind you – but I'm guessing by the fact that Kit called her Mother, that she might perhaps be ... Kit's mother?'

'Darling kiddlies.' Ginny is now smothering Buckley with kisses. 'You got so big! And so handsome! Just like your father!'

'Hello, Ginny.' Adam steps forward and gives her a kiss on either cheek. 'You're looking as glamorous and gorgeous as ever.'

'Why thank you.' Ginny laughs, coyly, not noticing Annabel because her eyes are fixed only on Adam, until she turns and spies Robert McClore sitting at the table. She stands still for a second, giving him a cool appraising gaze.

Kit leans over to Edie: 'Her radar for attractive men is still exactly what it was.'

'You'd better keep your boyfriend away from her,' Edie whispers back.

'He's not rich enough for her to be interested in him. Robert McClore, on the other hand, is much more like it, and he's much more the right age.'

'Didn't you say she has someone in her life?'

'My mother always has someone in her life. Until someone better comes along.'

'Does she recognize him, do you think?' Adam leans over, hearing their not-very-quiet whispers.

'I'm not sure. I think it's unlikely. If she did she'd start telling him about all the people they have in common.'

Adam grins. 'They have people in common?'

'Well, I don't know that for a fact, but given that Ginny knows the entire world, I think it's very likely. I'm surprised she didn't start his career.'

'What are you talking about?' Edie frowns.

'Kit and I used to joke about it. Ginny is convinced she's behind every huge star or success story. Seriously. If it weren't for her, you know, the Dalai Lama would never have the career he has.' Adam and Kit both burst out laughing at the memory of Ginny's words, before turning to see Tracy shooting daggers at Ginny.

'Oh dear,' Edie mutters quietly. 'I can feel a drama brewing.'

'Am I going crazy,' Adam whispers, 'or did I just see your mother actually bat her eyelashes?'

'Nope. She did. Clearly, the subtlety is becoming somewhat less subtle with her advancing years.'

'Advancing years? She looks about forty,' Edie says.

'So would you if you had that much plastic surgery.'

'What's she had done?' Charlie, slurring slightly now, leans over.

'What *hasn't* she, you mean. Eyes, nose, lips, face-lifts.'

'Really? Well, that makes me feel better. I did Botox last year.'

Now Kit knows Charlie's drunk. She'd never have admitted that in public, sober.

Kit turns to her in shock. 'Did you? You never told me.'

'Why would I tell you? It's no biggie. It's like going to the dentist. Everyone does it. Frankly it was so wonderful, I wish I could do it again but we can't afford it now. All I see when I look in the mirror is my frown lines.'

'What frown lines?' Kit peers closely, shaking her head in disbelief for she sees nothing.

'Sssh. Let's watch your mom in action.'

'Okay, but she's not mom. She's Mother. Actually, she'd much rather I just call her Ginny but I can't.' Kit sighs. 'This is pretty horrific.'

'What?'

'Annabel. My mother is so mesmerized by Robert McClore, she hasn't noticed anyone else, which means she hasn't realized Annabel is here.'

They turn to see Annabel, herself mesmerized by Ginny. But Ginny is not the slightest bit interested in anything other than the extremely attractive sixty-something gentleman standing before her with an amused smile on his face.

'Robert McClore. It's a pleasure,' he says, introducing himself. He takes Ginny's extended hand, leans down in a deep bow as if he were about to kiss it, but then he just raises it towards his lips, in a gesture.

Ginny is enchanted.

'Robert McClore? Now why do you look so familiar, Mr McClore? Have we met?'

'I don't believe we have.'

'Oh my goodness me!' She steps back. 'You're Robert McClore, the world-famous best-selling author!'

'Only on a good day,' he says with a smile. 'The rest of the time I'm just Robert McClore, Highfielder.'

'Hi, I'm Tracy –' Tracy attempts to interject, leaning over to be noticed, but she is no match for Ginny, who simply nods without interest and promptly directs the waiter to bring an extra chair. She squeezes in between Robert and Tracy, turning to face Robert and leaving Tracy completely in the cold.

Adam watches them before saying to Kit, 'Is it my imagination or has your mother developed a Southern accent?'

'It seems that she has, indeed, developed a Southern accent.' Kit starts to chuckle. 'Although it's hard to say, given that she's only said one word to me since she got here. Robert McClore is evidently far more interesting.'

'I was hoping she might have changed, but it seems people never change that much after all,' Adam says, reaching out a hand to give Kit's arm a gentle squeeze. 'I'm sorry. I thought we were doing the right thing, inviting her. I didn't believe she'd come, and I'm sorry.

Honestly, I wish now I hadn't told her about this. I never meant to hurt you.'

'It's okay. And frankly, it's great for the kids. They need to see their grandmother. As for me? I'm immune to her now,' Kit says, but the sadness in her eyes proves that this is not quite true.

'Your mom's really something,' Steve says, when Adam moves away to watch Ginny. 'What a beautiful woman.'

'That she certainly is.'

'Now I know where her daughter got it from.'

Kit smiles, and squeezes his hand, but there is something disingenuous about his comment, and it is this, she suddenly realizes, that makes her wary.

Steve says all the right things, does all the right things, but it is as if he has been trained. Kit cannot put her finger on it, but she can't help feeling that despite the constant stream of compliments, the constant gifts, he does not mean what he is saying.

And with a pang of loss, she looks at Adam, remembers how she always trusted him. How she trusts him still, despite the divorce. She shakes her head to dislodge the disquieting thought, for Adam and she are divorced, and she will not travel backwards in her life.

It is time now to let her mother know what is going on. Taking a deep breath, Kit stands up and walks over to Annabel, who has the little-girl-lost look on her face again as she gazes at Ginny, still locked in conversation with Robert McClore.

'Are you okay? Are you ready to meet her?' Kit leans

down and whispers in her ear, and Annabel nods slowly and stands up.

'Mother?'

Ginny looks up, to see Kit and a tall, attractive blonde standing by her chair.

'Mother, there's something I need to tell you. Someone, actually, I'd like to introduce you to. This is ... Annabel Plowman.'

Ginny draws a sharp intake of breath. 'Good Lord,' she says, quickly regaining her composure. 'I didn't think tonight would become quite the family reunion it evidently is.' Her voice is icily cold.

Kit is surprised, and upset. Upset for Annabel, who doesn't know what to say.

'Well, you've certainly grown into a stunning young woman,' Ginny says eventually. 'I have seen pictures of you over the years but, I must say, you are far more striking in the flesh.'

'Thank you,' Annabel says, her voice equally frosty.

Alice leans over to Edie. 'What exactly is going on?'

'I'm probably not supposed to say anything, but Annabel is Kit's long-lost sister, who has never met her mother, until, I would guess, now.'

'You're joking!' Alice's mouth drops open. 'How come?'

'She was adopted from birth, and she only tracked Kit down very recently.'

'God, how weird. So why are Annabel and her mother so cold to one another? Where are the hugs?'

'I'd say there's an awful lot going on that we don't know about, although I imagine we'll discover it quite soon. Oh dear. I do love other people's family dramas, but not when they're people I love so much.'

'Kit and Annabel?'

'Kit, certainly. Annabel, I hardly know.' Edie shoots Annabel a flinty look, and Alice thinks it better not to ask anything more.

Edie has been loving her role as the surrogate mother and grandmother in her neighbours' lives. She knows that Ginny sweeps in from time to time, but has never met her before.

And while Edie is secure in her role, secure in her friendship, in the love that both Kit and her children have for her, she cannot help but feel a little insecure with Ginny physically here.

Please God, she whispers in her head, let her not stay long. And please God, let her not cause too much damage, for the winds of discontent started blowing a gentle breeze this evening when Ginny appeared, and Edie prays they don't turn out to be a fully fledged storm.

'So,' Ginny picks up a glass of wine and takes a sip, 'what exactly are you doing here? Another stint in rehab go wrong? Your father deciding not to support you any more? Presumably, there's something you're after or you wouldn't be here. Money, again, is it?'

Kit's mouth falls open in shock. This is a side of her mother she has never seen. Her mother has been often dismissive, but never rude. Her belittling and invalidating of Kit came in the form of humour, jokes at her expense – 'Darling, are you sure you want to go out with hair like that? You look like you have a kitchen mop on your head' – rather than the caustic tone she is using tonight.

Annabel stiffens. 'My father said you were a bitch, but I never quite believed him until now.'

'Oh shit,' Adam mutters under his breath.

Everyone is now listening, everyone feels awkward, no one knows what to say.

'I will *not* be spoken to like that.' Ginny's voice is as cold as steel. 'Just *who* do you think you are?'

'I'm your daughter,' Annabel says, but she cannot hide her emotions, and as she utters the word 'daughter' her voice cracks ever so slightly.

'Ginny! I need to talk to you.' Kit doesn't bother calling her 'Mother' as she takes her by the arm and pulls her aside, out of the room and into the lobby of the restaurant.

'What the hell is wrong with you?' she says. 'I know you're not interested in seeing her, but you could at least have the good manners to be nice. This is your daughter, for God's sake.'

'You have no idea who she is,' Ginny hisses back. 'You are so naive, Kit. She is trouble.'

Kit shakes her head. 'I'll take you back to wherever you're staying tonight. You and I can have a talk on the way. Wait here. I don't want you going back in there. I'll get your coat.'

Annabel is pretending to be okay, but she is as white as a sheet.

'Annabel? Sweetie?' Kit crouches down by her chair. 'Are you okay?'

Annabel turns to her, and Kit can see she is fighting back the tears. 'Not really,' she says. 'I've spent my whole life trying to meet this woman, and I suppose, stupidly, I thought she'd meet me and want to be ... well ... my mother. I thought she'd realize how much she'd missed me.' Annabel laughs bitterly. 'I had this vision of her throwing her arms around me, and it would feel so real, I could literally feel what it was like – like coming home. And part of me never wanted to meet her in case that didn't happen, but I never thought it would be like this. I never thought she'd be such a fucking bitch.' She spits out the last words and Kit recoils slightly.

'Let me talk to her. Will you be okay with Adam?'

Annabel nods and looks up at Adam, whose face is filled with concern.

Kit watches her closely before turning to Adam. 'Would you drive Annabel home? Is that okay? The kids are still with you tonight, aren't they?'

'Yes. And sure, I can drive Annabel back to yours. If you need some time with your mom, Annabel can always stay with us.'

'Where will she stay?' Tory interjects, suspiciously.

'She could sleep on your trundle bed,' Adam says, with a vague hint of regret.

Tory's face lights up. She has been suspicious of her father and her aunt. Nothing she can put her finger on, nothing she can, at thirteen, name, yet there has been something that doesn't feel right; but all that is forgotten.

'Yes! That would be awesome! Will you? Say yes! Please! Say you will!'

'Are you sure?' Annabel flashes a look at Adam.

'Sure I'm sure. We'd love to have you.'

Steve pulls Kit aside. 'I was hoping I could come back to yours.' He nuzzles her ear.

'You can,' she says, although there are other things on her mind tonight, like how to talk to her mother, and how to comfort Annabel. 'Why don't you come over in an hour?'

'Will your mother be at your house?'

'I doubt it. My house has never been good enough in the past. I'm almost certain she's got a suite at Seasons Hall.'

A small Relais Chateaux, a couple of towns over, it is fiercely expensive and exclusive enough to satisfy even Ginny.

Steve raises an eyebrow. 'Seasons Hall? *Nice.*'

Kit doesn't react to Steve. She just wants to get out and talk to her mother, do something she's never been able to do before: vent her fury.

For how dare her mother be so dismissive? Kit can't even begin to imagine how Annabel must be feeling. Yet another rejection, after all these years, and this one in public.

How dare Ginny do this to her sister?

'You have *no* idea what she's like,' Ginny says, as soon as Kit pulls out of the car park of the Greenhouse and onto the Post Road. 'You think I've been rude and cold, but let me tell you, this girl is dangerous.' Ginny closes her eyes and sighs. 'I can't believe she came looking for you and found you, and I can't believe you've been so naive as to let her in.'

'What *are* you talking about?' Kit says derisively. 'She's not dangerous. She's a kid who's lost, who wanted nothing more than to meet her mother, and you didn't want to know. Not that I'm particularly surprised. It's not like you were ever going to win any awards for being a great mother, but you could at least have had the grace and the good manners to pretend you were interested. I've never seen anything like the coldness you exhibited towards her tonight.'

Kit's words pour out in a torrent. Words she has never dared say to her mother before, their relationship always having been distant and formal. But her rage is forcing her on, the years and years of pent-up frustration and fury finally coming out, finally being expressed in the open.

'I know I haven't been a good mother.' Ginny's reply is slow, measured. 'And I do feel guilty about that, and I apologize to you for not being around more, but do not point the finger at me about that Annabel Plowman.' She takes a deep breath before continuing. 'Do you really want to know who she is? Do you really want to know what kind of fire you're playing with?'

'Sure,' Kit says, knowing that her mother will attempt to justify her behaviour in any way she can.

'She's an alcoholic and a drug addict.'

'So? You told me that already and she and I have talked about it. She's been clean and sober for months.'

'That's just the beginning,' Ginny says flatly. 'She's bad news, through and through. She has only ever attempted to get in touch with me when she's needed money. This is a girl who does everything with an ulterior motive.'

'That's insane,' Kit says.

'Oh yes? And I'll tell you something else I witnessed tonight, which also seems insane: it's clear she's after your ex-husband.'

Kit snorts with laughter, although she saw how Adam looked at Annabel. 'Adam may like the look of her, but there's no way she's after him. It's ridiculous to even think it. Not to mention that he's my ex-husband. She would never ever do that.' But her voice falters. She isn't sure.

'I don't believe there is anything that Annabel Plowman wouldn't do if she decided there was something she wanted, and betraying a new-found sister is the very least of the things she is capable of. Do you know where your credit cards are? Does she have access to your computer? Your bank account?'

'Oh for God's sake.' Kit stops the car. 'This is the most absurd thing I've ever heard. And whatever you think of her, whatever ridiculous things you imagine she's up to, the fact remains: this is your daughter. A woman you've never met, never acknowledged. And what if you're wrong? I saw real pain in her face tonight. I saw pain, and hurt. Whoever you think she might be, she is still your daughter, and whatever her transgressions of the past, you owe her a chance.'

'Kit, I understand what you're saying, and perhaps

for someone else this would be true, but leopards do not change their spots.'

'At least will you think about it? Think about meeting with her so you can talk it over. Give her a chance. That's all I'm asking. If you're right, you never have to see her again.'

'And what about you?' Ginny demands. 'How will you protect yourself?'

'Let me worry about that,' Kit says. 'Let me worry about what her motives are with me.'

'Please, Kit. Watch her with Adam. It scares me. I know it seems to you like I'm being overdramatic, but this time I'm not. I'm horrified that she's here. It makes me think she has bigger fish to fry, and I just don't know what they are. Please, Kit, get her away from you. Get her away from the kids, from Adam. She isn't like you. She doesn't operate from a good place. You need to get her out of your life.'

Kit takes a deep breath, as if she is about to say something, and a picture of Adam looking at Annabel, gazing at Annabel, comes into her mind. A feeling of being unsettled, of emotional drama, suddenly overwhelms her and she bursts into tears.

And her mother does something she has never done before: she puts her arms around Kit and squeezes her tight, rocking her gently, rubbing her back.

'How will we know? What are we going to do?' The frustration and fear trickle down her cheeks in the form of tears while she relaxes into her mother's arms, for the first time in her life.

'I don't know,' Ginny murmurs. 'We need to talk

to Peter. He knows what to do about these things.'

Kit pulls back. 'Peter?'

Ginny smiles faintly. 'The man I'm going to marry.' She holds out her left hand, where a huge Asscher-cut diamond sparkles on her fourth finger. 'He was supposed to come with me this evening but had to make a detour to Europe for a business meeting. He'll be here in a couple of days. He'll know what to do. And I promise you, this will all feel better in the morning. We'll work it out. Now why don't you drop me off at the hotel? I'm going to need at least two sleeping pills tonight after this. And you probably will too.'

'I . . . I can't. Steve's coming over.'

'Steve?'

'He was at the dinner. He's my . . .' She can't say 'boyfriend'; she feels ridiculous calling Steve her 'boyfriend'. 'He's someone I'm dating.'

'Well, at least he'll help you take your mind off it.' Ginny smiles. 'But don't, for heaven's sake, tell him. Don't tell anyone anything for now.'

'Even Adam?'

'I don't know. Let me think about that one. My gut says do nothing until we talk to Peter. He was the one who found the private investigator for me. Let's just hold fire until Peter gets here and tells us what to do.'

26

It should have been a wonderful night, but instead . . .

Kit feels unsafe. Steve is lying in bed, snoring faintly, and Kit has been awake since three in the morning, at first hoping sleep would overcome her, and eventually getting up and going downstairs to read a book, to try to quiet her mind, take her thoughts to somewhere else.

Her life is usually terribly dull, but it occurs to her that every time her mother is around, a drama occurs. Kit hates drama, finds it unnecessary and unsettling, and strives to keep her life as balanced, ordered and calm as possible.

She watches other people she knows, women going through divorce, other mothers in school, get pulled into gossip and arguments, watches urgent, whispered conversations take place in the corridors of the school, and strolls past, grateful that she is not tempted to take part, and nor are her friends.

Already, women she knows, the ones who love the drama, are starting to ask her about Charlie. Is Charlie okay? Is it true? They're just concerned, *of course*. And Kit just smiles and says Charlie is great, and refuses to be drawn, refuses to take the bait, to comment any further. They may want the dirt, but they're not going to get it from her.

Charlie would do the same for her, *did*, in fact, when

Kit was going through her divorce. Everyone wanted to know everything, and Charlie kept quiet, a fact for which Kit will be eternally grateful.

But this is something different. The foundations of her life feel as if they are shifting. First with a sister she never knew she had turning up, then Charlie losing everything, and now her mother arriving and accusing her sister of being about as bad news as you can be. And Kit doesn't know what to do.

It can't get any worse, she thinks, but at the same time she feels as if she is on tenterhooks, waiting for the next bad thing. It feels as if she is living in an increasingly fragile house of cards which is being shaken with every new day.

The reading isn't working. Perhaps some tea. She makes it, appreciating her house at this hour of the day; it is six o'clock and absolutely quiet, no children, no noise, no errands to run or things to do.

Her mobile phone rings, shrilly, disturbing the silence, and she jumps, her heart instantly beating faster. When the phone rings late at night or early in the morning, and her children are not with her, she always presumes the worst, and picks it up with a shaking hand, trying to prepare herself for terrible news.

'Darling? What are you doing awake?' It's her mother.

'I couldn't sleep. What are *you* doing awake, and why are you calling? I thought you didn't get up until noon.' Kit gets a flashback of staying with her mother when she was young, and the staff tiptoeing round the house all morning for fear of waking her up. Ginny would emerge from her bedroom at around noon, in a cashmere robe and slippers, to have tea before stepping in the shower and getting ready for her day.

Ginny laughs. 'I've become a bit of a reformed character with Peter,' she trills. 'We're up at the crack of dawn every day doing yoga together on the terrace.'

'You *are*?' Kit is stunned.

'Oh yes. I've cut out all caffeine and we've gone organic with everything. I'm a new woman. Honestly, I feel twenty years younger.'

That might be the new round of Botox, Kit thinks, but doesn't say.

'I was going to leave a message. I just spoke to Peter and he said you ought to check all your things. Change the passwords on your accounts, that sort of thing.'

'Mother, don't you think that's a little excessive? Even if you're right that I should check, I just don't believe she would do that.'

'I promise you, Kit, she would. And isn't it always better to be safe rather than sorry? Just double-check that everything is safe. She's a clever girl, and it won't be the first time.'

'What do you mean?'

'She was caught stealing money before. It was a long time ago, and her father told me it was to fuel the drug addiction, but she was lucky. They didn't press charges. I always thought they should, because if there are no consequences, what's to stop her doing it again?'

'But ...' Kit splutters. 'Even if that's true, she isn't doing drugs now. Why would she do that?'

'Is she working?'

There is a pause. 'I don't think so.'

'So. Just check. That's all I'm asking. I understand how hard this is for you, you know, and I understand your loyalty, and that you cannot accept my not wanting to have anything to do with her, but let's talk again when you have done some checking.' Ginny pauses. 'I mean it, Kit,' she continues. 'You need to check your stuff, and Adam ought to as well.'

'I'll go upstairs now. She's staying at ... Adam's. With the kids.'

Even as the words leave her mouth Kit realizes that she's been burying her head in the sand.

'Oh God,' she attempts a laugh, 'I think I've been really stupid. You're right. There's ... something ... But ...' She tries to make sense of it. 'I just can't believe that anything has actually happened. Adam likes her, I saw that tonight, but it would be so inappropriate. Do you really think they are?'

'Oh darling.' Ginny sounds sad. 'Men are such shallow creatures, and she is a stunning girl. You're quite right that it shouldn't happen, but I'm afraid it probably already has.'

'What?' Kit starts to shake. 'Do you know something?'

'No, but I saw the way he looked at her. He's smitten.'

'You're wrong,' Kit says firmly. 'I can see that he's fascinated by her, but honestly, I don't think anything has happened. It would be like sleeping with a child, and however bad you think she is, I think she cares about me, and she knows that would be unacceptable.'

'She doesn't care about you,' Ginny says. 'I promise you, she doesn't care about anyone. She's a sociopath, and the only thing she cares about is herself. Oh, and money.'

'Even if that were true, that doesn't mean she'd steal my husband.'

There is a long pause.

'I mean, ex-husband.'

Ginny exhales before speaking slowly, choosing her words carefully. 'I think that's exactly what she's trying to do. I think you represent everything she's ever wanted, and she wants what you have. And I believe nothing will stop her.'

'Do you really think it's that strong?'

'I do,' Ginny says. 'I finally figured it out. She wants to replace you.'

Kit takes the tea upstairs and pauses outside the office, where Annabel has been sleeping.

Pushing the door open gingerly, she goes to the closet and riffles around. Annabel's clothes, and many of Kit's, are crumpled on the floor. She reaches further into the closet and pulls out her own favourite cashmere wrap. It has been shoved damply in the back of the closet, and Kit spits with rage as she discovers the irreparable hole.

'Oh my God!' She is instantly furious. 'How dare she?'

She sits down at her computer and gazes blankly at the screen, overwhelmed at the prospect of Annabel being dishonest. Could that really be the case?

And Adam. Could that be true, what Ginny has suggested? Could anyone be that duplicitous? To stay in your house, be part of your family, all the while knowing that sleeping with this person would hurt you more than you could ever imagine?

It wouldn't just hurt her, she realizes. It would be ... horrific. Even the thought of the two of them together – she allows herself a few seconds to close her eyes and imagine it, imagine Adam performing the moves she remembers so well, on Annabel – even the thought of it makes her feel physically sick.

Charlie asked if she had the hots for her ex-husband. She didn't think so. Thought that chapter was well and truly closed. But it's one thing choosing not to be with someone, quite another for them to choose to be with someone else.

With a start, she realizes that it has been easy to get on with Adam recently precisely because there has been no one special. Countless dates, and she is certain he has been getting lots of regular sex, but no one who was a threat to her, no one she had to compare herself with, no one who was mothering her children when they were not at her house.

She can go pumpkin picking with him and the kids, and pretend to be a happy family still, *because* there has never been anyone else. She was thinking of asking him to come along with them to the Christmas tree farm. It could be Steve who comes, but that would feel wrong. He barely knows her kids, her kids barely know him – the handful of brief meetings they have had don't exactly count. There isn't enough intimacy there, and –

honestly? – she doesn't even know if she wants him to come.

She realizes now that she has already envisioned the family outing to get the tree. They would head up to Maple Row in Easton, as they have done every year since the children were born.

They will all dress up warmly, thermal underwear, thick gloves, hats and boots, for it is always colder than they expect, and nobody wants a repeat of the year Tory cried non-stop because she was so utterly freezing.

They will start at the bottom, waiting in line at the food stand, and buy hot dogs and doughnuts first, hot chocolates for the kids, and warm apple cider for her and Adam, then sit on low benches around the fire, chatting with strangers, and Tory will fall in love with all the dogs that people bring along, and once again, as she has done every year for many, many years, she will beg her parents for a puppy for Christmas.

It has become a Christmas tradition, the begging for the puppy, the indulgent smiles of the parents as they explain, once again, why this year won't be the year Santa brings a puppy, no matter how many times Tory writes to ask for one.

Then they will hop on the hayride to go up to the top of the field, their legs dangling off the back of the old wooden flatbed as they trundle up frozen dirt paths, passing the tiny newly planted trees first, then the medium ones, all the way to the top, where the trees to be picked this year will be ready.

They will collect their saws from the small shed, and wander through the trees, each looking for the perfect tree, wondering why none of them is quite big enough, or perfect enough.

'Come and look at this one,' Buckley will shout, and they will all follow the sound of his voice, trying to think of a nice way of telling him that a tree with half of one side missing probably isn't the best choice.

'How about over here?' Tory will say, although it is invariably Adam who finds the tree, but pretends it is one of the kids.

'What do you think of this one?' Adam will say, when he has at last found the perfect tree, and the kids will pick up on his excitement and will agree.

Then Adam will lie down on the ground, inching his way in, to start sawing the trunk, and Buckley will lie on the other side, imitating Adam perfectly, instructing his dad to saw further to the left, or right.

Buckley will finish off the sawing, while Kit watches, a proud smile on her face, for Buckley loves nothing more than imitating his father, and they will tag the tree, hop back on the hayride, and wait for the tree to be brought down to the car, where they will hoist it onto the roof rack and tie it with twine, before bringing it home.

Adam will set it up in the corner of Kit's living room, and he will stay to help decorate, a Christmas playlist ringing out from the iPod as the children hang the ornaments, most of which will be rehung in a more organized fashion by Kit, once the children have gone to bed.

It is a tradition that stretches back years, and no one saw any reason to change it after the divorce, but perhaps that is also because there has been no one else. Would the tradition continue with another woman? A stepmother? Maybe not. And would the tradition continue if that other woman, that potential stepmother, was Annabel?

It is, Kit realizes, causing her a pain that is almost, *almost*, physical, and even before she suspected anything happening between Adam and Annabel, she was finding it hard to be around her sister, to see her getting on so well with her children, particularly Tory, who is so often, for Kit, a struggle.

Kit changes passwords on the computer, and, about to shut down, as an afterthought clicks on history. It is blank. Everything has been cleared, and since she is the only one to use this computer, the computer that is in the room in which Annabel has been sleeping, and she has definitely not cleared the history, she gets a plummeting feeling in the pit of her stomach.

Oh God. What has Annabel been looking at that she's trying to hide?

Checking that Steve is still fast asleep – the less he knows about this the better, and there's really no reason for him to know – Kit goes back down to the kitchen and softly shuts the door, picking up the phone and dialling a familiar number.

'Hey. It's me. I need to talk to you in private ... No, not on the phone. Is Annabel still with you? ... Great. She can babysit. I'll meet you in Starbucks in fifteen minutes, and don't tell her you're meeting me.'

27

Adam does not feel good about this. Not that he ever had an affair while he was married, but now, as he climbs in the car and starts the engine, he realizes this must be what people feel like when their illicit affairs have been discovered.

Guilt.

There isn't another word for it.

Although it's not as if he's doing anything really wrong. Okay, maybe a bit wrong, but it's not like Annabel grew up with Kit and Annabel was his sister-in-law throughout his marriage. That, he admits, would be wrong.

Despicable.

Unforgivable.

But Annabel is barely her sister. A sister you have only known about for a few weeks hardly counts. Does it?

He is trying not to think about the fact that up until he met Annabel, he was seriously starting to wonder about getting back together with Kit. Not that he even knew if she would be interested, but there is something so comfortable, so familiar, so easy with Kit. An ease that doesn't exist with anyone else, and he has often found himself gazing at her and wondering how it went wrong, thinking that of all the women he has ever been with, Kit is the one with whom he wanted to spend the rest of his life.

That was before Annabel crept into his brain, consuming whatever other thoughts he may have had. She is like a drug. He can't stop thinking about her, planning when he will next see her, keeping his Black-Berry next to his bed and checking it intermittently throughout the night, checking for her texts, her funny, flirtatious emails.

He adores her voice, her clipped English accent, her sarcasm that he usually misses first time around. He adores her hair, her pale, smooth skin, her enthusiasm and energy. He adores her mouth, her smell, her taste.

And however wrong he knows it is, he just can't get enough of her.

He could hear her and Tory last night, whispering secrets to one another as Annabel lay in Tory's trundle bed, and he fought a flash of resentment against his daughter, willed her to go to sleep so Annabel could come into his bed. He lay still, wound as tightly as a spring, flicking through television stations, unable to concentrate on anything other than when Tory would sleep.

And finally, finally, the soft pad of Annabel's bare feet as she came to his room, pushed open his door and locked it behind her.

'I had to be sure she was fast asleep,' she said, grinning as Adam pulled her on top of him. 'Proper, deep sleep, or I'd never have dared.'

He hasn't been able to think of anything other than Annabel for days, but this morning, Kit's phone call was a sharp jolt back to reality. She knows, he is sure of it, and for the first time he is thinking rationally.

How does he explain it to her? He knows he should stop, not least because Annabel's visa is running out soon, and she will be going home to England, but he doesn't want to stop, doesn't know if he can.

And what can he possibly say to Kit to make it okay? Kit, who, only a few weeks ago, he was imagining kissing again. Kit, who today he can only think of as a friend.

Should he deny it? Swear blind that nothing is going on? How could she possibly know, anyway? Would Annabel have told her? Absolutely not. And the children know nothing, of that he is certain.

So is it just guilt that is making him feel so ... guilty? So certain? But what else could Kit want to talk to him about so urgently, making him sneak out of the house early in the morning?

He crept into Tory's room, where Annabel was safely back in the trundle bed, and shook her awake.

'I'm running out to get stuff for breakfast,' he whispered. 'And I might go to the gym.'

Annabel was bleary-eyed. 'What time is it?'

'Early. I can't go back to sleep, but you should. I'll be back soon.'

'Okay.' Annabel yawned, reaching up for a sleepy kiss.

It snowed last night, not for the first time this winter, but for the first time it has stuck, and although it's barely there, just a fine dusting, perhaps less than an inch, it is already freezing, and Kit is driving carefully, aware that anything faster than a crawl could send her into a dangerous spin.

The roads are empty, and Kit crawls along, her mind spinning, not sure that she should tell Adam, and yet Adam seems to be the only person who can set her mind at ease.

Is there something going on with Adam and Annabel? Yesterday she would have laughed at the thought. Today it simply causes her pain. But the only thing she knows for sure is that she believes her mother, and she isn't sure why. Perhaps it's because Ginny, who loves drama, wasn't dramatic. She was cool and low-key and concerned.

Kit has never seen her like that before, and although there is a part of her that wants to believe her mother is wrong, she needs the proof, and right now Annabel's handbag and documents are at Adam's house.

She needs Adam.

Adam has a look on his face Kit has never seen before. Guilt. She is absolutely sure of it, and, in that second, she is sure that even if nothing has happened, it is not for want of trying.

He brings their drinks back to the table – regular coffee with half and half for him, and a skim frappuccino for her – and sits as Kit leans forward, her voice low and impassioned, and repeats, word for word, what her mother told her about Annabel.

Adam listens, sipping his coffee occasionally, as the torrent of words continues.

'So,' Kit says finally, 'mother is sure Annabel is here with some ulterior motive. She told me that Annabel had stolen before, and is convinced she's after money. And then I changed all the passwords to my accounts, and I just looked at the history to check –' she pauses, and takes a deep breath – 'and it was cleared. The only person who could have done that is Annabel. So I feel sick with wondering what she's been looking at. And my mother thinks she wants to replace me. She thinks ...' She stops, nervous as to whether or not to say anything; but she's come this far, she has to say it all. 'She thinks there's something going on with you and Annabel.' Kit looks up at him expectantly, hoping that Adam will instantly reassure her, say whatever words it will take to still the little voice that has been whispering to her since her mother arrived, the voice that tells her Ginny is right.

Adam says nothing. He sips his coffee, then looks at Kit, who notes in alarm that his left cheek is twitching with a nervous tic that only appears when he is stressed. Or angry.

'I think you are out of your mind,' he says finally, his voice low and cold.

'What?' Kit fights the tears threatening to well up in her eyes.

'I mean it,' Adam says. 'Your mother swans in here with her drama and her ridiculous stories, and you believe her. I think this is disgusting. It's a witch-hunt.'

'Look, I agree my mother has a tendency towards the dramatic, but I swear, Adam, she wasn't the way she usually is. I believe her.'

'I wouldn't believe anything until I had proof.' Adam snorts. 'It's ridiculous. Travelling under a false passport? Checking your bank accounts? Trying to replace you? Sleeping with me? If it wasn't so completely insane, I'd be sitting here laughing.'

'I agree, it sounds . . . unbelievable. But even if you think I'm insane, her handbag is at your house. Could you just check? Even to rule it out?'

'You're asking me to sneak around and look at her passport without her permission?'

'Yes. Maybe you're right. Maybe my mother is crazy. But at least that way we'll know.'

'So because she had some trouble in her past you want to judge her today based on her past? It won't tell you anything anyway, that's what's so ridiculous about it.'

'It will,' Kit says vehemently. 'It will prove she's lying, and if she's lying about that, then I can start to believe that my mother isn't completely crazy.'

'What's that supposed to mean?'

'It's supposed to . . .'

Kit's voice tails off as she looks at Adam intently, a cold shiver running up her spine as she realizes exactly why his attitude is so odd.

'Why are *you* so angry?' she demands. 'Why are you defending her so much? Why am I feeling like the one who's done something wrong?'

'What are you trying to say?'

'Fine. If I have to spell it out for you, I will. Are you sleeping with Annabel?'

Adam leans back, forcing a smile on his face. 'I knew

it. I knew that's what this was about. Your jealousy, still, even after we're divorced.'

'This isn't about jealousy. This is about the right thing. And any way you slice it, if you and Annabel are sleeping together, that is not the right thing. To sleep with your sister's newly ex-husband would not be appropriate in any way, shape or form.'

'Shall I tell you what I think?'

'What?'

'I think you're jealous.'

'I'm not jealous!' Kit shouts, and Adam shushes her. 'I'm just trying to get to the truth and right now it feels like everyone's lying to me.'

'I'm surprised at you,' Adam says simply. 'I'm surprised that you would believe your mother over Annabel. Your mother, who has done nothing but let you down your entire life, and you are choosing to believe her with this stupid tale of Annabel replacing you.'

'Adam –' the tears are almost there – 'I'm not saying I believe my mother. I'm saying I don't know who to believe. I'm saying I need your help. You've always been there for me, you've always helped me, and now, when I really need it, you don't want to know.'

'Don't start blaming me in this,' Adam says. 'This has nothing to do with me.'

'But it does! If my mother is right, it has to do with all of us. Me, you, our children. Don't be so damned blind, Adam. Whether you're sleeping with her or not, this has everything to do with all of us.'

'So what do you want from me?'

'You could start by answering the question.'

'What's the question?'

Kit wants to scream in frustration. 'Are you sleeping with her?'

'I can't believe you're still asking that.' Adam looks away, can't meet Kit's eyes, and that gives her the answer. There is a long silence, and eventually Adam turns to Kit, and she sees the guilt in his face.

'How could you?' she whispers.

'I ... I didn't mean ...' But there is nothing else he can say. Nothing that can mask the shame that he feels as Kit stands and walks outside then makes her way to her car, tears streaming down her cheeks.

Adam drives home slowly, sick with guilt. Oh God. He never meant to hurt Kit.

He stops at the grocery store and fills a basket with eggs, bacon, muffins, thinking all the time about the conversation he has just had, hating himself for not being able to restrain himself when it came to Annabel, especially when he knew – of course he did – that he was doing the wrong thing.

The house is quiet when he gets home. He looks in on Buckley, then Tory and Annabel, and all are fast asleep.

He will surprise them with breakfast, he decides, and goes downstairs to start cooking. At the bottom of the stairs is Annabel's bag. He passes it and shakes his head, thinking again about Kit's accusations, how she thinks Annabel may have been looking at her bank accounts.

He pours the coffee beans into the machine, and cracks the eggs into a bowl, then glances back at the bag. If he does the unthinkable, takes a quick look, he might be able to prove to Kit, prove to himself, that her fears are unfounded, for if Annabel is up to no good, surely there will be something in her bag.

Not that Kit is likely to ever speak to him again.

He lays the strips of bacon on the griddle, and looks at the bag again, then walks over. He can see some papers stuffed at the bottom. They are peeking out from just below her passport.

He stands over the bag and looks up the stairs. He can't hear anything. And if she were to come down-stairs and see him looking, he could just tell her that – well, he was removing her passport to put it somewhere safe. Everyone knows you don't carry your passport in your bag.

He is simply looking after her, making sure nothing happens to her. He stops breathing, listens intently for any noises upstairs, but there is nothing. He reaches down into her bag and pulls out her passport and wallet.

First her wallet. Nothing there that is interesting. His heart pounds as he pulls out a few credit cards. Her UK driving licence. All is as it should be. Annabel Plowman. He shakes his head. He can't believe Kit. Will have to phone her later and tell her that, as he suspected, her mother is nuts.

And then her passport. Burgundy. He flicks through to the picture page. There, as he thought, is a picture of Annabel looking just as beautiful as she always does.

Typical. Everyone else has a passport picture that makes them look like a washed-out, unhappy criminal, but Annabel looks glowing and gorgeous. Just as she is.

He reaches down and pulls out a sheaf of papers, and as he opens them he has to focus properly to understand what he is seeing. There are printed statements of a bank account and two credit cards.

Not Annabel's bank account and credit cards.

Kit's.

Oh Christ. He didn't expect this. Instantly, he knows Kit is right. Annabel cannot be trusted.

Annabel yawns as she comes into the kitchen, and she puts her arms around Adam, leaning her head against his back, but he stiffens.

'What's the matter?' she says.

He almost says, 'Nothing.' But it isn't nothing. It's very definitely something – he just doesn't know what to say.

'I tripped over your bag,' he says eventually. 'Some things fell out.'

Annabel's face hardens.

'What things?'

'These, for starters.' He picks up the statements, where they have been waiting, on the kitchen counter, and lays them back on the counter. 'What are you doing with Kit's bank statements and credit card statements in your bag?'

Annabel stares at the statements, and he can almost see her brain working furiously, trying to come up with an excuse.

'You didn't trip over anything,' she says slowly. 'You were going through my things. How dare you?'

'How dare I? I was trying to prove to myself that Ginny was wrong, and forgive me for going through something so personal, but that doesn't explain what the hell you are doing with Kit's statements.'

'I have no idea how they got in there,' Annabel says defiantly. 'I've been staying in her office and I swept some things into my bag that were on her desk. Those papers must have fallen in there by accident.'

Adam snorts. 'Is that really the best you can do?'

'No, that's the truth.'

'I'm not stupid, Annabel. And I'm not going to give you the benefit of the doubt. What the hell are you up to? I've just lent you money, which I presume I won't be seeing again, so what are you doing with her statements?'

'I told you.' Annabel sounds more and more like a child. 'I have no idea.'

'Annabel, this is a breach of trust, on every level. I can no longer trust you and, once I phone Kit, she will not be able to trust you either. You might as well tell me the truth.'

Annabel breathes. 'You wouldn't dare.'

'Oh no? I have to.'

'If you phone her,' Annabel says slowly, a glint of menace in her eye, 'I'll tell her about us. That her precious ex-husband is sleeping with her sister. I'm not joking. I will tell her, so if that's what you want, to ruin your relationship with your ex-wife for ever, fine. You go ahead.'

'First of all,' Adam's voice is steely, 'she may be my ex-wife but she's also your sister. I'll leave it up to you to decide which is the greater transgression. And second of all, she already knows.'

'What?' Now Annabel is shocked.

'So frankly, Annabel, at this point I have nothing further to lose. I suggest you go upstairs to get your things, and leave this house immediately.'

'Oh shit,' Annabel whispers, as the realization of what she has caused finally hits her. 'What am I going to do?'

Adam turns away. It's not what are you going to do, he thinks. It's what is he going to do. He has a lifetime to make amends, and make amends he must. The guilt and shame and regret are almost unbearable, and whatever he has to do to make it up to Kit, he will.

Keeping busy is what is preventing Kit from crying. Every time she stops to think about Annabel and Adam together she starts to feel physically nauseous, and she pushes it down by cleaning, by packing up Annabel's things, knowing that until every last trace of her is removed, she will not be able to relax.

Everything she looks at that belongs to Annabel seems tainted. Dirty. She strips Annabel's sheets off the bed and throws them in the washing machine, pulls her clothes off the shelves and packs them unceremoniously in Annabel's suitcase.

She finds more of her own things, jewellery, scarves, shirts, all stained and crumpled, or thrown carelessly around the room – one gold and moonstone earring, one of Kit's favourites, is lying in the corner of the room, the other has seemingly disappeared.

She sweeps up Annabel's stuff, removes hers, and cleans.

Get rid of her, goes over and over in her head, like a mantra. *Get rid of her.*

She uses Pledge on every surface to get rid of her smell, her perfume. Going into the bathroom she gets rid of the soap – even the thought of using the same soap fills her with horror. Kit doesn't want anything in the house that will remind her of Annabel, she wants nothing that Annabel has touched.

Compulsive, perhaps. But Kit needs to do this. Needs to clean up the physical evidence in a bid to feel clean herself, for right now she feels dirty and disgusting, and furious.

Her mother was right. She stole her statements and God knows what she was going to do with them. She has checked and rechecked, but nothing has been transferred, nothing changed. But to be on the safe side, she called everyone this morning and cancelled her cards, put her bank on alert for any unusual transfers.

And then there is the thought of Annabel and Adam. Again she thinks of it and shudders as she pushes the tears away.

There will be time for crying later. Right now she is furious. And there is work to be done.

Annabel pushes the door open, feeling sick. She doesn't want to go back to Kit's, but how can she not? Her time here is up. She thought, hoped, that Adam would rescue her, that he would step in and look after her, stand up for her, but the Adam that walked back into the house this morning was a stranger.

He wanted nothing to do with her. She saw his guilt, every time he looked at her, and nothing she said, whispering furiously so Tory wouldn't hear, seemed to change his mind.

It was over, he said. As quickly as it started. It was a mistake, he said. One he should never have made. He didn't know what he was thinking, he said. And then he said he was sorry, and the look in his eyes told her there was no going back.

So where is she supposed to go? She came here to find a new life. A fresh start. She came here hoping to re-enter her mother's life, to have the helping hand she never had during the early years. And when she got here, she found a family she wanted, but it wasn't enough to be the sister. She wanted to be Kit, to have what she has. She wanted Adam, the house, the kids, the security.

She wanted to belong.

Her suitcases are lined neatly by the door. She isn't surprised. It is exactly what she expected. The house is spotless. She smells beeswax and lavender and detergent, and as she stands nervously in the living room, unsure what to say, she hears Kit's footsteps, and Kit is there, in the doorway of the kitchen, arms crossed, body language telling Annabel that everything is closed. There is no going back.

'You packed my bags.'

'I did. I'd like you to leave immediately.'

'Can we at least talk about things?'

'There's nothing to talk about. I'm appalled at you. And more, I'm appalled at myself. That I let you into my life, and trusted you with my family, and you betrayed me in every way possible. I have no idea what you were planning to do with my financial information, but you'll find that everything has now been changed. As if that wasn't bad enough, I then discover you have been sleeping with my ex-husband. You make me sick, and I never want to see you again.'

Annabel, defensive when she walked in, starts to crumple in the face of Kit's cold fury. There is nothing she can say. No excuses she can think of. Only that she had an opportunity, and she has fucked it up more than she ever would have believed possible.

'I'm sorry,' she says finally.

'I realize that. I realize you're sorry now. I think you spend your life treading on people, and then saying sorry, and expecting the apology to make everything fine. I opened my life to you. I opened my home, my family, and you have exploited and abused me.'

'I didn't mean to hurt you,' Annabel says. 'This was never what I intended.'

'I don't really care whether you meant to or not. When you slept with the father of my children, you betrayed me, and hurt me beyond measure.'

'But ... he's your ex-husband,' Annabel attempts. 'I thought it was over. You have Steve. I thought you wouldn't mind.'

'Nobody could think that sleeping with Adam, ex or not, is right, or appropriate. And frankly, I'm not that interested in even discussing it with you. I'm sorry too. I'm sorry that it has to end like this.'

'But what does that mean? End? You're my sister,' Annabel pleads.

'A few weeks ago I didn't have a sister. Right now, I wish I still didn't.'

'Please let's talk about this?' Annabel's face flushes. She hasn't realized how much she cares, how unprepared she is for this rejection.

'I can't,' Kit says. 'Not now. I'm not saying never. Maybe in time we can talk, but right now I just need to regroup. I ordered a car for you.'

'But where am I going to go?'

'I have no idea. There are a number of flights out of Kennedy this evening. I'd suggest you make some phone calls on your way to the airport.'

'So … that's it?' There is panic in Annabel's voice but Kit ignores it.

'For now. Please give me your key.' And she holds her hand out, only realizing, as Annabel places the key in her palm, that both of their hands are shaking like leaves.

28

For other people, Robert McClore might look like the perfect exit route. Just as, once upon a time, Richard Stonehill had appeared to be the perfect exit route.

She had got away from Jed for a while. Had planned on staying away. And befriending him on Facebook after she moved to Highfield turned out to be the biggest mistake of her life.

When he first came back, he vowed things would be different. Everything was different, he said. She had a business, his business venture was going well, he was happy now, he'd never hurt her.

He'd been in therapy, he said. Had got help with his problem. He'd never lift a finger to her again.

For months things were wonderful. As they had been right at the very beginning, when they'd met, when she'd been little more than a child. He said he'd turned over a new leaf, no more crime, no more scheming, no more abuse – although he never called it abuse. He said he hated himself for raising a hand to her, but that it was her fault for making him so crazy.

That first time he did it again, she knew she couldn't stop it. When Jed was nice, he was the greatest man she'd ever met. But it was like watching Jekyll and Hyde. She never knew what would set him off, but he would sit simmering with fury, and there would be nothing she could do.

If she left, he'd be worse by the time she came home. Trying to calm him down seemed only to infuriate him more. It was a lose–lose situation.

After his explosions there is none of the contrition he showed in the early days. Now he is cruel. Disdainful. Vicious. She has heard women on television say they didn't leave bad boyfriends because they were scared of being killed by them. These days she knows what that is like.

There have been times when she has packed her things, with pounding heart, determined that this time will be the time she will make a fresh start, but she is the one with roots in Highfield, with a business, with friends. And where would she go?

His latest scheme has got bigger and bigger. As soon as he heard Robert McClore lived in Highfield, and one of Tracy's friends worked for him, he started to think of extortion. He just needed time to work out the details.

Tracy would seduce McClore, and he would seduce the assistant, get closer to McClore through the assistant, keep a close eye on the scheme to make sure he could deal with any unforeseen circumstances.

And then another idea, in case that didn't work out: raising money from people Tracy loved and trusted, to open a new yoga studio in Norwalk. His plan was to disappear with the money, but the financial world collapsed, and it was back to plan A.

A part of Tracy hoped Jed would fall in love with Kit, anything to get him out of her life. Not that she would wish him on anyone, but perhaps he would be different with someone else, someone stronger, someone who would stand up to him.

Not like Tracy, who hides in the bathroom for hours at a time. She feels safe in there, but doesn't recognize the woman she gazes at in the mirror. When did she lose her *self*? When did she become such a victim? So weak? How did she ever allow this to happen, particularly when she had known, as she watched her father hit her mother, that she wouldn't have stood for it, had known that if she were her mother she would have left?

Oh the innocence of childhood.

If there is anything good to have come of this, some small consolation, it is that Jed can't hit her when he is with Kit, and he can't hit her while she is at Robert McClore's. Moving in with Robert, Tracy has said, is an integral part of her plan, and she has had something of a reprieve – until the other week, when Jed vented his fury about something inconsequential, and no one was around to stop it.

The black eye is finally fading.

And in all this mess, this violent, dysfunctional, unhappy mess, there is Robert McClore. Robert McClore, who is the only bright spot in her life, who loves her for who she is. He doesn't seem to want her to be anyone else. For the first time ever she is accepted and adored.

And Tracy feels the same way about Robert.

Edie shakes her head and tuts when she hears Steve's voice on the answering machine.

'I still don't like him.'

'Well, don't worry,' Kit says with a sigh. 'I don't think he's going to be around much longer.'

'You've seen the light?'

Kit shrugs. There are so many things she's seen recently, so many changes; and having the wrong man in her life seems pointless right now.

For as blissful as it is to be having sex again, the more she sees Steve, the less she feels for him, and sex with no feeling behind it, is even more depressing than having no sex at all.

She doesn't know why she doesn't feel more. There is no denying that he is the most handsome man she has ever been with. He is thoughtful and considerate. He goes out of his way to make her feel special. He never turns up empty-handed, and professes to adore her.

And he is quite spectacular in the sack.

But it isn't enough. She isn't excited about seeing him. There is an initial thrill at having landed someone with his beauty, but it doesn't last. A few minutes in and she finds herself bored.

He hands her flowers, gifts, perfume, and she is starting to think, *again*? Please, no!

The more bored she becomes, the more Steve is pursuing her.

And the more she is pursued, the more she misses Adam.

Particularly now. When her life feels more unsettled than ever before, she recognizes that Adam provides a safety and security she desperately needs. Even with his betrayal, now that Annabel has gone, now that her house is her own again – oh Lord, how much she missed the peace and quiet! – she finds herself thinking more and more about Adam.

And she is not thinking about the fact that Adam slept with Annabel. The pain of the betrayal has subsided for she understands how it happened, and why. She understands that Adam doesn't owe her anything, and she understands how Annabel, when in charm mode, was almost irresistible. She fell for her herself.

What she thinks about, when she thinks of Adam, is the Adam that she loved. The one she loved being with, before he got so caught up in work he didn't see her any more, didn't hear her, didn't appreciate her.

Loving, she realizes, is a *verb*. It is an act. It is not enough to say you love someone, and then forget about them, or trust a relationship will stay strong simply because you share a house or children or a life.

Loving requires *acts* of love. It requires thinking of your spouse, doing things for them to make them happy. It requires acting in loving ways, even when you are tired, or bogged down with work, or so stressed you are waking up every night with a jaw sore from grinding your teeth.

They forgot to do that, she now knows. They *forgot* to love each other. They expected love to continue, without putting any work into it, and today she knows this is why her marriage failed.

And she misses it. She misses her marriage, and she misses Adam.

She misses lying in the bath and having someone to talk to. He used to grumble about having to stay in the bathroom, perching on the one uncomfortable chair in the corner, but he would stay as she luxuriated in the bath and chatted to him about whatever was on her mind.

She misses taking the kids to the diner every Saturday, a tradition they had since Tory was a baby. Misses hugging the owner when they walk in, knowing all the waiters and waitresses, having them crowd round the table to coo over how big Tory and Buckley have become.

She misses having a family, because without Adam it doesn't feel complete, doesn't feel like a whole family. And it's not just her. Buckley has commented on it too.

'One day,' he told her, 'I'd like to be a whole family again.'

'What do you mean?' Kit asked, horrified.

'I mean whole. With a mommy and a daddy.'

'But you do have a mommy and a daddy, who love you very much. We'll always be your family.' She smiled.

'No. I mean a mommy and a daddy in the same house. That's what makes a whole family,' he said.

She tried to tell him that wasn't the case, except she knew it was. She felt the same way.

She has been trying to tell herself that she isn't missing Adam, she is just missing *someone*. Someone to help, someone to be a sounding board, someone who will ensure she won't have to do everything, absolutely everything in her life all by herself.

But that isn't true. She has Steve, but she doesn't want him. He won't make the family whole. The only person who can do that is Adam. And as hard as it is to admit it, there is no question now that it is Adam she misses. She misses the way he makes her feel safe. He is the only person in the world to ever make her feel that way, the only person who has ever sheltered her from the storms of life.

Especially now. She walks around much of the time feeling horribly unsettled, a great cloud of anxiety resting on one shoulder. The only times she doesn't feel it weighing on her are when she is with Adam.

But her marriage is over. She forces herself to remember why they divorced; although it's hard to remember precisely why. He wasn't around, she reminds herself. He worked all the time, wanted a different lifestyle.

He wanted the big house, the fancy cars, the fast friends. She hadn't been interested in all of that.

He probably hasn't changed, she tells herself. People rarely do, unless they experience an event that is so traumatic, so life-altering they find they are different, through to the very core.

Would their divorce have done that for him? And even if that were the case, the likelihood is that he wouldn't want her back. There is too much water under the bridge. Too much Annabel.

There's no point even thinking about it. Not any more. It's just too damn late.

Robert McClore puts a coffee on Kit's desk, smiles at her and leaves the room. He is in a great mood. Come to think of it, he is in a great mood most of the time these days.

He is just a couple of chapters away from finishing the book. In one way it has been the easiest book of his life, but at times it has drained him emotionally. He realizes that he should have written it years ago. It has been cathartic, healing, has finally given him closure on something he has been trying to put behind him for years.

And now he is on the home stretch. His editor will be thrilled, his agent delighted, and he will be able to move on to the next book, the storyline of which is already brewing, the notepad he carries everywhere already starting to fill with scribbled notes as more and more of the story, more pieces of the puzzle start to come together in the most obscure of places.

Standing in line waiting for a taxi in New York City, an image comes to his head. He grabs a pen and writes it down. The villain's early life starts unfolding as he's sitting in a tiny, claustrophic stockroom, waiting to sign stock at a bookstore in Cherry Hill.

The motivation behind the hero coming back appears as he's sitting at the kitchen table, waiting for Tracy to finish getting ready.

Tracy. Yet another reason for his happiness. Her relative youth, her beauty and her care of him are consistently delightful.

Robert never thought of himself as a lonely man, and he never thought he would allow himself to fall in love with anyone again, not after Penelope.

But love changes as you get older. In his twenties it was mad passion, lust, excitement. And now, in his sixties, as well as the unexpectedly satisfying physical relationship, love is about companionship. It's about having someone by your side as you enter your golden years.

And Tracy is turning out to be a perfect companion. Her feistiness, the anger that so reminded him of Penelope, the passion in her he found so attractive, has given way to something far quieter, almost deferential.

She isn't who he thought she was. And he finds he quite likes this new Tracy. This is an easier Tracy. This is someone who would look after him, whom he could mould.

It hasn't been long, but he hasn't been this happy in years. Everyone is commenting on it. His agent. His publisher. He is sure Kit will notice, except she, poor woman, seems to be distracted and pale these days.

Perhaps a celebration is in order. Something exciting for Kit to organize. Perhaps he should make an honest woman out of Tracy at the same time. Solidify their growing commitment.

It doesn't need to be billed as an engagement party; this is the holiday season, after all.

It has been years since the house on Dune Road hosted a holiday party. A true holiday party, for friends, neighbours, colleagues. Almost like the Grand House of the village hosting fairs for the villagers. He could do something similar here: Robert and Tracy as the grand benefactors.

They could have, as they had when he and Penelope were married, a huge Christmas tree in the hall, swags and garlands festooning the staircase, presents for the children under the tree.

Perhaps Santa could even come – wouldn't that be fun? Santa and reindeer outside.

Robert is astonished that he feels a buzz of excitement at planning a party.

It is this book.

It has freed him. Has allowed him to come out of his shell.

29

'It's not you, it's me.' Kit is embarrassed even as she says this, those immortal words she never thought would come from her lips.

'But I thought things were going so well.'

'I think you're a great guy,' Kit says earnestly, wishing this would just be over. God. She hasn't had to break up with anyone in over twenty years, and she was never that good at it back then. 'It's just that I'm not ready for a relationship. I thought I was over my divorce, but I'm not ready for anything serious.'

Steve stands for a while, looking at her, then smiles and shrugs, and Kit feels relief. He will take it well.

'I could do a million times better than you anyway,' he says, and Kit's mouth falls open in shock.

'What?' she manages, as he turns to the front door.

'Oh please. You think I was in it because you're so great? This was out of pity, honey. I felt sorry for you. Middle-aged, divorced, no hope of anyone else. I thought it might be fun.' And he walks out through the front door, leaving Kit gasping in pain.

'Fucker!' Charlie spits with rage. 'What's his address? I want to go over there and kill him.'

'Great. So I dump my boyfriend, who turns out to be

a psycho bastard from hell, and then my best friend kills him and spends the rest of her life in prison.'

'But I can't believe it. I hate him. What a fucker.'

'Edie was right.'

'She never liked him, did she?'

'Nope, and she was right. It was like talking to a different person. I swear to God, he actually sneered at me. I've never seen such disdain in my life. It was horrible.'

'Oh Kit. I'm so sorry.'

'Don't be. I mean, yes, I've been feeling totally shitty about myself for the last few hours, but I was ending our relationship. I guess I just never expected him to be so vicious.'

'At least you've got something to take your mind off things.'

'What?'

'The party! Oh Kit. This is the perfect thing to stop you thinking about . . .'

'What? How shitty and empty my life is?'

'Oh darling. At least you haven't lost everything and have to move in with your in-laws.'

'You're right. Thank you for proving it could be worse.'

'So tell me about the party. How's it all going? Have you been able to breathe?'

'Of course you can do this,' Robert McClore said, seeing her face fall when he first told her of his plan. 'You have enormous style and you're my Girl Friday. You can do anything, Kit.'

'Girl Friday!' Edie smiled when Kit came home and told her. 'That's what he used to call me.'

But it is true, Kit can do anything she puts her mind to, and as overwhelmed as she was, surveying the list of things that needed to be done, she has needed the distraction now more than ever.

She has needed it so as not to think about Adam. She has needed it so as not to think about Steve. She has needed it so as not to think about Annabel. She has needed it not to think about the mess her life has become: unsettled, unsure, filled with anxiety, and then, with Annabel and Steve both out of the picture, empty, lonely and sad.

Thank God she has a party to organize.

And what a party. Lights have been strung in all the trees along Dune Road, culminating at the house, where large Christmas trees, covered in tiny white lights, stand on all the porches.

Wreaths in every window, and a single candle, burning bright.

And inside, garlands of bay leaves snake their way up the banisters of the sweeping staircase in the grand hall, the mantelpieces are filled with small galvanized-steel pots of paperwhite narcissi, white ribbons and glittered silver balls.

Silver balls, crystal icicles and clear glass ornaments hang from every chandelier, every sconce in the living room, giving the effect, even inside, of having entered the Snow Queen's Palace.

It is Kit's idea, one she gleaned from a magazine she was flicking through while sitting in the waiting room of the doctor's office. It has never occurred to her to do anything different for Christmas, just red, green and gold as she has always done, nutcracker dolls around the fireplace, popcorn strung in the tree.

But flicking through the magazine, she came upon page after page of colour-themed Christmas decorations. Blue and white rooms, glistening icily, still managed to convey, with beauty and elegance, the Christmas spirit. There were silver rooms, gold, pink, purple rooms.

Some were, admittedly, extreme. She laughed when she turned the page to find the interior of a decorator's home, beautifully done for Christmas in a style which included covering the many hundreds of books on her bookshelves in silver paper.

A little too *too*, perhaps.

But it gave her an idea.

In the entryway there would be a hint of traditional given a modern twist: garlands of gorgeous-smelling bay leaves twining round the doorways and stairs, large red ribbons, a huge tree in the corner with red and green balls, strings of popcorn, pretty wooden ornaments made by a local business in town – tiny hand-painted trees, steam engines, boats, jack-in-the-boxes, Raggedy Ann dolls – everything a child would love, all made of local wood, all delighting every child to see them.

And through to the formal living room, with the silver and crystal theme; then a different blue and white theme in the library.

She has done it herself, she really has done it on her

own, and she turns up to work every day, walking through and gazing at the rooms with pleasure, unable to believe she did it all herself.

She could have brought in a designer, but Robert would have quibbled over the unnecessary expense, and honestly, once she got used to the idea of organizing the party, she enjoyed tackling every part of the project and welcomed the distraction. Poring over menus, choosing the food, working out the bar, booking extra staff to help serve; buying presents for all the local children, finding a Santa with an authentic, natural long white beard, rather than one with a wad of cottonwool; sourcing the gifts and decorations – which involved hours Googling wholesale feather boas, silver-ball wreaths; shopping at HomeGoods, Wal-Mart, where every bargain, every reduction, every finding of something that she knew was a fortune somewhere else, lifted Kit's spirits, gave her a sense of achievement, took her mind off the rest of her life.

And now 22 December, the night of the party, is finally here, and she is feeling excited. Everyone she knows is coming. Almost, it seems, the entire town. The mayor, the entire staff of the Highfield Public Library, most of the police force and firemen, all the people who run businesses that Robert has anything to do with: bookstores, restaurants, pharmacies, liquor stores. Robert's doctors, lawyers, friends, acquaintances.

And naturally, friends and family of Kit's must be invited, he said. He wouldn't take no for an answer.

Charlie and Keith. Alice and Harry. Tory and Buckley. Kit's charming mother, and of *course* her mother's fiancé must come, particularly as he's flying in this afternoon. And that nice ex-husband of Kit's, who she still clearly gets on so well with? Adam? *He's* a good egg. Invite *him*.

She has, even though she and Adam have barely spoken since the Annabel fiasco. Adam waits for the children in the car, and the couple of times Kit has come to the door, he has just waved and smiled, and there has been nothing to say.

Instead of phoning one another, they send texts, short and to the point, or emails, but not, as they had been, long and chatty, funny and warm, but asking what time the children's dental appointment is, or is it okay if he drops them an hour later.

For the first time ever, Kit feels divorced.

Charlie walks out of her house and looks up at the sky. It is a dull white, and a few flakes are starting to swirl, but not like the brief flurry they had the other week. This is supposed to be the first big storm of the season, six to eight inches.

If this were any other party, no one would show up, but too many people are excited about seeing the inside of the house on Dune Road, Charlie included, and she suspects everyone will be coming, even if they have to shovel the roads themselves.

Charlie has kissed the children goodbye and left them in the care of her in-laws, who are babysitting. One of the unexpected pleasures of having in-laws in the same town is that you almost have built-in baby-sitters, but this presumes you *want* to go out with your husband, and while Charlie loves going out, she's still struggling to get on with Keith.

It is not made easier by the fact that he is now around most of the time. Luckily, Charlie still has her business, and although it is deathly quiet she has thrown herself into it with renewed vigour, attempting to drum up new business, posting ads online, offering discounted arrangements, donating flowers for parties as silent-auction items.

Why not? It gives her something to dwell on other than how much she hates her husband. And it may be all they have. The odd thing is, business isn't nearly as flat as you would expect from reading the *New York Times*, listening to all the reports on the news; but she knows it's going to get worse. Much, much worse.

Thousands of foreclosures are expected, but today Charlie only knows of a handful of people, herself included, who are being forced out. There have to be more. She knows there will be more. But people are clinging on, praying that there will be an upswing, hoping that their house will sell, that they will be okay in the end.

January would normally be bonus time, but not this January. And so many of the 'wealthy' families she knows live off their pay cheques and bonuses.

The pay cheques pay their bills, their mortgages, their car leases and school fees. The bonuses pay for their Birkins. Their diamond eternity rings. Their holidays in Great Exuma.

For many of those families it is, she knows, only a matter of time.

Spring will be telling; they are likely to see tons of houses coming on the market then. People are waiting for January, hoping that something will change and bonuses will come through. And although Charlie knows that for so many of them things won't change and their bonuses won't come through, none of this helps her forgive Keith.

Keith is going to the party tonight, but meeting Charlie there, later. He has been in New York this afternoon, going to see headhunters, looking at what he can do.

Everyone is saying the same things: the future is dismal; it is going to get worse before it gets better; the financial world will never be the same; the jobs just aren't there – everyone is laying off and no one is recruiting.

A new president brings new hope, and never has there been as much hope as with President Obama, but there is no such thing as an instant fix, and the economy is in such dire straits it will take a long time. The Stimulus Plan isn't looking quite as stimulating as many had hoped.

Keith is hearing the same advice from every single person he is talking to: if there is another business you could be doing, something totally unrelated to finance, now is the time to do it.

But what can he possibly do? At forty-five, all he has ever known is the world of finance. He went into it upon graduation, because that's what everyone did; that was the only way to make the serious bucks.

'*What do you do?*'

'I work in finance.'

What else can he possibly say to fit in, to have a hope of achieving millionaire, or billionaire, status, before the age of forty? To be, in short, like everybody else.

There is nothing else he has ever done, ever thought of doing. He has heard horror stories of men who worked on Wall Street, now working in Starbucks. He shivers with fear when he hears that. How can he possibly do that? Even if it were to cover health insurance for the entire family. *How?*

What are his loves, he was asked the other day by someone, a headhunter, who was telling him, just like all the others, to find something else.

His loves? His family. Shopping. Fast cars. Business – although the only business he has ever known is the business of money. Nothing that could translate into a new career.

He feels utterly lost. His work life, the thing that defined him for over twenty years, has been destroyed, and now he feels his marriage slipping away from him as well, and he doesn't know how to save it, doesn't think that he has the energy, for it's all he can do to get out of bed in the morning and make the pretence of looking for another job.

Right now, that's all he can do, and without Charlie's support, without her partnership, her friendship, he's not even sure how much longer he can do that.

'Oh my God! That dress is gorgeous!' Kit fingers the grey shift dress, trimmed with silver sequins, that Charlie is wearing for the party.

'I know. A remnant from my old life.'

'I thought you'd sold everything.'

'Most. The Consignment Store is stuffed with my clothes. It's so depressing. And I swear I saw Marianna Miller walking down Main Street the other day in my coat.'

'Why did you think it was yours?'

'How many people in Highfield had that exact Oscar de la Renta coat? I didn't get that at Rakers, I got it at Bergdorfs, and I don't believe Marianna happened to be in the city during that particular season, buying that particular coat.' Charlie sighs. 'So, most has gone, but I've kept a handful of key things, and the clothes that really won't get anything in consignment. This one –' she pulls the plastic bag up over the hanger completely – 'has a stain under one arm so it would be a reject.'

'Good job. I love it.'

'I know. Thank you.'

Kit peers at her friend closely. 'So how *are* you? Any offers on the house?'

Charlie snorts. 'I wish. Lots of people looking, but there's so much to choose from, why, it seems, would ours stand out? I keep telling the realtor they have to bring in more creative types who will appreciate the barn, or people who run a small business from home.'

'And?'

'And I think the realtors are just as desperate as us.'

'So you're definitely moving out?'

'Yup. In with the in-laws in three weeks, and I have to say they've been extraordinary.'

'So there has been something of a silver lining?'

'Yes. If it counts. It's just so frightening. And the business. How can I carry on the business without a space? My in-laws have offered their garage, but it's unheated, and not set up for anything.'

'Could you buy a space heater?'

'At the moment, I may have to.'

'And things with Keith?' Kit doesn't know whether she should ask.

Charlie shrugs. 'I'm working on forgiveness. I'm also reading the Kübler-Ross book on grief, on the advice of my old therapist.'

'You had a therapist?'

'Course. Didn't everyone?'

Kit laughs. 'No! I didn't.'

'Well, I did, and I phoned her. She said I was going through the grieving process for my old life, and I had to work through all the stages before reaching acceptance. She said reading the book would help me understand.'

'And does it?'

'Funnily enough, it does. It makes things a little easier, and I'm beginning to accept that anger is part of the process. But I've been targeting it all at Keith, which isn't fair. It's helping. Definitely.'

'Good.' Kit nods, satisfied. 'I'm glad.'

'So any word from Annabel?'

Kit shudders. 'No. Thank goodness.'

'You still feel that way?'

'I think I'm going to feel that way for a long time to come. When she arrived I thought she was family.

The fact that she was blood meant something special, bonded us immediately. I guess I was really naive.'

'I don't blame you. She was very likeable. Until she wasn't. And you do share a mother. I understand why you would feel a bond.'

'The thing is, I don't know whether I truly did. I really wanted to, and I tried to create one, but she drove me insane. Even before the whole Adam thing, I was beginning to question her.'

'Have you and Adam talked at all?'

'Barely. I think he's too embarrassed. He totally knows he was wrong.'

'And she didn't tell you anything?'

'No. I have a feeling our paths will cross again, but I'm not ready for her yet. She's someone who seems to come with a lot of drama, and I'm at a place in my life where I've made a conscious decision not to deal with drama. Blood or no blood.'

'You sound wise.'

'I *feel* wise. For as empty as I felt right after it happened, I'm also glad it happened. It made me question a lot of things.'

'Such as?'

'My family. My friends. My relationships.'

'You've really been through a rocky patch.'

Kit laughs. 'I have. But right now it feels like the sun is starting to shine again. Very slowly, and it's pretty damn weak, but I feel optimistic again, like good things are about to happen.'

'I'm sure they will.' Charlie smiles. 'You're going to be fine.'

30

For many, it is the first time they have been through the stone gateposts at the end of Dune Road, the ones that guard the gravel drive sweeping up to Hillpoint.

Tracy is upstairs as the staff put the finishing touches to the party. Jed has been in a furious mood since being dumped by Kit, and she has barely been back to her house, too terrified of what she will find.

When she has gone back home, she has wondered why she bothered, why she didn't just stay with Robert. She is finally happy, with a man she loves, but she has to figure out a way to get rid of Jed once and for all. She doesn't want to see Jed again, doesn't want to give him the power any more. Not now she has seen the alternative.

Jed thinks she will bring Robert down, but she could never do that, and she doesn't care about the money, has never cared about the money. If Robert lost everything, she would still want to be with him. She is safe here, and the only thing she wants is to remove Jed from her life, and continue without him.

Could she pay him off? Possibly. He has always been motivated by dollars. But would he stay away?

She dabs Touche Éclat on the hint of the shadow around her eye, and sweeps her hair back in a ponytail, brushing Mineral Veil over her face and adding a touch of dark red lipstick. She has adapted her look significantly since she has been with Robert.

From California babe, to girlfriend of best-selling author. It isn't as far a jump as you might think.

The only way to figure this out, she knows, is to tell Robert. She is going to need his help, and if he decides to leave her, because her betrayal is too much, she will survive. It will be hard, but she will survive.

She always has before.

The party is in full swing, a pianist playing traditional Christmas carols on the baby grand piano in the living room, everyone congratulating Kit on what a wonderful job she has done, people moving through the house to say hello to Robert McClore.

For those who are here for the first time – the wives and husbands of people he knows – Robert is not what they expected. Nothing reclusive about him, and so handsome! Far more handsome in the flesh, and such manners! Such charm!

Adam stands by the bar, and turns to see Kit on the other side of the room. It has been too long. They have to talk. He orders a French Martini for Kit and a Dirty Martini for himself, then holding both drinks high, he inches through the crowd towards her.

'What's this?' She is able to give him a genuine smile, for the party seems to be going better than she could have imagined.

And tonight she feels beautiful, in her black sequined cocktail dress, her hair falling in soft waves, and seeing

Adam come towards her is like the perfect end to a perfect dream, and she cannot stop smiling.

'Sustenance. You've done a wonderful job, and I thought you could do with a drink.'

'French Martini?'

Adam smiles. 'You think I'd forget?'

They exchange a glance, and hold on a second too long. Kit's heart lurches and she looks down. She can't do this, it hurts too much. It's too late for them now, given what happened with Annabel. It's way beyond the point when she and Adam might have been able to salvage something from whatever chemistry she thought remained.

'This is an incredible party. You've obviously worked so hard.' He looks at her gently. 'You look tired.'

'I do?' Her face falls. 'I thought I'd covered up my shadows expertly. I used Charlie's make-up.'

'You look beautiful,' he whispers, the smile fading from his face.

Kit's heart lurches again, and she turns away and sips her drink so he doesn't see the sudden flush.

'Darling!'

They both swivel to see the familiar figure of Ginny, shimmering in a silver dress, huge diamonds in her ears, her hair piled up, pulling a man along behind her.

'Aha. At last we get to meet the famous Peter!' Kit grins at Adam, the moment broken.

'Darling!' Ginny double-kisses both Kit and Adam. 'You two look so adorable together! Are you sure the divorce was a good idea? Honestly, you look like you were made for one another.'

'Oh Mother!' Kits says angrily.

'I'm sorry. It's just that I love both of you and ...' She sees the look in Kit's eye. 'Okay, I'll stop. Anyway, speaking of love, there is someone I'd like you to meet.' She smiles at the man. 'This is my daughter and son-in-law, Kit and Adam Hargrove.'

Kit thinks about correcting her, reminding her that Adam is her ex-son-in-law, but she doesn't. And neither does Adam.

'How do you do?' Adam smiles warmly and shakes his hand. 'So nice to meet you.'

'I'm Peter,' he says, turning to Kit. 'But nobody other than your mother actually calls me that. Everyone else calls me Plum.'

Plum? Plum? Why is that name so familiar? The clouds of Kit's memory start swirling as she attempts to place that name, and that face, that tanned, etched face, with startlingly white teeth, a face that somehow she sees as a young man's, only she doesn't know how, or why.

'And this is the most bizarre thing,' Ginny bubbles excitedly, 'Plum knows Robert!'

Kit looks at him, squinting slightly as if this will help summon the memory.

'From many years ago,' Plum says. 'I haven't seen him since the seventies.'

'Plum Apostoles!' Kit shouts out, as if she is taking part in a game show.

'Yes.' He raises an eyebrow. 'That would be me.'

At ten o'clock, Kit finds herself sneaking exhausted glances at her watch. She is so tired, wants to have a hot bath and crawl into bed, but can see no way of leaving this party until the end.

Tracy is ostensibly the hostess, but Kit knows that if there are any problems Tracy will have no interest in sorting them out.

So far tonight, when the ice ran out, and when they needed to rustle up a Band-Aid for a child, it was Kit to whom Robert turned, and while she has welcomed being so busy, now that she is able to stop, she is suddenly shattered, and she knows she needs to take a minute to lie down.

She slips through the kitchen, forcing smiles at the catering staff, who are busy placing tiny jewel-coloured petit-fours on silver serving trays, through the butler's pantry and into her familiar office.

She doesn't bother putting on the lights. All she wants to do is lie down on the sofa and close her eyes. Just for a moment. Just pretend that she is at home in her bed. A five-minute power nap. Her life has been so frenetic of late, organizing this party, that there hasn't been time to even think about recent events, and there is still so much unfinished business. With Annabel, Steve and, mostly, with Adam.

She needs a five-minute power nap that will replenish her energy enough to get her through the rest of the night, to enable her to pretend she is having a marvellous time.

She lies on the sofa, breathing deeply, trying out a meditation technique she once learned: visualizing a beach, golden sand, turquoise water, palm trees swaying gently in the breeze. She tries, but images of Steve and Annabel keep forcing their way into her mind.

There is so much she doesn't know. People enter your life and you take them at face value. People like Annabel. And Steve. And suddenly she realizes that she knows nothing about Steve. She's never been to his apartment. She doesn't know anything about his work. Nothing about his family, his friends.

But she assumed he was good, assumed he was like her, in the same way she made assumptions about Annabel.

When her world was turned upside down, the only thing that felt safe, the only thing she knew and trusted, despite his transgression – and she could tell it was something he wished had never happened – was Adam.

Is still Adam.

She continues trying to visualize the tranquil beach, turquoise water, golden sand, but now she pictures Adam instead, and instantly she calms down. She sees his reassuring smile, his ruffled hair in the morning.

Suddenly, she hears the click of the door and the light in the lobby outside the office is flicked on.

It is Robert. And Tracy. Standing just outside the open door. She knows she should excuse herself, but they are having a whispered conversation, and something tells her she should not be there, so she makes herself as still as possible, hoping they won't come into the office and find her, feeling guilty, but the moment for her to announce herself, if it was ever there at all, has gone.

'Darling girl,' Robert says. 'I've been wanting to get you on my own all night.'

'You have?' Kit can hear the smile in Tracy's voice.

'I have. An extraordinary thing happened tonight. Plum Apostoles is here, the man who was on the yacht the night Penelope died. He is someone I haven't seen for many, many years, and it's like a gift, that he is here tonight, a reminder of how different my life is now, and how happy I am now. Happier than I ever thought I would be.'

'Thank you,' Tracy says. 'I love you. And I'm also so happy with you.'

'So there is something I want to ask you. It is a question I never thought I would ask anyone again –'

'Stop.' Tracy's voice is a whisper. 'I have something to tell you.'

'What is it?'

'I . . .'

Tracy's footsteps move, and Kit can picture her pacing, prays she doesn't pace over to the sofa to see Kit lying there; she is now feeling guilty beyond imagination.

'. . . I haven't been honest with you.'

'What do you mean?' A note of confusion in Robert's voice.

'Oh Robert. I love you so much. I wanted to tell you everything but I couldn't. I was so scared you'd leave me.'

'Tell me what you're talking about.' The confusion in his voice has given way to coldness which, Kit knows, is hiding fear.

Tracy sighs. 'I don't even know where to start. Let me start by showing you.' There is a rustle of clothing, then nothing.

Kit has no idea what is going on, until she hears Robert's voice, horrified.

'How did this happen? What are these scars from?'

'They are the reason I insist on the light always being off,' Tracy says softly. 'This is so incredibly hard to tell you, but you have to know. These marks were made by a man called Jed. He was my first husband. But you know him as Steve.'

'Steve?' Robert is confused; Kit starts to feel sick. 'I don't know anyone called Steve.'

'You've met him. He's the man who has been dating Kit. Steve is a false name. It's . . . a very long story.' She closes her eyes, feeling sick with nerves.

'I think perhaps it's one you ought to tell me now, don't you?' Robert's voice is colder, fearful perhaps.

Tracy takes a deep breath.

'I'm horrified that I didn't tell you before. I *couldn't*. And I'm so, *so* desperately sorry. I wanted to, badly, but I didn't know how to. I met Jed in my twenties, which I guess should be the beginning of the story, but in fact it probably started much earlier, when I was a child. My earliest memory is of my father slapping my mother, and her crying. I would stand in the corner, terrified, not knowing what to do.'

Kit's nausea sweeps up, and she wants to run out, but she can't move; she lies there, frozen in fear, as she hears Tracy's story unfold.

There is silence in the room when Tracy finishes. Robert buries his head in his hands, rubbing his eyes, trying to comprehend what he has just heard.

386

He looks up, bemused. 'I don't know what to say. I just don't know how to take it all in.'

'Robert, I love you. You have to believe that. And I understand if you decide you can't see me any more, but I needed you to know the full story, and I also need you to know that at forty-one years old, for the first time in my life, I have fallen in love. I love you, and I want to be with you, but I will respect whatever decision you make.'

'I need a little time,' Robert says quietly. 'I think perhaps you should leave. I need to think about all of this.'

'Okay,' Tracy whispers, going over to him and kissing him on his forehead. 'I love you.'

Robert doesn't say anything in return, and Tracy goes back through the kitchen, bursting into tears when she reaches her car.

Robert stays in that safe haven, for a very long time, until finally he walks out and goes to find Kit, still unaware she is a few feet away, to ask her to tell everyone the party is over.

Kit walks out, eventually, when the coast is clear, on legs like jelly. She cannot believe everything she has heard, but of course it all makes sense. Tracy distancing herself from everyone because of the fear of being discovered. Steve's pursuit of Kit that never felt entirely genuine. She shudders with horror thinking about him. How could she have been so stupid?

And what is she supposed to do now?

The doorbell rings early the next morning, and Kit drags herself out of bed and down the stairs. She isn't expecting anyone, but through the sidelights she sees her mother, dressed down in a cashmere sweatsuit, the omnipresent diamonds sparkling in the morning sunlight, with two Starbucks' cardboard cups in hand.

'Mother.' Kit feels heavy, the exhaustion hitting her, the emotions of the last few weeks just too much for her to bear. 'What are you doing here?'

'I was worried about you. I watched you last night and you seemed like someone who has a very heavy cross to bear. I may not have been the perfect mother in the past, but I'm here now, and I want to help. Here –' she extends an arm – 'I have no idea what you drink so I brought you a Mocha Frappuccino. I think that's what it's called. I really don't understand those drinks at all.'

Kit takes the drink and thanks her, standing aside to let her mother in, and somehow, although she is trying to be resolute, her mother's kindness is too much for her; it is so unexpected, so needed right now, that Kit sits down to find the floodgates opening, and she tells her mother everything.

'Can I make a phone call?' Ginny says, when all is done.

'Who are you calling?'

'Peter. I want him to hear this.'

Two hours later, Peter, a man whom Kit instantly trusts, looks Kit in the eyes, leans forward and asks: 'Do you believe Tracy?'

Kit sighs. 'I do. I know she's been peculiar as hell lately, but I do. I wish I didn't, but I don't believe anyone could have talked the way she did if they were lying. There was something about her voice. It wasn't emotional, just completely flat, and I believe her.'

'And what about her love for Robert? Do you think that she sees Robert as a means to escape, or do you think she really does love him?'

Kit shrugs. 'I'm not an expert, but I think she does. I really do. I'm not sure she intended that to happen, but she's telling the truth. I would put my life on it.'

'Do you think she would talk to you if you reached out to her?'

'I have no idea. Things have been so difficult between us recently, although at least now I know the reason why.'

'I think you need to talk to her,' Peter says. 'I'm willing to talk to Robert, as an old friend, but I have to be sure I am doing the right thing, and for that, I need your help.'

Kit, apprehensive but determined, walks slowly into the yoga centre.

'Hi,' she says to Olivia, the girl on the desk. 'Is Tracy around?'

'She's in her office.' Olivia gestures upstairs. 'I don't think she's feeling well, though. She doesn't want to see anyone.'

'I'll be quick,' Kit says, knowing that Tracy is avoiding everyone, for she has left three messages, and none has been returned.

She knocks gently on the closed door, which in itself is unusual, and, hearing no answer, she pushes it open slightly.

Tracy is sitting in a chair which is positioned so that her back is to the door as she stares out of the window.

'Tracy?' Kit says, waiting for her to swivel round.

The seconds pass, and eventually Tracy turns, her eyes red and swollen from crying and lack of sleep.

'Oh Tracy.' Kit forgets whatever distance has come between them and rushes over, gathering Tracy in her arms.

Tracy bursts into tears. 'I love him,' she says. 'And it's over.'

Kit rubs her back softly, not saying anything, and when the tears gradually subside, Kit pulls away and cups Tracy's face in her hand.

'I know,' she whispers, and confusion fills Tracy's eyes.

'I know about Jed. Steve. I know about the abuse.'

'Wha –' Tracy frowns. 'How? How do you know? Did Robert tell you?'

'No. I was in my office and the door was open. I was resting and you were standing right outside. I didn't know what to do. I was going to get up but then it was too late, and I froze. I'm so sorry.'

'So you heard everything.'

'I did.'

'Kit, I'm so sorry I've been so weak. And I'm so sorry I didn't tell you about Steve, and I'm so –'

'Will you stop? Stop apologizing. I understand. I understand everything. You don't have to explain it to me. I just wanted to see if you were okay. I was worried about you.'

'I've been crying all night.' Tracy closes her eyes.

'I never expected to fall in love with Robert. Not like this. But now I have, and he doesn't want me.'

'That's not what he said last night. He said he needed time.'

'But he can't trust me after this. How could he?'

'I think you will be okay,' Kit says. 'I think he loves you too much to let you go, and this isn't your fault. You're the victim in this, not the perpetrator.'

'But I was in the beginning. I went along with Jed's plan in the beginning, before I thought about what I was doing. Before I cared.'

'That's in the past. Now we just have to figure out the future.'

'How?'

'I'm not sure yet, but we'll think of something. You really do love him, don't you?'

Tracy nods. 'I really do.'

The snow, still falling, covers the small Connecticut town in a blanket of white. It is a perfect snowstorm. Picture perfect. So soft and welcoming, it will cover up any ugliness underneath.

Dune Road is covered, apart from a set of tyre tracks leading up to Hillpoint. They are from a rented limo, which may or may not be able to get out of the driveway now that the snow is falling so fast, but the visitor has been inside the house for two hours, and shows no sign of coming out soon.

The driver presses his seat back and rests his head on the headrest for a nap. It doesn't look like he'll be going anywhere in a hurry.

Inside, Peter, or Plum, as Robert knows him, sits with Robert, chatting quietly in the living room. He explains how he knows, and assures Robert that Tracy is genuine. He made a few calls after he spoke to Kit, and there are some things he has firmly established.

The first is that Tracy is telling the truth, and there is nothing in her history to indicate she is part of a larger conspiracy: no criminal record, nothing damaging other than her affiliation with Jed.

He, on the other hand, is another story entirely. There are outstanding warrants for his arrest in the state of California, and a criminal record.

'A nasty piece of work,' Plum says, 'but a small-time operator.'

Robert smiles. 'Are you going to tell me you have people who would take care of him?'

Plum doesn't smile back. 'Are you asking me to have him taken care of?'

Robert shakes his head. 'I would not do that. I just feel . . . torn. What if I make a mistake? What if I am wrong about Tracy?'

'Pfff!' Plum dismisses him. 'What if I am wrong about Ginny? So I am wrong. Lord knows I have been wrong many times before. If we are wrong, we move on. Life is too short not to seize happiness when it presents itself, and you, my friend, have spent many years without knowing happiness.'

'It hasn't been that bad.' Robert attempts a smile, but when it comes it is forced, and false.

'I was there, remember?' Plum says, this time more gently. 'I saw how Penelope treated you. She was a wild

392

one, too much of a handful for you. I saw her fall and, although God will have to forgive me for saying this, I always felt relief for you. I assumed you would be able to move on without her. But I read about you in the papers, and you haven't moved on. And now, all these years later, I see you again, and finally you have a chance of happiness. You must seize it, for it is all we have. Why spend the rest of your years alone, when you have someone who brings you peace?'

He pauses for a moment, then shrugs.

'And if it doesn't work out? You will try again. The splendid Ginny is my fifth try.' He grins. 'And all of them have been marvellous in their own ways. Apart from number three,' he grimaces. 'She was a monster.'

'So what about this Jed Halstead? How do we make him go away?'

'Easy. Men like Jed Halstead bully their women because they have no balls. They always say if you stand up to a bully, you'll never be bothered again. I have a friend who is a producer on a big news show on NBC. I can put a call in to him, get him round with a camera crew. I promise you he'll disappear. Or I could just go and see him. Have a man-to-man chat. Tell him it would be better for everyone if he left, and stayed far away. It helps to be friends with the Governor of California.'

Robert laughs. 'You and Schwarzenegger? That I'd have to see.'

'So. In my opinion, you must give this Tracy a chance. And I can take care of Jed Halstead. If you will let me. For many years I felt that I owed you after

Penelope's death. I was not a good friend to you, too caught up in the problems in my own marriage, and I always felt bad about that. This is my chance to repay you.'

'Thank you, Plum.' Robert nods. 'You will never know how much I appreciate this.'

3 I

Edie believes in fate.

When Robert returned, alone, from his yacht trip around the Mediterranean, all those years ago, Edie's heart broke, but she loved them both, and she prayed that one day Robert would find his happy ending, hoped that fate would intervene to find him true love, for as much as she adored Penelope, she knew they were two people who should never have been together.

When Kit moved in next door, Edie knew she had found a family – Kit would be the daughter she always wanted, and Tory and Buckley the grandchildren she never had.

She knew that Steve was bad news, and had lived long enough to also know that life has a habit of working out, particularly when you're busy making other plans.

And so today, as she sits in the Greenhouse with Kit and Charlie, listening to them chatter away, she smiles to herself, knowing that everything is working out exactly the way it is supposed to.

They have stopped for lunch after a morning traipsing around the neighbouring town of Westport searching for the perfect outfit to wear to Robert and Tracy's wedding.

'It's tiny,' Tracy kept insisting. 'Just fifteen of us. Please don't go to any trouble.'

'Don't worry, we can't afford to,' Charlie reassured her, driving Kit and Edie off to Talbots, Ann Taylor and J. Crew, where each of them has found the perfect dress for a late spring wedding.

Into the shoe store for shoes, although Edie passed, preferring to wear her old comfortable sandals, and then off to the Greenhouse for a girls' lunch, where they stuff the bags under the table and treat themselves to flatbread pizzas and sweet potato fries – as Charlie says, they won't have to worry about squeezing into their dresses for another four weeks.

'So how are things, Charlie?' Kit asks, picking up a French fry and dipping it into the home-made aioli.

'Tough,' admits Charlie, 'but getting better. I miss having my own place, my own house, but it could be worse. At least we have family here. God knows what would have happened to us otherwise. Seriously. I sometimes think we would have ended up on the streets if they hadn't taken us in.'

'No, you wouldn't. I would have taken you in.'

'For about a minute until you realized you couldn't stand having four more people in your house.'

'You're right. I would then have sent you to Edie's.'

Edie grins at them. 'I'd have loved it.'

'And how's Keith doing?'

'You know, I honestly don't know. It's better than it was, but not as good as it was before it got bad, if that makes sense.'

'He's still working with you?'

Charlie shrugs. 'I need the help. And he has the time. It's working for now, enabling me to do more deliveries than I ever did before. I hate working in my in-laws' garage, but –' she looks around the restaurant and lowers her voice – 'there is something exciting coming up but I'm not supposed to talk about it.'

'Oh come on! You can't just say there's something exciting and not tell us anything else.' Kit pouts. 'Anyway, you've always been hopeless at keeping secrets.'

'Okay, but if I tell you, I have to swear you both to secrecy.'

'Done.'

Edie nods her consent.

'Alice and Harry are opening a second Greenhouse.'

'Another restaurant? Really? In these times they're doing that well?'

'It's not the restaurant that's doing so well as much as the catering. They're finding more and more people are asking them for prepared food, and when Boccas went out of business, they started looking at opening a food market.'

'So . . . what? You're going into the business of selling food now?'

Charlie laughs. 'I don't think so. It will be almost like the farmers' markets in California. Great, fresh, local food where possible, a coffee shop, a small restaurant – and a florist.'

'Aha!'

'Exactly. So they asked if I would run the florist.'

'Would you own it?'

'I would run it as a concession. It's perfect. It gives me a shop front but without the headaches of ownership, which is the best of all worlds. And there's great space downstairs in the basement to do all the arranging. We've projected an increase of sixty per cent once we're there, so I'm going to need Keith's help because, God knows, it's not like I can afford to pay anyone.'

'And how does Keith feel about this?'

'Surprisingly excited. He sees it as a real possibility, and we've also been looking at vendor licences to operate flower carts, so we could expand into other towns, or other areas in this town.'

Kit smiles at her. 'Charlie, this sounds great. Really exciting.'

Charlie shrugs. 'I hope so. We need all the good news we can get.'

Kit smiles coyly. 'I may have some good news myself . . .'

'You do! What?'

'Well –' A slow smile spreads on her face. 'Adam and I are taking the kids away next week. Adam's rented a house on Fire Island.'

'What do you mean, Adam and you?'

'I mean, Adam and I.'

'Are you two . . . ?'

'Together? No!'

'Okay, let me rephrase it. How many bedrooms does this house have?'

Kit looks away, but there is no disguising the smile in her eyes. 'Enough.'

'Have you and he *done the nasty*?'

'Oh please!' More peals of laughter. 'Not in front of Edie! And I hate to tell you this, Charlie, but how do you think Tory and Buckley were born?'

'I don't mean *then*! I mean *now*! Recently? Have you?'

Kit blushes. 'No. We haven't.'

'So ... have you kissed?' This time Edie asks the question, a twinkle in her eye.

'Well, no. We haven't.'

'Oh. So ... is this just you and Adam doing your usual thing and co-parenting sickeningly well?' asks Charlie.

'I don't know,' Kit says. 'But I do know that after this past year, I need a break, and Adam offered, and he and I are getting on better than we ever have. I like being around him again.'

'And he's around, which is, in itself, a huge difference.' Charlie smiles.

'Exactly. It feels very different now. He's *around*, not constantly running away to work, and he's really been there for me.'

'So do you think something will happen?'

'I don't know, but I'm excited. I have these nervous butterflies every time I think about it.'

'And the kids? How do they feel?'

'Thrilled. Tory was completely in love with Annabel, and she still doesn't understand how she could just disappear and not get in touch.'

'Poor kid. Will you tell her?'

'Not at the moment. There's no reason to. I just said Annabel had some things to take care of, and she was going through some hard stuff in her life.'

'Have you forgiven her?'

Kit shakes her head. 'No. And right now I can't see a point where I'll be able to.' As she looks at Charlie, then

Edie, she is tearing up slightly. 'You're my real family. Both of you. The people who surround me that I love. Not some long-lost sister with dubious motives.'

'What about your mom?'

'Funnily enough, this has brought us much closer together. And it helps that she's finally got a great husband. I think Peter's amazing. You know Robert's asked him to be best man?'

'Really?' Charlie and Edie are both surprised.

'And now they're even talking about buying a little house in the area – Peter thinks Ginny should be near her grandchildren.'

'That's great!' says Charlie, but when Kit looks at Edie, she can see the concern in her eyes.

'Edie,' she says gently, 'we love you as well. She isn't replacing you and, frankly, you're more of a grand-mother to my children than she will ever be, wherever she ends up buying a house.'

'Thank you for saying that,' Edie says, her relief apparent.

'And you're also more of a mother to me. You know that, right? Nothing will change if she's here.'

'Are you okay with her buying a house here?'

'Well, my first stipulation is that Edie has to be her broker, and the second is that I shall have to keep reminding myself that as long as I have no expectations, it will be fine. I will say that she's surprised me recently. I know that people don't fundamentally change, but she seems more at peace now, and she's really been there for me during all this in a way she never was before. And she's really a great grandmother. Much better than she ever was as a mother. I'm just going to sit back and see what happens.'

Charlie sighs. 'God, all these difficult relationships. Life is so goddamned complicated at times.'

Kit shrugs, then smiles with a twinkle in her eye. 'And so goddamned *good* at the same time. I'm glad for the hard times, they make me appreciate the good so much more.'

'Like right now?'

'Exactly. Like right now.' The phone rings, and Kit looks down to see Adam's familiar number flash on the screen, and as she picks it up, her eyes soften and her face lights up.

'Oh God,' Charlie groans, picking up her mug and downing the rest of her coffee. 'First love, round two. Here we go again.'

Also by Jane Green...

When Andi married Ethan she not only got the man she loved but also the chance to be a mother, to his daughters Emily and Sophia. Unable to have a child of her own, Andi saw this opportunity at motherhood as a precious gift. If only it were that simple.

For this is not a happy family, and the trouble lies with Emily. Her conflicted feelings towards her stepmother leave Andi feeling hated in her own home despite years of trying to reach out to her stepdaughter. And with each new drama, Emily drives Andi and Ethan further apart.

Just as Andi starts to contemplate a life without Ethan and the girls, Emily comes home with some shocking news. News that will change their lives for ever.

In 1996 Jane Green revolutionized women's literature with Straight Talking and its free-spirited heroine Tasha. Fifteen years later, Jane is a 2.5 million bestselling author, now a mother of four, married twice and dealing with all the things a woman in her forties faces on a daily basis, is releasing her best ever coming of age tale that will satisfy her most demanding fans

'Compulsively readable'
Sunday Times

Holly Macintosh is sitting round her kitchen table with her oldest friends
– friends she hasn't seen since school – now reunited by an unexpected
tragedy and catching up on the past 20 years.

On the surface, they are all successful and happy. But scratch
a little deeper after that extra glass of wine and it's not quite so
straightforward: Paul and Anna are struggling to have a baby, Saffron
the actress is still waiting for that really big break that – at 39 – is
looking less and less likely, and Olivia, always the wallflower of the
group, is newly single and mourning her lost love.

And what about Holly Mac? Can she and her husband Marcus get their
marriage back on track for the sake of the children? Or has someone
just come back into her life who will change everything forever?

'A corker of a story, sharply and elegantly told'
Heat

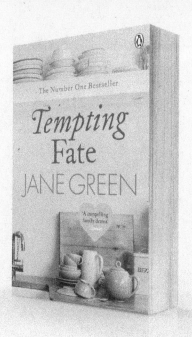

When Gabby first met Elliott she knew he was the man for her. In twenty years of marriage she has never doubted her love for him – even when he refused to give her the one thing she still wants most of all. But now their two daughters are growing up Gabby feels that time and her youth are slipping away. For the first time in her life she is restless. And then she meets Matt . . .

Intoxicated by the way this young, handsome and successful man makes her feel, Gabby is momentarily blind to what she stands to lose on this dangerous path. And in one reckless moment she destroys all that she holds dear.

Consumed by regret, Gabby does everything she can to repair the home she has broken. But are some betrayals too great to forgive?

'A heartbreaking tale of love and family, truly compelling'
Closer

Alice knows she should be happy.

After all she has a handsome husband, a beautiful house and
membership to all the most exclusive clubs in London. So what
if the rumours about her husband's skirt-chasing are becoming
harder to ignore?

When Joe's indiscretions force a transfer to New York, Alice hopes
it might be a fresh start. And when they find a beautiful old house
in Connecticut Alice is overjoyed. For a while she and Joe seem as
happy as newlyweds.

But then the late nights and unexplained absences start again.
What should Alice do? Stay and fight for him? Or leave with her
head held high?

'Green whips up a sparkling morality tale that points the finger
at bad boys and low-rent romance'
Independent

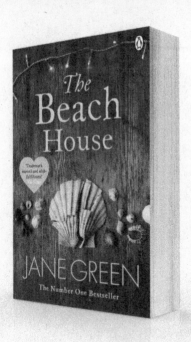

Nan, a widow whose family has flown the nest, is an independent, free-spirited woman who couldn't care less what people think about her living alone in her beloved beach house. But when she discovers that money is running out and she might lose her home, she knows it's time for a drastic change.

Nan decides to rent out rooms for the summer and people start moving into the house, filling it with noise, laughter and tears. Among them is Daniel, a recently divorced father, who's struggling to find out who he really is, and Daff, the single mother of a truculent teenager who blames her mother unreservedly for her parents' divorce.

As the house comes to life again, Nan finds her family growing. Her son comes home for the summer and an unexpected visitor turns up, turning all their lives upside down …

Compelling, absorbing and poignant, The Beach House is a story of friendship, love and those moments that can change your life.

'Fizzing with fast-and-furious dialogue, this is vintage Green'
Eve

Love is not an abstract idea. It is not saying 'I'm here for you, let me know if you need me'. It's making the decision, when someone close to you is in trouble, about what you will DO to fix as much as you can for them. It's a 'doing' thing. A verb.

For Callie, love is about looking after her family – her husband and two children – and their beautiful home.

For Steff, Callie's younger sister, love is about experiencing all that life has to offer without having to ever settle down.

For Lila, Callie's best friend, love is about finding a soulmate. And when she meets divorced father-of-two Eddie, she knows her search is over.

For Walter and Honor, Callie and Steff's divorced parents, love is about caring for the daughters they share.

Then Callie gets some life-changing news. And suddenly the whole family is about to understand what 'love' really, really means....

'A must-read summer delight'
Heat